Now hear the Forest Lord:

Had I no sentinels, the trees would be hewn down to feed fires or build shacks, the animals hunted to extinction, the whole ancient cycle of plenty torn asunder.

For now I must hedge my land about with horrors, that one day, when the works of men totter to their fall, I may receive them whence they never should have strayed. Then I shall throw open the borders of the Forest.

And that day may not be long removed. . . .

DON'T MISS VOLUME 1 IN ROHAN'S THE WINTER OF THE WORLD TRILOGY,

THE ANVIL OF ICE

"An exciting adventure . . . characters that live and breathe in a world of nearly convincing magic. This remarkable novel reveals a gifted writer of stories and pages turn as if by magic!"
JEAN M. AUEL, author of
Clan of the Cave Bear

THE WINTER OF THE WORLD

VOLUME 2

THE FORGE IN THE FOREST

MICHAEL SCOTT ROHAN

AVON BOOKS NEW YORK

AVON BOOKS
A division of
The Hearst Corporation
105 Madison Avenue
New York, New York 10016

Copyright © 1987 by Michael Scott Rohan
Cover painting by Yvonne Gilbert
Published by arrangement with William Morrow and Company, Inc.
Library of Congress Catalog Card Number: 87-11099
ISBN: 0-380-70548-6

First Avon Books Printing: August 1989

AVON TRADEMARK REG. U.S. PAT. OFF. AND IN OTHER COUNTRIES, MARCA REGISTRADA, HECHO EN U.S.A.

Printed in the U.S.A.

K-R 10 9 8 7 6 5 4 3 2

Contents

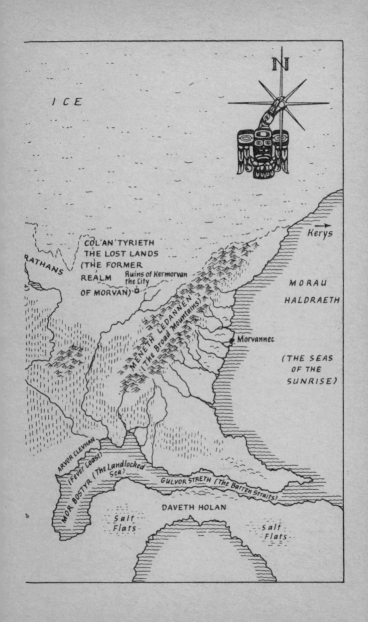

Prelude

Between youth and maturity comes a time of questing and discovery; between apprenticeship and mastery comes journeying. Of the strange apprentice years of the mage-smith Elof, their great and terrible achievements and their uncanny ending, the Winter Chronicles tell in the Book of the Sword. But when that storm was past, and months of sickness drew to an end, the desire of his heart awoke in Elof once more, and he was free to heed it. And it is of that desire, and the long quest it led him, even along the byways of the years, that is told in the Book of the Helm.

CHAPTER ONE

The Kindling

It was the seawind woke him, as his head drooped lower over the close-scrawled book. Through the open upper door of the smithy it gusted, flattening the hearthfire, guttering the rushlamps, and it breathed a sudden chill upon his bare neck. He sat up sharply, blinking in the wavering lamplight, with the queasy alertness of the suddenly awakened. He had been elsewhere, somewhere far away, black marshes or bleak mountains, chasing a shadow out of his past, a shadow that vanished before him, shifted shape in his grasp, reformed and reappeared at his back, forever close, forever out of reach . . .

There came the soft thud of a book closing, and impatiently he shook off the moment of nightmare. "How goes the night?" he asked, without turning his head.

"At its accustomed pace," came Roc's calm reply. "An hour before the middle hour it has reached, by my glass. Time you were abed, by Ils' iron command. Marja and old Hjoran are off long since. And tomorrow is my lord Kermorvan's day; sleep, if you would be fresh for that."

"I cannot sleep."

"A grand mimic you were, then, but a minute gone . . ."

"I mean, I dare not. Not now, with my mind so weighed down by thoughts and cares. My very dreams are poisoned."

"You've found naught to help you, then?"

1

Elof shook his head. "No, nothing. And you?"

Roc rose, stumped over to a bench heaped with great tomes, and slapped down the one he had been reading upon the highest pile. "The same. Much fascinating, much I do not understand, but nothing bearing upon your concern." He peered at the boxes of scrolls beside Elof's table, and leaned over his shoulder. "Not so many of those left, either. What's that one all about? Doesn't look promising. Pity our late unlamented master didn't bring more of his precious library south with him. It'll all be moldering away in the old tower now . . ."

"If the duergar have not seized the place," said Elof. "Or . . . others."

"The Ice, you mean?" said Roc softly, and glanced involuntarily out into the dark beyond the stable door. "Doubt the books have much to tell it."

"Aye, but there are other things there. We did not find that helm I made, the Tarnhelm, among the Mastersmith's effects. And that too was a work of power . . ."

Roc shrugged. "It had its uses, for passing unseen. And somehow shifting place, if what you saw the night of its making was right . . ."

"It was," answered Elof, heavily. "And on the Ice, also. Here is a scroll Ingar must have consulted in planning the helm—see, it bears the very chalkmarks from his soiled sleeves . . ." He stopped a moment, caught his breath. Roc said nothing. "This is a treatise on the power of masks, with annotations by the Mastersmith of much he learned among the Ekwesh, of transforming the wearer into his own living symbol. If I understand aright, such transformation must be the root of the helm's whole power. You remember the virtues he had me set upon it? *Of concealment, of change, of moving subtly and unseen* . . . It was that which haunted my dream, the understanding at last how that helm must act, how powerful it truly is. The helm is a mask, a perfect mask, a concealment shaped by its wearer's own image of himself. Let him think of shadow, and he is unseen. Let him think of a shape, and it masks his own. Let him think of being somewhere else, and he is masked in that thought; he is there . . .''

Roc swallowed. "A fell power to wear with a light heart. I think of many places I would as soon never be. Ach, but the duergar'll know what to do with it, if any can . . .''

"I do not think they have it."

Roc eyed him sharply. "You've reason, by your tone. What then?"

Elof sighed deeply. "You saw as I did, that last hour. Two swans flew up, flew eastward . . .''

"You made but one helm."

"Kara wore a cloak when first I met her, ere the helm was made, and its lining was black swan's down. But Louhi wore no such cloak. And why would they ride horses over such rough country, and when visiting an ally, if both could shift their shape and fly? It may be, it may well be that Louhi came that night to command the Mastersmith to make her something that matched Kara's power.'' He stood up, and the precious parchment crumpled in the convulsion of his powerful fingers, the rod of thick wood at its center creaked and snapped. He looked at it in annoyance, and cast it down upon the table, twisted as the ruined black blade before him. "You see now why I must follow her so urgently, whoever, whatever she truly is? Once more a great power of my making is put into evil hands. Once more must I find it, and if need be destroy it. And she is my only link to Louhi. Even if I did not wish to free Kara, still I would have to follow her, find her. Even if I did not love her.''

Roc pursed his lips and looked away, as he might from the sudden blaze of his forgefire. Gently he ran a finger along the tortured metal before him. "Well, for such a task you'll need your strange sword made whole, right enough. Few in the world could have cloven as that one did in your last need.'' He stretched, and yawned loudly. "But for now, do you try to rest, at least. Tired eyes may miss what's plain by daylight.''

Elof breathed out a long breath, and nodded. "True

enough. Very well. I'll try, but not this moment. I'll sit up awhile and mend the hilt, at least, if there's no more to be done now. Work of the hands will clear the brain.''

When Roc had gone Elof smoothed out the crumpled scroll and stowed it carefully. Then he sighed, and turned to the hilt. The sheer force of the blow that had twisted the sword had shivered loose the plain silvered wires of the grip; gone was their cloudy, stormy sheen, racing and beautiful as the marshland skies beneath which they were made. He thought a moment, reached for his precious tool pack and bore it to a workbench by the window. There Marja, old Hjoran's girl journeyman, kept her work. Instead of the blackened instruments of the forge, delicate grippers, thin files and fine-tipped burins were laid out in neat racks, for Marja was an accomplished jeweler. Elof chose a delicate blade and from a side pocket he drew a fold of stiff leather; a few dry leaf needles fell from one end, and he opened it with minute care. Within it lay a dry sprig of the redwood tree, almost naked of its needles save for one small twig, and this he carefully severed. He laid it upon a polished stone slab, brushed across it a subtle paste of eggwhite and gums thinned with strongest spirits, and laid across it a light leaf of hammered silver, finer than finest parchment. He breathed gently on this, till a ghostly outline of the twig showed through, and then with fine-tipped tools he began to smooth it down, patiently working it close around the outline of every needle, turning it over and adding more leaf till the twig was wholly encased, enshrined.

Now it looked like the talisman it had been. Little power seemed left to it, but it was too precious a thing to discard entirely. *While there are leaves on it, even withered and dead, something of the virtue of forests will cling to it . . .* He smiled. ''But no autumn wind shall unfix these last leaves. A silver season sets them in place, and I will bear them with me wherever I go.'' These words he spoke over his work, and then unwinding the wires he fastened the twig about the grip, and set the wires tightly in place above it once more. It felt as solid as before, but Elof scowled as he took it in his hand. What was it without the blade it bore? He tossed it down in disgust. The night was silent now, save for the rising whine of the wind, bearing with it the distant sound of the wavelets in the harbor, the clopping hooves of some benighted rider on the cobbled streets. Sleep seemed further fled than ever from his mind, so sharply the need to learn spurred him. Impatiently he snatched up another scroll. It proved to be a wordy treatise on extracting metals from ores, and, save for a long chapter on the strange forces set moving by iron and copper in corrosives, it was dull stuff. And before him on the table sat the sword, the precious blade he had not made for himself, but had taken from a long-dead hand. It lay there like a mute accusation. Was he worthy to wield such a thing, if he, a smith of craft and power, could not reforge it?

"But how? *How?*" He pushed the scroll aside and took up the cool metal in his hands. If metal it was, in truth. For no furnace would heat it, no file bite upon it, no hammer subdue its stubborn strength. Not all his smithcraft, all his long study, all his strength of mind or arm, neither the flames of his forge nor the fires of his need could make that blade anew!

"Greetings, worthy smith!" A sound of thunder rang through the smithy, rattling the heavy door on its hinges; still greater was the impact of the voice. The blade flew from Elof's fingers, the bench he sat on overturned as he sprang to his feet in fury and fright. But the latch was up, the lower door already swinging open, and Elof's anger slackened as he saw what manner of figure stood there, half hesitant in the shadows of the street.

The man was old, that was obvious. In the dim light from the forge his wide hat shadowed his face, its battered brim drooping across one eye, but it only served to stress the whiteness of the windblown locks and beard beneath. So also the heavy mantle, that had once been dark blue and was now sorely stained with travel. The shoulders beneath were bowed, and he leaned upon a great staff of smooth dark wood, crowned with its own bark. A strong support but hard, perhaps, to manage; Elof forgave him his clumsy knock.

"Greetings!" said the old man once again, and bowed courteously. "A wayworn guest asks hospitality of your hearth awhile, that shone out warmly from afar in these nightbound streets." The voice was gruff yet deep and resonant, with more than a trace of the northern burr. Elof smiled at his old-fashioned courtesy, but still he hesitated.

"Who is it that asks? Who has sought out my smithy in all this great town?"

The old man stepped slowly through the door, as if that had been invitation enough. The seabreeze frisked in with him, whipping up the forge charcoals, pulling puffs of smoke from beneath the chimney breast. "A wanderer only, so the world might call me. For indeed far and wide I have wandered, many long leagues across its face. And further still, it seems, I must go."

I doubt as far as I, thought Elof wryly, but said no such word, and moved to usher the ancient gently out. A beggar once within is harder to turn out, and the city was full of northern beggars now, young and old, who had slipped past the gate guards; he could not feed them all. Also, of this oldster's face he could see only a great hooked beak of a nose with a bright dark eye above it, and in that a gleam he did not altogether trust. Elof laughed, and fumbled at his belt for a coin, enough for a night's lodging. "Well, if you're called a wanderer, the last I would be to detain you. Here is alms, but I cannot . . ."

The old beggar paid him no heed, but advanced into the smithy with that same slow stride, his mantle sweeping odd swirls in the dust. Elof stopped, startled, and let the coin slide back into his pouch. He must once have stood very tall, this ancient; even now his head was on a level with Elof's, and the pale mottled hands that gripped the great staff were long and muscular. In the trembling fire-glow his shadow loomed enormous against the smithy wall. "Good man greets the journeyer gladly, aye, so it was said in the Northlands, was it not? For I hear them in your fair speech." Elof blinked at the mild rebuke, but

sought to bar his way nonetheless. The old man ignored
him, and turned toward the hearth. "So it was ever with
me, in the old days. Men made me welcome then, gave
me food and drink and even gifts. True men, they, not
scared to admit a stranger. Trouble fears, that trouble wills,
thus they said, and opened their doors wide."

"Troubles I have!" sighed Elof, resenting the nettle's
sting. "Why do you come to worsen them?"

"I would only sit by your hearth," grunted the old man,
lowering himself slowly and wearily onto the brick seat,
sighing as he laid his back against it and basked in the
warmth. "So! Since it is grudged me, this scant rest, I
must fee you for it as best I can, with wisdom. Much I
have seen, learned many things strange even to men of
lore; counsel of mine has lifted gnawing care from many
men's hearts. Ask of me what you will!"

Elof sighed. "Nothing is grudged," he said firmly, "but
I have many labors. Take the alms I offered, and leave me
to them. I need no counsel that you could give . . ."

The old man tossed his head contemptuously, and Elof
caught a glimpse of his face, lined but hard like some
ancient tree. "Are you so sure of that?" demanded the
stranger sternly. "Many who deem themselves wise fail
only to know the extent of their ignorance!" He poked his
staff clumsily at a pile of bound books. "You, you bury
your nose in dead words. You seek some secret, that is
plain. Words hold many, that is true. But not all!" Again
that dark eye flashed from beneath the ruined brim, quiz-
zical, mocking, and lit upon the crippled sword. "Ahh.
You seek a means to mend that blade . . ." He chuckled.
"A fine strong lad like yourself, can you not simply hammer it straight? No? Then however did you make it in the
first place?"

Again the dart flew straight and keen; Elof felt his ears
burn, his cheeks flare, and cursed beneath his breath. "You
do not know," mused the old man, cocking his great head
to one side. "You cannot have shaped the blade for yourself, then. It is not . . . yours."

Elof glared at him. "It is no man's else, I found it, where it had lain buried beyond sight or memory—"

The old man shook his head querulously, his shabby hat flapping. "So! Found is not freely given. Yet sometimes even a gift must be earned, must it not? A horse that one must learn to saddle before riding, a boat to rig before sailing. It is not for me to say, but such gifts might be given to teach the given new craft, or make him aware of that he already has. Thus truly he wins both the gift and the skill for himself, and stands free of all obligation save gratitude."

Elof stood very still. The forgefire was crackling now, whipped up by a breeze sharp as a storm's outrider. He looked askance at the old man, hard to make out against the smoky glare behind him. "Skill I have sought . . ."

"Aye, in books of another's wisdom. They have their place, perchance. But I had always heard that magesmiths of the north were such men as ever sought new truths, new wisdoms in the very ebb and flow of nature itself."

"Aye!" said Elof fiercely, stung now to the quick. "So we do! The mastersmiths, the great among us, they harness with their craft the many forces of this world. To heights and depths they put forth their hands, and grasp them, bind them in cunning work. The true mastersmith fears not to snatch those forces even from the hands of the very Powers that wield them!"

The old man laughed softly to himself. Then, with a speed that startled Elof, he hauled himself up one-handed upon his great staff and with the other clawed up the black blade from the table, heedless of its hair-fine edge. Outraged, Elof sprang to seize it, only to stop short with a gasp as the great staff, twirled effortlessly about, tapped against his breastbone. The hand he raised to dash it aside faltered at the slight cold sting where it touched him. His fingers closed more gently round the bark, found it a mere wrapping over a shape beneath, and chill meltwater coursed in his veins. It was an edge he touched, narrow, hard and tapering. This staff at his breast, hard on a strange wound's scarless site, was a tall spear, and in hands deft to wield it.

The old man nodded softly. "Proudly spoken, my wise smith, to set your kind against the Steerers of the World. Yet know you of what you speak?" He straightened suddenly, effortlessly, and the black shadows seemed to flutter round the forge, chill-winged on the freshening wind. "Over this world was set their dominion ere it was shaped. Over sea and land they rule, over sky, over stone, cloud and mountain, forest and lake, plain and river, over all that lives, plants, beasts, men. And over the Ice." The great staff that was no staff stretched out in a wide sweep before him, as if to score some mighty secret on the flagstones, as if to encompass the wide world. On the outflung arms the mantle billowed as if in the winds of the heights, and flew like a banner from the shaft. "High and wise they are, and surpassing strong, the least and weakest past measure of men. In their slightest glance is seeing, their least thought knowing, their smallest gesture . . . power." Outheld like some vast scepter, the staff's head glanced lightly against the flaring forgecoals. The smithy rang with a shattering sound, a blast of thunder that flattened flames and spat sparks stinging and sizzling into the smoky air. The floor shook, flagstones heaved, and a great blade of glaring light leaped between hearth and chimney; a thunderbolt burst beneath the roof. Wind shrieked, smoke rolled in blasted tatters across the room, the lamp, blown out, topped and shattered; the tools ranked upon the wall jangled and chimed. But amid this stood the old man, stern, unmoved, cold as a winter sky, his dark eye glittering in the shadow of his hat.

There was silence then, the strangely unquiet silence, still reverberant, that comes after cataclysmic sound. And in it, distant, faint but very clear, Elof heard what might be an answer, a faint crackling rumble borne from far off down the shrilling seabreeze. The gusting air, sobbing and rattling at the door, pressed chill against his stiffened spine, and he began to shiver violently.

"Well, cunning smith," demanded the old man quietly, "do you repent now of your pride?"

Mutely, holding his eyes on the old man with utmost intensity, Elof shook his head. But the strange wanderer only leaned wearily on the great staff once again. Shrouded still stood its crown, but in the rippling shadow the firelight cast upon the wall the shape of a broad spearhead stood out clear.

"Well enough that you should not. For—as I have heard the wise tell it—it is only those of the Ice, those who fail in their trust, who desire slaves, servants, subjects. The true Steerers cannot, being themselves doubly servants, to a cause and to an end. And that end is best served by those men who need their help least." He sighed, and turned toward the door. "I cannot fee you for your hearth-gift; you need no counsel of mine. I depart in your debt, as before."

Elof stared. "As before? How so, for I never laid eyes on you till now? And counsel I need! For I still don't know how to reforge the sword . . ."

The Wanderer had reached the open door; there he paused to look back, the picture of way-weary age. Yet his eye gleamed brighter than ever, and what lurked below the tremor in his stern voice seemed nearer mirth than misery. "You should not think to mock me! Have you not told me of it, you who aspire to clutch the forces of the world in the palm of your hand? The answer lies open to a child—were not children wont to fear!" He gestured contemptuously with his empty hand, and his mantle fell away from his arm. Beneath it gleamed blackness as dark waters under the moon, a breastplate and the hilt of a vast black sword. Then the old man ducked through the door and was gone.

"*You!*" yelled Elof. A sudden crazed anger seared away awe and fear, and he ran headlong for the door. "You again! Raven! Stay, you Wanderer, you get of a—"

From the blackness a bird's harsh scream answered him, a wordless essence of mockery, and the swift ring of shod hooves upon cobbles. And he knew that one of those hooves he had shod himself. Out into the street he burst, but it was a vale of blackness; many great storehouses and tall granaries of the Merchant's Guild stood here, and their shadows blanketed it deep. Only at the far end, by the harbor, he thought he saw for an instant the gleaming flank of that lofty warhorse. But it flickered again, and he saw it was only the herald of the approaching storm, lightning that leaped from cloud to cloud glittering against the pale stone. The wind blew hard in his face, the first cold droplets stung him; it was thunder, not hoofbeats, that drummed afar. The Wanderer had vanished as he had come.

The distant lightning awoke a reflection at his feet. There, glinting on the cobbles, lay the black blade. He snatched it up and stared at it, caught and baffled: what could the old fox have meant, to claim its secret was already his? A third of its length from the tang was so sadly wrung and twisted that the rest stuck out at the crazy angle of a broken limb. Thus indeed it felt to him, and one not yet set or splinted. Had it not defied every art he could summon up? Even the secrets he had learned of the duergar, who could look deep into the very form and structure of metal, had failed him. And if it was not metal? It had to be metal, it felt like metal, it could not be obsidian or any other glass, or any of the odd stones savages and poor men had once used. And yet, as he played it in his fingers, he became less sure. That gleam was undimmed, its edge undulled; even long years sunk in a marsh had failed to fault them. Could the hardest metal endure thus? But how to test it? With a lodestone? Many metals would not answer one. With corrosives? To succeed would be to damage it.

Elof stood there, his head whirling like the stormwind, and fought for calm. One might ignore what an old beggar mumbled, but surely this weird being said nothing without purpose. How might those words apply to him? He did not know what wisdom he lacked. He had the blade as a gift, but a gift that must be earned with new and daring skill. He could not assume that the lore of it was to be found in books, but more likely among the ebb and flow of nature. How? Where? Somehow he had said it himself! In fury he hammered at his brow as if he might reforge the mind within.

The storm crackled as it drew nearer the land. Above the harbor wall the dark outline of the Tower of Vayde stood out stark against the coruscating clouds: it woke intrusive memories in him, of fear and blood and pain, and of love found and lost. He strove to force them down and concentrate his thought. In angry defiance he had prattled of a magesmith being able to put forth his hand and grasp . . .

"Roc!" he yelled suddenly, and whirled round. Slipping on the cobbles, he dashed back into the smithy, yelling for his friend and wondering why he had to; that levin-bolt should have had the whole household hurtling from their beds. But the corridor was empty, and when he flung wide the door of Roc's chamber his friend was still a round hummock beneath the bedclothes. It was Marja who bounced up first from beside him, angrily clutching a fur counterpane about herself.

She had fled with old Hjoran, late her master, out of the north when their towns were sacked by Ekwesh marauders. When at last the great tide of fugitives had borne them to the Southlands they were as near starvation as any, but by good fortune they had fallen in with Roc; remembering Hjoran kindly, and knowing the worth of even a minor mastersmith of the north, Roc had taken them into his own forge. The partnership had prospered, but to what degree Elof had not guessed. Too impatient, though, to be startled or embarrassed now, he seized Roc by the shoulder. "Wake up! Didn't you hear it?"

"Hear what?" mumbled Roc.

"The crash! The bolt! Roc, it was the Raven!"

"The Raven?" cried Marja, gaping wide-eyed at Elof as if he were mad. Distant lightning whitened the shutters.

"The Raven?" yelped Roc, sitting up and looking wildly about. "Like you told me? The bastard's back? Where? In here?"

"Yes! Here in the smithy!" Marja cried out and dived beneath the bedclothes in a tangle of brown limbs. "Didn't you hear? It was like thunder . . . Never mind! Up with you, up, while I rouse Hjoran! There's work afoot! I can reforge the sword!"

"Now hold hard!" growled Roc angrily, pulling his arm free, and putting a protective arm round the heap of bedclothes. "Amicac's teeth, man! You come barging in . . . I know you're all agog, but there's nothing that won't wait for honest sunlight—"

"But there is!" cried Elof. "While it's at hand—oh, there's no time to explain!"

"At least send for Ils, and we'll see what she—"

"No time even for that! I'm sorry, Marja, but we must hurry or it'll be too late!"

Roc winced as the cold air struck his bare skin. "It'd better be good, that's all!"

It was a strange parade that scant minutes later made its uneasy way down the street toward the steps of the harbor wall and emerged at last, gasping exhaustion like landed fish, into the rain-sprinkled air atop the open summit of Vayde's Tower. The guttering linklight Marja held high trailed a splash of gold around the battlements, cast her spidery shadow down across the gallery where the Mastersmith had lurked among his looted wealth. In her free hand she bore Elof's bundle of tools, under that arm the ruined blade, well wrapped, and in the pocket of her man's smock the hilt and fresh rivets. As she came out under the sky she looked back with concern at the three men stumbling and gasping up the stair behind her, under the weight of Roc's strongest and heaviest anvil. By now old Hjoran could give no more than token assistance, and even Roc's dour strength ebbed. But Elof drove them on up the steps like a man inspired, taking ever more of the burden upon his own shoulders. Lightning flashed, the thunder hard on its heels, and he chivvied his friends furiously up the last few steps.

"If that Raven shows his face again," gurgled Roc, "he'll have this slung in it!"

"What I'd gladly know, lads," panted Hjoran, as they struggled out onto the summit, "is just how much further there's to go?"

"This is the place!" gasped Elof, lifting his face to the spattering rain. "And in time, it seems!"

"Here?" demanded Roc. "Why here? There's not even a fireplace . . ." But they were glad enough to set down the anvil, with a clang that struck sparks from the hard stone. Hjoran leaned on it, wheezing, while Marja comforted him.

Breathless, Elof gazed out over the harbor and the sea beyond. In the lightning's own light the stormclouds rose up immense, bastion upon bastion, like some great fortress of the Powers, seething with the energies it could scarce contain. Now their vanguard was almost overhead, and the rain was growing heavier, sputtering against the link's cover. A great curtain of it, opaque as a pearl, was sweeping in across the churning sea, no more than moments away. He set his teeth and looked down into the darkness of the stairwell. All the time they had struggled through it he had been willing some guidance from it, some sign such as he had once felt there. Now there was nothing, save perhaps watchfulness, remote and stern. A flash sent his shadow coursing down the steps; the thunder was so close he jumped. "This grows perilous!" he heard Hjoran grumble, and Marja's squeak of agreement.

"It does indeed!" Roc said. He took the bag of tools and unrolled it on the anvil top. "Leave the gear, Marja, get you back to the stairs, and you, Hjoran. I'll give him what help he needs . . ."

"It's given," said Elof quietly, unwrapping the blade. "Pass me a good hammer, if you please, the great slope-headed one of duergar pattern. Fit those rivets to the hilt, there, and lay them aside with a punch to fit. Then go with the others."

"You're sure?" growled Roc, rummaging through the clinking roll. "I smell another of your tomfool tricks—"

"Maybe. But fool or no, none save myself may try. Now keep back!"

Flash and thunder all but drowned him out. The few hulls at anchor rocked, plunged and vanished as the rain lashed across their decks. "Get below!" Elof yelled. "There's no more you can do! Later I may need you!" From the pouch at his belt he tugged the armor gauntlet he had made among the duergar, and Roc's eyes widened in understanding, doubt and awe.

"Do you make sure later comes, that's all!" he bellowed, and vanished smartly into the stairwell. An instant later the line of rain charged across the tower top, and all vanished in lashing confusion.

Elof stood fast by the anvil, fighting to keep his feet against the buffeting wind, struggling to hold the blade while he drew on the long gauntlet. It slid minutely over his fingers, inscribed and patterned plate molding smoothly to the close contours of his flesh, mail fine almost as cloth swelling and shaping around the very joints, till his arm was enclosed to the shoulder and his fingers could at last close firm round the flat faceted jewel at its heart. With that comfort he dared not pause to think, but sprang up upon the battlements and thrust his arm to the sky. Now he himself was the summit of the seawall, there was no higher point save the towers of the distant citadel itself. It must happen, it had to happen any moment now!

Then a thought unleashed a rush of cold perspiration. Quickly he spread his fingers wide and flat as he could, arching back his hand to raise the palm. If it should light first on a fingertip, anywhere but the palm . . .

The storm took him and shook him, the blast yelled at him not to be a fool, he felt it roll and swirl in the abyss at his back, down along the streets far below. Or was it at his back? He was no longer even sure which way he faced. All his courage was thinning and draining out of him, leached away by the icy rain. He had carried that anvil too long, he had no strength left; his arm was a taut hot wire of pain, his wrist an agony of tension, his fingers squalling to cramp shut. Another minute and he must abandon this lunacy, drop down and cower before forces he should never have aspired to defy, another second even . . .

Then it was as if storm and tower and all else vanished, and an infinite whiteness opened around him, a space that echoed with the single stroke of an incalculable drum. A vast weight descended, and for a moment he held up the whole vault of the sky on his palm, lest it drop to shatter the fragile glass bubble of a world beneath. It was cramp, not will, that snapped his fingers shut. At once the storm was buffeting him again, and he held some vast monster by the leash, that throbbed and trembled in his palm. He wavered, lost his footing and with a yell of madness leaped the only way he could. Hard flagstones slapped at his feet, he stumbled against the anvil and the black blade clattered down upon it. He was dimly aware of voices that clamored to him, but the throbbing grew within his palm till it seemed the very joints of his fingers must yield. With his right hand he edged the blade round to lie against the metal, and groped blindly for his hammer. The short haft came under his fingers and he seized it, feeling the comforting weight. Down above the black sword's twisted heart he brought his quivering arm, the clamped fist vertical, closed thumb uppermost. Then, feeling the faint ripple of fine rings clashing, he slowly released his little finger a trifle, as if he would trickle away a fistful of sand.

White fire purer than the shrouded stars poured down upon the anvil, a sparkling, blasting light that mere eyelids barely barred. A hundred high fosses roared there, cataracts louder than the storm. Roc yelled at something, but his voice was lost in the tumult. To the watchers at the stairhead Elof's sturdy frame stood out against the light in a single sweep of motion, the huge hammer swinging high to the top of its arc, descending with easy, leisurely grace. While the light still shone, the hammer plunged down into its midst, rose and plunged again, and a fountain of smoke spurted up for the storm to sport with. At the fourth blow or the fifth the light cut off abruptly, and Elof let the hammer fall. But the gauntlet, still clenched, he raised now on high, and sent his own closed fist hammering down in the hammer's place. A blasting light smote upon the anvil and leaped upward to the racing clouds, a great ringing clang shook the tower, and the smith staggered and sank down to his knees upon the glistening flagstones.

Whether it was the final escape of what had been captured, or simply the eye of the storm, a clearness opened overhead. The rain slackened to a fine drizzle, as if the clouds wept for their lost power. The watchers stumbled up from the stairwell and rushed to the swaying figure before them, fearful of injuries they might find. But though his garments smoldered in many places and his wet hair smoked, though his face was smudged and scorched, his eyes glittered with a wild exaltation. "See!" he shouted, and pointed with his out-thrust gauntlet. "You wise Wanderer, say, do I pass the test? And you from whose hand I took it, do you bear witness! Say now, is it not truly mine? From a dying hand it fell ruined, but by a living one it is made whole! On evil it was marred, yet it shines now straight and strong! To life again it awakens, to strike in its defense! Blind the unhallowed with your dark gleam, shatter the evil, strike down the false!" Shaking off the hands of his friends, Elof surged to his feet seized the hilt from the flagstones and stumbled forward. In the pale glow of the lancing flares overhead they looked after him, and saw. Hjoran cried out. Marja squealed, and Roc swore in a hoarse whisper. Straight indeed stood the black blade, for it was driven deep down into the very metal of the anvil.

Elof thrust the hilt down over the upturned tang and twisted the rivets home. Then, without staying to flatten them, he braced a boot against the iron and gave a single convulsive heave. With a scream of stressed metal, a shower of sparks, a loud triumphant ring, the blade tore free. The anvil, cracked now from top to foot, fell slowly into two and clanged upon the tower's dark stones, hissing in the reviving rain. *"So cleaves the smith's own blade!"*

Then Elof laughed weakly and turned to Roc and the others, and embraced them; clumsily, for he would not set down the sword. "Thank you, my friends, thank you! I am sorry it had to come so fast, and without explanation.

And Roc, I'll craft you trinkets enough to pay for a fine new anvil . . ."

Hjoran and Marja stood dazed and speechless, but Roc, more hardened to strange matters, simply shook his head in wonder, and set to gathering up Elof's tools. "That's no matter. Leave this where it lies for now, and let's be off here ere the heavens start some more smithying of their own!" He chivvied the others off down the stairs, clapped Elof on the back as he passed and exclaimed at the soggy thump his hand made. "Do you come back with us, man, you're soaked to the skin! We'll find you a stoup of mulled wine and a warm bed!"

Elof shook his head, still exultant. "I thank you, but no! I've trespassed enough upon you all for tonight. I'll turn back to Kermorvan's house and my own bed, and leave you in peace."

"As you will!" said Roc, putting his arm around Marja. "My respects to his lordship, and we'll be cheering him when he comes out onto the steps tomorrow."

"You're not coming to the ceremony?"

"What, to hear a crew of windbag syndics spouting for hours?" scoffed Roc. "I'll leave the formalities to you and Ils, you've the heads for them. Sooner pass the time in the alehouse, if there's any to be had in these days!"

Elof chuckled with the others. "If there is, I'll be bound you'll find it! Save some for us, afterward!" Letting the others press on ahead, he lingered in the musty darkness, finding its cool quietude pleasant after the storm above. The blade in his hands was cool also, and the gauntlet at his belt; scarcely conceivable it seemed that such forces had flowed through them not long since. He thought back to the moment of fire, to the brief glimpse he had gained deep into the matter of the sword. It was indeed no metal. Long black strands had glowed within it, coiled and twisted, set thick in a hard dark binding substance; glossy and lustrous they had seemed, like the locks of some long-dead beauty set imperishably, save that the blade's edge was finer than the finest hair. He stopped by one of the great stairwell windows, where stormlight yet glimmered, and held up the sword to gaze again. But its surface was once more a mirror impenetrable. A thought struck him, and he looked at the hilt, tilting it in the light. Once more it glimmered with racing cloud patterns, but they seemed gray no longer; they were black, potent as the storm-clouds whose living force had flowed into the blade's reforging. "I never named you before," he said softly. "I cannot have been sure of you, indeed. But now I am, and for the darkness that clings to you I will name you. The Bringer of Darkness be, Herald of Night, Gorthawer in the sothran tongue, and may you fall ever upon the eyes of my foes!"

On impulse he slashed at the air with the sword Gorthawer, and a voice sang in the darkness, high, exultant, clearer than of old. It spoke words to him that fired his blood, made him forget a moment wetness and chill and the weary walk that lay between him and the bed he yearned to collapse on. "A dark road lies ahead," he breathed. "But at least I have won back one true companion on it. I wonder what others I may find?"

CHAPTER TWO

The Casting

The wind came howling across the Marshlands with a million savage voices, driving dark clouds in a swathe before it, scything down the brown reeds of autumn in its path. Again he cowered fever-ridden behind the rattling door of his forge, hearing on the blast the echoes of ancient battles upon the fens, the distant, hungry cries of the myriad dead who lay beneath them, arisen now and hunting, hunting along the gale. Gusts hammered on the wood like huge hands, huge as the blackened and crumbling fist from which he had snatched that sword . . .

He awoke abruptly, and lay shivering a moment before he became aware of the soft bed beneath him, the worn richness of the counterpane under his clutching fingers. The chill was all within his dream; the Marshlands lay far behind him. But he knew he had not been wholly dreaming; he listened a moment, with a leaden swell of apprehension. The bedhangings were dark silhouettes against a faint graying of the darkness; not even a tassel stirred, yet the howling was still in his ears. The threadbare rug slipped underfoot as he swung himself out of bed, the cool air stung his skin and the smooth slabs his feet as he padded over to the outward window. But this was narrow, and the grille stopped him leaning out far enough to see. The house, like most of any size or age in the Old City, faced inward around its own quadrangle and presented as blank an aspect as possible to the outward world. He turned and sprinted past the door curtain, out into the open gallery and up the stairs that led to the roof. By the time he came out among the dilapidated tiling his head was swimming, his heart laboring, a familiar ache burning deep in his chest; the night's labors had spent his strength. He had to steady himself a moment on the crumbling stone parapet before leaning out to look.

The city below lay in deep shadow, but bright flecks of firelight flickered here and there—surely too brightly for this ashen half-light at night's end. And though the air hung still as a dusty tapestry, the stormy voices were clearer than ever now, closer, louder, a hungry, savage baying that made him shudder where he stood.

The touch of something soft and animal on his bare back made him jump. "Small wonder you're shivering," growled Ils' voice. The duergar girl reached up to drape a robe round his shoulders. "On your feet no more than a month, and you're gallivanting around in your skin!"

"I'm all right!" he protested, with a resentful shrug. "This would be a warm day, where I was born!" But he slid his arms into the garment nonetheless, grateful for the warmth of the fur lining. The winter, they said, had been the fiercest in the city's memory, and this spring was hardly warm yet.

"Good!" she said firmly. "After all, you cannot heal from fevers in just a moment!" Elof smiled thinly, glad she was ready to make a joke of the matter. That sudden closing of a mortal wound had opened a wider gulf, that moment of strange recovery had briefly stood like a barrier between him and his friends who witnessed it, like a bare blade tossed on the table between hands poised yet hesitant. Ils, for all her care of him, had grown warier than any. Only the racking sickness that had come swiftly upon him, a symptom of humanity as it seemed, and some price paid for so terrible a wound, had dispelled their doubts. They had remembered what manner of blade struck the blow, and blamed all strangeness upon that. He did not gainsay them; but as his mind cooled he knew it was not so. Yet even now his thoughts blurred as he probed them; he understood it no better himself, no better . . .

"The row woke me, too," she muttered, calling him back to himself. "What devilry are the humans up to now? It comes this way, by the sound."

"I don't know. I fear . . . Listen!" They heard it clearly, the sound of footsteps, pounding steps stumbling on the dawn-slick cobbles, running as a man does at the end of his strength or a quarry a length ahead of the pack. Around the corner of the street below staggered a young man, a boy almost, long-limbed and very thin. He ran with the reeling stride of desperate exhaustion, his copper-skinned face suffused with blood, his breath rasping in his throat. He dived into a gap between the houses, stopped short with a despairing flutter as he saw the stone wall of the citadel blocking the alley's end, and turned to flee. Then he sprang back in fright as a wave of yelling men with torches poured in upon him, blocking his escape. In an instant he was overwhelmed, kicked and beaten to the ground. The horrified watchers saw a rope slung over the grille of a window in the wall below. Struggling and screaming, the helpless youth was being dragged over to it.

Ils cursed, turned to the stairs, but stopped. The street was four circuitous floors below; by the time they got there, even with weapons, the victim would be past help. Elof looked around desperately. Many of the heavy roof-tiles of glazed earthenware were missing, others looked loose; he seized one, and it came away in his hand. Wolf-ish baying laughter arose; one of the mob was about to drop the noose round the boy's neck, others to throw their weight on the rope. Elof poised the tile, and threw.

The sureness of his aim startled even him. With a loud smacking sound the tile took the noose-man on the side of the head and stretched him flat on the ground. *"Good!"* yelled Ils; an instant later her tile clipped the arm of the first man on the rope, and he fell down screaming among its coils. The other rioters looked up with angry shouts, but dropped back in alarm, guarding their heads from a lethally accurate shower of tiles.

Then from the street sounded fast hoofbeats, horn-calls, shouts, and suddenly a tall man on a great white warhorse plunged in among the rioters, calling orders in a clarion voice. A sword was at his side, but he laid about him with a huge drover's whip, his bronzen hair flying, and screams arose from the crowd as it milled this way and that to escape hoof and lash. Behind him streamed men in the armor of the City Guard, and they fell upon the rioters, striking about with their pikeshafts.

Before the pikes the mob's killing mood changed at once to panic. They dropped their victim, boiled about and scattered, tripping over him in their hurry to escape, and horseman and guards wheeled off to break and disperse them. Elof breathed his relief, only to see a straggler suddenly turn back, stoop over the sprawling youth and with brutal precision thrust a long knife through his stomach. Elof's last throw caught the slayer only a glancing blow to the thigh, and with a savage gesture he hobbled off. Before Elof could react the horseman came cantering back through the mêlée, but the youth's writhings had stilled. At the rider's word a pair of guards ran up. One bent over the bodies of hangman and victim, looked up to the rider and shook his head.

By the time they had made their way downstairs Kermorvan was already in the courtyard, leading his horse to the stable and calling loudly for breakfast.

"I don't have such an appetite," said Elof grimly, as he followed the warrior into the cool gloom of the Lesser Hall, where a wizened old servant was setting out a few plain dishes. "Not now." Ils, who had herself cut down men without the least qualm, nodded agreement.

"You should keep your strength up," said Kermorvan dryly, tearing at the loaf of hot cornbread before him. "After tossing half my ancestral roof into the street, you must be exhausted." He washed the bread down with a swallow of strong cider and smiled, more sympathetically. "I know, it was the only thing to be done. But jesting apart, spare the roof if you can; those tiles are old, and costly to replace. As for the boy—you did right to fell those roughs, but console yourself; it was a kind of justice nonetheless. It was that lad and two others who set on and robbed a shopkeeper, earlier this morning. An old man, who may well die.''

Almost overhead, on the high seaward towers of the citadel, ringing trumpets mirrored the sunrise in their tone, signaling the beginning of the city's day. Elof rubbed his stubbled chin. ''So? When it could only stir up more trouble between city and northerners, another riot? You are sure?''

''We took one of his complices, and he confessed. They were starving, he said, and I believe him, skin and bones that he is. But they also thought to avenge that northerner who was robbed on the outskirts last week. Avenge! Twelve more that I know of have died in the uproar this morning, ten of them northerners. By now it may be more. Do you wonder I insist these things are stamped out the moment they begin, and thoroughly? There is no end to them, they breed.''

''Aye, but have a care!'' said Ils darkly. ''You're brewing trouble for yourself, making yourself unpopular with the rabble. Ask Roc, ask Ferhas; they hear the gossip, and it's that you're too soft on the northerners. They were herding that one here to string him up on your window. A little love gift, since you like them so much. And you're still only Marchwarden-elect, you've not the full powers yet.''

''Till noon today only. And have I not been given every encouragement to use the rightful powers of office to the hilt and past this last half-year?''

''That's not what Bryhon and his bullies will be shouting,'' said Elof.

Kermorvan shrugged. ''If others will not act speedily enough, I must, Bryhon or no Bryhon. There have been riots enough with or without provocation, Elof; the first came in midwinter, while you yet lay ill. Then we thought it was a passing folly, a brief outburst at the inflow of northern fugitives when we were ourselves in need.'' Kermorvan shrugged. ''Now we know better. Every day it grows worse, and every day more come, as the Ekwesh rampage through Nordeney. The common folk fear; they cannot believe our land will feed them all. I begin to wonder, myself. And so fear breeds hatred in both sides, and hatred leads to crime, crime to riot—''

''And to madness, all!'' snorted Ils, tossing her thick black curls. ''You men are all daft, to wish such miseries upon your fellows, and to suffer them so lightly. Look at us! Did we not come, we three, through danger upon danger to succor your folk? And what thanks do we find? Oh, you, Kermorvan, you they laud and applaud—or most of them, anyhow—you they make Marchwarden, and well they might. But us? Even your own precious faction point the finger at Elof as some kind of northern warlock, benign enough maybe but not to be trusted. And me they call his familiar! I can hardly walk abroad by myself. And that's your friends! What your enemies say—that moonstruck Bryhon and his rabble . . .''

''But that's mere malice!'' protested Elof. ''It's so obvious Bryhon seeks only to settle an old score. Surely few save his own close faction believe—''

''More than you think!'' said Ils sharply. Her dark eyes flashed. ''They don't want to believe they were so short a step from defeat. Nor that they had to be rescued by foreigners. And there's more like them every day. Well, I have had enough. I go, and soon! Back to the hollow hills I, and this city may slide into the sea for all I care!'' The men sprang up, protesting, but Ils sat back, face set and stubborn. ''Waste no more words! I endured this long only to see Elof made well, and the success of my healing.'' Her round fingers knitted together a moment. ''He needs me no longer. My mind is made up.''

Kermorvan sighed. ''And you, Elof? What will you do, now you are well? I hope you at least do not wish to depart. My house is yours for as long you wish it, and the city folk do respect you; with your fair skin they forget you are a northerner—''

"Will I?"

Kermorvan flushed in embarrassment. "Do not take it so! I meant only that you may help overcome their foolish distrust of northerners. Remember, the first copper skins most have seen were on Ekwesh, and your folk look much like the reivers—too much, in eyes that saw the horrors of the siege. But if you and I can open those eyes to the old kinship, there is a chance . . ."

Elof shook his head. "I'm sorry. Oh, it's true enough what you say, but no. My prime purpose, my heaviest duty, ended when that evil I unleashed was undone. Another promise claims me now. There's another place I must go."

Kermorvan frowned. "What place?"

"I don't know." Elof looked out into the courtyard, to where the first long rays of the sunrise warmed the courtyard's cold paving. "I know only whither it lies. That way, in the path of the dawn, whither I must go. To wander. To roam across the whole wide world, if I must. I do not wish to tarry long. I dare not."

Kermorvan nodded. "I understand. But you will stay at least for today? And you, Ils? At least come to the ceremony, both of you, ere you settle your minds to any of this. There you may hear something to make you think . . ."

"I doubt that!" muttered Ils.

"She'll come!" grinned Elof. "She wouldn't miss it for the world, any more than I. Will it be you saying all these things?"

Kermorvan stood up, rubbing at his stiff back. "I appreciate the honor of my position less during early alarms . . . Yes, some of them, at least." He sucked in a long determined breath, and his face hardened. "I mean to make myself heard. The syndics have been dragging their heels over this matter of the northern refugees. We must settle it, secure their safety, and quickly. At whatever cost." Then his grimness faded to a smile. "Linger over your food as you wish, but I must be at the Syndicacy well in advance! Ferhas, my robes! Come, I beg you, both of you! For if this day goes as I think it may, I shall have need of my friends." He strode away from the table and up the wide main stairs, scabbard slapping at his riding boot as if to punctuate his shouts for his squire. Elof gazed around the gloomy hall, following the peeled and faded murals, the portraits darkened by centuries of smoke from the hanging lamps.

"He values us, you know," he said. "Admirers he has now, aye, and flatterers in plenty. No family at all . . ."

"I know," said Ils, and sniffed disapprovingly. "A poor place to grow up in, this, with only a few old women to look after him, and his father's squire for a tutor. A wonder he did not turn out odder than he is."

"I think he has few friends as close as we," said Elof. "And this ceremony must mean a lot to him. Will you not witness that, at least? Then you can tell your folk that they have one friend among our rulers, mad and savage though we be . . ."

"We? Never number yourself among these folk! Nor among your precious northerners!" retorted Ils. "You're another breed entirely, whatever blood flows in your veins. And him also! He is wise to grab hold of his Marchwarden's place while he may, hard and thankless honor though it is. The tide of gratitude that swept him into it neglected to provide wealth to patch even his own roof, let alone sustain the people's. In these parts it seems gratitude's a beggar child, starved into an early grave. What will be left of it after he puts down a few more riots? It'll be back to what drove him out in the first place, his partisans and Bryhon's breaking each other's heads in the streets, and the ordinary citizens damning them both. Ferhas says there are whispers even among his friends . . . Only this time there's the Ekwesh waiting to sweep up the bits! Well, since you insist on going to the ceremony, so will I also, for all my heart counsels otherwise. I fear, Elof, I fear . . ."

"You? What could you fear?"

"Anything. Nothing. This great warren of men oppresses me, it dims my wits as the sun does my eyes. I start at shadows, that's all.'' She tossed a hunk of bread onto his plate. "Eat, and pay no heed.''

But as they emerged into the sunny street an hour or so later, Elof could well understand her feelings. The bustle and roar of Kerbryhaine the Great City swept at him and over him like an inrushing wave, carrying with it the sound and scent of men a millionfold. From the clifflike crag of the citadel overhead to the first low slopes of the hazy hills around, all, everywhere, was a great sea of men, walls and houses rising above it like summits of coral along a reef, and writhing coils of smoke. Vast and stately as were the works of the duergar, they stood quieter, emptier by comparison; there was no such sense of fierce vitality barely pent, nor of such bitter unease. Yet he understood it a little better than Ils, and what aroused her contempt awoke in him a measure of pity. The city folk had been terribly shaken, first by the sudden and devastating assault when they had thought themselves so rich and invulnerable, and then by the vast inpouring of northerners fleeing the Ekwesh. The people had looked to their lords for some wise word, some simple gesture that would turn time back to the days of their smug security. But now they were growing impatient, beginning to suspect what might well be true—that there was no such word or gesture, that there was no going back, ever, to what had been. In such a time it was easy to seek scapegoats. They had heard Kermorvan cheered to the echo as he left the house, but now Elof saw heads turn in the crowded street; he heard, or guessed at, the dark mutterings, ribald whispers, sniffs of sternly self-righteous disapproval, sensed fingers pointing in stabbing gestures of distrust and fear. By popular prejudice duergar were regarded as vermin, on a level with beasts of the gutter, and he as some kind of necromancer for walking with one. He swung aside the bag of tools that he was taking to finish some work for Roc, and took her arm. It was tense against his side. Nowhere among all this, not even behind the walls they had just quitted, could she feel even remotely secure.

Fortunately, the way to the Syndicacy was not long.

Kermorvan's ancestral roof, dilapidated as it was, stood tall among the houses of the Old City, against the rocky crags of the citadel's northern flank. Before its gentler eastward face there opened a wide quadrangle all paved with white stone, the square of the citadel, and along one whole side of that ranged the massive gray frontage of the Syndicacy. High though it stood, it was outwardly stark and plain, its only ornament a line of austere pillars which ran out around the great main doors to support a lofty canopied porch towering on steps above the heads of the throng in the square. Ils flinched nervously at the noisy crush around the steps, but strode beside Elof as if she had no troubles in the world. The crowd parted swiftly to let them pass, as if fearing the contact, and she smiled sardonically. "Even vermin have their privileges, I see."

When they entered the portico the Syndicacy's air of austerity vanished, for all around its inner walls were rich mosaics, male and female figures depicted in swirls of vibrant color. Elof guessed by their size and their heroic aspect and distinctive attributes that they must represent the Powers most revered by the folk of Bryhaine: there was Niarad with his nets, succoring mariners, and Ilmarinen, as it seemed, releasing lava to shape the citadel rock, and many others he did not know. He looked in vain for a figure in black armor or blue mantle, till Ils pointed to the summit of the great doors ahead. Above their wide arch rose a great sun in gold, pouring down gilt radiance, and across its disc, flying with open beak, a vast raven. To Ilmarinen Ils bowed as they passed, but at the Raven Elof glared.

The doors beneath were blackened wood, of great height and thickness, and width enough to span almost the whole floor of the chamber within. At most times they stood shut tight, shielding the deliberations of the Syndicacy from common eyes, but upon rare days such as this they were flung wide to vouchsafe the crowd a glimpse of its solemn ceremonial. Ferhas, Kermorvan's squire and steward, awaited them there, white mane bobbing nervously: he ushered them swiftly up a marble stair to places kept for them at the front of the crowded public gallery, overlooking both chamber and doors, but himself chose to stand some way behind. Elof smiled wryly. Even wise old Ferhas was as much a city man as the worthies on either side who edged discreetly away; much as he valued these proven friends of his master's, he had long held the city view of northerners as bumpkins at best, at worst barbarians, and still less could he shake off the violent prejudice against duergar. The conflict left him perpetually ill at ease in their presence. It was chiefly more traveled men, Northland traders such as Kathel Kataihan, who held broader views; there were not so many of these in the city now, and among the four hundred-odd syndics fewer than a score. And even of those how many could Kermorvan rely upon to side with the refugees, if the majority would not?

Elof scanned the wide empty chamber below, the banked rows of seats carved from fine stone and gilded wood, set about with signs and blazons where the place was held by ancestral right as well as wealth. The many-colored windows flecked the chamber with glowing warmth. All in all a noble sight, yet to his eyes it looked cold and hard, entrenched, unyielding. So also too many of the syndics seemed as they filed in, proud in the sweeping splendor of their robes. Too many faces reminded him of the Headman and elders of Asenby. Strong and even capable men those had been, but blind to all of the world that did not concern their immediate interests; so also these seemed, and from all he had heard, in defense of those interests they could be selfish and quarrelsome as children.

Green robes marked the landowners and men of property, gray the scholars and officials, brown the merchants and tradesmen, but they varied wildly in shade and pattern and ornament, sometimes as a mark of faction, more often as a display of wealth. The two great factions, once nobles and commoners, now old nobility against new, generally wore darker or lighter shades of their particular color, but still they vied in ornament. Some of the gray robes were most richly and garishly adorned of all, while many of the scarlet robes of the warrior order, worn over armor and the weapons they alone might bear in the assembly, seemed positively old and threadbare. Not so one that was borne by a dark man of great height, taller even than Kermorvan. Light red it was, and marked at the breast with a device of a claw and broken chain. Its discreet border of worked gold and baldric of golden mail bore out his air of prosperous ease, as did the smooth joviality with which, pausing by the doors, he acknowledged the loud acclaim of a good part of the crowd.

At last men of the City Guard called for silence, and a wide door at the rear boomed open. Syndics and spectators alike rose to their feet, and the crowd surged forward to see. In came the two elderly Marshals of the city in gray robes, their faces uneasy, and behind them in scarlet and armor the Wardens of the Eastern and Southern Marches, flanking Kermorvan as Warden-elect of the North. But at sight of him a swelling cheer from without faltered and dwindled to a great babble of astonishment, for the robes he wore were not scarlet but black, trimmed and collared with heavy gold, and over his heart in gold was traced the emblem of the Raven and Sun. The guardsmen hammered their staves on the marble floor for silence as the procession swept toward the center of the assembly, leading Kermorvan to a tall seat one place to the right of the Marshals' chairs. But ere they could reach it there was a rustle of robes, and the dark man was on his feet, his gangling frame towering over the Marshals and blocking their path.

"One moment!" he cried, his deep voice echoing through the chamber. "One moment, my lords! By what authority do you admit this man to the Syndicacy, and lead him to a place? And by what authority is he permitted to bear those robes?"

The astonished Marshals gaped at him, while through chamber and square alike a buzz of dispute arose. Many of the crowd, and even some in the gallery, howled abuse at the tall man till across the floor another man rose, in brown robes trimmed with fine furs that only emphasized his stoutness, and his rich mellow voice rode over the uproar. "By the unopposed vote of this assembly under the rule of war, these six months past—that would be how, my lord Bryhon! And in recognition and reward for great deeds done. Which is more than I recall you were ever voted!"

"And those remarkable robes, my lord Kathel?"

"M'm, as to them . . ." The merchant's voice was honeyed as ever, but it had lost something of its first certainty. "Well, they are of his choosing, and I know of no law that prevents him."

Kermorvan raised his head calmly. "My lords Marshal, they are the robes my great-grandfather last wore in this assembly, as was the ancient and unquestioned privilege of our line. By what authority has that been changed? And by what authority are these questions asked?"

"By the urgent need to question a decision forced through in haste and folly," said Bryhon with equal calm. "And consequently, perhaps, to impose some grave penalty." Sharp whispers, astonished and aghast, ran across the chamber, echoes rustling like dead leaves in the domed roof, and outside the crowd rumbled contention and discontent.

"But—but he has not yet taken his seat in the assembly!" blustered the leading Marshal, a stout, red-faced old man with bristling white moustaches; his blue-gray eyes were not penetrating like Kermorvan's, but bulging and opaque.

"Looks like a dead fish," muttered Ils, "only with fewer wits."

"Let him stand, then," said Bryhon quietly, "as must all brought here to our judgment." A wild chorus of dispute broke out, and Elof could hear that neither in chamber nor in crowd was it all on Kermorvan's side; scuffles were breaking out, and files of guardsmen went hurrying down to deal with them ere they spread. The harassed Marshal conferred with his colleague, a younger edition of himself; they shook their heads at Bryhon and Kermor-

van alike, and when the guards had eventually enforced
silence they announced that all should take their seats for
now, but without ceremonial, and Bryhon should have the
right to speak. He smiled and bowed graciously, and
stepped to the middle of the floor.

"My lords Marshal, fellow syndics, for any discourtesy
I crave your pardon. But it seemed to me the only way to
forestall what might not easily be undone. Master Kathel,
in justifying this strange act of the Syndicacy you mentioned the matter of some great deeds done by this man.
But the people of this city are driven to ask, were such
deeds ever done?"

"W-what foolishness is this?" stammered the Marshal,
into a shocked silence.

"Yours, I fear," said the dark man coolly. He rounded
on the other syndics, "What do those deeds amount to? A
skillful claim, aided, it shames me to say, by some within
this city, to have compassed the defeat of that whole savage army which besieged us. How?" He shook his head
in apparent wonder. "By the slaying of one of their leaders! And by the shattering of some savage totem, which
he claims they relied upon. But I ask you, look again without panic and credulity at the events of that sorry time.
That we were beaten back by the first attacks, that is little
wonder, for they came upon us without the least warning
and we a people at peace, unprepared. But given a day or
so to muster our full force, to plan our strategy, we sallied
out, and we drove them back into the sea. As you would
expect! For how could such savages stand against the
forces of this city? Ask of yourselves, must we really hare
after miracles to explain their defeat? Are we ourselves
grown so savage, are we sunk to the level of simple northerners that believe in magical mutterings over metal?" His
cool eyes swept the chamber with mild scorn. "It seems
we are. For from a sideline of the battle a man stages a
clever show with the corpse of a slain chieftain and a broken weapon—were there not enough of both, that day?—
and with some small encouragement we fall at his feet.
Some encouragement, no doubt, from those who would

gladly turn aside the people's allegiance, that they might more easily be oppressed. Turn it aside from their chosen leaders. From *us.*'' The word was spoken no less quietly, but with the spitting intensity of water on hot steel.

Elof sat silent, held in icy thrall by the pattern of what was unfolded before him. It was shaped with cunning to appeal to all that was narrowest and most insular in the sothran temperament, and the typical syndic most of all. They would know, if they remembered truly, that events had not been as Bryhon described them; for one thing, where had the lightning come from, that blasted their walls? But he was presenting them with every inducement to disbelieve and distort their own memories, even an open appeal to their naked self-interest, a hint that Kermorvan threatened their power.

As if scenting success, the tall man's manner grew more jovial; he grinned, and fingered his bushy beard. ''And after all, why should we believe such a man, whom we knew even in his first youth as a vicious brawling braggart? Was this assembly not on the point of trying and exiling him, save that he slunk away in disgrace, to avoid a formal sentence and the seizure of his property? Such as he has. And what did we hear of him then? Tales that he had taken up with a pack of starveling corsairs, and then vanished from their ken, until, two years later, he reappears amid a sudden onslaught of savages. An onslaught he had been threatening us with for . . .''

''Warning,'' said Kermorvan, equally quietly yet so unexpectedly that all started. ''Warning, not threatening.''

Bryhon inclined his head. ''As you will; it mends nothing. Warning us, then, for years in an attempt to spread a panic, panic that would bring him power. As in the end, it seems, it so conveniently has!'' The change in his voice was startling, so loud now that it overbore the first cries of protest. ''Those brown-skinned reivers took us by surprise, that is true. But have you not, any of you, asked yourselves how such a thing might come to pass? How a pack of sea-roving savages could dare assault, let alone manage to breach, the walls of the greatest city in this land? How else," Bryhon answered himself simply, "save by treason?" And he looked from Kermorvan up to the gallery, straight at Ils and Elof.

Elof felt his ears and face flame hot as if he bent over a forgefire. He sprang to his feet at the gallery rail and shouted, "And do you call me a traitor? What manner of man, then, skulks on city walls at dead of night? What manner of man tries to murder those he meets there in secret, though all they ask is to be brought before authority? And there's witnesses enough for that!"

The crowd seemed to snarl like a slide of falling rock. Kermorvan flashed him a sudden warning glance; Ils plucked him down by the sleeve. Bryhon did not so much as look at him; his voice was calm and smooth as the stuff of his robe.

"Which brings us to the manner of this singular return. Did he come openly and in brotherhood, offering to take his place among us as an equal? He did not. At dead of night he came slinking over an embattled wall. And he came in strange company. A northern vagrant, the first of many, and, though one would hardly credit it, a creature of the mountains, a race accounted as savage as the man-eaters and still more beastlike."

A rush of memories awoke in Elof, of halls rich and noble in the hollow hills, clam rivers mirror-dark under stone, strong faces lined with lifetimes of wisdom and great craft. Of a folk who had succored a desperate unknown in flight from his own destiny, and set the power in his hands to forge it anew—

He was ready to spring down, to spit his contempt in Bryhon's face and dash his fist after. But to his surprise Ils at his side remained calm, though her heavy brows were drawn tight. "Be still!" she hissed, and he remembered suddenly how much older than him she must be. "We are but ciphers here, conceits in a debate, no more. It is not for us to answer, but Kermorvan."

"Then may he do so soon!"

Bryhon gestured at Kermorvan. "What do you think the ancestors he vaunts before us would have made of him

then? Much what I did, I fear. And if in the days since
that return he had proved me wrong, with all my heart I
would have made amends, and been the first to follow him
today. But has he? What has he brought us since? Help
and wisdom in our need? Hardly. Instead he has encouraged a flock of carrion crows to settle upon our already
devastated fields, under guise of a kinship long forsworn.
His pack, for do they not hang upon his every word? And
how many more of them are there to come, when the
Northern Marches are in his hands? Shall the Northlands
be emptied for us to feed? See how the half-savages he
shields steal among you, the northerners who scuttle
southward from their cannibal kin. See how they slip the
very bread from before the mouths of your hungry children, the smallest wealth from your pocket, the roof from
over your heads. A strange way to treat a city he professes
to care for! Either he is mad, or he has a purpose. And
what can that purpose be?'' He waved a hand in Kermorvan's general direction. "I am grateful to him, in his arrogance. For so vast was his pride in what he thought his
hour of triumph that he has saved me the labor of convincing you. For he stands revealed in his purpose! Is he
not clad in its colors?''

Elof could not guess what he meant, but that barb struck
harder upon the city folk than any gone before. There was
a moment of stunned silence, and then a roar like a great
wave breaking. Elof could hear cries both for Bryhon and
against him, for Kermorvan and against him also, but it
was as if the same feeling fed them, a ravening anger that
seemed to convulse both crowd and chamber, syndics and
spectators both, as a lightning flare leaps from cloud to
cloud. Blows flew freely among the crowd, brawls sprang
up and spread outward like ripples in a pond. Anger rode
upon the shoulders of the crowd, anger whose very cause
and moment seemed forgotten in its own mad onrush. It
was like a wave indeed, driven on from behind by shouts
and milling brawls. The great crowd surged forward, up
the steps and spilled through the doors into the Syndicacy
itself. Elof shuddered as he heard the rising growl of that

most savage and monstrous of beasts, a mob. Syndics sprang to their feet in fury and alarm, but their shouts went unheard in the row. His formerly stolid neighbors in the gallery were on their feet also, shouting first down into the chamber, and then at each other and others around. Feet clattered on the stairs, and a tide of rioters spilled into the gallery. "Mad!" shouted Ils, ducking down as blows were traded above her head and Elof's. "Stark mad, the whole pack of—"

Then a heap of struggling, cursing bodies tumbled between them, and they were forced apart. To either side of Elof the spectators scattered in panic, stumbling over the stairs and each other, and he saw one almost toppled over the low stone balustrade. "Ils!" he shouted, and heard a faint voice cry out, *"Elof, beware! At your back!"* He whirled, and saw a knot of tall men forcing their way determinedly through the crush in his direction, five copper-skinned northerners, all with faces hard and fell. They saw him even as he them, and plunged down on him; he saw steel glint among their garments, and his hand flew to his side for the sword that was not there. He cursed, seized the heavy bench he had been sitting on and with a heave tore it free as the first knife reached out for him; it stuck in the wood, and he upended the heavy seat and smashed it down upon the wielder's head. Another threw his weight upon the bench and tore it from his hand, and the rest sprang forward. Elof looked desperately for some weapon, saw at his feet his toolpack spilled open, and seized the huge hammer with which he had forged the sword. Short in the haft it was, but terrible weight was in its high-peaked head, as long as his forearm and cored with strange and turbulent metals of great weight, which the duergar alone knew how to refine and contain in safety. Swiftly he straightened and with wild strength he swung it against the nearest blade; there was a sharp shattering ring, and the long knife splintered against its wielder's hand. Icy pain lanced into his side, he felt a blade snag in his jerkin, fell back and struck out once again. With a frightful muffled sound the hammer struck deep into flesh, and the man fell choking and writhing to the floor. Another loomed over him with upraised hand, in it no knife but a short sword; Elof's arm was seized from behind, and the crook of an elbow snaked round his throat. Then it was suddenly torn free, as if somebody had hurled the man away. With no room to swing the hammer, he drove it straight into the swordsman's stomach; the man doubled, and it was Elof's hand that rose and fell, once. The cry came again, he sprang round and saw Ils by the balustrade, struggling half-choked in the grip of the remaining two killers who were striving to force her over. So it was she who had freed him! From the chamber below came the ring and clash of swords, but he paid that no heed and barged through the crowd toward her. The killers saw him, pulled her back from the balustrade, but instead set her before them as a shield and charged up the gallery steps toward the door. Without stopping to think, Elof whirled his arm and let the hammer fly, as he had the tile. A handspan above Ils' dark hair it flew, and one man yelled in horror as the other's head was dashed into a spraying pulp. Ils' arm was free, and even as Elof sprang and shouldered his way through she caught her attacker by the throat and hurled him to the ground. He sprang up, snake-lithe, unfolding a claspknife from his sleeve, but Ils seized his arms. The knife slashed past her throat, she heaved, and her duergar strength told. The man cartwheeled down the steps, struck the balustrade and slid, screaming and scrabbling, over its brink.

Elof stood gasping, staring. How many attackers had there been? Then they saw the man whose sword and hand he had shattered run for the door, holding old Ferhas off with a knife. He had all but reached the stairs when there came a clatter of arms beyond; he sought to spring back, but a robed silhouette blocked the opening. With horrific suddenness a bright sword leaped out between the man's shoulder blades. Then a mass of guards poured through, and set about subduing the rioters and herding them toward the stairs.

Elof looked at the dead attacker, and at the red-robed

man who had run him through, now stooping to wipe his sword on his victim's jerkin. The newcomer glanced up, and raised an eyebrow. "Brawling again, sir smith? And in the Syndicacy, too; no tiles here! Be warned by the fate of this one! But it appears that you took some small hurt; we shall call that lesson enough."

Elof looked down; only when he saw the bloodstain in his side did he remember the sting, and feel it anew. "A scratch, no more. And glad as I am to see you quelling disorder for once, Bryhon, you were not quite timely enough. As before, we had to do most of the work ourselves."

Red flame burned in the dark man's cheeks. "Fitting enough," he shrugged, and kicked at the copper-hued arm. "Northerner, slay northerner. Your friend put paid to another two brace on the chamber floor. Perhaps he is learning wisdom. Guards, remove this carrion."

"Northerners?" muttered Elof, following the guards who were dragging the corpses away down the stairs. "I wonder—I grew up among them, remember? These have brown skins, yes, but look at the hard faces of them, and the scarring! Do they not sooner resemble—"

"Amicac's guts, yes!" roared Kathel, stumping over to the door with Kermorvan at his heels. "Ekwesh! And the ones down here also! Where in Hella's name did they spring from?"

"Stragglers from their foraging bands, perhaps," said Kermorvan thoughtfully, "left behind in the rout, slipping into the city in the guise of refugees to seek revenge. Seeing their chance in the disorder caused by Lord Bryhon's unruly followers. But there is another, darker chance. They could be spies, assassins deliberately sent among the refugees from the Ekwesh settlements in the north. In which case . . ."

"We cannot afford to admit any of them?" broke in Bryhon. "It seems you learn wisdom indeed!"

"You mistake me, Bryhon. It proves my point, not yours."

"And what point is that?"

"You will hear when the session begins anew. And the sooner you call your mob to heel, the sooner that will be. I suggest you set about it."

A mirthless grin gleamed in Bryhon's thick beard. "I have not yet had my full say. But better, perhaps, that you stand convicted out of your own mouth. Speak on, then."

"Well, you make progress," croaked Ils to Elof as they climbed wearily back up to the gallery. "Bryhon speaks to you instead of at you. Wonders will never cease! Speaking of which, a wonder you dealt with that one behind you. I strove to help, but I was already half throttled."

"But you did help!" said Elof, gathering up his trampled tools from the gallery floor. "He was pulled away—"

She shook her head firmly. "Not by me. He only turned to me after you threw him off."

"Who, then?"

But Ils only shrugged. "Perhaps he slipped." She avoided the bloodied end of the bench as she sat.

Elof shook his head. "I cannot explain it. But they were certainly assassins; they knew their targets. What will Kermorvan have to say about that?"

The chamber and the crowd alike were hushed as Kermorvan stepped out to speak. He looked at them a moment, and then at Bryhon, and his gaze grew very cold. His words rang clear against the marble of the chamber. "Syndics and people of Kerbryhaine! This day you have heard my lord of Bryheren lay many grave charges against me. Or have you? I know this man of old, and I took care to listen to his actual words, not the dark things he implied. For the most part he simply struck a spark with subtly worded questions, and led your minds to blow them to a blaze. For well he knows that such cloudy and insubstantial matters are harder to dispel with solid truth! But truth is the best I have to offer you, and I warn you now, it will not be the truth you wish to hear! Yet it will avail nothing to riot or shout me down. For truth is truth, and if you stopped my voice forever it would not alter by one jot the forces I see at work. Save perhaps to hasten them." He looked at Bryhon scornfully. "I have ample answers for the trifling charges this man made, but I will content myself with an example or two only for now. Take the matter of the corsairs. I joined them only because they were willing to fight the Ekwesh, when all others in this land laughed at the idea that they could be a threat, or chose to believe Lord Bryhon's insinuations at that time, which were that I sought to win military power for myself by building up a false menace. Those corsairs are in this city now, having won pardon, and we have testimony enough that they fought the Ekwesh, and valiantly.''

Bryhon inclined his head mockingly. ''I bow to your authority. They fought, aye—for booty already riven from our folk.'' Elof bit his lip; that was sadly true, though not as it was put. But Kermorvan was undaunted.

''Did I say it was not so? Yet I thought that better, much better, than nothing, for even such small opposition might discourage the reivers from the Southlands long enough for this city to see its peril. And I could at least put the wealth gained thereby to building up a fleet. A small hope, and as I eventually realized, a false one. When I heard of a matter more urgent, the mysterious mindsword, I turned to that instead. For another example, take the manner of my return. How in the world could I have returned openly, as Bryhon suggests, to a city besieged and partly taken? What other way was there but quietly and in darkness, when it could not be said for certain who held which part of the wall? The suggestion is absurd, as Bryhon must know. Yet see how he used it to color the gravest charge of all he dares to bring against me.''

Trouble passed over Kermorvan's lean features like a cloud, and his voice was stern and bleak as a cold wind from the north. ''He has deftly avoided making that charge openly. But through his words I stand accused, in sum, of having sought by some means or another to use the events of the siege to seize power within this city. To set myself up as ruler, as tyrant over you all. As your king.''

Elof's first instinct was to laugh, but the deadly stillness quelled it; the crowd hardly seemed to be breathing. This was something they took with deadly seriousness. And looking at Kermorvan, he saw that his friend did also. A great hush filled chamber and gallery alike, and the silence seemed itself a clarion, calling from the deeps of time. Kermorvan lifted his head, and there was a fierce smile on his lips, a grim pride in his voice. "But why should you believe this? The child of kings I acknowledge myself. But this was never their kingdom."

Elof blinked as if he had been struck, hardly aware of the uproar that washed over him. "I saw before Andvar that he must be some great noble," he murmured to Ils, "but a *king?* Of where?"

"But did you not *know?*" hissed Ferhas in his ear, detachment forgotten in the excitement. "His name, don't the glory shine out of that, all alive? You in the north, sir, have you quite forgot them, the Lost Lands and their great city of olden times, greatest there's ever been in this land?"

"Y-yes—the Strandenburg he called it, the City by the Waters—but his name? He called himself plain Kermorvan then!"

"Ah," breathed Ferhas, "and he stuck to your northern tongue? That'd be when he wasn't right sure of you—if you'll pardon me saying, sir!" he added hastily, with a furtive superstitious gesture. "But you've the sothran well enough, sir, can't you see now? *Kaher,* or *ker,* that's a walled city like this; *mor,* a great lake or sea, and *mor ouhen,* that's the waterstrand. So *Kaher-mor-ouhen—*"

"*Kermorvan?*"

"That was the city's name, sir, and so of its kingly line— what remains of it. The name alone's not uncommon, for there are younger branches that bear it. But Keryn, now, that's one of the kingly names, for first-born of the true line only. Put the two together, and he'd have been telling you who he was at once. It was among the corsairs you met him, wasn't it, sir, and them sothrans? He'd not risk naming himself clear in that company! T'wasn't you he distrusted, sir, t'was them."

Ils was nodding slowly to herself, as if at a suspicion now confirmed. But Elof stared down at his friend as if he had never truly seen him before. Kings were hardly human to him, benign or frightening figures in childhood tales, remote figures of worship and majesty or wicked tyranny. This lean young fighter he had first met barefoot upon a beach, rubbing shoulders with a hard-bitten corsair crew, hardly seemed to fit either image. Yet even as Elof formed the thought, that mantle of infinite age seemed to settle about the tall young warrior once again, as it had in the courts of the duergar before Andvar their lord and had diminished even his grim presence. Kermorvan, his face mild and calm once more, advanced to the center of the floor, and the light from the windows gleamed in his thick bronze hair, so that he looked in truth a king already crowned.

"It may be, though, that you will not believe what I say. Or, more subtly, you fear that the enmity of Lord Bryhon and his friends will force me to fight for the dominion of Kerbryhaine, whether I will or no, and so plunge the state into civil war. That indeed might come to pass . . ." He raised a hand to quell the swelling protests, and repeated more loudly ". . . *might* come to pass, if— *if* Bryhon forced me to it, and *if* I thought such dominion worth the winning. But I do not! Never for good or ill would I seize their rule! Why? Because though I dearly love this realm, these lands in which I was born, I believe that the days of their greatness are ended, that even the time of their enduring draws to a close. As well seize a sandhill around which the tide is washing! For I truly believe that this city is doomed. I believe that the downfall of Kerbryhaine is at hand!"

The sense of shocked disbelief was so tangible in the chamber, Elof almost expected laughter. But it was a cry of fear, as much as anger, that arose from the crowd outside and wiped any laughter from the faces of the syndics. Then Bryhon sprang up and rounded upon the crowd. "Pay no heed to the man! Is not his purpose clear? He seeks to fright you like children with shadows! To scare you, that you may come clinging to his skirts!" Now indeed cries of anger arose, as rumor of Kermorvan's words and Bryhon's were tossed and bandied about, no doubt with exaggerations, among those too far back to hear. Again the growl of the beast awakened, but even as it did so Kermorvan strode to the door, and his commanding cry echoed across the square.

"Be still! Be still, and hear!" And astonishingly, the crowd indeed fell silent.

Kermorvan rounded on the syndics and pressed home his words as a fighter feeling his enemy's guard falter. "The Ekwesh, they are our doom! They have seen our walls breached, our strength falter before theirs! They have tasted blood, they have tasted wealth, and worst, they have tasted defeat and flight! That at least will unite them, now that fell sword cannot! They will return, and soon—before the eldest who fled is too old to fight, and redeem his honor in his clan! And before our scars can heal. At best, in ten years—at worst, in one! And how then shall we sustain such another siege? In ten years, if we have them, the city may build new walls, new ships, new houses— but how can it regain its sons?" The weariness in his voice now was more moving than any trick of oratory. "We were unprepared. The blame for that . . . is not our present matter. But, as well as fighting men, to the tally of our slain it added women and children. Within these walls more than a fifth of both perished. And the country folk, being first set upon, fared worse. Let us ponder on that, we confident syndics! As our folk grow old and die in their turn, who shall replace them? What does it mean for our numbers?" The assembly stirred in deep disquiet, but no word was spoken, not even by Bryhon. The dark man looked baffled a moment, then sat up sharply, as if seeing Kermorvan's intent, and looked as worried as the rest. Kermorvan nodded.

"You see? Our wound festers and worsens; our numbers will dwindle further. For my part, as Warden of the Northern Marches I would be fortunate in years to come to raise half the levies the last Marchwarden had. And he and they were slaughtered out of hand." He rounded furiously upon his audience. "By Kerys' Gate! Need you wonder now why I welcome the fugitives from Nordeney? I would do so even without the demands of mercy and the bonds of kinship! But those bonds exist! Look!'' He gestured up at the gallery. Elof glanced round to see who was meant, and realized it was himself. "Elof, my northern friend, to whom the true glory of the siege's ending belongs!" Elof, feeling his face redden, smiled sheepishly. "But he is also a reminder, if you must have it, that northerners are our kin, as they have been since the founding of great Kerys itself. What if they are chiefly brown-skinned now? What may the skin tell against the man beneath it? They at least had the sense to welcome and succor fugitives when they themselves were weak. Shall we be less wise?" The rumble from the crowd had little enthusiasm in it, but less anger. Kermorvan nodded. "The northerners will fight beside us, and hardily, if we have the wit to accept them." The chamber was silent still, but Elof could feel the change of mood. He became aware that his neighbors were looking at him hesitantly, unsure, almost shamefacedly. But Kermorvan did not seem heartened; his voice was if anything more sad. "Think on it, my friends! And be as honest as I have known you. And yet I fear even that may not be enough."

"What will, then!" burst out Bryhon. "The placing of a king over us? As our ancestors of old so wisely shunned? Never!" Other voices echoed him in angry refusal, many syndics among them. Even Kathel and Ourhens, the other leader of the merchants, looked anxiously at Kermorvan, as they might at a customer who carried the haggling too far. But Kermorvan appeared not to notice them; he was staring into the many-colored windows as if into an infinite distance, a gulf of years as well as leagues.

"I mean, Bryhon, that we need more folk, and a greater vision. We must reunite northerners and sothrans, Runduathya and Penruthya, Svarhath and Arauthar that should never have been sundered. But we must not stop there! We must unite all our scattered kin. All!"

The syndics looked at each other in puzzlement. "But who d'you mean?" demanded Kathel. "There is only us!

Those that fled here from the Lost Lands, us first and northerners after! Who else is there?''

''That you have forgotten is small blame to you,'' said Kermorvan, with a thin smile. ''Few in Kerbryhaine would remember, for their ancestors fled westward long before the victory of the Ice. But others endured longer, until the glaciers were at the very gates of the ancient city itself. Then the king sent many more westward, his queen and his infant heir among them, from whom I am descended. Then as now there was strife, and many fled northward to settle Nordeney. But they recorded that the king had sent others east, to the small ports they had on the coast, as we do on ours. These were not so far from the Ice, and very small, but shielded to some degree by mountains. So perhaps their descendants also have survived.''

The chamber rumbled with excited comment, and among it some incredulous laughter. ''A few, perhaps,'' chuckled the elder Marshal. ''But what are they to us? We cannot send them word, let alone summon them . . .''

Kermorvan's gray eyes glittered. ''Why not?''

Now indeed there was laughter, and it spilled over into the crowd as Kermorvan's words were repeated. ''Why, man,'' demanded the other Marshal, ''have you lost your learning, or your wits? Have you forgotten what lies between? The whole span of the land of Brasayhal, nigh on a thousand leagues!''

''Aye!'' shouted Ourhens the merchant. ''And most of the way through the Great Forest, by all accounts. Such a place that claimed half of those who set out westward!''

''Yet half were not!'' Kermorvan threw back at him with a snap. ''Half, many a thousand, came through, for all they set out ill prepared and in haste, burdened with families and great store of possessions. And more than half of the northerners came through, though they were even less ready.''

''So indeed,'' nodded an arid old man in plain gray robes. ''But they drew no maps. They were so crazed with fear they would scarce talk of it again.''

''All the more reason that some be drawn,'' said Ker-

morvan grimly. "We may be wanderers again, if the Ekwesh return too soon!"

"But there's nobody mad enough to set foot in the Forest nowadays!"

Kermorvan smiled. "I have, though it scared me, and
my friends . . ." He paused to catch a shout from the
crowd, that other voices took up. "What's this? Another?"

"Try Kasse the Hunter!" bellowed a rough voice from
the foreground. "He's always boasting about it!"

"Then let him come forward!" For a moment it seemed
he would not be taken up. Then a dark-haired man of
middle height was more or less bundled through the throng
and up the steps, and stood there sullenly, seemingly ill
pleased at finding himself the center of attention. "Well,
man? What know you of the Forest, of Tapiau'la-an-
Aithen?"

Kasse scowled. "That you'd best keep that name to
yourself beneath the trees, for one. Yes. I've been in it,
and often. My master's estate stretched to its very shadow
ere the Ekwesh torched it and him, and my father and
grandfather before me's hunted there. You learn, there are
things to do, things not to do. You watch your step, keep
your nerve and you're well, and the hunting's good."

Kermorvan nodded. "Well then! So you at least would
brave a journey into it?"

"Well . . ." Kasse's leathery face twitched, and the
crowd laughed; he scowled again. "Not alone!" he
barked. "Who would? Not you bastards, for sure!"

"You would not be alone," said Kermorvan. "A company would be sent—"

"Is this not the idlest folly of all?" cried Bryhon, and
awoke clamoring assent from parts of the crowd. "How
do we know there is anyone left alive in the east, or that
they are worth the finding? They could have dwindled to
nothing by now—"

"Or be as free and strong as we should be. I agree; we
know nothing. We must find out. We must send a com-

pany eastward, scout and embassy both, and without delay.''

Bryhon threw up his hands. ''Can we in our need spare some such costly mission, let alone the huge war band it would require as escort? Its mere absence would weaken us, let alone its most likely loss. He has told us we bleed, which we knew full well already; now he seeks to open our wound still further. And in pursuit of what?'' He shrugged. ''The shadow of a memory. Or something worse.''

''My lord Bryhon,'' sighed Kermorvan, ''I conceived of no such great enterprise. Apart from your most wise objections, so great a force could not stir a league in those dark lands without drawing the attention of every perilous power. Or Powers.'' The emphasis was clear in his voice, and many stirred uneasily, and shivered in the noon warmth of the southern sun. ''A small party we need, of men well hardened to wandering and to peril, yet led by those who can speak for the city, and perhaps also the north—''

''And do we not have such a man before us?'' demanded Bryhon, not bothering to conceal his triumphant smile. ''For you must be a most accomplished vagrant by now, and some, I feel, may account your absence welcome, your loss small. As to speaking, you have presumed to do little else this last half hour! So, my lord Kermorvan, I say to you go, and take with you the discord you have sown in this city! If your idea has one virtue it is that it would rid us of you. Lead this embassy of death, and I will gladly support it!'' Breathing hard, the dark-haired man sprawled back in his seat among the cheers of his followers, grinning with delight at having so entrapped his adversary. Elof clenched his fists, and Ils cursed hoarsely; Kermorvan would have to refuse, and so appear to betray his own idea. But the warrior bowed solemnly to his adversary, and held the floor.

''I thank you once more, Bryhon, for saying what I wished said, though somewhat garbled. But I counsel you, do not measure me by the extent of your own ambitions,

Bryhon. I have no wish to become your king, and nor do I enjoy sowing discord for its own sake, as it seems you do. Never, *never* will I be the center of bloody strife and division among my own people! Sooner than that I withdraw from among you, as I did before, and seek another way to help you. I will lead our mission eastward.''

Both within and without the great chamber syndic and spectator alike stared in dismay and disbelief. The sight of them, agape like so many fish in a trawl, had Elof chuckling silently to himself. These great folk were as insular as his own villagers, unable to imagine an exile once returned ever leaving of his own accord. They had known Kermorvan's worth well enough, were glad enough to have his valor as their shield, but imagined they could treat him like a mere watchdog, tame him and chain him, if need be, with the threat of exile. Well, now they knew better. Even some of the syndics who had applauded Bryhon most loudly seemed alarmed, glaring openly at the dark man. But Bryhon sat stroking his curling beard, his long pale face calm, expressionless, with only the faintest glimmer in his narrow eyes.

''B-but my lord Kermorvan . . .'' stammered the younger Marshal. ''There was no thought of . . . We need you, the city needs . . .''

''Lad, lad, how can this be wise?'' barked Kathel, and then, because he knew his man, ''How can it be honorable? To toss away your life on such a shallow venture, when your city needs you? That way east, it's a hundred deaths, plain and fancy. Chance is we'll never see you more! And then, if you're right—I believe you, mind—if the Ekwesh do come back—''

''Then trust to the northerners!'' said Kermorvan curtly. ''That defense I leave you, if only you are honorable in accepting it. And you, Kathel, shall hold the Northern Marches in my stead. Hearken well, for that is my herald's fee, my price for peace. I exact it as a pledge from all present—you, Bryhon, most of all. You shall decree and depose an oath that from tonight you shall no longer close your gates against the northerners, but treat them with honor and justice. You shall admit them as citizens and equals, subject to the same rights and laws. And you shall allot them land in the country to settle and grow food for themselves and the city; we have it, and to spare, since so many were slain.''

"But if they bring more Ekwesh among them?" shrilled a youngish man in ornate green robes.

"Now they are on guard, I think you may leave it to the northerners themselves to stop that rat hole," said Kermorvan, with grim humor. "Remember, a mere likeness of skin will not deceive them! What better guards could you wish? Enough, then! Will you swear? Or are you so eaten away by old hatreds that you will see the city fall to slake them?" He spoke to the assembly at large, but his glance fell clearly upon Bryhon Bryheren.

The tall man shrugged, and met Kermorvan's gaze with a grin. "I'll swear," he chuckled with jovial contempt. "It may just be worth a few northerners to be rid of you. We might even civilize them, in time. I'll even suffer a merchant to be Marchwarden, in these upended days. Why, I'll go so far as to wish you success in your venture, scant though I fear the profit will be."

"Strange how once Bryhon has sworn, the mood of the syndics eases," Elof muttered to Ils, as he heard them take the oath without a word more in dispute. "And yet his followers are no majority."

"They have been more concerned with avoiding clashes between Kermorvan's faction and Bryhon's," she whispered back. "At any cost, for it might upset their own comfortable lives. Who was right, and what was best for the land, that walked a long way behind. Small wonder the Ekwesh caught them napping."

The session lasted only a little longer, time enough to make formal the decree and to install Kathel Kataihan as Warden of the Northern Marches. For all Bryhon's jibes, he was a popular choice; from his travels he knew the northern borders better than most, and though not a warrior he had made a wise commander in the siege. But that he was so easily accepted marked the hold Kermorvan had gained upon the syndics.

"You see, I learned my lesson well among your folk, Ils," he smiled as he met them on the steps outside. "That one may get what one wants by bending before a wind, as well as standing up to it."

"You did well," said Elof soberly. "The northerners are deeply in your debt. But the cost to you . . ."

Ils nodded fiercely, forgetting her aches. "To exile yourself again, and so soon—did I not say these men were ungrateful? Among my folk you had more honor than this!"

Kermorvan threw back his head and laughed, a rare thing in itself. Then, still chuckling, he rested his forehead against a cool pillar. "And to think one of my ancestors forbade nobles to perform upon the public stage! Do you not see? Why else do you think I maneuvered Bryhon into demanding it? This is what I want!" And indeed he looked happier and more carefree than he had for many a day. "To be no more a focus for strife and intrigue, to be no more an intriguer myself! Can you not guess how great a burden that has been? To be free from the follies of this place, and wander through the world once again, on a great quest . . . The east! Long have I dreamed of seeing its shores, and the wide ocean over which men first came here from ancient Kerys! And you will come with me, will you not? Did I not say you would hear matter to make you think?"

Elof stared. "I must follow—"

"The path of the sunrise, aye! And where do you think I go?" insisted Kermorvan. "I need men of mettle in my company! Why should we not set out together? Face the perils of the inner lands together as we did the mountains and the sea? We will surely fare better together than apart! Well, do you hesitate?"

"Not I!" Elof laughed. "I was taken by surprise, that is all. Of course I'll come, and glad of it! It was loneliness I'd come to fear the most."

"And you, Ils?" Kermorvan turned to her. "Will you . . ." But Ils had vanished from the steps. Many in the streets had seen her, heading back to Kermorvan's house, and when he and Elof returned there the servants assured them she had come in, and not since passed the gate. Yet when they looked for her she could not be found; gone from her room was her scant gear, nothing left save a simple message on a table. *"Fare you well, and may the Shaper speed you! And may we meet again . . ."*

"She has gone, then," said Kermorvan unhappily, passing the note to Elof. "As she said she would, and secretly lest we entreat her too greatly to come. Well, I cannot blame her; she has deserved better of this city than it has given her. May we meet again, indeed!"

But that night in his bed Elof drifted out of dreams, vaguely aware of a shadow that seemed to slip across the floor and bend over him as he lay. "Ils?" he mumbled.

A quiet chuckle. "I awaited the safety of the dark, when I can see and you humans cannot. Where better than here? But I could not resist . . ." She bent down, and her lips pressed hard against his a moment, he breathed her breath. "Fare you well indeed!" she whispered, and crushed his hand to her. Her wide eyes gleamed in the blackness. "It's only that I cannot . . ." She rose and vanished. He sat up, suddenly awake, but heard nothing, not even the faintest footfall on the stairs. Only the heat of her breath seemed still to course through him. He found it hard to sleep again.

Next morning he was unsure whether or not he should tell Kermorvan. But when he went down to breakfast he was saved the decision, for he found Kermorvan deep in conversation with a rotund man, blond of hair and beard, and was startled to recognize him as Ermahal, skipper of the corsairs.

"Well now, sir—sirs," he corrected himself, with a respectful nod to Elof, "there's all kinds of reasons. See, we all of us bought off our outlawry by rescuing the women, fine. And we 'ad a fair whack in booty put by; there's some of the lads turned their share to good use and settled down. Some stopped one in the siege, rest their scabby souls. But others, well, they've shed it one way or t'other, through gaming or skirts or whatever."

"Would I want such fools as followers?" inquired Kermorvan.

"Ah, but they're not all of 'em fools," protested Ermahal, tapping his long nose. "Some're just plain wild, money or no. Fact is, there was reasons we were outlaws, all of us, and we ain't changed in a day, no, nor a year neither. Piss-poor citizens we make, but corsairs, adventurers by sea or land, well, that's another matter." He drummed his fingers on the long table, managing to look at once sly and diffident. "You were our real skipper, sir, no gainsaying that, not that I ever resented it. We've followed you before, and it wasn't us as ran off an' left you, was it, sir? But we'd be glad to take up with you again. And you, sir smith," he added hastily, bouncing up to bow to Elof. "We've seen your mettle too."

Elof smiled. "Lord Kermorvan alone is our leader, not I. But how many do you speak for?"

"Ah," said Ermahal, and began to reckon on his fingers. " 'Bout twenty, sir, there being some downed by drink or disease."

"Too many, I fear," said Kermorvan. "Our company must be small, its members men of experience—that huntsman Kasse might prove useful, for one. And there should be some northerners among them, to show that we can fare together in peace. I am having it cried both through the city and the northern camps that we seek such men. Our company must be ready to depart in a matter of weeks."

Ermahal shrugged. "Well, sir, the pick's yours. But I've sailed rivers as well as seas, and that might be useful; I'd be glad if you'd count me in, and Maile the bosun, you know what a hard nut 'e is . . ."

Kermorvan nodded in amused remembrance. "So be it! I'll start my choice with you both." He cut short the skipper's grateful protestations with a lifted hand. "Remember, this is no wild venture, wagering peril against a chance of plunder! Death weights the scales, and the greatest prize on our side may simply be survival.''

Ermahal plucked at his scanty beard. ''Aye, well, I'll settle for that. I've always had a fancy to cast an eye on that Eastern Ocean. Might be they're short of corsairs in those parts.''

Elof laughed, but Kermorvan's smile was sterner. ''Or they may have an excess of gibbets,'' he said. ''You are a great rogue, Ermahal, though a brave one. Leave your corsairs' ways here in the west, lest I hang you myself.''

The fat man chuckled. ''Like I was sayin', sir, we ain't all changed in a day. But I'll skip to your tune till journey's end.''

''Do so, or you may dance your last. But you will not go unrewarded, if it is in my power.''

When Ermahal had gone Kermorvan suggested they take the sun upon the roof awhile. Elof sensed why; from there they could look out over the whole city, across the wide squares and high buildings of the Old Quarter, down along the plunging streets of the newer circles to the half-repaired breach in the outermost wall and beyond it the dark shading straggling over the plain that was the northerners' town of tents and huts. The sun above was warm, the breeze light, and yet where sky met distant mountain gray streaks mustered. ''The clouds gather,'' said Kermorvan. ''And while we are gone they will surely close in further still. There is little enough time left us to save this place. I did not say this to the syndics, for fear of closing their minds altogether with scorn, but it may not, as they think, be a matter of summoning easterners westward. Our wounds are too bloody, our healing too slow. If the Eastlands can offer any refuge at all, it is we who may be forced to flee.''

''Eastward, aye!'' The smithy was hot, for they were casting silver. But nonetheless Roc shivered. ''Over the mountains and into the Forest—brrrh! League after league of it, and full of who knows what. Run north and there's the Wastes and the Ice. Run south and there's the Wastes and the desert. Freeze or burn. Or worse.''

"That's just what I need!" laughed Elof. "Encouragement! It's all very well for you, you're not going—"

Roc put down his ladle with a clatter. "And who in Hella's name'll stop me?"

Elof stared at him. "Are you serious? You are serious! Roc, you're daft! Here you're well settled, you've the best smithy in all this town and Kathel for a patron. In a year or two you'll be rich."

"Aye, and when I told you as much, it didn't stop you, did it?"

"Well . . . But I've a purpose, Roc . . ."

"And haven't I?" growled Roc. "I'll be rich, says you? Aye, just in time for the Ekwesh."

"Yes . . . But Roc, this journey must take more than a year at its swiftest. What about Marja? Doesn't she have some say?"

Roc shrugged. "I never promised her anything, she's no claim on me. She'll have the smithy, of course, with old Hjoran; they'll manage fine till I get back. She waits. Or she doesn't."

"Roc, you well know there's a chance you never will get back! I don't want to drag you away . . ."

"Understood," grunted Roc, "but it's my decision, nobody else's. If you're too daft to stay, someone's got to keep an eye on you. And I fancy a share of the sport this time, see? You won't shake me like you did before!" And indeed when, some three weeks later, the time came to depart, Elof was no nearer managing it.

It was a motley group of callers that came knocking on the gates of Kermorvan's house that evening as the sun slid down behind the clouds of early spring. First to arrive were two tall men clad in rough green and russet, marked as northerners by their copper skin. Gise and Eysdan were their names, and they hailed from villages far inland, on the margins of the dense northern woodlands; they themselves were foresters, men accustomed to rove freely under the shadow of trees, wise in their lore as few sothrans were. They both bore broad falchions, Gise a short bow of strong wisant horn and Eysdan an immense long-hafted axe. They were quiet men, exchanging only curt greeting with the noisy corsairs who came straggling in soon after. Though they had obviously been celebrating their departure, it encouraged Elof to see them no worse than merry. Besides Ermahal and Maille, Kermorvan had judged only three others sound or trustworthy enough to make the journey; they were all sothrans, men of the sea but with some experience of wandering on land. Dervhas, Ermahal's helmsman, and Perrec had been deserters from Bryhaine's small war fleet, and Stehan a hand on a trade ship; Borhi, the youngest, had been a fisherman till exiled for killing a man in a drunken brawl. After them came the hunter Kasse, slipping shadowlike into the courtyard, and then three more northerners, Tenvar, Bure and Holvar. Lighter skinned than the foresters, they were burghers' sons of Saldenborg who had fought in that rich port's brief but heroic defense, and made their way south through many hardships, passing scatheless through the Forest's arm. They too were merry, but what worked on them like wine was new hope, a fresh light in eyes that had long worn the dull gaze of the fugitive. Their new garb and weapons put swagger in their step and flourish in their salutes to Kermorvan, seated at his ease beneath the yellow-crowned locust tree in the center of the yard. Last to arrive were Roc and an older sothran of somewhat the same aspect, Arvhes; chosen at Kathel's suggestion, he had been a trader of his caravan when Roc and Elof met it, and spoke the northern tongue well.

When all this company was assembled, Ferhas brought wine. Kermorvan pledged each of the company in turn, and they drank his health. It was no time for greater ceremony; thoughts of the paths they must tread weighed upon them all, and the only words exchanged now were quiet inquiries about gear and provisions. "We must do our best to slip away unnoticed," Kermorvan had decided. "For one thing, Bryhon's rabble might gather to bid us a warm farewell; for another, if there are any spies about, better they cannot say what time we left, or by what roads."

A file of ponies was led out of the old stables, and they

busied themselves loading their baggage. Their vestigial side-hooves marked the beasts as of the Northland stock, short of leg and coarse of coat against long-limbed sothran breeds, but Elof and the other northerners rejoiced to see them. The sothrans were not so sure. "Sight too free with the flamin' teeth for me!" grumbled Ermahal, skipping awkwardly out of one irritated beast's way.

"Don't haul so on the girths, man!" laughed Bure. "It's no longboat you're loading there!"

"Would it were, that I'd 'ave somewhere to kick you off! Give me a solid beast of Bryhaine any day, these jades are 'alf rat and about as well broken."

"But they will bear even you," grinned Elof, "over ways where your solid Bryhaine beasts would stumble every second step, and leagues long enough to burst their hearts. Not even Kermorvan's great white warhorse can match them in endurance."

"True," acknowledged Kermorvan. "I would never think to lead her on this rough a journey."

"It's said there are wild horses east of the mountains," said Tenvar mischievously, "giant ones. Maybe they're tamable. They sound better suited to bear a man of your, hmm, presence, sothran."

"Presence?" growled Ermahal, purpling and rounding on the young northerner. Tenvar stood his ground, smoothing his small moustache nonchalantly, and his fellows moved to join him. Kermorvan's genial voice cut into the silence.

"And of mine! My long shanks lose grace on these little beasts; I am close to walking. But we will miss them soon enough, I reckon. Once within the pathless Forest no horse can help us, and we must be our own beasts of burden then." It was a sobering thought, and turned each man to securing his baggage once more.

But Elof had some skill in reading Kermorvan's impassive face, and whispered, "That was a cut well parried!"

"Aye, but spare me any more such! Those Saldenborg lads are fools to jest so, though they meant no harm. Ermahal would hardly be a corsair captain if he were a safe man to mock. Elof, you are a northerner of much their age, and they are used to heeding smiths; do you take them in hand!''

''I'll have them as rearguard, then, with Roc, away from the corsairs.''

''Do you so. As well to have sharp eyes and live minds there, in any event, on the dark paths we must tread.'' Kermorvan gazed about the gloomy courtyard. ''Now the sun is all but down, the city's voices grow quiet. The time of our going is here. Home of my fathers, night and silence claims you once more. Shall I ever rest at ease in you again? Yet it must be, it must be . . . Elof my friend, it may be that all our trials and troubles so far have been no more than a prelude to this.''

''I was thinking the same,'' acknowledged Elof. ''But of my own quest in particular.''

Kermorvan nodded. ''May that prosper, whatever else betide. Well, all farewells are said save mine; I must not linger.'' Then Ferhas and Kermorvan's few other servants came and knelt before him, a thing done rarely in north or south, even before great lords. Yet there was no servility in the gesture, but more of love, for clearly they wept. And when Kermorvan handed over a great ring of keys to Ferhas, they shook and rattled in the old man's hand. Elof saw then something of Kermorvan's shaping, for it was these old servants who had brought him up, as the deaths of his parents and his family left him increasingly alone. He was a lord shaped by vassals, a king molded in the image his followers sought to believe in, all the more so in an age and a place where kingship was no longer welcome. Such an upbringing might have turned out many ways, but in him, to Elof's mind, it had tempered pride and strength with compassion and restraint, and the urgent need to command with reason and respect for those commanded.

''Aye, agreed,'' said Roc. ''Couldn't have been easy, though, growing up a prince with no domain past these four walls. Small wonder he was wild as a lad. But like I told Marja, there's few men else I'd follow where we're bound.''

Ferhas was fumbling with the keys now, and even as the gates creaked open Kermorvan, Gise and Eysdan began to lead out the line of ponies. As had been agreed, the travelers pulled cloaks and hoods about themselves, and slung weapons out of sight; leading rather than riding their mounts, they would look like many another party of weary fugitives.

Ferhas saluted Elof as he had the others, but plucked at his arm and whispered vehemently, ''You'll have a care of him, won't you, sir?'' The idea of himself guarding that fearsome fighting man seemed absurd, but Elof could not laugh at the old esquire. He nodded, clapped him on the shoulder, and passed on. The long caravan ahead was silhouetted against the pale stone of the mansion opposite like figures on a moving frieze, as if already they merged with the faded chronicles of times past. The young northerners were on his heels; he heard the gate creak to, and awaited the sound of the lock. It did not come, and although he would not turn his head he held clearly in his mind the image of old Ferhas standing there in the wall's black shadow, listening, straining his ears until the last faint hoofbeat had utterly died away.

The night was cool, the streets fast emptying. City folk hurried here and there with their smoking linklights, few sparing an eye for the drab procession that clopped and clattered across the cobblestones. The square of the citadel, where tall braziers burned, they skirted, and also the Merchant's Quarter, still busy and aglow with everything from crystal candelabra in high windows to rush dips and little charcoal ovens in the street stalls. He thought of Kathel, now on the northern borders ordering his new domain, and smiled; the merchant had not gone without giving Roc and himself strict orders to report on the wealth of any eastern lands, and their dearth and surplus of a long list of commodities. ''You seem very confident we will find somewhere,'' Elof had said.

'' 'Course you will, lads!'' Kathel had puffed cheerfully, and then, remembering perhaps his claim to be the Honest, added, "But, well, it's a poor pedlar doesn't knock on even the rickety doors, eh?"

He would miss the man, thought Elof. And if he too was honest, he realized, he would miss this whole huge sprawling city as he had never dreamed he would. He rested a protective hand on the saddlebag that held his baggage, meager but heavy; a few garments, a change of boots, but chiefly the things he most valued, a certain gauntlet of mail, his precious tools, and with them a crook-tipped rod of worn bronze, the strange cattle goad that was his only inheritance from his first youth. He had brought that on impulse, not for any use it had. But now he knew why; to here also he might never return. Once a tiny village had been his world, then a lonely tower; the first small towns had seemed overpowering. But this, this teeming human hive, it could have swallowed them up a thousandfold. And for all its sins he had come to see that only out of such a community of men could arise the order and strength of will that was their best shield against the oncoming Ice. It made the wild lands beyond its bounds seem that much wilder, and himself more foolish to seek to venture into them once more.

Others seemed to be feeling the same. Bure, fond of his food, kept scuttling over to stalls they passed to buy last portions of local delicacies. Elof found it hard to blame him, for the northerners had eaten poorly enough before being chosen for the company. But then he saw Borhi the corsair slip across to a winestall, and Tenvar begin chatting to the market girls walking alongside, and he called them back into line. "That's well done," said Roc. "There's some as'll know us, and talk."

"For which I'll wager Lord Bryhon has ears listening!" agreed Arvhes, dropping back. "The happier I'll set out without flagstones flying round my ears."

"There's that," admitted Bure indistinctly, munching spicy chunks of fowl from a skewer. "Gate's not so far, though, now."

"A step is full far enough, with a mob in the way."

The shadow of the high gate tower might have concealed one easily enough. Now, though, there were few folk about in its shadow, and most of them sentinels of the City Guard. But the figure who stepped suddenly out of the shadows was clad in tunic and cloak of richly worked red velvets, and he was very tall. Elof exchanged horrified glances with Roc, and moved swiftly down the column to Kermorvan's side.

"A shame on you, my lord of Morvan," was the newcomer's jovial greeting, "that you sought to slip away thus! Did you think it could be kept from me?"

"I had my reasons, my lord of Bryheren," Kermorvan said coolly. "You, among others. What have you to gain by hindering me?"

Teeth flashed in Bryhon's beard. "I? Hinder you?" He sounded affably hurt. "I came only to wish you well!"

Kermorvan sighed, and rested an arm across his pony's back. "My lord, I fail to understand you. That we are hereditary enemies is of little moment in these times, but if the law permitted I would cheerfully slaughter you for all the wrongs you yourself have done my family. You have ever sought to thwart any plan of mine simply because it was mine! You are no generous adversary. Am I expected to believe you now?"

Bryhon shrugged. "If you are right, you bring us some small benefit. If you are wrong, you cost us little. I hope you do find survival in the east, most sincerely I do. Is that to be a crime in your kingdom?"

"Hardly. I accept your good wishes to the extent you mean them, and return such thanks as they are worth. Though from one who sought to murder me in secret . . ."

Again Bryhon shrugged. "In the best interests of the city—as the troubles that followed have proved. But we are warriors of the same high order, you and I. I would not fear to face you if I could, Keryn Kermorvan."

"Nor I you, Bryhon Bryheren. Now may we pass?"

Bryhon's deep laugh was wholly genial. "Am I preventing you? But for all the world I would not! Go, succeed, or be damned to you!'' And, still chuckling, he turned and strolled off into the dark.

Elof glared after him. ''For a moment I thought that human mantis meant what he said!''

''In part, perhaps,'' mused Kermorvan. ''We are of the same order, the same discipline, that one and I; we have endured the same trials, and may speak of them to each other as I may not even to you, a friend. That bond even hatred cannot wholly expunge.'' He smiled. ''But you and I, we have shared our own ordeals, and others no doubt lie ahead. At least we need skulk no longer! Mount up, all, and follow! Guards, there! Open the gates!''

''Open! Stand aside for a lord of the city!'' cried Roc in his powerful voice, and the other sothrans joined him at once. The northerners, who had known no authority stronger than town elders or guildmasters, smiled to see how the guards scurried to the immense windlasses and set the long weight-chains clanking down over the stone, the heavy gates grinding inward. As the first gap appeared it seemed to Elof that a deeper darkness came spilling in, like the shadow of some vast beast lurking, and a light but chilling breeze. He shivered, but when Kermorvan led the column forward beneath the deep arch he followed gladly enough; he thrilled to the clink of the smoothly metaled High Road beneath his pony's hooves, the grating rumble of the gates closing behind them. It was exciting, after all, to be a wanderer once more.

He looked up. The sky above was pearled with a full moon rising, but the city walls barred its light. The company plunged into shadow like deep water, dark and cold. Roc looked back at the Gate ramparts, and nudged Elof; a lone watcher stood there, outlined in silver. ''You've good sight by half-light,'' he grunted. ''Who'd that be? Ten for one it's that bugger Bryhon.''

Elof looked, and smiled wryly. ''A poor wager, Marja.'' Roc snorted violently. But he dropped back a little, and a moment later, when he thought Elof was not looking, he turned and waved, and for many minutes he would surreptitiously look back.

Across the plains of the city the caravan trotted, that Elof had first seen as a gaming board of fields, spacious and rich. But over them had passed the Ekwesh, plundering and destroying beyond all reason, and after them the refugees. They had made their pitiful camps of tent and shack there on land that should have grown food to help support the city. The camps cultivated only a few scant patches and at poor yield. But the blame was the city's. Much waste could have been avoided, if it had accepted the northerners and made use of their willing labor, instead of branding them beggars. The thought angered Elof. Kermorvan was right; why had he needed to fight to prove it? What made men so blind to their own best interests?

It was long before they passed the last of the little campfires, but longer yet before those fires faded from his thoughts.

CHAPTER THREE

The Ocean of Trees

Little was said of their route, for little could be said. Those who had fled westward had not lingered to make maps, nor sought to perpetuate any memories of their ordeal. It seems that such maps as the Chronicles preserve were all made at a much later time, for it is certain that Kermorvan found none to guide him; the charts of Bryhaine ended at the Shielding Mountains. He had, however, conferred with Kasse and all other folk he could find who lived in the lands nearest the range, eager for any word of what lay beyond. But few could tell him much. All along the foothills lay the western arm of the Great Forest that they dreaded, and from their own experience Elof and Kermorvan could hardly blame them. Few save outlaws and wild, solitary men dared cross the margins of the trees: fewer still ever returned, and their tales were fantastic and contradictory, full of strange sights and visions.

In the end, though, Kermorvan found he had few choices. He had to pass the Shieldrange somewhere, and only in two places could he venture that without going through the Forest's arm. He could circle the mountains to the southward, by Orhy Lake on the Gorlafros, the great river Westflood, where the rich lands ended and the increasingly barren Wastes began. But those few who had stood atop the summits of the Shieldrange had all reported sight of other summits on the horizon across the river.

"And they make it a poor risk," Kermorvan had concluded, tracing with a finger the rough map he had compounded out of many accounts. "If those mountains can be seen from so far off they are at least as high. We cannot tell how passable they are, or how far southward they extend into the Wastes. But it seems they do not continue northward very far—not as far as the passes in the west of the Northmarch, level with Iylan and Armen, our northernmost towns. And between those passes and the Westflood, we know there lie the Open Lands, hilly and lightly wooded, easy enough going. So that way lies our road, I guess."

"But could we not turn further northward still?" wondered Elof. "Are there not wide gaps in the Shield there, where the rivers come down?"

"Aye, the Shieldbreach, but that is past our borders. Those are the Debatable Lands still, doubly debatable now the Ekwesh hold so much of Nordeney! And see what lies west of them! Those uncanny Marshlands of yours; through those gaps run the rivers that feed them, swelled by the meltwater of the Ice and all it brings with it. That is no safe way for us!"

Elof shrugged. "What is, since we seek the Forest? And once I felt almost at home in those strange fens. But I agree. Wastes to the south, war to the north; by all means let us seek a middle way!"

The trek north and east was long, for at first they had to take the coast way that skirted the Forest's westward arm, but on the High Road the going was quick and sure. Only shelter for sleep was wanting, for all the roadside inns and post houses had been devastated by Ekwesh foragers, and the dwellings in the lands around, from peasant cot to high mansion, had fared little better. These grim reminders along the wayside, like so many hollow teeth, sharpened their vigilance; some of those foragers, stranded by the sudden flight of their fellows, might still be lurking in the land. Such folk as had returned to work their fields dwelt behind hasty palisades, greeting all outcomers with anger and suspicion; and in truth, they had little enough to spare for hospitality. Outside some gates brown-skinned bodies dangled on gibbets, and whether Ekwesh or northerner none could tell. Travelers on the Roads were even less trusting and many fled precipitately at the very approach of the company, or at the sight of darker skins among it. Such troubles eased as they turned steadily further inland, where fewer reivers had reached; at the ford of the river Yrmelec, boundary of the Northmarch, they encountered a strong guard of the Marchwarden's garrison, posted there by Kathel to watch for strays.

It was in these inland regions that Kermorvan had thought the outlivers of Bryhaine should seek refuge in wartime, rather than in the overcrowded city, and Elof could see why; they were rich warm lands, untouched as yet by war. The company fared more comfortably awhile, but came at last to the ending of the Roads in the upper valleys of the Yrmelec. Sound tracks carried them a few leagues further along the steep grassy slopes, and after that, paths maintained by the little farms they served. But one hot morning when they stopped to buy refreshment at one of these, on high ground above the Yrmelec's narrowing gorge, they found no onward path; dense woodland spread across the slopes ahead, growing thicker and darker the further the eye followed it. They had come once again to the margins of Aithennec, the Lesser Forest.

"That'ud be right, me lord," croaked the little old man who poured their ale. His speech was sprinkled with dialect words the northerners found hard to make out. "Further paths there were once, one or two even when I was a little lad, but they're long gone, long sunk back under grass, like the crofts they served. But 'twas not that way they led." He plucked at Kermorvan's sleeve, ushering them all across the cracked and weed-grown flagstones to the rear of the cottage. "Long gone, now, the crofters, their children off to the *kahermhor,* that High City of yours. The last I am now, all alone and naught at my back but fell and forest and barren *ygeldhyrau.* "

"He means . . ." began Kermorvan, but his voice dwindled. Nothing indeed lay at the back of the cottage, save a high plain, a sea of whispering green grass, and beyond it a smudged line of darker green. But above that, towering craggy and gray-white against the hazy blue sky, rose the vast peaks of the Meneth Scahas, shield and boundary of the realm of Bryhaine and all the western lands. Out to the southern horizon they stretched, an immense jagged rampart against the wild lands beyond. Northward, though, the mountains seemed to tumble and fall sharply away. From the last of them a ridge plunged down, ending in high steep hills, gray and misty and generally treeless, save around the river gorge that plunged between them. But beyond it another ridge swept upward, and the mountains continued their northward line.

"Aye, me lord, that's all there is now, the Wild. Times are even now, on a dark night or in a wintry storm, it come a'creepin' and a'tappin' round my door. And when I'm gone, why, it'll stroll in an' make 'isself at home. Old Edhmi down the valley there, he'll be the last then, and it'll go call on him." He gave a wheezy laugh. "And when 'e goes, what then? Where d'you think it'll fetch up, one day? Eh? It's only got to wait! We go, my lord, one by one we go, and it takes another step."

They took their leave of the old farmer, and set out across the wide plateau. Its whispering grasses brushed at their legs as they rode, as if seeking to hold them back from the wilder lands beyond. Even the ponies seemed to sense a change in the air on this easternmost margin of their land. Camp that night was lonely and windswept, and they huddled gladly round their fire. By the next day they were at the plateau's end, a downland slope ending in a stream that was marshy and hard to ford, and a shallower rise to the high hills beyond. These the company found no more comfortable, their grass short, dotted here and there with scrub and sparse trees, but boasting no better shelter. The company's tents of oiled leather and fabric could keep the spring rains out, but the wind chilled them mercilessly; in the days that followed, mountain and sky above them vanished all too often under weeping cloud. One such drizzling afternoon they saw atop the summit of the hill ahead a great irregular slab of dun stone, a tangle of bushes about its base. It had an eerie look to it, upthrust thus against the gray overcast sky like a giant's forbidding hand. Elof and Kermorvan, sure it could not be natural, rode ahead to examine it. Even before they reached it they saw it bore some inscription. But it was soft sandstone, and time had run rain and rough mire down the deep-graven letters, blurring them into mere rain furrows that could not be read. Disappointed, Kermorvan urged his mount round the far side of the pillar, and called back to Elof. "We may guess what it spoke of, anyway! Come see!"

Beyond the stone the hillside fell away sharply and steeply; the valley below, like so many they had passed through, was enshrouded in rainy mists, its further slope invisible. Or was it? Even as Elof strained to see, the shifting breeze whipped the shroud away, and unveiled for a moment the lands beyond. There was no further slope; the hills were at an end. They had come through the pass, and to north and south he saw for the first time what few men living of the Western Lands had looked upon, the eastern flanks of the Shieldrange. Out into the Open Lands they curved like an embracing arm, and below them, as far as he could make out in either direction, a rough-cut ribbon of blued steel lay stretched across the land, spreading here and there into thin threads and broader curls. This could only be the Westflood, its threads tributaries and its curls lake and mere. Between mountain and river the Open Lands were as Kermorvan had predicted, rolling and sprinkled with patches of light woodland. But it was what lay on the far bank that caught his gaze and gripped it as does the void beyond a cliff edge. That was what the stone had spoken of! There was blackness, an ocean of it to the gray horizon. Elof stared at it balefully, knowing it for what it was, straining his stinging eyes into the depths of the rainstorm for some break, some gap in its grim solidity. But save for stray threads straggling from the Westflood, there was none. Over all the lands before them the Great Forest, Tapiau'la-an-Aithen, still reigned supreme.

A new onrush of rain swallowed those distances, and Kermorvan pulled his pony's head round, calling to the company and pointing downslope. Not far below them was the only woodland for a league or more dense enough to afford them shelter. "We may still reach it ere the worst of the storm comes over! But though it is not yet the Forest, be you on your guard!"

They found it hard to remain so as they urged their bedraggled beasts down the steep slope, hooves skidding and sliding in the slippery grass. At last they had to dismount and lead the poor brutes down, broad flanks steaming in the sharpening downpour, and they were well soaked ere they reached the sheltering eaves of the wood. The downpour beat upon the outer leaves, hung there and dripped down in long rivulets, driving the company on deeper beneath the treeroof. A heavy twilight gathered. "I'm almost missing good old Nordeney snow!" Roc grumbled, stifling an immense sneeze. Kermorvan gestured curtly for silence, and sent out Eysdan and Kasse as scouts. The huge northerner slipped through the trees every bit as silently as the smaller man, and only the softest of rustles betrayed how they circled round among the dense bushes, seeking the slightest trace of danger. Meanwhile the company huddled against their beasts for warmth, and sought to forget how tired and hungry they were.

Water trickled suddenly down Elof's neck. He glanced up irritably; it was falling from an opening among the leaves, where a little patch of sky showed gray. Some great bird swooped and wheeled across it an instant with brief grace, and vanished. He pulled his pack off his saddle, and fumbled in it for his hood. Then he heard a soft crackle behind him, a sudden tang of smoke and the thin midgesong of damp wood steaming. He spun round, to find his townsmen heaping up twigs upon little tongues of leaping red; a thin thread of white was already blowing here and there among the branches above. Holvar squatted on the ground, happily clicking his flint and steel. "You thrice-damned idiots!" growled Elof.

"Listen, you may want to catch your death here, while

my lord makes up his precious mind,'' said Tenvar thinly,
''but we don't!'' Elof moved to stamp out the fire; Tenvar
and Bure barred him, and he thrust them staggering aside.
Holvar sprang in front of the fire, and Elof, unwilling to
start a fight, stooped for an armful of leaf-mold as a
smother. Something sang across his head, and he heard a
startled gasp from Holvar. But it ended in a gurgle, the
tense legs buckled and Holvar sank to his knees. A wash
of blood welled from his mouth and pattered onto the
mold, flooding the arrow that transfixed his throat. Its
black and white fletches turned scarlet, and Holvar toppled
face down into his own fire.

Elof was no longer visible. At first sight of the arrow
he had dropped, pulling Bure and Tenvar down with him.
He hugged the ground, slinging the heavy pack over his
back, and shouted, ''Down! Down and to cover! *Ek-wesh!*''

A sinister wind whistled among the branches, the leaves
jerked and whipped as black streaks hissed among them.
But the stunned company had that moment's warning, and
ere the next arrow could land they were flinging themselves from their saddles, diving wildly behind trees or
into bushes. Yells and shouts mingled with the thud of the
arrows striking. A high scream froze Elof's blood; one of
the baggage ponies bucked and toppled, breaking its reins,
and lay kicking. The others, with arrows thudding into
loads and saddles, plunged and bolted as one, whinnying
with terror. There was a sudden eruption in the wood
ahead as dark-clad figures sprang up to escape the threshing hooves. ''So that's where they lurk!'' growled Gise,
and loosed two swift shots of his own; one shape leaped
high and fell. Bushes crashed behind them, and he whirled
round with a curse. But it was Kermorvan, still mounted,
ducking past lashing branches as he spurred his pony forward. ''Up, Westmen, on your feet, and rally! They come!
Morvan! Morvan morlanhal!''

Elof and Roc sprang up as he passed, running at his
heels, and behind them Tenvar and Bure, faces ashen, tear-
streaked but murderous. Ermahal was up, bellowing to

Maille and the corsairs. Ahead of them Kasse whipped up an arbalest and fired. A shriek told of a mark found, and then the dimness was flickering with shapes, crashing this way and that. An impact almost yanked Elof from his feet; the jagged limb of a fallen tree, hidden by brush, had snagged his belt and all but jarred the wind out of him. He snatched at his sword, found it entangled in thorny twigs. A shadow loomed up before him, a spear glinted from behind a painted shield; he ducked, swung the pack from his shoulder and dashed it at the shield. The shield cracked, the spear flew up, its tall wielder staggered back and a gray-gold blade crashed down on his head; he toppled beneath the hooves of Kermorvan's mount. It stumbled as a warhorse would not have, and Kermorvan fell heavily from the saddle. A copper-skinned warrior rushed forward with spear raised, and took Roc's mace full in the face. Elof struggled to free himself, till a dull gleam caught his eye among the spilled pack at his feet. It was the great hammer. He had not replaced it in his tool-pack; even scoured clean many times, some taint of death still seemed to cling to it, clouding the identity the true smith must feel with his instruments, and he had feared lest somehow it contaminate the rest. Now it seemed to blaze before his eyes, and there was no denying its power.

"So be it!" he cried. "Smite metal no longer! Come, and temper men!" It felt almost as if the hammer leaped into his hand; through branch and brush it smashed, and barely in time he was free. Three shapes closed in, two spears crashed where he had been; he felt hot fire sting his leg and it leaped to his head. With a yell of sheer anger he caught the hammer in both hands and swung a great scything arc, whirling on his feet with the impetus of it. Momentarily the world became a smashing, shrieking blur, and then he was bounding clear and striving to get his bearing among the sudden skirmishes that erupted through the dense thickets.

Then it was as if time stopped. A new sound rang through the clamor of the wood, a discordant, blaring cry of menace in the near distance. Heads turned, blows faltered on both sides; it seemed to Elof that neither side knew what to make of it.

From behind him came a bloodcurdling yell. Maille the bosun rushed madly past, whirling his cutlass about his head, and fell upon an Ekwesh warrior as huge as himself, who stooped and thrust with his spear in one serpentine lunge. Maille's jerkin burst asunder, and the spearhead leaped out between his shoulder blades. But the force of the corsair's rush bore him down the shaft, his heavy blade chopped once, convulsively, downward, and the warrior's head sprang from his shoulders. They tumbled together among the moss. Another Ekwesh poised his spear, and Ermahal leaped to catch it. For an instant they swayed, struggling, then the captain's massive shoulders flexed once and turned the Ekwesh spear down into its wielder's body. More Ekwesh rushed on him, then flew apart like windblown leaves as Kermorvan surged out of the bushes. Elof stared, astounded, at what followed; well as he knew Kermorvan's skill, he had never seen the like of this.

Into the thick of the foe Kermorvan plunged, hewing to left and right of him, cutting, thrusting, bounding, twisting, whirling around to counter some new blow, always that trace faster yet minutely precise, never still yet wasting no movement. It might have been a dance, a dance of death, for spear and shield splintered where he struck and his sword trailed scarlet streamers in the air, which seemed to float on an unfelt wind. This was slaying made a craft, a discipline and art deeper than mere strength, speed or valor. All those the tall Ekwesh had, yet Kermorvan passed unscathed among them and all who stood against him bowed like reeds to the sickle. Terrible in its energy, it was more so in its eerie grace and most of all because it could not last. If the Ekwesh did not break, it could have only one end.

And even now a huge white-haired warrior, a chieftain evidently, ran up with one of the bowmen, pointing frantically at Kermorvan. Elof gathered his wits and sprang to aid his friend. The archer took swift aim, but even more swiftly Elof whirled the hammer and flung it. The archer whipped round and fell, bow and breastbone shattered as one, and the chieftain, taken aback, sprang away. Elof caught up the hammer and thrust it into his belt as he ran, ripping twigs from Gorthawer's hilt. At last the black sword sang loud and deep from the scabbard.

It was as if it found answer. Once more that jarring call rang among the trees, much nearer now. The Ekwesh heard it, heads turned and they fell back. With three quick strides Kermorvan was through their ranks and away among the trees, crying out, *"To me! To me, Westmen! Rally and we'll hold them!"* He turned to Elof, who pounded up beside him, and added, "If we can! These are no mere foragers, there must be nigh on a hundred! And they were lying in wait!"

"But how?" gasped Elof. "And where are the others? Maille's dead—"

"I know!" snapped Kermorvan, spitting blood from a split lip. "And the rest scattered, with the Ekwesh hunting us down! We must gather—"

A wall of painted shields swept out from behind the trees. Elof swung Gorthawer high in a spray of severed leaves to hew down at the shield before him. Then it dropped and he saw the taut feral grin, the spear poised at his unguarded breast. But suddenly it was as if a swift cloud rippled across the scarred face; the Ekwesh, startled, clutched at his eyes, and Gorthawer smashed straight down upon the line of its own black shadow. They fell flailing into the undergrowth, but only Elof scrambled up. There was crashing and shouting in the trees all around, but he could not see Kermorvan anywhere. A twig snapped, and he whirled about. Eyes and teeth glittered in the gloom, he heard a fierce hissing breath and swung up Gorthawer, but too late; the heavy shield slammed into him, his feet skidded in the mold and he fell. A thornbush raked Gorthawer from his hand, and he crashed upon his back, winded. He had a brief glimpse, too fast for fear, of the huge white-haired chieftain above him, a great steel-fanged club descending, slowly as it seemed, relentless, unstoppable.

Then the stroke flew wide, the Ekwesh leaped and cart-wheeled over him, hurled by the force of the spear in his back. And all around him the trees shook with the cry, a hundred warhorns snarling in fierce insistent rhythm. Feet drummed among the mold, figures loomed up in the twi-light, sprang over him without a pause and were gone. There were shouts, a brief clashing of metal; he rolled over and struggled up, bruised and wheezing, and scrab-bled to retrieve Gorthawer from the churned mire. The cloudy patterns in the hilt glimmered if anything more clearly in the tree-gloom, yet shadow seemed to drip from the blade. There was power in that talisman yet. He looked around sharply, expecting some new peril. But the uproar was hidden by the line of trees before him, and moving still further away. Save for the chieftain's corpse he was alone.

A sick fear gripped him for his friends, and he hobbled after the noise, hacking furiously at the undergrowth that barred his way. When he made out a clearing ahead, he set his sword before him, and with laboring lungs he burst through the last screen of brush.

Armored figures stood there, leaning upon spear and axe, but none made a move against him. He stopped, half crouching, and then he could have laughed aloud with his relief and delight. He gazed upon the squat forms, the stern faces more lined and gnarled than the tree bark around them, with something like love. He lowered his sword and gasped for his poor stock of duergar words, but they simply gestured to him to pass. He nodded, still breathless, and strode through their ranks; he saw now they were a guard, watching a flank of the wood for any Ekwesh who might seek escape that way. Beyond them opened a narrow avenue of trees; looking down it he saw faces he knew, faces of the company, and he began to run again, waving and shouting. Tenvar sprang up from the ground, and across from him Arvhes and Bure. But into his path sprang a small solid figure, so close they could not but collide. Strong arms seized him in embrace, and all but swung him from the ground.

"Ugh! You've grown heavy!" gasped Ils, and she laughed and wept all at once. Elof whooped with delight, crushed her to him and kissed her so hard the light helm she wore tumbled from her dark curls. Then he stopped, looked up and around in renewed concern.

"Ils! How . . . But Kermorvan, Roc . . ."

"Still hard on the hunt, with my folk! Most of your company is safe, I think. They . . . we feared you might have been taken . . ."

"No. The fight passed over me, that was all." He hugged her again. "But how by the Powers came you and your folk here, at the moment we needed you most?"

She snorted, and jabbed a mailed fist into his stomach, none too gently. "You're as bad as those Ice-worshiping man-eaters! Never give the mountain folk credit for being able to look downward now and again! We count these lands between mountain and river ours, though it's seldom now we fare abroad in them, save to seek wood. I came this way homeward and found the land alive with Ekwesh, a huge force of them hurrying south, combing all the lands west of the river, setting pickets on every path an east-bound traveler might take. There was hard doing then, I can tell you! I was driven well out of my way southward, but I reached the mountains at last. Our gate garrisons thought the Ekwesh too strong to challenge without good reason, but I guessed you poor fools might try these passes. So I had them set a special watch in the hills and sent word to Ansker."

Elof rumpled her hair. "And your watchers saw the fight, here in the deep woods? Sharp eyes the duergar have gained, this last year . . ."

"No, loon. Our sentries saw an Ekwesh band enter the trees, as if to set a picket. The watch were only awaiting the dark to come down off the hills and deal with them. But the sentries saw your company approaching, and summoned the garrison in haste. Did you not hear our horns, as we hurried down the track? We knew we might be too late, so Ansker ordered them blown in the hope of scaring the savages off."

"Ansker? Your father? He's here?"

"Indeed I am, journeyman," said a deep voice.

Elof released Ils and whirled round; he seized the hard calloused hand held out to him and sank to one knee, wondering. "My master! Again you step in to save us!" The hard planes of Ansker's face were as stern and intense as ever; but the smile playing about his thin lips and his dark wise eyes hinted at the depths of kindness beneath. Behind him, flanked by grim-faced duergar, others of the company came straggling out of the trees—Kermorvan, Roc, Ermahal, Kasse . . . the greater part of the company, alive. Ansker had indeed saved them, and their quest. "But you should not have risked yourself in war!"

The great duergh laughed, and raised him up. "I would hate to see my good schooling go to waste!" He rubbed his shaven upper lip, as if to suppress a sly smile. "In any event, it was my duty. I fear we may soon face these new-come men in our northern passes. As well the lord of the duergar should learn something of how they fight."

"The lord . . . ?"

Ils grunted. "They chose him in succession to Andvar. He thinks it a blessing not undivided."

"So it appears we have a friend in a high place," said Kermorvan, and added dryly, "or a deep one. But you, Elof, I am glad to see you whole! He had you, that spear-man, but they all fell upon me ere I could help! How did you escape?"

Elof told them of how he had set the talisman, and Ansker asked to see. His gnarled fingers, like twigs of old oak, chased the dark clouds as they coursed across the hilt, traced the outline of what lay beneath. "I marvel. You were wise not to throw this thing away. But have a care! There is much of you in that blade, and in binding it there you have bound the Forest close to you. More than one virtue is held here now."

"Useful enough, was that one," said Roc cheerfully. "Seems you and my lord here kept the Ekwesh chieftain too busy to order his attack proper, left us time to split up and leg it. Then it was raining these good folk and the

man-eaters legging it in their turn, and still running, I'll
wager, those as can. A rare scare they've had.''

"Rare, indeed," said Kasse the huntsman, his normally
saturnine face keen with wonder. Then it clouded. "A
shame, that this sword of yours could not throw a shadow
on that fire the young fools lit. It was that called the savages down on us.''

"They were not to know!" said Elof sharply, seeing
Tenvar flinch and Bure turn away. The death of their friend
would weigh heavy enough on them, they needed no further flaying.

"They were already waiting for us, Kasse," said Kermorvan, massaging his neck. His face was grim. "They
were only choosing their moment to strike. Leave the lads
alone, and let us take muster. Holvar is slain, and Maille,
grievous enough. Are all the rest of us here?"

They looked, one to another, faces crusted with mud
and mold and smeared blood, some grim and stern, some
haggard with shock. Shoulders sagged, or quivered with
shock and tension suddenly released. Elof felt himself
shivering, suddenly weak, but there was only one more
face he could not see. Ermahal jerked his thumb. "Perrec's over there. Spear through his thigh meat, but the little
men are caulking him fine.''

"Good!" breathed Kermorvan. "I feared it might be
worse. And the ponies?''

"We catch maybe four, five," volunteered a duergar
warrior, "maybe more now. Bags were torn loose among
trees, many. We gather them also."

Kermorvan bowed his head gratefully. "Then we may
be in better state than I feared. And ever more deeply in
your debt, my lord.''

"Friends need not talk of debts," smiled Ansker. "As
you said yourself once, we fight a common foe. Well, you
are weary and hurt, but we must not linger; these lands
are alive with the barbarians, and those who fled will summon a mighty horde. You must go with us a short way at
least, northward beneath the mountain shadow. If the eat-

ers of men tread there by night they will not live to learn
better. Come!"

It was a weary group of travelers who filed back out of
the wood and up into the hills. Many already looked long-
ingly at the last glow of sunset in the skies above their
own fair land. But the young northerners looked back toward the wood where their comrade had fallen, and the
corsairs also. The smoke of a larger fire arose there now,
twisting skyward against the weeping clouds. Ermahal
scowled. "Let the savages see it! And make feast on their
own, if they've stomach!"

Though it was less than a league the duergar led them,
it seemed miles uncounted to the travelers, their limbs
leaden, their wounds pulsing fire in the cool breeze. But
when they staggered and slipped on the rocky slopes, a
short square-built figure was always at their elbow, saying
no word but bearing them up with care. The men gazed
wonderingly at these stern creatures, whom they could no
longer think of as vermin or idle legends. Ils held by Elof's
side, and he was glad of her. Only Kermorvan, striding
out with Ansker at the fore, seemed not to be weakened
by their ordeal. But as he turned to look at the smoke of
the burning and the wreck of his company, the horror and
anger that seethed behind his eyes were not hidden from
Elof.

The duergar brought them to a little dell among the
slopes, hidden from view behind a screen of scrubby
birches. A spring rose there among tall stones, but there
was no more to be seen till one of the stones was tilted
smoothly back into the hill, to reveal a wide stone chamber in the rock. "Shelters like these we make for our
watchers and woodcutters," said Ansker, ushering them
in, "when they go abroad in these lands, or into the Forest. Here you can rest and be healed of your hurts in
safety." He looked at Kermorvan, still pale and grim,
standing apart from the others. "And we may take counsel, perhaps, to help you on your way."

A fire could be lit in the wall-hearth, its smoke cunningly dispersed above the rushing waters. The company

hastened to slump down around it, but Elof turned to Kermorvan, and with him Roc. Ils joined them, bearing water and salves to tend their wounds. Kermorvan sat silent and unspeaking. "You need not reproach yourself," said Elof. "How were you to know such an ambush was prepared? You took precautions enough."

Roc nodded vigorously, but Kermorvan shook his head. "I was careless, nonetheless," he said quietly. "Too much concerned with the perils of the Forest, not enough with what might be nearer at hand. But you mistake what most troubles me now. Ils, the Ekwesh force was hurrying south, you said?"

She nodded, tending a gash on Roc's cheek. "At a killing pace, even for their long limbs. A large band; those you faced today would be a tenth part of it, no more."

Kermorvan's face hardened. "So. Then they had some tryst to keep. And what, other than with us? They knew we were coming. They were summoned to picket all the likely passes, and waylay us. Summoned, aye! Another treason, another betrayal! There are still spies within the city!"

Roc swore. "And able to send word northward damned fast!"

Kermorvan nodded. "Exactly. This is no tentative gesture; it smacks of swift and deadly scheming." He shivered. "Did I hope for ten years' grace ere the Ekwesh returned?"

Roc nodded grimly. "We'll be lucky to have one! And what worth does that leave our journey? You might be better employed shaking some sense into the city . . ."

Elof fought to force down the laughter that welled up in him from a spring of sudden hope. "And that's what's weighing you both down? You doubt the worth of the journey? But are you too weary to see the other side of that coin? We may not know the worth, but it seems our enemies do—high enough to have them send a thousand men running to forestall it, for a start!"

Roc thumped fist into palm, Ils breathed sharply. The growing fire crackled and blazed under a caldron of water, and as Kermorvan looked up slowly the flames shone golden in his gray eyes. "Yes. Yes, it must be so. It must! I was too weary indeed to see that, and stricken with grief." He smiled suddenly, lopsided because of his cut mouth. "Very well, we press on! And my next command as your leader is that you, Elof, and you, Roc, sit tight and let your hurts be tended. At once!"

"And you?" scolded Ils severely. "That torn mouth won't wait if you keep wagging it! You're next in line, my long lad."

That night they slept the deep sleep of utter exhaustion. The stream's rush lulled them, or perhaps there was some healing herb mixed in the strong wine of the duergar, for all were strangely free of pain or dreaming, all save Elof. He awoke near dawn from a vision he would not tell of, though his face was streaked with tears. He had seen black swan's wings again, wheeling northward against a scarlet sky of dawn, and then, just before they vanished, eastward once more. And when after daybreak they conferred with Ansker, northward was the route he bade them take. "Southward, downriver, that is barred to you now; the hunters know you are about, and can follow you out of our range. But if you turn north we can shield you awhile, and cover your tracks with our own."

Kermorvan sat deep in thought. "That is kind indeed, Lord Ansker. I thank you for it. But our way lies eastward; sooner or later we must cross the Westflood and enter the Forest. Why not here?"

Ansker nodded. "Sooner or later you must, indeed. The duergar do not often enter Aithen the Great, but we know something of it. It is a place of deep shadow and deeper mysteries; many spells and many secrets, small and great, are worked in the gloom beneath its dark canopy. It is not a land into which I would willingly send a friend. But since your quest leaves you no choice . . ." He drew a small brass case from the sleeve of his tunic, and opened it to unfold a long sheet of the duergar reed paper. Craning over Kermorvan's shoulder, Elof recognized the snaky backbone of the Shieldrange, drawn in finer detail than he had ever seen before. Ansker's blunt finger traced a long blue line running alongside its eastward face. "Here is Gorlafros, which flows from the very margins of the Ice to the southernmost borders of your land. Swelled by the meltwaters of the Ice, it has carved itself many wide lakes and outflows. This one, the greatest, flows through the Shieldbreach and feeds the Marshlands that Elof knows; doubtless it disgorges there many of the terrors it bears from the Ice. This far south of it the river is wholesome enough. And not so far north of here there is another outflow, almost as great. But this one flows eastward."

"Into the heart of the Forest?" exclaimed Kermorvan in excitement. "But how far, Lord Ansker? And is it navigable?"

Ansker nodded and smiled. "You are quick to grasp my meaning. Indeed it is, for vessels of shallow draft. But as to how far, I cannot tell you; the duergar have not penetrated so deeply into Tapiau'la within living memory. It is said to end in a lake, within sight of some tall mountains. That is all I can say."

"My lord, it is vastly more than we knew!" exclaimed Kermorvan, his pale face flushed, his gray eyes agleam once more. "You have given me a surer road, where I thought to find none . . ."

"Surer, but not safer," cautioned the duergar lord. He hunched his broad shoulders uneasily. "You may have slipped the Ekwesh from your scent, but there are other perils, perhaps worse ones. No road is safe, beneath the trees."

"But this one we will venture," said Kermorvan softly, as a silken surcoat over steel. "And since you have recovered so much of our baggage, and beasts enough to carry it, we will heed your advice, and leave soon. Within the hour, if your folk are ready."

"What about Perrec?" put in Elof. "He can ride, but he won't be fit to walk far for a long time."

"Him we must send back, I fear," said Kermorvan. "He can take such of the riding ponies as we can spare; we will keep only the baggage beasts, and set them free to make their own way south again, or into your land, Ansker. From this point forth we will fare better on foot." He touched his mouth gingerly. "I have proof of that. Beware of galloping among low branches!"

Perrec protested bitterly enough, but underneath it the corsair seemed glad enough now of an excuse to withdraw without cowardice; the broad Ekwesh spear had torn his leg so terribly that none could dispute his reason. They saw him off an hour or so later, mounted on Kermorvan's strong pony, with two other beasts and an escort of day-hardy young duergar to see him across the hills in safety. "He will say no word in the city of our chosen route," said Kermorvan grimly. "Tidings of that, at least, will not reach the ears of spies. Now let us be on our way!"

"At least we won't lack much!" said Tenvar, who had seen to loading the ponies. Elof patted the bulge of his recovered tool-pack reassuringly.

"Aye, naught but what's most needed," grunted Roc. "Do you wait and see!"

But he too was cheered, for it was a fine morning, and the sun warm and soothing upon their aching limbs. Most of the duergar, save Ils and some younger warriors, pulled hood and helm low to shade their eyes, and muttered about being frozen one minute, fried the next. Elof and Kermorvan sympathized, remembering the seasonless cool twilight under stone, and were happy enough that the duergar's chosen route north led them for the most part under cover of thick woodland, or in the twilight. "For the Ekwesh have the long sight of sailors," Kermorvan observed. "And their shamans, it is said, may call upon the service of other eyes."

Elof thought of the swan, but said nothing. He looked at Ils, deep in some converse with her father, and remembered the biting suspicion in her voice. *She is this Louhi's,* Ils had whispered, *and not yours . . .*

After a quiet journey of many days following the river, the travelers came to a fair-sized lake, the first of those that Ansker had mentioned, and passed through the dense woodlands on its banks. When they reached the far side, in the light of a gray morning, they found themselves beneath the outermost curve of the Meneth Scahas, and looking across hilly country, bleak and treeless, to a whole chain of lakes.

"Here the Open Lands live up to their name," Ansker told them. "Too open for the duergar, I fear, and too far from our mountains. It is here we must part."

"My lord," said Kermorvan fervently, "already you have done more than we would have dared ask. I cannot imagine how I could repay you, but we will not forget . . ."

"Hmmph!" was Ils' comment, though Ansker frowned at her. "And your folk? True, they can't forget what they won't learn!" Kermorvan flushed scarlet, with shame or anger, and she chuckled and jabbed a plump finger into his ribs. "Oh, don't worry, long man; I know you mean well . . ."

"And not just him!" put in Ermahal unexpectedly. "We've learned, us. And we're not what you'd call the cream of our folk. More like the dregs, all 'counts rendered! If we can, so'll others. Or take a sore brain bone, on account!"

Ansker bowed with great gravity. "We are honored, good sir. But as it happens we have thought of some repayment you can make now, high though the cost may seem."

Kermorvan looked guarded. "What might that be?"

"A hand in this venture of yours. That you let us share its hazards and its success. We also came from the east, many long ages before you men. The roads we took lie now under the Ice; as well we should find some new ones, and learn how the Eastlands now stand."

"What he means," snorted Ils, "is that if we want the crackbrained thing to get anywhere, we'd damn well better take a part in it!"

"You already have!" protested Elof. "Where would we be without you?"

"Toasting on an Ekwesh fire, I've no doubt," said Ils,

with a certain relish. "But we won't be so easily at hand in the black bowels of Aithen the Great, not unless we come along. Or one of us, at least."

"You?" cried Elof in delight. "But I thought you could suffer men no longer!"

Ils squirmed slightly. "Not the city mob, indeed. But this crew of yours is not so bad, though rough. I'll endure them."

Kermorvan held his features as impassive as ever, but Elof almost laughed aloud to see how delight and dismay chased across them. "My lady," began the warrior with strangled formality, "you would be welcome, most welcome . . . But the, the unknown, the dangers . . ."

Ils made a ferocious face, and thrust out her buxom breast aggressively. "Are you implying—my lord—that I did less than my part in our last little jaunt together?" She ran a speculative finger along the silver-inlaid axe blade at her belt. "Because if you are . . ."

"I believe that is settled, then," said Ansker smoothly.

Elof looked at him. "It is no small treasure you send with us, my master."

"Treasure!" snorted Ils corrosively. "Little enough loss to those stuffy caverns, when there's real work for the duergar in the wide world."

"I fear she is corrupted," said Ansker with mock severity. "She grows more human every day. Well that she has a chance to weary of it. But in all seriousness," he added, a little sadly, "I feel as she does. We have remained hidden too long, retreating before the changes of the world. We cannot retreat forever. Our numbers dwindle, our young folk can look forward to nothing new. Even our smithcraft grows weaker in our eyes, when such as yours, Elof, burgeons now among men. Something must change, and perhaps this journey is its beginning. Few of us are more able than Ils, and fond enough of men and their daylight to share in it." He smiled. "I shall miss her, yes. But I would not hold her back from it . . . even if I could!" He turned and embraced her, briefly as it would seem to men. But both these creatures were old, far older than most men, and Elof guessed at the flood of feeling behind their light manner, flowing as deep and strong under its calm surface as their dark waters beneath the stone.

"We will take every care of her!" he said, dodging the blow she aimed at his midriff.

"I know!" said Ansker, and took his hand, and Kermorvan's. "Farewell then, my lord! May your high ancestors guard and guide you in their paths. And farewell, my journeyman. Strive still for mastery; of what, you know full well. But have a care, study the gentler skills as well as you have the fiercer, if what I hear is true. Anvils are expensive!" He laughed, but Elof bowed his head. "Now the sun rises, to hammer hotly on our poor brainpans! Come, my duergar, the mountains call us! It is time we were away!"

And as the travelers watched and waved, the duergar warriors drew their hoods over their heads and wrapped their cloaks tight about them. Then they bowed, once, with stiff courtesy, and seemed almost to dissolve among the shadows of the wood, so silent was their going. But Ils looked up at Elof, and smiled.

He smiled back, uneasily. "You had some other reasons for leaving the city, that you would not say . . ."

"Oh, those!" Ils shrugged. "As bad away as near, I found. That's all."

Elof understood only that she would say no more, and changed the subject. "Ansker said the duergar also came from the east. When was that?"

Ils' reply was stark. "When the first men set foot on its shores. We fled you, as you the Ice."

Going among the ponies as they made ready to depart, stooping to check a loosened girth, Elof heard a voice he recognized as the corsair Borhi's. "Not such bad little tykes, them, eh?"

"Have them, for me!" said a harsh voice that could only be Kasse's. "If you'd been a hunter like me, you'd know. There's more than one thing walks the woods in a human shape. Some you steer clear of, some . . . well,

you can treat with 'em. But duergar, they're uncanny
wights, and good riddance to 'em, say I!''

"What about the lady?" That was the coxwain Dervhas,
with his coarse chuckle. "Her shape not human enough
for you?''

"Bouncing prow on 'er!" agreed Borhi enthusiastically.
"What's ado, Kasse, feared of 'er axe? Aye, and she can
swing it, by 'counts!''

"I'll bed a human woman or none!" growled Kasse,
displeased. "My sires'd slaughter any duergar vermin they
found, and string 'em up to dry on the trees. Leave that
bitch to the northerner, the tinker boy. He's near as uncanny, him . . .''

They moved off down the line, leaving Elof boiling with
rage. It was as well, perhaps, that Kermorvan gave the
signal to move off just then. Yet even as they emerged into
the Open Lands, Elof had no eye for the view, no taste for
the fresh breezes. He walked by himself at the back of the
train, and neither Tenvar nor Bure dared disturb him. In
the corsair's coarse words he found no harm, and even a
certain admiration; but every word of Kasse's he longed
to ram back down his throat, and his teeth after. He embodied the sothran's worst prejudices; he had a mind of
mud and filth, that man, despising those who had come to
help him, reducing Elof's friendship and affection for Ils
to the lowest level, and to him the most obscene. As if it
could be so! For a moment Elof lost himself in a hazy
distance, a waking dream of Kara, Kara slender amid peril
and moonlight, the gleam of her dark gaze, the last agony
of loss. Then other dark eyes rose in his mind, another
thought, a stealthy intruder, tore him out of his dream all
unprepared, undefended. What he felt for Ils he knew,
indeed; but what might Ils feel for him?

The idea clawed at him. She was not even of his race,
she was older by a lifetime than he and much wiser in the
world's ways, with all the might and craft of her ancient
race at her back. And she knew of Kara, had glimpsed
her, perhaps, in the Tower. What could she ever feel for
him, young, rootless, homeless both in body and in spirit?

Even his name was of his own bestowing. Impossible, and yet . . . He looked at her now, laughing and joking with Arvhes and Ermahal up ahead, never so much as glancing back at him who walked silent and alone. Elof lashed the thought from his mind. The very idea was absurd.

It was nine days' march through the Open Lands, and the mountains lay far behind them before they came in sight of the largest lake in the long chain so far, and knew it for their goal. On the map Ansker had given Kermorvan the jagged duergar script named it the Spearhead, for its shape, but high up as they were, they could see no more than its southern shores, its northern expanse lost beyond the horizon. The slaty waters lifted in the wind, flecked by a sweeping cloudburst; reeds hissed and bowed around the western shore, but all along its eastern flank a dark blur dipped and swayed. This was the wall of the true Forest, Aithen the Great, and its foliage shimmered under the clouds.

"You're not telling me we've got to cross that?" shuddered Bure.

"No, indeed!" smiled Kermorvan. "Only the river south of it, and there are fords and islets enough on Ansker's map; it will not be too arduous. But we must turn loose our ponies."

"And after that?" asked Eysdan bluntly. "We have provender enough yet, with what the small folk gave us, but we cannot bear it all on our backs."

"Strong servants await us there on the far bank," answered Kermorvan calmly. "Strong enough they look to bear not only our provisions but ourselves, for many long leagues on our way."

"What do you mean?" asked the others eagerly, seeing that he had some scheme in mind.

"I mean the currents, and the trees. We have in our baggage tools and tackle to fashion strong rafts, such as you northern foresters use for your timber. I had wit enough to foresee that need, at least! But first comes foremost; we must seek out our crossing. Come!"

By midday they had found the first of their fords. The

Westflood here flowed from the lake in many narrow channels which merged and separated and merged again, creating a patternless marshy maze a mile or more across. But Ansker's map led them straight and true; by evening they found themselves on a narrow wooded islet no more than a bowshot from the eastern bank, and the walls of the true Forest.

"But the wall is breached!" said Kermorvan. "See that wide channel there, that crooks away from the others, past the islet about a mile downriver? Thenceforth the trees hide it. For that is our outflow, the river that flows deep among the trees."

They made camp there among the trees that night, and even with water as their chiefest sentinel they kept their fires small and sheltered, and set a watch. Elof took the first hour, watching the faint fire glimmer on the long bare trunks of the firs around him, listening to the rush and swirl of the wind in their greater kin beyond. Even when Ermahal had come to relieve him, he lay long awake in his blanket by the fire, listening to the corsair skipper humming some slow chantey over the embers, wondering what other songs might be sung beyond that wall.

The next day Kermorvan, who had taken the last watch, roused them all at the first trace of light, and set the company in a flurry of activity. The ponies were loaded at once, and, stumbling in the gloom, the company made its way down to a stand of huge old willows on the bank that marked the last ford. It was a poor ford; a slip on the weed-slimed rocks meant a plunge waist-deep into chill water and a strong current. The sure-footed ponies fared better than their masters, who had often to catch hold of their traces to avoid a ducking. The corsairs, hardened by colder ocean, would have laughed at the others' discomfort, save that the looming rampart of trees cast a shadow in their hearts; nobody felt eager to make much noise, and they even cried out and cursed in whispers. But when at last they reached the far bank the dawn glowed behind the trees, with a welcome promise of warmth. It was easier to remember then that the lowering wall was, after all, only trees, and not some sinister fortress.

Kermorvan, wringing out his cloak, seemed well pleased, despite the others' complaints. "We need every moment of daylight for our toil. It must needs make noise, and attract attention. By day, and at the Forest's edge, I guess the risk is not so great. But when night falls I would sooner be far from here." Then, shivering with more than cold, the others agreed.

The strongest and most practiced of the party, himself included, Kermorvan set to seeking out and felling suitable trees. They did not need to search far; even at the Forest wall there were many of good height. Though the giant redwoods of the coastlands were rarer among them, there were firs and cedars and spruces aplenty that seemed to burgeon in their absence. Elof touched the furrowed gray bark of the first fir, gazing up at it. "These are noble trees. I wish we did not have to fell them."

Kermorvan, stripping off his tunic and hefting an axe, nodded with some regret. "I feel as you do. I would kill no living thing I did not have to."

"Tree's a tree," said Gise the forester, faintly surprised. "Some fall, others come up in their place. The Forest's the thing. Look at it that-wise, fell sparingly and far apart as you can. Don't wound the wood too grievous and you won't turn it 'gainst you."

"I have heard similar counsels of kingship," said Kermorvan, amused, and struck a well-placed blow that made the tall tree quiver from stem to crown. Small birds fluttered scolding from the leaves; a large squirrel bounded to a neighboring branch and clung chittering with rage. But Gise's blows followed Kermorvan's and a low cut chopped out the wedge. On the tree's far side Roc and Elof, under their direction, began to cut the notch that would determine its fall. The pungent reek of resin flooded stingingly into nose and eye. Not far away another treetop jerked and sprang at the bite of axes as Eysdan and Ils, aided by Dervhas and Kasse, set to their task with equal vigor. Elof found time to wonder amusedly if Ils had also shed tunic and shirt for her labor; that, if anything, might alter Kasse's view of her humanity.

So hard did Kermorvan drive the felling parties that by the sunny mid-morning five tall trees lay by the bank, and a sixth trembled on its half-hewn stump. It was just as the sun reached its zenith that the tenth tree dropped along the line of its own short shadow, and the fellers let go their blunted axes and collapsed into the shade. Only Kermorvan stayed afoot, goading on the others of the company whose task it was to trim branch and root and, with the ponies, to drag the trunks to the river. Though his lean frame ran with sweat and his voice had thinned to a croak, his endurance seemed endless. An hour or two later he came striding back from the riverside with a leather waterbag, and splashed it over the exhausted fellers. "Come and marvel!" he called cheerfully, in his normal ringing voice. "You will have days ahead to lie idle!"

Groaning and cursing, they struggled up and shuffled after him. But when Elof reached the bank, he was indeed surprised that so much had been done in so short a time. There, bobbing high in the current, two long rafts were tethered; the others of the company were toiling with hammer and nail, cord and chain, fastening the second together. Ils came along to join him, curls straggling from a refreshing douse in the river; he noticed she was fastening her tunic. "Look solid enough, don't they?" she laughed. "Four good trunks for each, with the half of a fifth on either side, and both longer than that little courier boat of ours. And see what the northern lad's about!" On the completed raft Tenvar was even putting together a makeshift canopy, roofed with leafy branches. "We'll ride like lords!"

By the late afternoon both rafts had their canopies, indeed, and all the baggage was aboard. All that remained was for Gise, with Arvhes and Tenvar, to turn the ponies loose upon the western shore. Even Kermorvan in all his impatience was loth to abandon those game little beasts under the Forest's shadow. In the Open Lands they would find good grazing, and perhaps make their way back to the Northmarch, where they would fare well enough, wild or tame. But leading them back took time, leaving Kermorvan anxiously eyeing the sinking sun. At last, as the shadows lengthened, they espied the three drovers picking their way back across the last difficult ford. Arvhes fell in once, and Tenvar many times; Gise plucked them out by the scruff of their necks, like puppies. "They're too small! Heave 'em back!" jeered Kasse. But his raucous laughter rang alarmingly loud among the trees, and the others glared at him.

"Quiet, Kasse!" commanded Kermorvan sharply, as the three came straggling ashore. "All well, Gise? Then to your rafts, and cast off!" He drew on one end of the forward mooring line, the knot slipped free, and with long poles they thrust the leading raft's blunt bow out into the current. The line that linked it to the second raft thrummed taut, and Elof jerked the moorings free. An eddy sucked at it; the blunt-nosed logs ground and jarred against yellow mud, and the water grew suddenly thick as milk. But poles, and the pull of the leading raft, freed it and together, as the sun fell behind the trees, the rough craft leaped out into the smooth onrush of the Westflood.

Its flow was faster than it had seemed from the shore, and they found themselves hurled forward at a smart pace, with the breeze whipping at their hair. The younger folk of the company whooped with excitement, Ils loudest of all; Roc's cry went almost unheard till he seized Elof's arm and jabbed a hard finger at the receding shore. "There!" he hissed, to be heard through the river's rumble and rush. "There below the cedars! Can't you see 'em?"

"Not a thing; no, a few boughs shaking, perhaps. Some beast . . ."

"With suchlike eyes? They were watching us, no mistake, really watching. But not like a man's neither . . ."

"Green? Cat-like? The Forest folk have such eyes . . ."

Roc shuddered. "Naught so wholesome. Just . . . two gleams. Slanting, yellow. Maybe they caught the last sun,

I don't know. But they sent a proper chill through me, they did.''

Elof looked around. Nobody on the leading raft seemed to have seen anything, and nobody else on their own. Ermahal leaned unconcerned on the steering oar; Tenvar and Bure sat in the bows, enjoying the ride, and Arvhes dozed peacefully on the baggage. Only Kasse gazed at the shore, and he gave no sign of having seen anything. "I believe you, nonetheless," said Elof quietly. "Whatever they were, they prove one thing; Kermorvan did right to goad us hence so fast. I would not now care to linger by that ford, after dark.''

Roc nodded. They were glad to see Kermorvan ahead of them shift his weight on the steering oar and take the raft further from the bank, aiming it straight down the center of the stream that flowed down the divergent channel. Their own matched it smoothly, as Ermahal followed suit. Kermorvan's way with boats he had gained chiefly at sea, so he had taken Ils to advise him, skilled at sailing the shadowed mountain rivers, and put Ermahal in charge of the second raft. The skipper was probably the most practiced waterman of them all, whether on sea or river, and he seemed glad to be at a helm again. His screwed-up eyes scanned the river ahead with keen appraisal, watching every little shift in the water's flow as they passed between islet and shore, and when they rounded the sharp turn at its end it was he who called the first warning.

Ahead of them, like an outstretched limb of the island, a low shelf of rock thrust out halfway across the river, just below the surface, so that the water bubbled and foamed across it, like a natural weir. It was onto this that the current was carrying them, faster already than a horse could gallop, and with no chance whatsoever of steering for the clear channel. "Down, and grab 'old!" yelled Ermahal. Elof saw Kermorvan fall on his steering oar and sweep it from the water, and after that there was little any could do save throw themselves flat upon the logs. With a booming crash, a dreadful scraping, the first raft hit, slewed sideways a moment so Elof feared they would strike it amidships, then it was lurching up and over. Elof saw its stern bounce and settle, then the impact took and shook him, rattling his very teeth in their sockets. His raft tilted and water sluiced along the logs; there was a roar of rage from Arvhes as the awning toppled onto him, then that terrible scraping once again. Elof felt the logs judder under him, heard the crosspieces creak with the strain, and then the whole craft slid bouncing and splashing into the wider channel.

"Well," said Kermorvan as they strove in the fading light to set the rafts in order again. "That is one feature your father's map did not show, Ils! No doubt there will be more; we must keep a proper watch, especially when faring on through the dark."

"You'd no thought of doing that tonight, had you?" inquired Elof, among groans and protests.

Kermorvan shook his head. "No, tonight we are all too weary. We will find somewhere to moor and sleep if we can. There are some islands marked a way downriver, too far perhaps for tonight. But we must find somewhere safe."

All of the company understood him, for in rounding that bend in the river and crossing the weir they had lost their last sight of the Open Lands, and of the west. Both banks now were high walls that closed in as completely behind them as ahead. Wherever they looked, they saw nothing save rank upon rank of trees, upthrust at the sky above, mirrored in the river below. Aithen the Great, the Forest realm, had closed its gates behind them.

So it was that as the last light faded from the sky, the rafts glided on down the stream. It was a clear night, but warmer as the wind fell. The Forest was beyond sight for the moment, dark upon darkness, but never out of mind; the wafting odors of pine sap and tar and damp humus bespoke its awesome presence, and the myriad scurryings and snufflings of its small night-dwellers. Then the stars came out, and the moon arose, dusting the treetops silver. Their dark reflections narrowed the river, but the rafts sailed on serenely down the strip of sky mirrored at its center, across shoals of glittering cloud and deeps of starry blackness. By then most of the company not on watch lay asleep, but Elof could not; he moved astern to sit by Ermahal, who seemed quite happy to go on steering.

"And why not? Grand night to be out on the river again, like when I was a lad. Grew up on a river barge, I did, d'you know that? Used to borrow the tender to take the lasses for rows on a moonlit night like this." He chuckled. "Worked a treat, did the moon. You ever do that?"

Elof shook his head regretfully. "Nothing but swink and study. There were no lasses where I grew up. Save one."

The corsair nodded, not unkindly. "Aye, 'er you seek, would that be? Guessed as much. Must be quite a lass, to 'aul you so far."

"She is."

Ermahal was obviously expecting more details, but when none came he sighed and scratched his head. "Ah well, I might've felt the same when I was your age, if only for the adventure of it. Not now I'm old."

"You? You are no graybeard yet!"

"Five winters short of my 'alf-'undred. Twice your age, if I guess aright."

"More or less. I cannot be sure of it myself."

"Well, there you 'as it. Precious few lasses'd fetch me out into the wilds now. Save one, p'raps, 'er I used to go with that many years back. Pretty's a picture, all long blond curls to her waist and a bold blue eye on her like a summer sky. A fine shape, too, that a man could get a hold of. 'Er beckonin' me to come, and I wouldn't, not me, seein' I was on first watch an' all. Funny, that. Seeing 'er again, after all these years, just the same, beckonin', beckonin' . . . On one of them big willows down by the ford. Fancy."

Elof looked up in astonishment. Ermahal looked much as he always did, if anything calmer and more serene; the moonlight seemed to have smoothed away some of the salt-hardened lines from his broad face. Perhaps that was why he was wandering in memory, seeming to talk of his memories as if they were only of last night. "Sittin' on the tree limb, out over the water bold as brass, swingin' those plump little legs and beckonin' . . ." His voice tailed away, and when he spoke again it was of another and less innocent memory. He did not mention the girl again.

They had at last to accept that they could not reach any islands that night, and chose to moor on an out-thrust sandspit, wide enough for them to sleep on but narrow enough to be guarded by one. Ermahal, still apparently unwearied, offered to take the first watch once more, and was not opposed; even Kermorvan was stumbling with weariness. But Elof, though he also wished to sleep, was concerned enough to seek out Kermorvan, and tell him of Ermahal's words. Kermorvan also looked concerned, but not unduly so. "I know of few men less given to fancies than he. Perhaps it was only weariness that spoke, and the strains of a long day. Still, we should have a care for him. You travel on his raft; watch him, and if anything seems worse about him, summon me at once. And now I must have some sleep, if I am not to start babbling also."

Elof agreed with Kermorvan's judgment; the corsair skipper was a hard man to daunt. At their first encounter he had feared anything that might have strayed off the Marshlands, but he had not been afraid to fight it. Sitting on watch now, leaning on his steelbound halberd, he looked the very image of solidity and strength. But when he awakened Kermorvan for the second watch, some two hours later, Elof also awoke. The corsair rolled himself in his blankets, grunting comfortably, and appeared to drift off at once. But only a few minutes after, when Kermorvan's attention was fixed upon the wood, Elof saw the skipper sit up, clutching his blankets nervously to him, and stare fixedly across the dark waters around. Then with a disappointed sigh, he lay down and at last began to snore.

The night passed without incident, and the next day's sail, save that the Forest seemed to be closing around them ever more closely. Open patches of bank were scarcer; the trees were growing down to the water's edge, many over-hanging it with their long limbs. Some had broken, or partly torn away, and lay rakelike below the water's surface, perilous snags for any craft less solid than the rafts. That night they did not moor, but set full watches and sailed on; Elof chose his with Ermahal. The skipper seemed cheerful enough, but nervous; he started violently when an owl plummeted silently from the trees to pluck some small beast shrieking from the bankside grass, and once again at a sharp splash from the calm waters astern. They looked, but saw nothing save wide circles of ripples spreading outward from a deep place in the moonlit water, and the flickering dance of nightmoths above them.

"A fish rising for a moth," Elof remarked. "They must grow big in these pools with none to fish them. We should try trailing some lines astern one of these nights; our supplies . . ."

He stopped. In the strong moonlight Ermahal's face was aglisten with sweat, his breath labored as if with some great effort. But all he said was, "Might be an idea, that," and turned the talk to other things. When they went off watch he took gladly to his blankets, but Elof watched him lie for a long time on one elbow, gazing into the black river, till finally his head nodded and he sank into unfeigned sleep.

All the next day's sailing Ermahal seemed in high good spirits, as if some weight of worry had been lifted from his mind. He was as pleased as any when they rounded a bend and espied a fine flock of deer ahead, drinking at the bank. Gise leaped for his bow, but they fled too quickly. "No matter," Kermorvan said. "I had hoped that we could hunt for our food by the river, and this proves it. We shall find other drinking places, and lie in wait." He looked at the mud churned by hooves, and at the trees beyond. "Interesting, though, that the beasts fled so readily. As if they were accustomed to being hunted by men. Or folk like men."

Ils bit her lip thoughtfully, looking at Elof. "You mean the tall ones—the Children of . . ." She seemed reluctant to speak the name, and here beneath the frowning treewall Elof was of like mind. He felt suddenly very vulnerable out in the open, and acutely aware of the power within the woods. Memories came to trouble him, the gaze of green eyes, a voice over vast distances, ravens riding a storm-wind, and for that time they obscured his other concerns.

Toward evening of that day they came upon the string of small islands the map had promised. They were nearly as thickly wooded as the shores, but seemed safer in their isolation. The company chose one well apart from the rest, and in deep water. Here at least they could search the brush, climb the tall willows and other trees and be sure neither man nor beast lurked there in wait. They found nothing, not even snakes, and settled down to sleep with only one on watch. When Elof's turn came, not long past the middle hour of night, he was happy enough to sit with his back to the smooth bark of a tall tree, a maple of a variety new to him, and think his thoughts. He listened to the soft windrush overhead, imagined it sweeping across an incalculable plain of treetops, like a green ocean, and wished he could sail over them as easily. But he was not minded to complain. Despite the horror of the Ekwesh attack, his own quest had proved lighter by far than he had feared. Instead of wandering alone and aimless into the wild lands, he had traveled fast and with friends, and in relative peace. Whatever the terrors of the Forest, it seemed they might not extend to the river. He wondered how long it flowed, how far it would bear them, whether they might not find other rivers flowing eastward and so be whirled safely right through these menacing lands . . .

He stiffened suddenly. Something had moved, softly, heavily, among the bushes behind him. Hand on sword hilt, he twisted about, crouching on his knee with the trunk as shelter. A bulky shadow stepped softly, hesitantly, among the undergrowth, away from the camp. He caught his breath as he recognized Ermahal; it had to be him, as broad as Eysdan or Gise but not so tall. What was he doing? His errand might be natural enough, yet he was stopping and looking about, as if searching, or listening. Cautiously Elof slipped out from behind the tree and followed. Over the low ridge of the island they went, Elof keeping low among the leaves lest he be seen. But the skipper did not look back once, only turned his head urgently, as one who seeks something lost. And gradually, as they went, Elof grew aware of a faint sound in the air, floating as it seemed high among the branches, then falling, rippling like laughter along the water. It was a sweet, soft sound, yet it plucked at his ear almost to the point of irritation, as the whine of some insistent insect. But that thought brought the shock of recognition with it, for that was no insect; it was a voice.

Ermahal changed his pace suddenly, went blundering swiftly down the slope to the bank, then halted, hesitant again as he emerged onto the shore. Elof followed more cautiously, for the moon was slipping down the sky, and his way was no longer so clear; he was crawling now on all fours to stay hidden among the low brush, straining his eyes to seek some trace of what held Ermahal in such thrall.

It was only when she moved that he saw. He had been looking at her for some time, perched in the crook of a great willow, without distinguishing her shape, so still had she sat. It was a pose of tense, crouching energy, knees to chin, so that her long hair fell draped about her legs; it was as she lowered her feet, to dangle beneath the branch, that Elof saw her in truth. There she sat, a slender figure of a girl, naked, her long legs hanging over the black water of the still pool beneath, playing, dancing with their reflection and that of the silvery moon beneath her feet. The song was hers, high and soft, a yearning, winsome song whose words he felt but could not understand.

In truth he understood nothing, and did not dare move, so still was the scene before him. Her beauty alone held him, as graceful as the deer and as fragile; almost he feared that she might vanish as they had. Yet some part of him remained aware, and perceived that this was not the girl Ermahal had described. Her legs were hardly plump, but long, slender, her toes pointing as if to dance on the very water; her arms were lean and strong, enticing as they beckoned. Her hair hung long, yes, to below her waist, but straight, almost lank, not curling and blond; even by moonlight it had a strange sheen. And as for a bold blue eye . . . He shivered abruptly. They gleamed and glittered in the dying moonlight, those eyes, altogether too brightly, with the rainbow sheen of fresh-landed fish scale. Could Ermahal not see that, blundering forward thus to her beckoning arms?

It happened too easily, in the instant between Elof's foreseeing it and his shout of alarm. Ermahal plunged on with reckless abandon, right out along the sagging bough, his heavy face held up to her proffered lips which were poised not to kiss but curved in a strange sweet smile. In that instant her legs snapped straight, toes a downward spearpoint, and she slipped smoothly off her perch, all her weight bearing down into the corsair's straining arms. And as she slid down, so also the moon dropped behind the jagged summit of a tree. Utter shadow blotted out the pool.

Elof sprang up and rushed forward, but in the darkness he tripped among the damp vegetation and fell to his knees by the bank. The splash he awaited did not come, even to his keen ears. His swift eyes pierced the lingering moonglow, but nowhere could he see another human shape, or any stirring save the faint tremor of leaf and blade in the night breeze. The pool's black surface showed him only himself, staring ashen into a mirror undisturbed by ripple or bubble. He flung himself at it, shattering the image, plunging his arms in to the shoulders. But his fingers raked only among slimy tangles of riverweed, and when he thrust his face beneath the surface he could see no more. Ermahal was gone.

"It is useless, then," said Kermorvan wearily, glaring up at the bright sun of noon. "We must rest." He leaned against the willow, while the others slumped exhausted to the ground. Since Elof's first shout, in the dark hours before dawn, they had searched high and low for Ermahal, or the slightest sign of what had befallen him. Even in darkness they had taken grapnels and strong lines and dragged the pool below the willow, and a long way both downstream and up. But, like Elof, they found only weed and slime and small water creatures, and once the bones of some great beast sunk in the mud. They had crossed to both shores, but there was nowhere among the trees a man so big might have landed without leaving traces the foresters could pick up. With that against them, there was little point in searching deeper into the Forest; which way, after all, should they turn among such a trackless desert of trees?

"Had we had only some trail to follow, a mark even!" growled Dervhas painfully. "Then I'd tear up every bloody tree in our way to find him! Even if it took a year!" He shook his head. "But now, do we turn this way? That? Never dreamed a man might be lost on land as surely as at sea! Lost and gone to Amicac!"

Kermorvan nodded. If I thought he lived, I would not now be resting. My heart tells me that he is far beyond any seeking of ours."

Elof sat sunk in misery, thinking of his first swift clash with Ermahal, his equally swift acceptance and their share in the seafight. He had liked the fat captain, for all his past misdeeds; a rogue, but a friendly one and capable, a loss to his land, a loss to the company. "As I told you," he said dully. "That was no human creature that enticed him. I saw her . . ."

"Then why did he not warn the man, or us?" growled Kasse, and spat in Elof's direction, with a curious averting gesture. His eyes were narrow with suspicion. "I don't like that. I don't like it at all."

"No more, Kasse!" said Kermorvan sharply. "That is fool's talk, or churl's. Elof's trust is past question."

The huntsman looked to the others for support, found none, and scowled. "Well, there's nothing in the Forest ever hurt me, that's all I'm saying. Me, I've walked in it half a hundred times. You've just got to do the right things . . ."

Kermorvan stood up, stretching, and shook his head. "Spare me your superstitions, Kasse. You were fortunate, perhaps. You know, as I do, that many others were not.

No, you heard Elof; he warned me, he tried his best to help Ermahal at the last. But I wonder whether any of us could have saved poor Ermahal. For how could we have guessed what threatened him, till it showed itself? And then, as Elof found, it was too late.''

Stehan nodded. ''Wouldn't have thought he'd fall for a suchlike lure.''

''I might have thought it of others,'' agreed Kermorvan. ''But not of him.'' Elof fancied that Ils stole a glance at him, then, and perhaps also Roc. ''Strange, what may linger within a man's heart. Well, he is gone, and we must live on. Ils, you have the skill; do you take his place on the second raft. We must be gone in haste.'' He turned to face the company, and they saw that with his long hunting knife he had graven deep in the willow's bark the day and year, and the name of the man who in adversity had been his friend. ''Back to the rafts now and let us quit this unhallowed place! But henceforth let none of us be deceived by any vision of our past returned!''

There was a general growl of agreement. But as they returned to the rafts they spoke no more than was needful. Out into midstream they turned once more; the island slipped away behind them until it was no more than a fleck of darkness upon the waters, as lost to them as the years of their own youth.

CHAPTER FOUR

Hunters and Hunted

The chronicles tell little more of that river journey till its end, though it lasted many days more, and bore them some hundred and fifty leagues at least into the heart of the Forest. Rapid and shallow they passed with no desperate troubles, for their rafts were strong and stable and brought them through where fleeter boats might have been lost. Their journey was swift, for now they seldom cared to moor, but sailed on throughout the nights as long as they had a glimmer of light to steer by. Only when moon and stars failed them were they driven to seek the land in the hours of darkness, and there they slept on the rafts, close together, with a strong watch set. But although for that time the travelers were assailed no more, care still lay heavy on their hearts.

"Wonder if all those lost folk didn't just starve!" grumbled Roc. "Could be hunger's the worst terror in this land."

"Terror enough for me!" muttered Bure, eyeing the dwindling hummock under the awning. They were on half rations now, which must soon grow less. Kermorvan had intended that they live by hunting, such supplies as they carried serving chiefly to tide them over and provide some healthy variety. All the company could hunt, some with great skill, not least himself; but save for a few fish, even they had caught nothing. It was not that Aithen was empty of beasts; by day and by night they could be heard at a distance, living their lives among the trees, part of the vast cycle of growth and life that was the greater life of the Forest. But save for those first few deer, no living animal had shown itself. For two whole days the huntsmen had lain in wait by the bank, at what they all agreed was a well-frequented drinking place. They had chosen their hides well, disturbed little and covered track and scent with consummate skill, yet not so much as a sound of a living beast did they catch. But even as they took to the rafts again, angry and dejected, pinched with hunger, the murmur of the Forest reawoke around them as vigorous as before: small blue birds chased one another here and there, and a high whickering screech sounded mockingly from the bushes.

"It's not canny," grumbled Borhi. "All them beasts steering clear of us. Not natural, like. Evil."

"How'd you know what's natural and what's not?" grunted Kasse. He and Borhi were sitting dawn watch on the first raft, leaning across the steering oar. He spoke softly, but so still was the brightening air that Elof heard him clearly, lying half awake in the bows of the raft behind; evil dreams had hounded him from sleep. "I know these great woodlands, me," rasped the huntsman. "I've walked in Aithennec, remember? I *know.* They're not like the piddling little woods these Nordeney oafs are used to, or our high-and-mighty young lordling. You can't just go astroll in these glades and expect to make free of the hunting. There's a good many others dwell here. You've got to get the word from one of 'em, see? With their hand against us, our luck's turned, and no game'll come near us."

Borhi sounded very uneasy. Elof could hear him twisting this way and that on the logs, scanning the inscrutable trees. "Whose word? How? What do you tell me? That you know some evil's abrew?"

"Something, aye, but why evil? Not evil to demand your due, is it? There's the *Helgorhyon,* now, the Hunt; you want luck in the chase, stands to reason it's their leave you must ask. Get a good word said upon your weapons."

"You mean . . . there's other men here?" asked Borhi dubiously.

Kasse tapped his nose wisely with a finger. "Ah, I didn't say that, mind. There's some, but you don't want no truck with 'em. But the Hunt, they're . . . natural forces, no more: naught to fear, long as you know the right ways. Sound ways, old ways; I had them from my granddad, he from his uncle, and so on down a long line, great hunters all who never lacked kill and keep." He darted a look back over his shoulder at Elof, who kept his breathing slow and did not stir. "Listen, you're a bright lad, want to bring yourself a spot of hunting luck? Tell you a thing you could try, it's simple enough. Do you take two good arrows, another that's already struck its mark. Catch you a bird or some other beast alive, large or small, no matter long as it has eyes. Then at moonrise stand in a tall tree's shadow and lay the arrows crosswise, take your catch and a third arrow in hand and speak a hunter's blessing, thus . . ." He began to chant softly.

> *Watchers, that in darkness wake,*
> *Guardians of the shadow-brake,*
> *What be offered, hunters, take,*
> *On this sign I bid you slake*
> *Thirst for—*

"That's an ill sound for a blessing!" Borhi broke in uneasily.

"Ach, don't be a damned whey-belly!" grunted Kasse. "Just trying to help a fellow sothran, aren't I? With these Nordeney louts ready to spit on us! And my fine lordling, he just encourages them! One in the eye for the lot of 'em, it'd be, if—"

"Enough, Kasse!" The bark of Kermorvan's voice startled even Elof. He whom they had thought asleep was up and on his feet in a single movement, glaring down at the huntsman. "I numbered you in our company only for your boasted experience. And of that, the more I hear, the less I like! I know you for a grumbler and a superstitious fool:

take great care I do not come to think you something worse. Upon your peril, Kasse!''

The huntsman growled, spat some word and himself surged to his feet, slipping on the uneven logs. "Comes to that, my dear young lordie. I've about had my bellyful of you! And you, Borhi, you'll suffer this pup to kick our faces, who rates his own folk lower'n a tinker and a duergar bitch?'' Elof scrambled up, hand on sword, ready if need be to jump the gap; Kasse's hand rested too near his knife. Heads lifted from blankets, came awake in a flurry of movement, believing it was some new peril.

But Borhi only looked coldly up at the huntsman, and spat into the stream. "Do you fight your own fights, Kasse! And don't come running to me if you take a hiding! You and your mucky little hedge-wizardry! What good's that to me?''

The blood drained from Kasse's face, and Elof saw a cold glitter grow in his narrowing eyes. "Hedge-wizardry, is it, my lad? Is it, eh?'' He looked sulkily at Kermorvan, and the other travelers rising uncertainly. "But stop you till you've starved enough under the boy's yoke! Then you'll all come begging me for my wisdom! On your knees!''

Elof gritted his teeth; the moment was ugly, Kasse strove to sow discontent, imperiling their unity and inevitably their lives, yet he could hardly be slain for mere words. But then, facing forward as he was, Elof caught the flicker of movement among the trees ahead, and forgetting all else he hissed and pointed so fiercely that all eyes turned to follow.

"A prey!'' breathed Kermorvan. "Gise! Kasse! To your bows!'' Anger forgotten, the huntsmen ducked to the weapons they kept at hand. Kasse yanked back the cord of his arbalest and dropped a quarrel into the channel; Gise's horn-bow was strung in one fluid action, and Kermorvan snatched a longbow and quiver from among the stores. Elof's fingers itched, though he had no love of the chase or the kill for its own sake; he was a fair shot with a birdbow, but knew these were the likeliest marksmen.

The deadly barbs glinted as the archers notched and drew, seeking an aim in the uncertain light; the watchers quivered tense and taut as the bowstrings. At this gold there might well be no second shot.

But when they saw their mark clear, no arrow flew. With the rest the hunters stared dumbfounded at the monstrous shape the growing sunlight gilded among the leaves. Elof knew no beast like it, and neither, by their gasps, did the others. "Kerys, is that a bear?" whispered Roc.

"Then it could breakfast on any I've seen," hissed Ils. "Even the giant cavern-dwellers . . ." Slowly, almost painfully it seemed, the great beast lumbered down the bank. Its long lank hair, reddish with a strange green cast, hung from limbs bowed but as thick about as a man's body. Abruptly it reared up; all flinched, the bows jerked ready as it rose on its haunches and spread its vast forelegs in menacing embrace. "That's no bear!" breathed Ils. "It has a tail, see! And that long head? And by the Shaper's grace, see the paws on it!"

Elof's mouth dried as he saw a single hooked claw unfold from each massive inturned forepaw, huge black sickles open to hook and slash. Then, quite unconcernedly, it grasped the overhanging limb of a linden and bent it down to its open mouth: a long red tongue unreeled to curl greedily about the heart-shaped leaves and the sweet flowers between, plucking them into the grip of the narrow horselike jaw. The shift from menace to bovine placidity was almost hilarious; Ils smothered a breathless giggle. But then a single humming note sounded, a harpstring plucked, and two arrows soared up over the shimmering water and plunged like bright-beaked hawks upon their prey. The dead snap of the arbalest sounded, and the quarrel, flatter in its flight, hissed low and fast across the bank. They saw the broad back flinch at the first impact, then stared as one arrow glanced across the rough hairs and vanished at a tangent among the leaves, and the other spun off into the bushes. The quarrel struck with the ringing bite of axe in wood, hung a moment and then fell slithering through the fur. With a high bleating cry the beast whirled about and went lumbering and crashing away through the undergrowth, still shrilling in panic.

"It's a demon!" yelled Borhi, and threw himself flat upon the logs.

Ils pulled him up by his tunic. "Don't be a great fool! It must have tough hide, that's all. Or even bone within the skin, like those little grassland creatures you have in the south."

Elof snapped his fingers. "That harness the Forest folk wore! It might have been made from such a hide. We could land and go after it . . ."

Kermorvan stared after the disappearing beast, and shook his head. "We could only hope to slay it at close quarters. We might go far astray before cornering such a brute; it moves fast enough now. And what then? Spear and blade against those sickle claws, on limbs that can bend a tree so lightly. Scarce worth the risk, I fear. But Kasse," he added, turning to the hunter, "I see Borhi was bitten deeper than he allowed by your bogeys. But can you explain why such a curse cannot stop us catching fish? When next you hold forth on hedgecraft, do you also trail some fishlines! You may find the fish more gullible."

Elof joined in the general laughter, and was glad to see that Borhi did also. Kasse glared at the young corsair a moment, then very carefully laid down his arbalest and returned to his seat by the steering oar. But Borhi did not join him; instead, he rummaged among the baggage for the fishing lines. Kermorvan and Gise unstrung their bows, and the others not on watch returned to their blankets to snatch what little sleep they could in the growing light. Elof stood for a moment, undecided, and then he caught Kermorvan's eye. The warrior nodded, and sprang effortlessly across onto his raft. He looked around, and spoke low. "So something still concerns you. Something worse than a diet of fish?"

"I fared little better in the Marshlands, and was content. No, it is simply that . . . well, field lore such as Kasse's is one sign of our decline. Scraps of true smith-craft debased, mean and slight, with power only to work petty ill. And that only for those who have a touch of the true craft in their blood.''

Kermorvan's eyes widened. ''And Kasse has? Why did you not tell me?''

''I did not see it in his eye till now. It is not strong in him, it shows only in his anger. Nevertheless, it is there—not to fear, only to be wary of. And I also find it strange that the whole life of this Forest shuns us so thoroughly.''

Kermorvan nodded. ''Do you, indeed? And have you considered that the cause might be more natural than bewitchment?''

''Of course! But I cannot think what!''

The warrior smiled without mirth. ''Why, that it is not us the beasts shun. We know that others hunt here; might it not then be them the beasts fear?''

''But why should such hunters always be near us . . . oh.'' A sudden understanding grew in Elof, and he raised his eyes to the Forest above them, a shadow against brightening dawn, a lowering cliff face of trees. He realized then how much they had changed, day by day, as the company sailed by. Rare now were the redwoods of the coastlands, and rarer all the great evergreens. Lindens stood high and shady among their ranks, the honey fragrance of their flowers drifting down to him, and massive sycamores. The solid masses of green and grayish brown were broken by the bright leaves of many maples and red oaks, and by silver birch trunks and blue-gray beeches. Yellow birch leaves shone golden in the misty dawn against the somber black hunks of walnuts. Fair and rich was the canopy of the Forest in the hues of early summer; but the fairest garments might conceal a blade. ''You mean . . . we are watched?''

Kermorvan nodded. ''I do. By those who normally hunt the Forest beasts. They hide from us, but not from the beasts because hunting is not their present purpose. So wherever we pass, they do also, and the beasts flee or fall silent in their lairs. And as to who they might be, these hunters, I believe you guess now as I do.''

''The . . . Children,'' said Elof uneasily. ''Watchers

who can travel among the trees, and so pace the rafts. But why have you not told the others?''

"Dare I? How will they behave, if I tell them the trees may be full of unseen eyes? You and I and Ils know they need not be hostile, but the others? The corsairs especially, after what happened to Ermahal? I do not wish our hotheads loosing bolts at every bough that quivers; one strike might draw a rain of spears from the Forest folk. Thus far they seem content only to watch. That is why I was so reluctant to let us stray far into the Forest; it might be what they await.''

Elof was still scanning the trees, though he knew he need expect to see nothing. "If we could evade them somehow . . .''

"Aye, that would be different. But we cannot, for now. When we reach the lake we may contrive a chance. Until then, do you keep silent about this. Save to Ils, perhaps.''

Over the next day or so even Elof grew weary of fish. In these lower, deeper stretches of the stream the fish grew large, but the flavor of their flesh seemed muddier. The commonest catches were monstrous catfish of a kind not seen in the coastal rivers, fierce fighters and often too heavy for one man to land unaided. The sight of their immense toadlike mouths, leering and barbel-hung, as they snapped and thrashed at the line, was disturbing in itself. And since Kermorvan still would not allow the company ashore, they had to await suitable islands to cook and smoke their catch. It meant that often they had to do without a hot meal after a difficult day's rafting, or dry clothes after rain, and there were many grumbles. But Elof was relieved that none sought to gainsay Kermorvan's word.

He and Ils took care now to watch the trees in twilight and the dark. More than once they believed they spied foliage jerk and quiver as if some large creature swung between trees, and once Ils was sure that she had seen a hand and a face emerge. Kermorvan was pleased. "They do not guess we have good night eyes among us, then, and grow careless. Now we must seek and seize a moment when we can travel faster and further than they. If only we could come to that lake soon!'' He pounded the logs impatiently. "If only!''

By all the accounts it was indeed no very great time before their voyage met its unlooked-for end; it may even have been that same night. It is sure that the first warnings came while Elof still had his friend's words very much in mind.

He was on night-watch with Dervhas and Tenvar when Roc hailed him from the first raft; a wide bend in the river was approaching, and they must stand ready with their poles lest the current swing them aground on land or sandbank. But as they probed cautiously for the depth they felt the stream pluck at their poles, eddies seek to twist them under the logs, and they heard the rush and chuckle of the water against the blunt bows grow suddenly louder.

"There's no bottom with this pole!'' called Bure. "Not even mud!''

"By Amicac, the lad's right!'' muttered Dervhas to Elof. "It grows wider and deeper all of a sudden, and yet flows faster—now what's that mean, on a piddling little inland flood like this? Rapids? If only the skipper were here, he'd know! His lordship might, or the lass? Do you give her a shake . . .''

But then Roc hailed them again, and pointed, and they knew some change must be near. They were rounding the curve now, swinging wide across the rushing waters, and for the first time in many long and weary nights the dark trees no longer narrowed to nothingness ahead of them. Instead a bright gap opened, widened as if the trees were curtains drawn slowly apart, layers of curtains and each thinner than the last. For through them, between the trees, shone glimmers of the same silvery light, ever broader and brighter. From out of a cloudy sky the white moon blazed down upon an expanse of water wide and calm, silvering it like a mirror save where the wooded hills beyond cast their shadows.

That single hail had aroused Kermorvan, and even as he bounced to his feet he was calling the others. They too came suddenly awake at the sight of the breach in the walls they had come to hate. Some even whooped and pranced with delight on the uneven logs, till Kermorvan's hissed command called them to heel. "Do you dream yet, that you think us free of danger? Perhaps it only begins! All of you, gather up your gear and all the supplies you can carry! Be alert, be ready to abandon the rafts if need be and spring or swim for shore!" His sword flashed in the moonlight. "If danger threatens I will part the rafts; one may survive, if the other is overset." He scooped up his own pack and a heavy foodsack, and turned to Elof, standing on the bow of the rear raft. "Now, how fares the current?"

"Faster still, and neither Dervhas nor Ils can explain it."

"Nor I," muttered Kermorvan, gazing about the widening channel. "I did fear some hazard between us and that lake, at worst falls or rapids. But I can see nothing to cause this strange current. Ils, what of your sight?"

She scrambled onto the oar mounting, one plump hand shielding her eyes from the moon; Elof steadied her as the raft surged anew beneath them. "Little enough! A small turmoil in the water, around slender things upthrust, like reeds or twigs—"

"In water this deep?" cried Kermorvan, and threw his weight upon the steering oar that thrummed now like a gale-struck sail. "Down, all of you! Hold as you can! There is some hidden barrier!" And as the oar rose creaking from the water he drew his sword and hewed down at the stern. The taut cord sang apart, and the first raft sprang forward as the glittering water opened out around them.

Face down on the planks with pack and foodsack on his back, frantically clutching the stout crosspiece under his chest, Elof felt the weight of the sodden logs lift and buck under him, as if some immense hand took hold and hurled it like a javelin at the unknown target. *And has not all my life been thus?* In a moment of futile rebellion he glared up at the sky beyond the treetops whipping by, half expecting to see something there, for good or ill. But the stars blazed ice-cold in blackness, remote, indifferent, bitterly alone. A sudden shout came from the raft ahead, then with a deep grinding crunch its bow heaved upward like a drawbridge, and split; the scream and crackle of stressed wood dwarfed the petty voices of men. Spray rose and spattered him, he gritted his teeth, and then the shock shivered through him, shook and slammed him violently against the wood, the rough bark scouring skin. The logs rolled and flexed under him, the stout bough that was the crosspiece writhed and twisted like a living serpent in his grip. Despite Kermorvan's swift action, the current crashed the second raft sidewise against the first, driving it as hammer on chisel against the unseen obstacle. The churning surface erupted, mud and filth sprayed skyward, and a wave of creamy water washed over the second raft. Elof clutched wildly at his handhold as it dragged at him and plucked and twisted at his pack. The raft lurched forward, bucked, twisted crazily sideways and tilted, sweeping him across the logs at a wrist-wrenching angle. Mud spurted up between the logs and was whipped away into the foaming maelstrom. He heard Ils cry out, but could see neither her nor any other in the spray. Something lashed stinging across his face and clung. Then it seemed that the obstacle beneath the logs gave way, and the raft was shot forward, whirling about in the current. The looming trees fell away, the wheeling stars overhead slowed and steadied, the log beneath him settled and rode level.

For a moment he could only lie there gasping, the thing that had hit him a curtain of stinking slime across his eyes. He sought to brush it free, and found his fingers entangled; he panicked, and tore at it, and grew more entangled. Then his fingers touched another's amid its tangles, that pulled it away from his face. His heart leaped as he saw whose hand it was; Ils at least was safe. He caught her hand and raised himself on one numbed elbow; there were the others, as dazed as he felt. Dervhas and Tenvar still clung to the steering oar, spitting out water and weed; Arvhes was covered in fragments of the ruined canopy. The raft was clear now, drifting out across the calm silver of the lake waters. A faint current seemed to be carrying

them into a little bay ahead. Elof looked about urgently
for the first raft, and found instead a loosening tangle of
timbers astern, wheeling slowly in the current, a sorry
sight. The collision had sheared off two logs and by the
look of it the steering gear, and broken the for'ard cross-
members. But he could see figures picking themselves up
and sliding swiftly along the logs, striving to make them
secure. He scanned the water quickly for floating heads,
found none, and glanced back to see what had so nearly
destroyed them.

The whole rivermouth had changed. The water level had
fallen, and was now even with the lake; a new strip of
bank glistened with exposed clumps of weed. The barrier
stood revealed now as a thick tangle of stick and bough.
The double impact of the rafts had smashed a wide gap in
it, through which a muddy torrent poured. "A beaver
dam!" gurgled Arvhes. "Biggest that ever I saw! I've
heard they have giant beavers in the wilds of Nordeney!"

Ils looked at him acidly, and thrust out what she had
taken from Elof's face. "Do they use nets?" The men
gaped in horror, for net it surely was, crudely woven of
some coarse fiber. They stared again at the channel; on
either side of the breach the ragged edges of such a net
straggled useless in the current. Then amidst the heaving
water Elof saw a sudden arrowing swirl, and another.
"What's that?" he demanded of Dervhas.

"Amicac, how'd I know? Eddies, most like. Glad
they're nowhere near, though. Sooner we're off this pond
the better I'm suited."

Elof nodded, shivering in his soaked clothes. "At least
we're not far away from the bay; the water should grow
shallower there. If only the others can hold on . . ." He
looked back, and worse than the night breeze chilled him.
He cried out, pointed. The swirls had appeared again,
dark folds in the calmer water, streaking out against the
current. It was the first raft they pursued.

None there had heard. Elof struggled up on shaky legs,
but even as he opened his mouth to shout he saw the
wrecked raft judder and halt abruptly in its wheeling, and

clambering silhouettes stagger and fall. Then, quite slowly as it seemed, its huge logs parted at the bow and spread out wide like the fingers of a giant hand. Helpless, Elof listened in horror to yells and screams, saw two tall figures bestride the logs, haul others out of the water and then begin fastening cords and chains to the logs, meaning to secure them lest the raft break up altogether. But even as they leaped across to the outer logs the water swirled again, and Elof glimpsed a curved bulk that arched up and vanished, the back as it seemed of some fair-sized creature, mottled or dappled like fish or seal, glistening under the moon. Then, with that same easy, deceptive slowness that was horrible to watch, the logs jarred and swung together again. The leapers landed, but skidded; one caught himself by the chain he bore and fell along the log, but the other missed his footing and slid down its flank into the water. He caught himself by a branch stump, the other flung himself forward, but even as their hands met the huge logs bounced together. Beneath the dull boom there was a single crunch, a cry cut short. When they bobbed apart again, one figure knelt there, staring down at nothing. "Eysdan!" cried Kermorvan's voice, and then Gise's, but there was no answer.

Elof and the others stared in horror, forgetting for one instant too long that they also might be in peril. A cry from behind was their warning. Whirling about, Elof caught the black sword from its scabbard and threw himself slithering down the logs. Dervhas clung still to the steering oar, but frantically now, for both legs trailed in the water as if some great weight hung from them. Elof threw himself down, clawing at the man's collar, but the oar bent, cracked and splintered. With a despairing cry Dervhas let go and grabbed hold of the outflung hand. The weight on him was appalling; Elof braced his feet against the oar mounting to avoid being dragged in himself. Dervhas gasped in agony; the veins on his brow stood out as if he was on the rack. The mounting snapped then and Elof slid forward. Dervhas sank chest-deep and dragged him out over the black water. But Elof's free hand still held Gorthawer, and he speared it downward, once, twice. It struck, the water convulsed and darkened, and Dervhas was suddenly lighter, sagging in the water. Tenvar and Arvhes reached them and helped Elof haul him in. But as his left leg came over the edge of the log they cried out in horror, for the flesh had been stripped from it and the leg bones laid bare. Ils, shuddering, whipped off Dervhas' heavy belt to loop it round the thigh and stem the spurting blood, but hesitated, let it fall, and shook her head. Dervhas was a limp weight in their hands, and the spurting had stopped. Then she cried out and flung herself forward to the raft's edge. The patterned blade of her axe hewed downward. Elof felt its impact in the sodden wood, and saw a ghastly thing leap like a landed fish and go slithering severed across the logs in a spray of dark liquid. A broad frond of waterweed it might have been, save that thick ridged fingers writhed within the brownish web, tipped each with a short claw, and the dappled coat of it was sleek fur.

He had but a moment to see it. Then the whole raft heaved, as if on some invisible wave it could not crest. It listed, tilted, sloping ever more steeply. "They'll slide us off!" yelled Bure.

"And overturn the raft on us!" cried Ils. "Spring clear while you still may!" None lingered to argue. Elof sheathed his sword, braced his feet against the slanting logs, and kicked out with all his strength. Sky and shore whirled about him, and then icy blackness lashed his face. Just behind him a great bulk like a breaching whale slapped at the water, and a wave engulfed him; struggling, he sank, fighting for breath and imagining every instant the clutch of webbed claws about his limbs. The weight of his pack pulled him down, but never for a moment did he think of casting it free. He bumped something solid, slimy, cold, and threshed in panic a moment before he realized it must be the lake bottom. He pulled his feet under him and kicked upward. Almost at once his head bobbed free, he could tread water and cough up all he had been swallowing, suck in a painful, blessed breath. Then he had time to be surprised; he must be in the shallows already. There indeed were the dark walls of the shore, not far off, and other heads bobbing across the silvery water, too far to aid or be aided. He kicked out to follow them, but had swum hardly a stroke when the water boiled before him, and a rounded shape broke surface.

It was an eye, an eye the width of his whole face, and it fixed him as it rose. It was set high like a frog's, in a socket above a huge rounded head, and the look of it was glassy, impersonal, utterly unhuman yet acutely aware. That same dappled fur clad the head, sleek and seallike; water spilled from the smooth dome as it arose, running in streams over strands of weed that hung like mocking garlands about the head and straggled down past the corners of the wide lipless mouth, fixed in a false sated smile. There was no chin, no neck; the lower jaw curved downward to massive shoulders and a great tun of a body.

Desperately Elof groped for his sword, fearing it had fallen from its scabbard, but the cold hilt came to hand. He drew, but hesitated; if this thing had a mind . . . He held the blade up for it to see, a shadow upon the water, and motioned it aside. The creature answered clearly enough; its mouth gaped, a ghastly grin that bared rows of long teeth, and it glided slowly, tauntingly, forward. Elof thought of Dervhas, and shivered; the intensity of purpose in those eyes was more frightening than any rage or hatred. Then anger colder than the lake welled up in him, and he struck out between the glinting eyes. The blade bit and bounced free, the water convulsed and boiled up darkness. Elof gulped air and jackknifed down; he felt a huge body surge overhead where he had been. He slashed at it, but the water slowed his stroke. The shadowy bulk stooped upon him; he twisted about and thrust upward with all his strength. The blade bit deep, and a violent threshing hurled him this way and that in the water, till his chest labored and his head grew tight and dizzy with pain. At last he managed to twist the blade free and find the air once again. But even as he drew breath his knees scraped painfully into gravel, the sword chinked against a rock. He stood, found himself scarcely chest-deep, and floundered on, fumbling with vague anxiety at his pack. Still there, still closed, he could feel no more. The water fell away from him, leaving his body a dead weight, his wet clothes leaden. When the last wavelet lapped his ankle a sudden agony lanced through him, deadly fear for Ils, Kermorvan, the others. But he could bear the weight no longer. He dropped where he stood. He strove to raise himself, found himself staring into dense undergrowth above the bank. In among it eyes stared back at him, eyes unlike the lake creatures, or any other he had seen: eyes just as Roc had described them so many leagues past, narrow, slanting gleams of yellow, unwinking, impassive. He struggled to lift the sword he still grasped, but the instant it scraped upon the gravel the eyes blinked out, vanished utterly. He stared a moment, then slumped down upon the pebbles. Darkness took him.

Hard fingers clutched him, and in panic he snapped awake, flailing wildly around. "Hold hard, there!" said a protesting voice in his ear, and to his equally wild relief it was Ils. He grabbed and hugged her hard, and felt her sturdy shoulders quiver in his embrace. But she snorted impatiently, and pushed him off. "Napping quietly on the shore! Just like you, when we were combing the place!"

"And close to giving you up!" grumbled Roc's voice. "Fond of making life awkward, aren't you? Why'd you head so far out?"

Elof sighed and sat up, blinking through gummy eyes. The night was past, the gray dawn lighting up the trees, and he was looking out across the bay water, so still and black and heavy it might have been an oil pool. Only a faint swell upheaved its smooth surface, like the flank of some slow-breathing beast, giving no hint of what had lately happened there and what yet lurked beneath. He saw that he was on the outermost tip of the headland; he must almost have been dragged out into deep water. "Then you were not . . . beset, any of you?"

Ils caught his arm. "No! Were you? You took no hurt?"

"None, I think, save bruises and near-drowning. Was I the only one? Are Kermorvan and all the rest safe?"

Roc nodded somberly. "Aye, he's ashore and gathering the others; we saw a fair number, and maybe the rest are just late sleepers like yourself. Come, if you can walk we'll go and see."

Elof nodded silently, willing his stiffened limbs to move. His first attempt to stand brought on a tearing attack of cramp, but when that subsided he was able to limp along the stony shore to the wider middle of the beach. It was a bedraggled, dejected group of figures that sprawled there, but they sprang up swiftly and gladly enough when they saw him. "Are we all escaped, then?" he asked anxiously, when the excitement had subsided. "Save Dervhas, that is, and the other who fell . . ."

"That was Eysdan," said Kermorvan harshly. Elof was shocked: he had never seen the warrior so haggard, his lips drawn and bloodless. "I had his hand even as the logs took him; one instant more and . . ."

Gise shook his head grimly. "No blame to you. You did what you could. Well that you did not follow."

"Aye," said Roc. "Rest of us clinging onto that hank of firewood by our fingertips, and he somehow gets it ashore on a sandbank so close to shore we can all but walk. Seems shallows don't suit those brutes. Did what he could, and still blames himself. Never mind saving all our skins . . ."

"Did he so?" demanded Kasse sardonically as ever, though his face was gray, as if he labored under some great terror. "Did he indeed? All?"

"Stehan?" demanded Borhi. "Where's he got to? We forgot Stehan!" As one they turned to look out across the little bay, scanning water and shoreline for the least trace of another human form. Borhi cupped his hands to shout, but Kermorvan cocked his head at the looming palisade of trees above them.

"Wait! I have not told you this before, but it is meet you know now. We have had watchers, whom I guess we have evaded in crossing the lake. Best we do not draw them to us again.'' And swiftly he told them the little he knew of the Children of Tapiau. "We must search indeed," he concluded, "but swiftly. And above all, silently."

Like morning shadows they slipped along the shore line, questing even beyond the bay for some trace of their companion. Once Elof espied something far off across the waters, but it was only the second raft, overturned but whole, lodged on some remote sandbank. Its wet logs glistened as empty as all the waters between. Softly they lapped at the pebbles by the searchers' feet, but no trace of the lost corsair did they yield. At last Kermorvan had to call a halt to the futile search.

"Aye, why not?" muttered Kasse to Arvhes. "It's just another poor sothran! Five gone, just you, me and Borhi left! It's clear who's borne the brunt of this little jaunt—"

Then he sprawled flat on the stones, clutching his mouth, Gise standing over him with his great fists clenched and his dark face purple with rage. "And Eysdan?" demanded the forester in stolid outrage. "And the lad Holvar? But I'll add one sothran more to the tally any time you say, Kasse."

Kasse, face contorted, scrambled up clutching a jagged rock, only to have Borhi snatch it from him, so that he fell down again.

"Enough!" barked Kermorvan, pushing Gise back. "You, Kasse, you brought that upon yourself."

"Aye," said Borhi, ignoring Kasse's glare, and making no move to help him up, "save your bile for them things as did the killing, eh? Murdering brutes, to attack for no cause!"

Elof shook his head unhappily. "Not so, Borhi. That was their dam we shattered, their fishtrap I guess by the net. It must have cost them much labor, for since they cannot come on land, they must have worked only with driftwood. They may have thought we were attacking them. And as to slaying, Ils maimed one, and I wounded or slew another. We could not talk with them, that was the pity."

Silence fell, and many looked out at the lake once again. From oil to steel it turned as warmer light spread up the sky behind the wooded hills, and from steel to gold as the sun itself rose. Soft wisps of mist drifted over the waters, as if to flirt with its mirrored clouds. Small birds began to chirrup and twitter in the bushes around them, and the horrors of the night hung less heavy about them. But Kasse sat apart on a stone and spat blood through puffy lips. "Well," demanded Ils, who had no great love of sunrise, "what now?"

Kermorvan held up an urgent hand for quiet, and gestured to the Forest. Elof heard it then, a distant echo along the lake, the trample of many hooves, harsh snorting breaths, the crackle of large bodies moving through the brush. "A herd of some kind," he said, with the ring reborn in his voice. "Nothing alarms them, so we have evaded the watchers for now. But if we wish to stay free, we cannot linger here, and we must hunt to stay alive. So . . ." He shrugged. "You ask what now, my lady? We press on. What else can we do?"

So it is told that as the rising sun shot the mists with pale gold the company passed at last beneath the eaves of the Great Forest, Tapiau'la-an-Aithen itself. And since the river had borne them nigh on a hundred and fifty leagues from its western margins, they stepped at once into the very heartlands of that domain. To Elof, weary and grieving, it was a stranger experience than he had expected; he felt as if he entered some immense hall of worship, some mighty tomb or mausoleum such as he had seen in Kerbryhaine the City, but infinitely vaster, infinitely more imbued with ancient presence. The towering trees upheld it as pillars, sustaining an immense vault-work of interwoven boughs, a roof whose greens and yellows shone far richer than coppered domes or tiles of gold. Even the sun must defer before them, bowing down in narrow beams to pick small patches of the Forest floor out of its reverential gloom, or scattering into glimmering green shades upon the many-textured trunks. Rainbow iridescence it awoke, like the shadows of stained glass, from the water droplets that glistened on every leaf and moss patch, in every crevice of the trunks, that hung heavy in the unstirring air. For this was a place of water, a forest of rains, ever remembering the last shower or looking forward to the next.

Now Elof was on land he could see how much the lesser trees had changed, as well as the greater; among the more familiar dogwoods, junipers, tall hollies and black cherries he found slender quaking aspens, sumacs, spreading mulberries already heavy with their unripe fruit, and a hundred others he hardly knew. Willows and alders arched over the little streams they passed, but between them lifted madder and red osier, shrubs in his homeland grown here to trees. Indeed, tree and shrub, evergreen and seasonal alike, even the creepers that draped them like rigging on high masts, all were grown more tall, more rich than any he had ever seen, so that it felt to him as if it was he and his fellows who had dwindled, and were become like little beasts that dodged and scuttled through their brief lives among the roots. And it was not only the imposing trees that diminished humanity, but something greater that dwelt in this place, that ancient presence he had felt from the first.

"I keep thinking there's somebody else around," muttered Roc, who was walking by Elof's side. "Not spying on us, more like . . . It's hard to say. Like there was someone in the next room, or round the corner, and you always knowing it. Someone . . . important."

Elof nodded. "I feel the same. But more acutely. As if I walk steathily past that someone's door, or behind his back. A little excited, a little afraid, as when I was a child, and sought to avoid my master or mistress . . ." He shook his head, puzzled and daunted. In Vayde's Tower, on that first dark night, he had sensed something of the kind, but more remote, a vast emptiness of anguish remembered. This was different; the thrill of it, the nervous tickling tingle, was so strong it recalled the touch of the Ice, to him agony, to Kermorvan only chill and unease. Here Roc and the others felt no more, and unease was natural enough. "Well," Elof sighed. "We have worse problems for now. But if you ever begin to feel we are about to turn that corner . . ."

"Or that someone's about to turn round," agreed Roc. "Aye, I'll tip you the word. And you me. If the river was that bad, I reckon we've got to be ready for 'most anything here."

But that first day, as the travelers cast about for the track of the herd, they saw nothing save the small life of any ordinary forest, though even those creatures were larger and sleeker than they had seen before. The very jays that swooped chittering and scolding were larger, blazing arrows of color among the heavy foliage.

"How can they fly so fast in this air?" panted Tenvar, pushing back his streaming hair. His clothes, like everyone else's, had obstinately refused to dry out entirely. "It's like soup!"

Kermorvan smiled, though his own hair hung lank and grayed with dew. "Would it were as sustaining! But it is rich in other ways; scents linger even for feeble human noses. I am sure we draw near the track of some large beasts, large enough to yield us food for many a long league more. So do not grudge the effort, Tenvar! And may a full belly be the least of your rewards."

But though the other hunters felt as Kermorvan did, they still had not picked up the trail by the time the light began to fail. There was nothing to be done save camp and await the dawn. Kasse, most skillful with snares, caught them two rabbits, and this, with roots and herbs gathered by Elof, who knew most about them from his sojourn in the Marshlands, was all they had to sustain them that day. They found a dell, little more than a patch of earth among great tree roots, that was drier than the rest, and there Kermorvan made an earth-oven, covering it with leaves to damp down the smoke. But though it worked well, and the rabbits were unusually large, they made a small meal for ten weary travelers.

"Made sure it was three I saw you take up, huntsman!" Borhi remarked cheerfully as he gnawed the last fragments off a bone. "Not hiding one all for yourself, are you?"

Kasse curled his lip. "Two's what I caught, two's what we've had! If you want any more, get out and take 'em yourself. I give you leave!"

"Quiet, the pair of you!" grunted Arvhes, normally the most patient of men. "Do you save your energy for the hunt; then you'll be able to feed your faces all the better! Me, my back pains me, my legs are leaden, my heart sore, and I'd swear I'm catching an ague from the wet clothes. I care only for sleep."

"So say we all!" said Kermorvan wryly. "This is as dry a place as we shall find, and I think as safe. Rest you, while you may! The first watch is mine."

Elof rolled himself in his cloak, clammy as it was, and pillowed wet hair on damp arm; he was so weary that despite the chill he slept almost at once. But it was an unquiet sleep, full of strange dreams, of the solitary redwood in its lawn of flowers, of the great gusty voice that called from afar. And eyes moved through his dreams, eyes with a snakelike glitter, eyes pallid and staring, narrow, slanted, yellow . . . He awoke, shivering violently in the dark, looked around for reassurance as a dreamer may who opens his eyes from inner turmoil. At least they had a sentinel . . . but where was he? Nobody sat up. Kermorvan was curled up not far away, his lean features just recognizable in the faint glimmer of starlight that penetrated the canopy. Angrily Elof reached out and shook him. "Fine watcher you are!" he hissed, and jumped as Kermorvan uncoiled like a snake. In the blink of an eye he was squatting by Elof's shoulder, peering about.

"But I am not the watcher!" he murmured. "It is past the middle hour, and I bade Kasse take my place. Where might he be, I wonder?"

A branch rustled, feet scuffed in the mold; they both sprang up. A stocky shadow moved out from behind a tree. Kermorvan sighed, and slid his half-drawn blade back into the scabbard. "Where have you been?" he demanded in an angry whisper.

"Where d'you think?" grunted Kasse ungraciously, and

settled down to his watch once more. The others looked at one another, and shrugged.

Elof was just settling down under his cloak when he saw Kermorvan stop, whirl about and jerk Kasse to his feet by the front of his heavy jacket. "You! Where were you, indeed, watcher?" hissed Kermorvan. The fury in his voice startled Elof. "And what has become of Borhi while you were gone?"

Elof looked across the circle of sleepers and with a sudden thrill of alarm he too noticed the empty place. "How'd I know?" gurgled Kasse, feet almost leaving the ground in the force of Kermorvan's grasp. He threw back his arms in protest. "Not my fault if he wanders—" Elof saw the faint glimmer, flung himself forward on all fours and wrenched at the hand as it swept inward toward Kermorvan's side. Even a hunter's wiry strength could not match the grasp of a smith. Elof caught what fell, and held the knife up for Kermorvan to see.

The warrior nodded; his face took on a look Elof knew, remote and hard as a stone carving. "You will take me to Borhi," he said, very softly, and Kasse began to struggle wildly in their grip.

"I don't know . . ." he gasped, and stopped, for Elof seized him by the hair and twisted his head round.

"Then why the blade? I counsel you, huntsman, answer! Lord Kermorvan is noble and just, he would not carve strips off you with your own traitor's weapon, but me, I am of no birth, and I am not so damned sure!" He held the knife before Kasse's eyes. "Speak! Where's Borhi? Alive or dead?"

"Alive!" choked Kasse, half-strangled. "But danger . . ."

Kermorvan hurled him back hard against the tree trunk. "Then all the more reason you take us to him, now!" He swept out his sword. "Obey!"

The struggle, though in whispers, had aroused the remainder of the company by now. But Elof bade them stay where they were and keep watch, and as an afterthought to kindle fire in the oven, and prepare torches. "A good thought!'' whispered Kermorvan as they marched Kasse out before them into the darkness of the wood. "Though I would risk it only if peril is already upon us. How far, Kasse?''

It was less than five hundred strides he led them, though many times he claimed to be lost. But the point at his back was a powerful lodestone, and at last, coming around the trunk of a great storm-blasted laurel oak, they found Borhi. In the finding, though, they stood for a moment stunned.

He stood against the trunk, or rather hung, for his arms were lashed loosely round the bole, and his chin propped up on two crossed quarrels dug into it. A flood of dark liquid glistened on his head, and no better light than the stargleam was needed to know it for blood; the smell was enough. Elof feared him already dead, but suddenly he jerked upright in his ropes, and began to struggle and whimper. It was not his blood; behind him on the broad-ridged bark hung the mangled corpse of a rabbit, pinned there like . . . Elof bit his lip. Like some kind of offering, and what did that make Borhi?

He drew Gorthawer, then hesitated, startled, as Kasse began to shout. "No! Leave him! You must, it's danger-ous, deadly, you don't understand! Deadly danger! Leave him, let him bide, I can't stop it . . .'' Elof turned away contemptuously. The black blade flicked out, once, twice and Borhi slumped forward, moaning with relief.

Then shock clawed at Elof's heart. *"Kerys!''* choked Kermorvan, his clear voice gone hoarse and hollow. The howl that cascaded down the air shivered their thoughts as a stone a sheet of glass. So powerful was it that it awoke a single sight in both their minds, a sudden glimpse of long reeking jaws agape against the moon. Ravening hun-ger, fiendish menace echoed in that wailing cry, the voice of no man or beast they knew, and it was not far off. Kasse was shrieking now, fit to wake the whole wood. "Don't you understand, don't you understand? There had to be one! They had to have one! *I can't call it back!''* Ker-morvan hooked a powerful arm round the huntsman's neck and struggled to silence him, while Elof heaved Borhi to his feet.

"Can he walk?" barked Kermorvan, clamping Kasse's jaws shut. "Then back to the camp! Be still, fool!" he hissed, as Kasse whimpered and renewed his struggle. "If there is any safety for you now, it must be with us!"

They turned and ran for the dell, Kasse a limp foot-dragging bundle in Kermorvan's grasp. Borhi, an arm round Elof's shoulder, plucked off the leather rag that had gagged him, unleashing a flood of terrified babbling. "He . . . bastard . . . tol' me he'd show me what he'd done with other rabbit . . . good use . . . show hunters' lore worked . . . belted me . . . strung me up . . . Ah, Saithana come to us, *what's that?*"

The howl shimmered among the trees again, this time nearer still, and again from off to the side. "The Hunt!" screamed Kasse, and abruptly became a frenzied flurry of limbs. Kermorvan stumbled, his grip loosened and Kasse was off, bounding like a fright-maddened deer over root and through brush.

"Let him go!" gasped Elof. "Help Borhi!" Together they scooped him up, sprang for the dell, and tumbled gasping into the hands of their friends.

With a howl like the stormwind, something went crashing through the undergrowth behind them, something large and behind it others, their stride a bounding, loping sound like dog or wolf, but longer, wider. And all who heard thought that they went not on four legs, but on two. Past they streamed, while those terrible howls pierced the travelers' hearts, and then it seemed that the last of them turned aside and came padding, more slowly, in their direction.

"The fire!" gasped Kermorvan. "Light torches, all! Stay well within the firelight!" Then in the shadows beyond it another and most fearful howl shocked the travelers rigid as rabbits before a weasel. Somebody kicked aside the leaves, the firepit blazed up in yellow flame as the torches were thrust in, and the clear glare scoured the darkness from the dell. At its margins slivers of another light awoke, and Roc and Elof shuddered to see again the pale foxfire gleams that had so startled them among the undergrowth. Only now they floated in the darkness higher than a man's head, and they were not alone; other pairs of eyes appeared, moving this way and that to the sound of soft feet padding, pacing like fell beasts encaged. Ils moved close to Elof, and he heard the tremor in her breath. She seized his free hand, and he squeezed hers hard. Defiantly Kermorvan stretched out his sword. A low growl answered, and such was its menace that the travelers all shrank together. But the eyes came no nearer, pacing back and forth, back and forth, just beyond the reach of the light. For a long hour it lasted, till Elof thought his nerve could stand no more; it did not help to hear the trembling chatter of Borhi's teeth. But then, abruptly, it ended.

From far off to the north of the silent Forest came a rending scream, a human scream, and then another, louder even than the single triumphant howl that blended with it. The eyes swung away as one, northward. On it went, a frenzied, mind-cloven shrieking that rose to a single long thin note, and then died away to nothing. Feet crashed in the bushes, a sudden gust of wind pressed down fire and torches; shadows rushed in. But Kermorvan dashed forward, swinging his torch, and hurled it out high into the dark. Like a blazing starstone it fell, and in that brief streak of light they caught one glimpse of a hunched shadow higher than a man, yellow fangs foam-flecked in a narrow muzzle, a long flank pelted in black, wiry and close-curled. Then the loping feet passed swiftly northward, and were gone.

Kermorvan let out a long, shaky breath. "They could have run any man down in moments. All this time they must have been toying with him."

"Till dawn!" said Ils tremulously. "Praise the Powers, it nears." And Elof too saw the faint promise of light in the sky, and drew breath more easily.

"Well, Borhi," he sighed. "It seems he has himself paid dear for the bad turn he meant you . . ."

But Borhi, huddled against a root, seemed scarcely to

hear; he shivered and knitted his fingers. "An offering, 'e said . . . they'd have it t'set foot in the woods . . . or him instead . . . his bargain with 'em . . . their price for a good hunt . . . like the rabbit . . . clear trail an' a sure kill . . ." And they saw that hanging round his neck were two more of the black steel-headed quarrels from Kasse's arbalest.

The heavy bow itself lay on the ground where its owner had laid it. After only a moment's hesitation Kermorvan picked it up. "I wonder what manner of blessing was laid upon this? But we cannot lightly abandon a good hunting weapon. Tenvar, Bure, do you help Borhi! He must recover as best he can afoot. Our need bids us begone, ere we starve."

They moved out into the growing light, and a forest that seemed a different place, the least likely shelter for the horrors of the dark. But they were not yet quit of them. Gise, the most practiced hunter left them, claimed to find some promising scents on the breeze, so they followed it westward. A little way on a towering fir rose before them, and when Gise and Elof rounded its great bole they beheld a thick spattering of blood, still fresh in the mold. They looked up, and sprang back with the shock. Elof gestured frantically to keep Borhi away, but it was too late. He also had seen, and stood staring, his face as dusty gray as the bark. There, propped high beyond reach among the upper branches, hung the body of Kasse. Of his clothes, of his flesh, rags alike remained, like a pitiful carcass worried by a scavenger pack. Yet one arm, more whole than the other, was laid across a bough, stiffly outthrust in the direction of a trail that opened out eastward before them, sloping uphill among the trees.

Kermorvan inclined his head grimly, his gray-green eyes cold as the sea they resembled. "So justice of a sort is done, it would seem . . ."

Elof looked at Borhi, and shook his head. "Justice?" he remarked. "Say rather, an offering is accepted. Even if it was not the one intended."

Kermorvan looked at him sharply. "You may be right.

In any event, there is no more we can do for him, not even bury him. And that trail leads eastward, which is our road in any event. So let us press on, at once!''

''Aye,'' said Borhi quietly. ''That's best.'' And from that moment he seemed to recover his wits; it was his good cheer that never quite came back.

Their scant meal of the night before had only served to sharpen hunger, and for all their hurts and aches, and the persistent dampness of their clothes, they moved swiftly and eagerly up the shadowy trail. It was a strange hunt, for they followed no spoor; only that macabre signpost, and what Gise read in the breeze, gave them any assurance. But ere long Kermorvan, too, caught the scent, and wrinkled his narrow nostrils. ''Not an unclean smell, but strong. I guess that we follow a herd, but of what, that is another matter. Perhaps Gise may . . .'' He stopped. Gise, padding along the trail just ahead, had ducked hastily behind the bole of a stout red oak. Now he was gesticulating furiously to the others, beckoning them on yet waving them to stay down. Cat-quiet, they crept forward taking every pain to avoid the least rustle or crackle; the last few paces they all but crawled, and crouched down behind the thickest bushes, quietening even their breath. Now the musky, earthy reek of the mysterious herd was in all their nostrils, and none would dare be first to alarm the creatures. The breeze had freshened, as if the trees grew thinner; strange sounds it carried, the thudding of heavy hooves upon the earth, the creak and snap of boughs, and underneath them all, now and then, a soft rumbling snort, deep enough to come from the very stone underfoot. Very cautiously they peered over the leaves. But it was as well the breeze was in their faces, for despite their care they could hardly help but gasp at what they saw.

''What are they?'' whispered Arvhes in awe, almost too loud.

''Deer, idiot!'' snarled Ils under her breath, clutching at her axe. ''Scare them and I'll butcher you instead!''

''But such deer!'' breathed Elof, and even Kermorvan nodded agreement, his eyes alight with the wonder of the sight. This far up the slope the trees did indeed seem thinner. The summer morning sent a torrent of light between the trunks, and it spilled down hazy and golden upon a host of high antlers. There, basking among a drone of dancing flies, was the herd they sought, and it was vast.

In shape they were not unlike the red-coated deer of the Western Lands but, like all else in Aithen, grown regal and immense. Their bodies had the bulk and majesty of the great bulls Elof had once herded, but they stood far taller, higher at the shoulder than a tall man could reach. Broader and heavier than a bull's were those shoulders and the neck they bore, and small wonder when such antlers crowned the long head. They did not rise in narrow branchings, as in lesser deer, but swept out to either side in a vast flattened spread, upturned at each end like fantastic many-fingered hands. Their coats were shaggier and lighter than western deer, a dusty dappled bay that was hard to make out among the denser clump of trees. There were perhaps forty or fifty of these giants in the herd, chiefly does that browsed in little groups. Many had fawns by them, leggy and light-spotted. The immense stags circled the outskirts of the herd, browsing among the coarser undergrowth; one stayed to pull at some bushes near them, and Elof's mouth grew dry with awe. A crown in truth he thought those regal antlers, for one branch alone would span almost his own height.

"I've got that feeling again," growled Roc softly as they sank back behind cover. "As if it's myself that's shrunk . . ." Gise nodded calmly, and flexed his bow to be sure of the string's tension in the wet air.

"How may we dare attack such monsters?" muttered Arvhes, swallowing with difficulty. "One kick from those hooves would shatter a man, one sweep of the antlers fell us all . . ."

"Yet we must," whispered Kermorvan bleakly, tugging at the arbalest's thick cord and working the cocking lever, his face pitiless as the hunger and care behind. "There is more to be seen out there than deer. Look up, past the treetops."

Elof followed his glance, and stiffened with surprise. The branches stood out against the clear blue of summer, but over them loomed a vaster bulk, gleaming white in the brilliance like cloud castles made solid. With sinking heart he realized that their eastward way had led them to a range of mountains, jagged and high, capped with snow even under that blazing sun. They seemed impossibly sudden and close, as if they had only this minute sprung out of the earth as a new and daunting barrier. Thus it was that Elof first looked upon the Meneth Aithen, the Forest Mountains, the backbone of that vast realm and guardian of its most cherished secrets.

"We would have seen them from far downriver, had we not had the Forest over us," rasped Kermorvan. "To north and south they spread, as far as I may make out. There will be no going round them, I am sure. We must find a pass, and cross." He looked around at them all. "You understand, then! There may be scant game up there, or none at all. We need to find and prepare as much food now as we can. This nearest stag . . ." He said no more, but dropped a quarrel swiftly into the bow. Gise nocked an arrow, and together they slithered silently into the last wall of bushes, slowly and in no rhythm. More hesitantly the others moved after them, crouched on tense legs, ready for a rush. They froze as they heard a sudden angry snort and saw antlers toss above the leaves. But the great deer was only striking at a persistent fly, and the antlers rose and fell gently once again as it returned to cropping the bushes. Elof's heart sank as he saw Kermorvan rising on one knee, taking careful aim; the quarrel seemed minute, hardly more than a fly sting to that bulk of muscle. He would as soon have attacked thus the monstrous mammut they had encountered in Aithennec. But as Kermorvan's finger curled on the trigger there came a sudden screeching cry, and from among the branches behind them a winged flash of red arrowed upward, crying alarm and havoc. The antlers jerked upward, the pendulous muzzle tossed back in a cloud of steaming breath, the huge nostrils flared rigid and the stag gave a loud blaring cry that was at once challenge and warning. The other stags trumpeted to the echo, the does stared, ears twitching, and bounded to herd in the fawns, who jumped and stumbled on overlong legs. Gise and Kermorvan sprang up to shoot, but it was too late. All at once the giant herd was surging about the clearing, hooves churning in the damp soil, bunching and milling together in a tight ring.

Elof turned to glare at whoever had alarmed the bird, and so saw the true cause. He had barely a moment to shout a warning and spring aside, the others spilling after him. A deep coughing growl sounded; Borhi tried to spring up but Elof and Tenvar held him down. Kermorvan caught Gise's arm and they dived headlong among the bushes, barely in time. Then through the brush there burst three brindled beasts as big as ponies, and more bulky, bounding heavily on their thick legs. Their flat heads were held low, the wide jaws agape, their long fangs outthrust like assassin's daggers; claws sprang out on the wide paws. They spared the travelers no glance, but sprang into the clearing and, crouching low, circled about the herd to pen them in. The stags bellowed deafeningly and struck out with hoof and antler, but the attackers moved too fast, the does panicked and the herd became a milling stampede. One tall stag, a fraction slower than its fellows, passed the wrong side of a tree and was thrust out from the threshing cordon of hooves. Then the killers struck. It was a clean, expert kill, almost graceful save for its deadly end. One daggertooth sprang at a kicking rear leg, dragging the stag to a halt; another leaped for the muzzle and hung there by the wide lip, dragging the head down and hindering the deadly sweep of the antlers. Then the third lunged up at the lowered neck, twisting in midair to embrace the throat in its long forelegs, hung there and bit. Deep into the thick mane sank the long fangs, stabbing down into the great veins, and the jaws clamped shut about the windpipe. Blood fountained among the sandy fur; the stag struggled and threshed and gave great snoring moans, but the killers clung, scrabbling upward with huge hind claws at belly and flanks the antlers could no longer defend. Their sheer

weight held it in place while it stifled in the iron grip. Its
long head threshed back once in anguish, then the pillar
legs bent and folded, the great beast sank forward, kneeling, and toppled sideways with a crash. The killers rolled
aside between the quivering legs and fell on the spilling
belly, ripping at it with muffled snarls of satisfaction. The
herd, relieved of its pursuers, wheeled about and went
streaming off into the distant trees, and the thunder of its
passage drummed long in the earth.

"Now!" shouted Kermorvan suddenly, dropping the
bow. "Now, if ever!" And leaping to his feet, he tucked
his cloak over his arm, so that it flared out around him,
drew sword and went charging out into the clearing.

"He's gone clean daft!" cried Roc, horrified.

"No!" shouted Gise and Elof together, understanding
Kermorvan's purpose. "No, after him! And make all the
noise you may!" Elof sprang forward, crashing through
the bushes with a wild yell, and after him Ils with the same
exultant shout that had greeted the Mastersmith's downfall. In their wake streamed the company, shrieking and
yelling and brandishing weapons. But Kermorvan was far
ahead of them, already at the kill. The daggerteeth turned,
dripping jaws asnarl, and cuffed at him with paws as large
as his head. But their very size made them slow, and he
slid between them like quicksilver, slashing at the outstretched claws. Growling and spitting, they fell back from
the sweeping blade, but one leaped up on the carcass and
poised to spring. Elof grabbed for his hammer, but even
as its front feet lifted there came a snap, a hum, and it
tumbled kicking among the trampled weeds. Gise brandished his bow, cheering hoarsely, and charged forward
with the rest. It was too much for the other killers; their
nerve broke, and they slunk back, roaring and snarling to
cover their retreat. Right to the clearing's edge they snarled
and struck at their tormentors, but once within the tree
shadow they whirled about and went crashing away through
the brush.

The company fell upon the stag almost as raveningly as
the daggerteeth, but Kermorvan himself leaned on his

sword a moment to catch his breath. Ils stopped, and passed him her water flask. "I've seen you do brave things enough, long man. But was not taking on three of those brutes the prime of both?"

"Not so!" gasped Kermorvan. "Common enough in the wild that scavengers drive a killer from his kill; wolf packs often do it to daggerteeth, so why not we? It seldom comes to a fight. And I feared famine among the mountains far worse." He smiled thinly. "Well, scavengers let us be! The daggerteeth may yet return. We must butcher the poor brute swiftly, and bear off all we can carry to some safer spot."

Swiftly they stripped the flesh from the great deer, cutting it into pieces of a size they could carry. "Umbels and bones we will leave to the daggerteeth, if they return," said Kermorvan wryly. "They prefer those, anyway. Their dead fellow, also; meat eaters make poor flesh themselves." But Gise took the fangs for a trophy.

They left that clearing, and climbed on through the wooded hills till the near edge of night. The ground grew drier as it rose, though cut and crossed by many small streams and rivulets. At every ridge they came to, the mountain tops seemed to loom nearer. But as the warm summer twilight closed in about them they found a sheltered spot to camp, and could at last cook and eat their fill. They sank down then where they sat, and slept; but Kermorvan did not fail to set a watch. For two days more he bade them rest, gathering their strength and making ready their great store of meat for the journey ahead. Much of the venison they dried and smoked in thin strips, but Roc found a hollow tree trunk full of honeycomb, and the rest they cooked, chopped and mixed with this, berries and wild herbs that Elof and Bure gathered, to make a long-lasting reserve of food.

Those days were to Elof an endless time of peace. "Strange not to be forever in motion," he remarked to Roc as they watched the steaming clay oven at their feet, "pursuing and pursued, hunter and prey. To have leisure to think, and dream, dream of a life that was beyond this Forest . . .''

Roc grinned. "And that will be, I hope!"

"Will it?" Elof stood and stared up into the rooflike tracery of dark branches, hung with glowing leaves. "I can scarcely believe it. I feel as if the past has dwindled, as if all my greatest joys and greatest pains alike have faded away into the distance, and there's a barrier between them and me. A barrier of trees . . . always trees . . ."

"Ach, it's not that bad," muttered Roc uneasily. "You dream too much, that's all. Work under your hands, that's your need! Come tend the oven, though it's a poor substitute for forge and furnace!"

But the sense of isolation only grew in Elof. The times of his youth and his first meeting with Kara he could summon up as glimpses through shifting foliage, one minute bright and dazzling, the next obscured, faded, unreachable. He knew that no more than a year and a half had passed since last he saw her, and yet it might have been in another life. With heart, with mind he reached out to her, but it seemed to him that they were astray, both astray, wandering far apart among darkling trees. He gazed up at the patches of blue sky overhead, seeking, he knew not why, a sweep of wings. But the trees stooped and whispered, hid the sky from his sight and showed to him no more than the mountain tops that he must soon cross.

The morrow's dawn came very clear and bright, for the clouds did not hang so heavy over the hill forests as below at this season; it seemed to them all a good omen, bidding them rise early and make good speed. Even that small time of rest had made a great difference to them. Food had hardened failing thews, filled out hollow cheeks; new hurts had healed, old scars grown less stiff beneath clothes that had at last lost their clammy dampness. Roc even began to whistle, as Elof remembered him doing on their boyhood journeys with the Mastersmith, and though Kermorvan cast a wary eye at the trees he did not rebuke him. High reared the mountains before them, and in that day they passed out of the hills and in among their lower slopes. Yet their path never took the company quite out of the shadows of the woods, for the trees grew thick over all the land that was easiest to pass, and the Forest was always with them.

CHAPTER FIVE

The Halls of Summer

Of all that long and terrible journey, least, perhaps, is recorded of the crossing of the Meneth Aithen; yet those peaks were accounted the highest in the land, and a terror to travelers long after this day. It may well be that there was in fact little to tell, that in the mind of one who looked back to it, one day seemed scarcely different to the next. Day after day of trudging on up steep wooded hillsides, following small rivers that had sought or cut easy routes down the slopes, over loose soil and jagged stones that slipped away under scrabbling feet—thus the company wound a long and weary way between the looming mountain peaks. All the passes, all but the very highest slopes were smothered by the Forest, as it seemed to Elof, till he fell idly to wondering how the heights could sustain themselves under the onslaught of so many trees, their roots tearing at the very bones of the rock. But he found this part of the Forest less oppressive, for at these heights they walked once more chiefly among the evergreen pine-woods he knew, the air rich with the same tang of tars and resins as in the Northland forests, though many of the trees themselves proved strange to him, or odd variants of familiar kinds. The cooler, drier clime he found invigorating, and he all but forgot the looming presence he had been so conscious of in the lowlands. Equally heartened were the others from such lands, Roc and Ils and Gise, who was as close to joyful as he had been since the death of his friend; here his hunting skills were at their best, and by his catch and Kermorvan's the company lived well enough without relying too heavily on their precious store of venison. Best of all, perhaps, it was now high summer, and that worst of perils, the weather, was held firmly in check; even the winds in the high passes were moderated by the trees. It seems, therefore, that many long days slipped by without incident, until, passing between two high peaks, they found that no higher ones reared up beyond, and that the trees led them toward a downward slope. Then the company began to believe that the end of their crossing was nigh.

They camped that night in a little valley between two lesser peaks, and set out the next morning, tingling from a bathe in the pools of a mountain spring, eager for some glimpse of the new horizons eastward. But ere they had gone very far downhill they found that the trees came to a sudden end, and even the ground beneath. Beyond them was nothing but blue sky heaped white with cloud castles, as if they had come to the world's end. They guessed it must be the edge of a steep slope or a cliff, the trees growing to the very brink, and they hastened forward, full of excitement, seeking what might be seen from this high place. Kermorvan's stride, long and light, carried him ahead of his companions, and when Elof reached him he stood poised on the very brink, gazing out to the far horizon. Elof prudently caught hold of a hanging pine branch as he stepped out to join him, and caught sight of Kermorvan's face. His look was strange, grimness and great wonder struggling for mastery. Elof turned quickly to see what moved the warrior thus, and in finding his footing he looked down.

The world dropped away from under him, and he was seized in the empty clutch of the abyss. He gazed down upon treetops as tall as those that waved and whispered above his head; it was unnatural to see them so tiny and remote, as if he looked somehow through the eyes of a bird, soaring against the sun. Right to the foot of the cliff they grew, unbroken, as if that wall of stone had been suddenly thrust up out of solid forest, without toppling a single tree. So the Forest was here also, and awaiting them . . . Then understanding flowed like the Ice into his blood; he clutched the branch with convulsive strength. He had guessed Kermorvan's thought. If the Forest came unbroken across these mountains, then where did it end? To the distant horizon he raised his eyes, across all the broad lands between, and all was dark with trees.

Back to his childhood the sight took him, sitting on the hillside among the herds, gazing out over the immensity of the Western Ocean and wondering what lands might lie on its far shores, if shores it had. This too was an ocean; the wind drove waves across it, the scudding clouds swept purple shadows over it as they did over the green ocean. And this, too, held no promise of a further shore. All they could see was Forest unbroken, unending over this whole face of the world.

"The distance, that I knew!" breathed Kermorvan, his face suddenly very young and uncertain. "But this makes it real, real and terrible! From here to that horizon we must travel many times over ere we could hope to find the Forest's end. And how far beyond that to what we seek?" He shook his head. "I begin to wonder if I shall ever find that. If it can be found."

"The Eastlands?"

Kermorvan hesitated a moment. "I fear not. Oh, it may serve Kerbryhaine to find them. Or it may not. But I, I see now that I sought something more, a thing for which the east was only a guise . . . Some shadow perhaps of the glories of old, when my ancestors were kings. When I would have been a king!" He grimaced angrily. "A shadow indeed! And folly cast it. A phantom of things that are not, that never were, perhaps. Nobility, heroism, true kingship; have they fled the world? Or were they never truly in it? Were they always lies and glosses by chroniclers upon the folly and malice of men? If I were borne back to Morvan of old, would I find it any better than Kerbryhaine? Or Kerys itself any greater than Morvan, save in power and pomp? Can the hearts and minds of men have changed so much in the passing years? I fear not!'' The youth faded from his features, their lines deepened and set; years beyond his own settled upon him like motes of graying dust. As harsh and ancient as the raw granite below them was his face now, and as unyielding. Thus he had looked in the court of the duergar; but now it was against himself he turned that stony judgment. ''I hunted a dream, that lies not eastward nor any other way. And whither has my false quest led you all? And at what grave cost?''

Elof looked up at him. ''Not all dreams are false! I also seek one. To follow the sunrise I am pledged, till I find my life's fulfillment, or its end. The others also have their dreams, I do not doubt, of wealth, honor, adventure if nothing else; they knew their peril, if not its nature, and chose to follow regardless.''

''But you have touched your dream, and it lives. She lives. Of mine I am no longer sure . . .''

''Is that any reason to cast it aside? Give it life! Make it live! Give it your life, if need be! Even if you fail, it need not be wasted. Make some part of it true, at least, and you may inspire others. But my lord, I tell you this! In all my wanderings I have met no man more able to bring such a dream as yours to birth than are you yourself. You owe yourself the attempt, yourself and all the others we have lost.''

Kermorvan stiffened. He said no word to Elof, but glanced quickly at the others ranged along the cliff, staring unbelieving at the expanse of trees before them. When he called to them his voice was clear and strong. ''A barrier indeed! But our forebears crossed it, women and children, young and old, all alike. Shall we deem ourselves so much weaker than they? They found ways, and so shall we! For a first step, why not a safe path down? Let us search!'' He turned away from the brink, and as he faced Elof he smiled his thin smile. The gray years had passed from his brow.

''A way there must be indeed,'' muttered Roc to Elof, as they and Ils made their way along the cliff top. ''But by all accounts, there were plenty never came through that crossing! Let's hope it's not their way we find.''

"Indeed," said Elof. "But perhaps the way mattered less than they who trod it. Those who came safe to the west had great leaders, this man Vayde for one. And that is our strength also. It is his doubt I fear, the division of his will.''

Ils grunted. "Better a captain who knows doubt than one who doesn't, as is that creature Bryhon!''

"If only doubts do not consume him," said Elof. "As within sound steel a tiny flaw may spread, or a bright firecoal burn away from beneath, and fall to ash.'' To that the others made no answer.

It was long leagues of uneven ground before they found their descent, and the bright clouds of morning had been ousted by dark fleets racing southward before the wind, trailing drizzle across the treetops. The cliff face had no sudden end, but turned gradually to a steep slope with many patches of perilous scree and only a few pine trees, chiefly foxtails and whitebarks bent and tormented by the prevailing wind. Finally the slope became a broken surface of shelf and outcrop, a natural stair. Trees grew on every ledge that could bear them, providing welcome handholds; on steeper passages the travelers found themselves all but swinging from one branch to the next, never trusting the grip of their feet on smooth stone and shifting soil. Once Bure slipped and went slithering away across the rock, but fetched up against a stout pitch-pine sapling with only a few scratches. "As well you've been on shorter commons of late," laughed Tenvar, "or it might never have stood the strain!''

It was early evening before they at last came to more level ground. They were all weary, but still in good humor. It was something to have come through unknown mountains without worse hazard, and with the promise of rain in the air they were even glad to be back beneath the shelter of the trees. Within a stand of tall firs they found a spot that was dry and well floored with soft needles, and none could see any reason to go further that night. They had not hunted that day, but there was still plenty of dried venison to be stewed with herbs. The travelers sprawled around the little earth-oven as the shadows lengthened, resting their aching limbs and feeling secure and dry after their exertions. The faint scent of cooking, rich and savory, seemed the promise of a very banquet.

"Here comes the rain!" said Ils sleepily, as new gusts of wind ruffled the Forest around. She was always most aware of the weather, being least accustomed to it. "Hear it rattle down!"

"Down here we can snap our fingers at it!" sighed Elof, stretching contentedly. But even as he spoke he felt a sudden qualm, as of something forgotten that should have sprung to mind. He looked around uneasily. Roc raised himself on one elbow, peering into the gloom beyond the trees, and leaned over to Elof.

"You asked me . . ." he began, unusually hesitant, as if he feared to seem foolish. "You asked me to tell you if I felt . . . well, that that Someone was about to turn round. Well, that's the feeling I've got." He shivered. "How the storm blows!"

It seemed to be racing straight toward them; at every gust the rustle and creak of boughs grew louder, nearer. And with that thought Elof's qualms became a chill stab of awareness. "How it blows, indeed!" he cried. Kermorvan stared at him, their eyes met, then as one they sprang up while the others gaped.

"Up, all of you!" shouted Kermorvan, drawing his sword and snatching up his pack. "Up, and run! Run from the wind!" Even as he cried out a great gust raced upon the stand of trees and seemed somehow to circle it, so that the boughs above stooped and nodded, and raindrops spattered in. "Uphill! Out of the trees! Go!" Then came a hiss, a thud; he stumbled back against a trunk. In the ground before him a long spear quivered. The least step more and it would have impaled him. Tenvar dived for another gap in the trees, then fell flat with a yell as spears hissed by his head. Arvhes, about to dodge behind a tree trunk, stared aghast at the gray-fletched arrow that sang in the bark a hairsbreadth from his fingers. Gise's bow was drawn, Elof's hammer in hand, but Kermorvan's clear command froze them even as they sought their mark.

"No! Hold your hand! Do you not see?" Another gust shook the bending boughs, the foliage rustled softly apart; long low sunbeams poured in and set strange leaves glittering upon every tree. Slowly Elof let the hammer sink; thirty or forty there could be up there, arrows or spears, what matter? It was too many to fight, surrounded as they were. He cursed himself for failing to remember that trick of stealing up under cover of a rain squall; it was no comfort to guess that Kermorvan must feel much the same. "Stand your ground!" the warrior commanded them, letting fall his pack. "If they wished to slay us, they could already have done so."

"Be these your watchers, then?" demanded Bure, peering up into the trees. "Shy of showing themselves, aren't they?" Scarcely had the words left his lips when a loud rush of leaves made them all jump. The thud of feet on earth and suddenly a ring of shadowy figures barred the gaps in the tree circle. Tall and gangling they seemed, their stance oddly bowed, but keen eyes gleamed, the colors of the trees. Kermorvan lifted his head in silent recognition.

"These are they. We have met them before, Elof and Ils and I, and come to no harm. Be still, that they may see we mean none to them." Slowly he folded his arms and leaned back against the tree. The figures nearest him stepped warily forward, and as they moved into the light many of the company gasped.

"The Children of Tapiau, indeed!" said Ils softly. Two advanced, the reddening light glinting upon their hair, long, luxuriant, redbrown in hue; they were women, like as close kin to those they had encountered in Aithennec in the west. In their way they were fair, their faces lean, wiry, but smooth and unlined, strangely expressionless; only their eyes glittered with animal intensity. Their garb, or lack of it, was the same; no more than harness of studded leather about thigh and breast; Elof heard Roc chuckle appreciatively, and Ils warn him he might soon snigger on the other side of his face. Others followed them, men and women both, and to Elof's surprise they were less alike. Some were taller, padding along on limbs so long they seemed spidery, others shorter and more human in shape, though the least of them matched Kermorvan and Gise, and clad in plain short tunics of green and brown. One girl had hair as dark as Elof's, though her limbs were long and her eyes were that wild catlike green. She stepped up to Tenvar, peering at him, and put up a hand to touch his face; he flinched when he saw it, the least human thing about her, the fingers twice the length of his own, the thumb short and set low.

"Steady!" Elof told him. "It must be your dark skin, she may never have seen it before."

Gise nodded stolidly. "Aye, I can believe that! Their own damned hides are as milky as sothrans'."

"He's right!" said Ils. "I thought so before, and now I see more of them . . ."

"But not their hair," said Elof, considering. "No red or blond, little black . . ."

"Aye indeed," said Roc curiously, running his fingers through his own flame-red crown. "It's mostly that bronze shade, like 'twas a blend of all . . . I've seen but one head that shade, know it well, but on whom, now?" Then he caught sight of the others' faces, and together their eyes turned to Kermorvan, and the women who stood before him. A likeness deeper than the shade of their hair leaped to Elof's startled eyes, though he could not say whether it lay in some general thing such as the proud set of the lean faces, or some true semblance in the bones beneath.

Then a shout from Borhi distracted them. One tall Forest man had scooped up his pack, and was casually rummaging around in it with his long fingers. "Get your thievin' mitts out of there!" yelled Borhi, moving to snatch the long wrist away; he jerked his head back, choking, as two broad spears clashed at his throat.

"Easy, man," said Kermorvan reassuringly. "Let them look! Would you not search strangers loose in your lands? See, he steals nothing." And he reached out a foot, and tipped his pack toward one of the women. She flashed him a wary glance from under her thick eyebrows, then ducked down and twitched open the straps. Quickly but carefully she pulled out strips of dried meat, spare garments and some lesser oddments, sniffed at a box of salves and bandages. Then she hauled out a large and heavy parcel of oiled leather that Elof remembered well; Ils, too, by the anxious glance she shot him. He could only bite his lip and shrug; had Kermorvan meant her to paw at that? He saw his friend's fists clench hard as the woman idly peeled back the leather, and metal rang within. Unwrapping the dark helm and mail, she gave Kermorvan a sharp glance, but let them spill carelessly on the ground as she spied the gleam of gold within. Kermorvan's frown deepened. Then her gasp of astonishment was clear as the damascened breastplate spilled into her hand, its crest a flaming web of gold in the dying fires of day. Up to the watchful trees she brandished it, and the travelers heard a soft sighing cadence, a breeze like a low breath of awe, run through the foliage. *"Margherren'ac athail!"* she said softly, and Elof gaped.

"Raven and Sun!" he breathed in astonishment. "Kermorvan, she knows your crest!"

Kermorvan nodded, looking slightly dazed. "So I see, though I cannot understand her words. How may you? Is it some arcane speech?"

"Arcane? Man, it is your own!"

"What?"

"Aye, listen! In ancient books I have seen it written thus. It is your tongue as they spoke it of old, the words the same, only their sound differs. Listen!" Elof turned to the woman, and spoke as slowly and clearly as he could. *"Krythen'a margran ac eyhel, e'yn! Yn'a Kermorvan Arlath, kanveydhe?"*

"You I understood!" barked Kermorvan. "The crest is mine, I am the lord Kermorvan . . . But did she?"

The woman looked at them both, cocked her head at Kermorvan, her mouth silently forming words. Then suddenly she darted forward, peering down into his face with an air of startled recognition. Abruptly she turned and shouted something. There was a flurry of movement, and Elof felt long hands seize him; he struggled to reach his sword, but fingers of steel wire clamped his hand crushingly to the hilt. He heard Ils cry out, had a brief glimpse of Roc and Borhi threshing and struggling in the grip of four tall woodsfolk, then he was plucked from the ground and hurled straight at the wall of foliage overhead.

Even though he knew now that he was being swept along by those elongated arms, swinging from bough to bough, it was a dizzying, sickening sensation; branch after branch hurtled crazily straight at his face, into his eyes, at such a speed it must dash out his brains, and he flinched in fright. Then at the last moment it would be whisked aside and the next one lash at him. The rush and sough of the wind around him rose to a shrieking gale, speeding cold droplets that stung his cheeks like hailstones. The mad rush of the air seemed to choke him, stifling breath and mind alike, though of falling he felt no fear, knowing too well the effortless strength of the hands and feet that held him. He could hardly cling to coherent thought enough to wonder or worry about his friends, or where they were being taken, or how long the journey was; only the failing light gave him any sense of passing time. He guessed they were moving downslope, but never for a moment could he be sure. Then, as abruptly as it began, it ended. He felt a sudden, jarring halt, swung for a moment in shadowy emptiness, then saw a greensward, as it seemed, rise up under his feet. Hard ground slapped them a crisp blow; unable to stand, he fell on all fours and clung to turf that heaved under him like a ship. Someone groaned beside him, and he saw Borhi sprawled there, staring at him with white-rimmed eyes, face bloodless, mouth working. On his other side was Roc, sprawled gasping upon his back, and beyond him Kermorvan clambering unsteadily to his feet. But suddenly the tall man rested on one knee, gazing upward, his thin lips parted, his stern features softened with the open wonder of a child. Behind him Arvhes staggered up, only to cry out, point and drop once more to his knees, his round face no less rapt. Swiftly Elof heaved himself up on one elbow and followed their gaze. Then he understood, and felt the same awe swell up in his own heart at this unlooked-for vision.

It was evening still, the sun hidden now by tree and cloud, yet shedding a last pale glimmer through the storm-cooled air. They lay on a broad space of level ground, for their mad journey had indeed borne them down into the eastern foothills of the Meneth Aithen. Those slopes arose above the travelers now, crested and carpeted with tree-tops tall and ancient, their foliage thick and shadowdark. Into the very rainclouds they mounted, that swept racing and boiling by, up to heights hidden behind the trailing veils of rain. A fine fast drizzle beat down upon them and from their whipping leaves a haze arose that scattered the pallid stormlight into a hoard of soft gleams and sudden sparkles, glowing droplets upon every shadowed leaf and bough. Solid they seemed, those tossing trees, as the stony soil they gripped, yet in their files there was a breach and their summits were overborne. For from the end of the greensward a way opened between them, a wide grassy way flanked by great cedars, curving up to the middle slopes of the hill. And there, wall upon wall, roof upon roof, all across the hill's wide flank a majestic hall arose out of the Forest.

Towers and turrets thrust up above the waving treetops, arched garrets and peaked gables; down upon them gazed windows uncounted in a multitude of walls, and between those windows ran many galleries and walks. Yet it was clear that all this was part of one great building which spread among the trees but did not sprawl, and seemed strangely suited to its situation. Noble and strong were those walls in the gathering twilight of storm and sunset, graceful those angled roofs as the treetops they crowned. And even as the last gold of day slipped from the walls, a thousand windows sprang alive with twinkling light and warmth behind the cool tossing of the trees. "A very town it might be, in one building," marveled Roc. "A mighty citadel . . ."

Kermorvan shook his head. "No," he answered absently, "no citadel this, though as imposing. It was not made to withstand assault."

"Nor to confine?" asked Elof quietly.

"No more that!" answered Kermorvan decisively.

Ils nodded, her round eyes peering far into the gloom. "If it has defenses, that place, they are not in its walls. Yet my heart tells me that defenses it will have."

Elof glanced warily around. All the company were there, at least, and their baggage also; thankfully he snatched up his precious pack. He felt suddenly weak and famished, and found himself pining absurdly for the food left steaming in the little glade. But now their captors were helping them to their feet, gently enough, and urging them toward the grassy way. No gate barred it, but on either side were tall hummocks of green, like banks or thick hedges; only as he drew closer did Elof see patches of gray-white beneath. They were walls, stone walls, heavily overgrown with creepers and a kind of ivy; one even began in a stone pedestal, such as he had seen flanking gates in Kerbryhaine, bearing statues or other ornaments. But opposite it there was only a half-formed heap of rough stone blocks, hardly visible through the weeds.

The cedars grew so close to the sides of the way that high above it their branches met and entwined, lightest and airiest of vaultings, but nowhere did their roots intrude upon the smooth grass. So strong was the feeling of order that in the gloom Elof could almost believe himself walking in duergar halls or the calm cloisters of Kerbryhaine, between pillars of stone, beneath arches of carven foliage. But ahead of him a sudden light spilled out along their trunks, outlining a tall gate opening, and out from it, in slow procession, came files of lesser lights, torch and twinkling lanthorn. Into the way they streamed, and by their shifting light he saw more clearly those who bore them. Very tall and stately they stood, grace and dignity in their bearing, and the torchlight flickered mellow over rich patterns and broideries in their garments, picked out rich jewels adorning the shadowed faces. Scant sound they made, save the soft sigh and rustle of gown and robe

against the short grass, the murmur of fair voices lowered
as at some solemn occasion; a woman's laughter bubbled
up, light and clear as moonlight, and as swiftly vanished.
Along the flanks of the walk they ranged themselves, as if
the shabby travelers were a procession that must pass between and through the open gate.

The travelers stared wide-eyed; some might have hesitated, had Kermorvan not strode on so firmly, his keen eyes
alive with wonder. Elof, dry-mouthed, fought down his own
unease; what else, after all, could they do? At their backs
loped the ones who brought them here, and all around them
was the trackless Forest. But that thought only heightened
the unreality of all he saw, this noble hall and lordly company
before him; it was too much like a dream.

Suddenly Kermorvan halted, so sharply Elof almost
barged into him. Out of the gathered ranks a tall figure
had stepped, and advanced toward the company; he doffed
the cap he wore, and bowed deep before the travelers. Elof
studied him keenly, seeing a face longfeatured but wholly
human, lined and weary, yet serene. Tall and slender he
stood, unusually so for a man yet far less than the woodfolk; hand and limb were of human measure. He gazed at
them for a moment; then he spoke, and his speech was
warm and clear. *"Korhemyn, arlathain! Er heroth devyes
lysaiau'an aithen! Korhemyn!"*

The language was sothran, and less archaic than that the
woman had spoken. Elof swallowed his astonishment, and
whispered urgently to Kermorvan, "He welcomes us as
lords! And names himself—"

"I heard!" said Kermorvan crisply. "As chosen herald
of these woodland halls! Chosen by whom, I wonder? But
we must answer him, in all courtesy." And speaking as
clearly as he could, he returned the greeting, and named
one by one each member of the company, making as much
of their qualities as he could, and last of all those who
stood by him. To each the herald bowed, but when Kermorvan named Ils a great lady of the duergar, a ripple of
excited comment ran through the ranks of watchers; many
among them sank to one knee or made solemn obeisance.

Ils' eyes widened, and she hastily bowed in return; Elof
saw how greatly such courtesies impressed her, she who
had found scant honor among ordinary men. It was to Elof
next that Kermorvan turned, naming him a smith of great
lore and greater craft for all his youth, and a valiant fighter
at need; that also seemed to impress the watchers. "For
myself, I have led this company out of the distant Westlands, and Keryn, Lord Kermorvan, is my name." And
as he spoke it the woman of the woodfolk darted forward,
sank on one knee before the herald and held out the breastplate in her long arms, shining clear in the torchlight.

It seemed then that a single gasp, a single sigh, arose
from the shadowy watchers, running like a rushing breeze
among the torchflames. Even the herald stared as if bereft
of words. Then they surged forward, torches held high,
and some among the company laid hand to weapon, though
they could never hope to fight such a throng.

But the press parted suddenly, and a man taller than
most shouldered his way through. They fell silent and drew
back; seizing a torch, he strode toward the travelers, looming up over them like a young tree, his mantle and hose
flaring dark green in the yellowish light, and rich goldwork
gleaming in his tunic. "Keryn!" he cried, "Keryn, is it
truly you? Do I find you here at long, long last? Where I
had long since lost hope of your coming?" His deep voice
faltered as he looked upon their uncomprehending faces,
Kermorvan's set grim as granite, "Keryn? Is aught amiss?
Do you bear some grievance against me? Or are you ill,
then, that you offer me no greeting? I, your own brother!"

Elof stared around at the few faces he could make out,
seeking laughter or pity in them, as at some harmless dot-
ard or madman. But nothing of that did he see in the long
countenances, nothing but a deep interest, a tinge of concern. Kermorvan's gray eyes glinted wide in the torchlight,
and his voice dripped a bitterness Elof had hardly believed
the man could feel. "I can give you no other answer than
this. My parents are dead, my mother in bearing me, her
firstborn and her last. I never had a brother."

"But how is this?" demanded the newcomer. "Does

some thrall of blindness lie upon you? Oh, this is bitter
cruel, bitter as the very heart of the Ice! Do I not know
your voice, your face, as well as my own? Look upon my
own, and tell me I lie!'' He held the torch high, and the
first Elof saw by its light was the gray-flecked bronze of
the man's hair, the tracks of tears upon his gaunt cheek.
Kermorvan stared up into those long features, and slowly
his stern mouth lost its set, his lips parted, seemed to
tremble. Ils gasped aloud, almost a cry; a sudden deep
chill sank into Elof's stomach. Distort either face, lengthen
Kermorvan's or shorten the other, and they would mirror
one another. It was as if each mocked the other, yet both
were noble, proud, even fair in their way, inescapably akin.

But Kermorvan shook his head. ''Sir, I have never set
eyes upon you in my life.''

''No!'' stammered the man. ''How may this be? You
are Keryn as I remember you . . . But that should not be!
As if no time had passed! As if you . . . he . . . had grown
no older, while I, I who was younger . . . How? How?''
His voice cracked in horror and confusion, and the torch
shook violently in his hand. Deep lines were scored on
his face, wrung as if by agony. Kermorvan, without thinking, reached out reassuringly. The sudden gesture startled
them both, and they stared at each other again; it was
almost an intuitive acknowledgment of their kinship.

''You . . . he . . . remained,'' murmured the stranger,
and to Elof it seemed that a tension grew among the
watching throng, the string of a tuned instrument wound
slowly tighter. ''Remained behind, when our last defense
was overborne, when the Ice itself came finally against
our very walls, and all along the shore the stout stones
cracked and shattered like nutshells. There was a fearful
sight indeed! Did we deem something so weighty would
move slowly, as till then it had done, inching its way forward day by relentless day? No; not in this, its final assault; not after that night, clear and cold, without wind or
cloud. So still the Waters lay, still as a mirror under the
moon, on the far horizon reflecting those cruel white crags
that reared over once-fair fields and woodlands. Yet even

their turmoil, their storms and roaring avalanches, whole ice cliffs collapsing into the Waters to become great floating mountains, even that was stilled then awhile. Fair I thought it, and an omen of peace . . .'' He shivered suddenly, violently. ''Then . . . it was as if the moon breathed upon the Waters. For that whole great landlocked sea clouded as would a mirror. And in the very beat of my heart it turned all to silver, and thence to white! I knew then that our doom stood at our gate. Our very ships were crushed in their harbors, our islands overwhelmed; terrors flooded across the Ice, troll and dragon and other fell beasts and fell men and half-men behind them, that then laid siege to our very walls. And behind them, whom we might yet have withstood, the crags themselves advanced. No longer did they inch along; across that frozen sea they glided, as fast it seemed as a man might run, and a howling gale was their herald, their banners a vast wave of rubble and stone they bore before them. Its own creatures the Ice overwhelmed and cared not. It bore up against our shoreward walls, and the stones, the strong stones, cracked like shells, shells . . . Then my brother bade flee all the followers that were left him, his loyal lords and counselors, his soldiers and his people, all their families who remained. And when we would not, he commanded us with all his force to fare, some eastward with tidings to my own realm, but most, myself among them, westward. For thither he had already sent his young son, in charge of our sister Ase and the great Lord Vayde. His son must grow up to build a new realm in the west, far beyond the reach of the Ice, and there reunite the sundered kindred; he had sent the high scepter with him, but he would have need of more tangible force if he was to assert his kingship and his power.'' The man stared at them now with eyes that burned. ''We were to make our way west as best we could, and if we could come there, serve the holder of the scepter, his rightful heir. But my brother, he himself would not come, for in his city, he said, lay his destiny, to live or die with it. And he took the crown, and two old warriors of his guard, and went from among us. What could we give him then, but our last obedience? We took what we might gather and made a great sally from the landward gates, scattered the besiegers there and won free. But even as we ran free across the hills, we turned and looked back and saw the white crags grind across our walls, scrape them from sight as the edge of a hand wipes clean a slate. The tall towers, the bridges and battlements, the rows of rooftops, we saw them leap up in thunder and turmoil before the advancing walls, and topple or be crushed. Then all was ground down into silence. All that had come down to us across long centuries, that only days past had seemed to us mighty enough to withstand as many years more, strong enough to scorn the challenge of mere Ice, all that we saw crumble and vanish before us in a mere shred of time. All the mountains of the earth falling could not have obliterated it more completely; the very dust that escaped the Ice its gales took and scattered in mockery. Many among us slew themselves upon their own weapons at the sight, or cast themselves down from the heights. For it seemed to us that all the shielding Powers had forsaken us, and that the world's ending was come."

Elof, standing silent and dumbfounded, heard a soft sigh arise from the watchers, like an echo from some dark deep of pain revisited. It awakened in him memories he hated, the destruction of the little town of Asenby where he had grown up, his guilt at having so fervently wished it. Beside him Kermorvan, left gaping as wide as any, at last found voice. "M-my lord . . . who *are* you?"

The gray-blue eyes so like his own flashed at him, and the voice rang like some dark-toned horn. "I? I am Korentyn Rhudri, Prince of the House of Kermorvan, High Steward of the Realm of Morvan, Sealord of Kermorvannec. All this by the will of my brother Keryn, High King of Kermorvan the City and the realm of Morvan, one hundred and sixty-fifth in that line since the Flight from Kerys."

Elof, torn between anger and amazement, could not forbear. "How can any of this be?" he burst out. "Tell me that, my lord, when he who stands by me is well-nigh two hundredth of his house, the thirtieth born in the Western Lands! And when, since the realm of Morvan fell beneath the Ice, nigh on one thousand years have passed!''

A rumble of disquiet ran among those who watched, and the man rounded on him, his face a set mask of anger. It was alarming how like Kermorvan the expression made him, but Elof met the cold gray eyes firmly, and almost at once the anger faded. "Elof you name yourself,'' murmured the man, "One Alone, that would be, in the ancient tongues. Strange, then, that you also should remind me of someone . . . not so closely . . . of whom, I cannot think, but it is strong . . . and what you say . . . ach, this is madness, madness . . .'' Again the man's face knotted and twisted, as if in the throes of some terrible struggle; he lifted shaking hands to his temples, choked as if some word trembled on the edge of speech, some word that failed him. The silence among the watching throng hardened, as if no breath should stir the air. Then a sudden trilling note, liquid and beautiful, broke it, the call of some nightbird in the whispering foliage around. The tall man raised his head as if to listen, and Elof also harkened in great wonder, for it seemed to him that in the song there was a tremor of meaning which shaped itself into words within his mind.

> *Within the woodshade*
> *I sing of all life*
> *Ever renewing*
> *Coming to flower.*
>
> *Worry is folly*
> *Doubt is deceiving*
> *Serving what lives not,*
> *Slaves to its power.*
>
> *Look to the Forest*
> *Here in its hallow*
> *Time shall bring fullness*
> *Never decay.*

Under its shelter
Fear not the season
This and this only
Passes away.

The rain had ceased now, and the clouds parted upon a cool summer night. As Elof listened to the birdsong, he felt less oppressed by the Forest, less wary of it, ever more acutely aware of its living beauty. On a nearby bush a cobweb's pattern was picked out in raindrops which the emerging moonlight turned to white gems; he found the craft of it almost heartbreaking, it and the silvered leaves that bore it far surpassing any counterfeit from human hand. The air itself was so fresh it seemed to sparkle as he breathed it, rich with the myriad scents of the wood. He felt weariness and hunger fall from him like soiled mantles, and new strength flow in his veins. The tautness faded from Kermorvan's stance, and he flexed his weary back and limbs; Roc gawked around him open-mouthed, as if seeing the place for the first time, and all the others of the company seemed suddenly more at ease. Ils breathed deeply, and rubbed her eyes gratefully; even after so long above ground she much preferred moonlight to sun. The man called Korentyn listened most intently, as if hearing even more than did Elof in the song; little by little the anguish faded from his face. The last liquid trills died away among the bushes, and he turned to them with nothing in his face but grave courtesy and concern.

"I pray you pardon me. I am grown discourteous, that in my sorrow at not finding him I looked for I should so disquiet another close kinsman!" He smiled with calm delight. "To that name your face is title and patent beyond all dispute. And you remind me of him in more than face; what else need I know? I should have remembered that few in the Forest meet by chance. I bid you welcome, in the name of the Preserver who has led you hither! And these your worthy companions, no less; long is it since we had a great smith amongst us, and never before any of the mountain folk. Honor our halls, if it pleases you! Find here refreshment, rest, slumber without fear, joy in waking. For all are welcome, by the Preserver's will! Come!'' He stepped aside, smiling and eager, and gestured them to pass through the ranks of watchers and up to the gate. ''Come!''

It was in Elof's mind to hang back, to ask more. Thresholds could be decisive things to pass, most of all where there was metal and a smith. Ils, he could see, was of like mind. The others were anxiously looking to them for guidance. But Kermorvan glanced about a moment, and Elof guessed what was in his mind; if good was intended they could cause offense, if ill, there was little enough they could do against such numbers. The warrior stepped forward, and the weary travelers after him, glancing nervously at the throng as they passed. But only grave bows greeted them, and graceful courtesies. Kermorvan returned them with becoming grace, and Tenvar and Bure as well-born northerners also, but Elof felt rustic and abashed, and dared not try. Ils, by contrast, beamed all over her broad face. ''Strange day,'' she laughed, ''When a duergar lass gets so fine a greeting among men! I may begin to like this place.''

''Among men?'' murmured Elof. ''I wonder.''

As he spoke he felt the grass grow thinner underfoot, heard his steps ring on buried stone; one step more and he trod bare flagstones, hollowed like hands from long wear, as were the broad steps leading up to the gate. A towering arch of carven stone it was, high and fair, yet as Elof stepped up to it he stood startled, for it seemed to him that beyond it there was only the Forest once more, a grove of trunks overshadowed by the immense and ancient oak at its end. Then he saw his error, but marveled all the more; the trees of the grove on either side were the two great gates of wood, cunningly carven and contrived to draw the eye within when opened, counterfeiting depth and distance. But the oak was real, though it rose out of the paved floor of a wide court whose walls were high. Many roofed galleries ran along them, but the oak rose still higher, its topmost branches waving free against the moon.

Kermorvan strode through the gate, and warily Elof followed, admiring its work as he passed. The man called Korentyn noticed his interest, and smiled. "Closed, they still seem open and inviting, and they are without lock and bar. But we rarely close them, save against rough weathers; here there is no worse enemy to fear. For this is Lys Arvalen, the Halls of Summer." He held his torch aloft, and around the high walls lamps awoke in answer, soft steady glows of many shades that swelled in a moment to fill the court with radiance, broken and dappled by the oak leaves into a mild summer twilight. From the galleries many voices called down fair greetings through the cool air, and spilled down great profusion of sweet-scented flowers and petals upon the travelers. Snatches of song beguiled their ears, glimpses of fair faces caught their eyes, and above all these the sheer majesty of the building.

"This is a noble place indeed!" breathed Kermorvan in quiet admiration. "Larger than anything in Kerbryhaine save the citadel, and more majestic. A fair sight, and a fairer welcome!"

"But one as strange as the other!" Elof reminded him. "Still, it is work to rival even the duergar, is it not, Ils?"

"Not quite!" remarked Ils, amused. "Do you not see? The walls—" Then she could say no more, for they were surrounded in an eddy of tall folk, pressing close about them, eager to make themselves known.

"My lord Keryn?" said one man, shorter and broader than Korentyn, yet of the same cast and color. "Welcome, welcome again! I am Lord Almayn, a cousin of your house, and this is the lady Dirayel." Tall and fair of hair, she reminded Elof uncomfortably of Louhi, though her smile was warm. Another and younger approached, smaller of stature, her delicate catlike face framed by straight auburn hair, a startling contrast to the flint-faced giant on her arm, whose hair streamed fire-red as Roc's about his shoulders. "And by her side the lady Teris, and Merau Ladan, who was a distinguished guardsman of King Keryn."

"Merau Ladan?" repeated Kermorvan, astonished, taking the outstretched hand. Elof glanced down at it in dismay; the fingers seemed longer even than Korentyn's and the arm, though still massive, matched it. Kermorvan seemed about to ask the man something, but Almayn was beckoning to a wiry man with tanned complexion and dark-brown hair not unlike Elof's. "And may I present another cousin of Prince Korentyn, who was once our foremost captain of the seas, Svethan—"

"Svethan!" cried Kermorvan in astonishment. "He who drove the hordes of the Ice from the Middle Isles? Who met Amicac himself upon the open ocean?"

Svethan chuckled. "And who came close to outrowing the breeze in the other direction! But I am done with the sea now, kinsman. Welcome! Say how it is you know of me, and I not of you?"

"I read of you in the lays of Morhuen!" whispered Kermorvan. "You, and Merau Ladan. And if this is the same Lady Dirayel . . ."

Svethan laughed outright. "Morhuen! Well, well! Wait until we tell the old fool his fame has reached even these Westlands of yours! Beside himself he will be!"

Kermorvan's eyes narrowed. "My lord Svethan, they did indeed reach us. These many centuries past."

A slight frown crossed Svethan's brow, and Merau Ladan shook his head firmly. "Hardly, my lord Keryn. An old fool is Morhuen indeed, but you may meet him yourself later, and judge!"

The lady Teris sighed. "May it drive him to play something once again! I miss hearing him, of late."

"Not I!" said the guardsman firmly. "My lord, and you, sir smith, and your friends all, when these courtly folk will weary you with their lays and their dances and politeness, do you come hunting with the Guardians and myself! For there is better sport to be had in these woods than in even the parklands of Morvan, and I hear there is a huntsman among you." Elof waved to Gise, who was evidently laboring to understand this archaic form of the sothran tongue, and translated the guardsman's words. Gise launched into a positive torrent of northern speech which, to Elof's surprise, Merau Ladan evidently understood very well, and replied in a fair attempt at a Northland accent. Teris began discussing poetry with Kermorvan, classical works Elof had never read; Ils was suddenly encircled by chattering gallants, Borhi and the northerners by pretty girls, and even Arvhes was busily discussing the commerce of the Westlands with Almayn. Elof felt absurdly left out. But then Korentyn appeared once more, gathering up the travelers, a hint of kindly amusement in his resonant voice.

"My friends! You are weary and worn after your long journey; who should know that better than we? So we shall set by court and celebration till you are rested, and may share in them. Food awaits you, and better rest than the Forest floor has provided. Come!"

He ushered them briskly through the press of folk, who seemed in truth loth to let them go. Teris in particular almost ran to keep up with Kermorvan, her long gown of soft blue scuffing across the flagstones. "Like children bereft of their new playthings," said Ils amusedly.

Roc laughed. "Not much changes in a forest. Like as not we're the first things new here for a long time!"

"Like as not," agreed Elof, but he found no laughter in himself.

Korentyn led the travelers up a broad stone stair to the first level of galleries and round to the far end of the court. There, in a wider balcony whose windows looked out onto the Forest, he sat them down in high comfortable chairs round a long table raised upon a dais; his own chair had a carven canopy, and so also the one on its right hand. There he placed Kermorvan, and as the warrior sat he glanced at Elof, placed opposite him, and raised his eyes meaningly. In the center of both canopies was a design of the Raven and the Sun.

To Elof's surprise it was the long-limbed woodfolk who came to wait upon them, bringing them water to wash, then loading the tables with trenchers of meat and other foods, simple but plentiful. Kermorvan bowed formally to his host. "On behalf of all, I thank you, my prince, for the hospitality of these your halls."

Korentyn smiled, and helped him to meat. "I thank you, but I am not the lord of this place. A steward or castellan, perhaps, if such things mattered; but here they do not. I am only the leader of such as survived our flight from Morvan; we were drawn too close in that terrible time for rank to matter so greatly. Merau Ladan's courage and resource kept many alive who would surely have perished, so what counts it that he was only a sergeant of the guard? We are of one rank and quality now. The only true lord in these halls is he who found us wandering and near death in his domains, that ancient Power who gave us the very heart of his realm to dwell in. He the Preserver, the Lord of Forests. He who is Tapiau." And he gestured out to the shadowy trees below.

"He gave you this place?" asked Ils quietly, from her seat at his left. "But who built the hall?"

"Ourselves," smiled Korentyn, with some pride. "I doubt that Tapiau has much appreciation of buildings. But we were fortunate in having Torve still with us."

"Torve the Builder," muttered Kermorvan, as if in a dream. "Of course . . ."

"And did he plan the walls thus?" asked Ils. "Stone up to this level only, and above . . ." She gestured. Elof twisted round to look out across the gallery, into the court beyond, up to its roof and the towers and rooftops he could glimpse beyond. Once mentioned, it seemed obvious; he would have seen it sooner, even without keen duergar eyes, had it not seemed so improbable. Of all this enormous hall, almost everything above the level of this gallery, a mere second story, was made of wood.

Korentyn sighed. "Not precisely, no. Poor Torve! He swore to make this place great, a monument to Morvan that was no more, the fit center of a realm that would be a haven for all men. And he fired all of us with his vision. Man and woman, lord and lady, not one scorned to help in any way they might." His mouth twitched. "It might surprise you that a prince of Morvan made a fine feller of trees and digger of ditches; me it certainly surprised. A hard labor it was, and a long one . . ." His eyes grew distant, vague, his voice sank almost to a murmur. "The Guardians were there to help us, of course; but they were fewer in number then, and the quarries of good stone were so far off, so far . . . Many grew weary, many, and Torve spent the fire of his heart all the sooner in striving to rekindle theirs. Ever more seldom we saw him, until at the last . . ." He shrugged, and slowly his eyes regained their keenness. "There were still some with fire enough to continue what he had begun, myself among them, but not in stone, not when Tapiau'la affords us wood aplenty. And strange as it may seem to one of the wise stonefolk, we have grown to love wood. It keeps the strength and warmth of living things about it, and it is as fitting here in the Forest as stone must be in your deep delvings."

"What happened to this Torve, my lord?" asked Elof. For all his misgivings he had eaten ravenously, and found no lack of anything he could wish for. After so many weeks on scant food, and then the sparse sufficiency of a hunter, it seemed marvelous beyond belief to eat a rich and varied meal, and to sit now supping at some light wine and watching the play of the leaves below the windows. "Did he simply . . . wander away?"

"No!" smiled Korentyn. "Few would do that, who have once breathed the air of this realm. He went to live with the Guardians, that is all."

"The Guardians?" inquired Elof. "Those that Ils' folk call Tapiau's Children?"

"A fair name," nodded the prince, "and a true one. But we call them Guardians, or in the Northland tongue I perceive you grew up with, *alfar.*"

Elof sat up in surprise. Had the meaning altered? That name did not mean Guardian now; he above all should know, who had once borne it in contempt, who had been named Alv—the changeling. But he thought it better, then, to say nothing of that. "What are these Guardians, my lord? What does the name signify? Are they servants? Slaves? Or . . ." He waved a hand. He had been about to ask, *or jailers.*

Korentyn looked slightly shocked. "No such demeaning thing! Here no man need be what he does not wish to be, so long as he does no hurt to others. They are our friends. A simple folk, as you may see, but with many skills and virtues among that simplicity, and very dear to us. They have no greater joy than to hunt, to gather, to till the soil in their own rather crude fashion. And having Tapiau's favor, that is all they need to feed both themselves and us in abundance. That and their service they give to us with love and reverence, and to Tapiau all that and great awe, for he is their lord. They guard his domain and its bounds, keeping a watchful eye on intruders even as they hunt and gather, and so are they named. It is no poor life they lead; many of us, like Merau Ladan, may spend days or weeks away hunting with them, and find it deeply refreshing, a rest from the court. You may, also.''

''It sounds so,'' smiled Kermorvan, stretched out at ease in his chair. ''Have you ever gone out with them, my lord?''

''Aye, often,'' said Korentyn quietly, and once more it was as though a veil fell across his eyes. ''Often, and for long, so long that I have thought, at times . . .'' He shrugged, smiled again and dismissed the thought with a wave of his hand.

Elof looked from him to Kermorvan; he had been waiting for his friend to ask one question, one vital to them all. Better that it should have come from him, but at all events somebody had to ask. ''My lord Korentyn . . . did you not name yourself Prince of Morvannec? Is that not Morvan's eastern port? And far from the Ice?''

Korentyn set his wine cup down carefully, and for the first time since his outburst at their meeting something other than kindness and merriment played over his face. ''It was, sir smith. And so I name myself, empty honor though it be.''

''You believe, then . . .''

''Could poor little Morvannec stand, when Morvan fell? Messengers were sent, as I told you. But since that time none has come westward, not one. Beyond doubt the east is dead, gripped and ground down under the hand of the

Ice; far or near, the power of men unaided could not save it. My brother knew what he was about in forbidding us to return there, and so waste our lives. Do you take heed, wise smith!'' The gray gaze flashed in the long lean face. ''For not only yours to hold is your wisdom, to risk or throw away as you will. You must not waste it in a light cause, a doomed adventure. You owe it to the men who are to come, you hold it in trust for them as I hold my own scant store, that I may leave more than a mere life behind me.''

Elof rose and bowed, to relieve his question of any sting. ''Then you are a prince indeed, my lord,'' he said, for he was deeply impressed by the sincerity of the man, much as he had been by Kermorvan's at their first meeting. But next to this man, Kermorvan might have seemed young and callow had Elof not known better.

When all had finished their meal, Korentyn and some of the *alfar* led them out of the gallery and across a covered bridge which joined the hall to a high slender tower some way upslope. The moonlight was so bright now that Elof could follow his rippling shadow across the treetops below. He looked around, hoping to see further from this height, but there was only the far side of the vale, and above it the stars. He felt then that he might as well hope to reach them as the Eastlands.

''Tonight you will all lie like princes,'' said Korentyn, his good humor restored, ''for this tower is my home. And yours, if you will, until such time as you choose dwellings to your taste.'' He brought them up many winding stairs to a balcony set with chairs, and behind it a long broad corridor, paneled in some light wood and lined with louvered doors. Behind each was a small bedchamber, the beds well strewn with furs and bright dyed blankets, so inviting that many began to yawn. A silver bowl and pitcher in an aumbry of fragrant cedar were all the other furnishings of Elof's alloted bedchamber, but these, though old and much used, were of work so rare it almost distracted his attention from Korentyn's parting words. ''Sleep or wake as you wish, come and go as you will. We gather for our meals in the galleries of the court, but

if you wish food here or anywhere, you have only to ask
the *alfar*. They may understand your northern speech better, for it seems less altered. For now, your time is your
own; but some weeks hence we have one of our great
festivals, to mark the height of summer. Many now absent
with the Guardians will be returning for that; there will
be feasting, songs, dancing to beguile many a long hour.
I bid you attend as our guests''

Kermorvan seemed slightly dazed. "You do us every
honor already, lord," he said, and bowed.

"On the contrary," said Korentyn. "You honor us, and,
in truth, you will add new zest to our revels; it is rarely
now we have newcomers to welcome. It will recall to us
a little of what is no more. And for you also, perhaps, it
will cast some faint shadow of the glories that dwelt in
Morvan of old. But you shall see. A fair night to you, my
brave guests, and sleep you well.''

With many polite good wishes the travelers watched him
stride off across the tower, heard a door open and his footsteps mount a stair. Then they were surrounding Kermorvan and Elof, deluging them with questions that Tenvar
summed up in demanding, "What *is* this place? Are we
safe to sleep here, or should we seek to flee? Who are
these folk?''

Kermorvan sat leaning on the balcony rail, gazing out
over the trees below; he shook his head ruefully, and a
strange slight smile played across his thin lips. "Do you
ask me, of all men? When ancient heroism and tragedy,
signs and symbols that all my life have inspired me, that
have shaped my will to this very venture, stand living before me? When old tales I was raised on have taken my
hand and spoken with me? When names a thousand years
dead are given to the young and hale? How could I dare
trust such a place?'' Suddenly his fist pounded the rail.
"And yet I do! I must! Against all reason! My heart leaves
me no choice, it will not let me gainsay them. These *are*
the heroes and legends of old, come alive.''

"The legends?'' asked Elof quietly. "Or the people?''

Kermorvan stared at him, then nodded. "A shrewd stab.

All I can tell you is this, that there were once such folk as we have met or heard of tonight; they lived, all of them. Almayn the Wise, Svethan the Mariner, Merau Ladan, that bard Morhuen, Torve, many others, and Korentyn himself not the least; Korentyn Rhudri they called him, the Red-head, or the Firebrand. In the realm and city of Morvan they dwelt, and perished with it; so the annals of Kerbry-haine record. Their deeds and works have passed into legend, into folktale; they themselves should have been dead and dust these thousand years gone. Those who confront us now are not ideal figures, not legends. But the cause that legends are, that I could believe. And whoever they may be, they breathe humanity.''

Borhi shivered. ''We've only seen 'em by night,'' he muttered, and his meaning was clear.

''But we've met these Guardians or Children or whatever by day,'' said Ils firmly. *''And* drawn live blood from them in fight. And in all reason, do they *seem* like phantoms?''

''Yet they are no ordinary folk,'' objected Bure. ''So tall, so . . . drawn . . .''

''But so fair!'' said Arvhes reverently. ''I could well believe we had shrunk in stature since their day!''

Kermorvan shook his head. ''Not by such armor as survives.''

Gise nodded. ''They say we of the north have grown taller by the mingling of our blood with the men from oversea.''

''But do you not see . . .'' began Elof, and then checked himself. Ideas turned in his mind as flotsam in a whirlpool, too fast to grasp completely.

''What?'' challenged Tenvar sharply.

Elof shook his head. ''It is nothing, perhaps. I . . . will take counsel upon it. One matter, though . . . Kermorvan, are all those you recognized from the same time? Do the annals say they all lived in Morvan in the same years?''

The warrior glanced keenly back at him. ''I know not what led you to ask that question, but it struck full in the gold. That fair lady, Dirayel, if she is the same . . . and after her the name was deemed unfortunate, and rarely if ever given . . . she is well remembered, as one of the great ladies of southern Morvan. *She* was lost on the first flight westward, that led to the founding of Bryhaine, a good two centuries before Korentyn and the others were born! She should be as dead to them, as they to us.''

A long silence fell, broken only by the rustling of the trees and the living sounds of night, bird cries and the croak of frogs, bats shrilling, insects humming, small things scuttling and scrubbing among the leaves. So recently such sounds had seemed alien, even sinister, but within this fastness of walls they spread a sense of serenity and peace. This was the voice of the Forest, the soft insistent murmur of its myriad lives busy about their own intense concerns, and it spoke to them now, steady and untroubled. Before it, fears and tensions seemed to recede. Once more the full weight of weariness settled upon Elof, but as a calmer, kinder sensation, something fitted to hour and circumstance. In the end it was Kermorvan himself who spoke. ''Tenvar, you asked if we will be safe to sleep here tonight. That at least I can answer; we may not safely do aught else. We do not know enough.''

Gise snorted scornfully. ''One thing we know, that they could have left us carrion on the Forest floor, if they wished us ill. Why offend them now?'' Others voiced agreement, and Elof was surprised to hear Roc, normally most suspicious of new things, among them.

''That is what I meant,'' agreed Kermorvan calmly. ''We cannot judge; we must know more, and for that await the morrow. But what the mind cannot unravel, the heart may measure. And mine tells me that here we have found a haven of peace, a bastion of living might against what would ravage the world. I shall sleep as I have not for many a night.'' He rose and turned regretfully away from the view. ''In peace.''

Elof looked at him in some surprise; peaceful or not, was the mighty mystery at the heart of this place to be dismissed so lightly? But the others were of Kermorvan's mind, turning toward the bedchambers, yawning and stretching as happily as in their own homes. Elof held his peace then, but sat obdurate till only he and Ils remained. "A haven . . ." he grated. "At almost any other time I would trust Kermorvan's judgment, whether it sprang from heart or mind. But not here. He is too deeply wrapped in ancient glories, he desires them true!"

She answered him softly. "And may they not be, after all? Slow I should be to remind any human of this save you, Elof, but we duergar may live three times your short span, and more. Andvar was little short of his three hundredth year. Yet we are close kin. Is it then so impossible that . . ."

He turned on her, and the concern he read in her dark eyes angered him further. "Longer, yes! Not forever! And not unaged, unchanged! Andvar was ancient, not hale as these. Can you see no difference between three hundred years and a thousand?" Impatience drove him from his chair. He glared at the hillside beyond, carpeted so thoroughly in trees that its contours could be seen only in their summits; in just the same way must this place reveal the mystery at its foundations, if only he could trace the shape. "Kermorvan says we do not know enough, and I agree. But in such a mood what will he learn? And you others are as bad!" Ils put a plump hand on his shoulder, but he shook it off. "Go, sleep then! Dream your dreams with the rest! I'd sooner be sure when I am awake!" He repented his discourtesy even as he spoke, but as he turned with an apology on his lips a door closed softly, and he was alone.

That night there were no dreams for him; no sleep would come, though weariness burned in his limbs and his eyes grew sore outstaring the darkness. At last, as faint grayness glowed in the door louvers, he slipped from his bed and pulled on his breeches. A thought struck him, and he looped his sword belt over his shoulder before padding out barefoot onto the balcony and down the stairs, keeping to their margins lest they creak. But they did not, so solid was their making; he felt the polish of the wood under his bare feet, and wondered how it was maintained. All un-

bidden, there arose in his mind a vision of feet passing
back and forth, the bare feet of the Guardians, the light
court shoes of the others, back and forth, back and forth,
while in the world beyond the Forest centuries paced by
. . . He bit his lip in irritation. He had come to the galleries round the great court; better he should stay alert.
But when he peered down into its shadows, he saw nothing
stirring save the foliage of the vast oak, and he made his
way very carefully down onto the cold flagstones beneath.
He eyed the branches as he tiptoed over the stone and into
their deeper shadow; he could imagine *alfar* asleep in
them. But he saw nothing. Still he hesitated; was he not
being precipitate, risking offense to seek what might be
shown him in due course? Should he not wait? But he
dared not abide that risk, to himself or his friends; he was
bound to try. Drawing a deep breath, he pressed both
palms to the ancient trunk before him.

He felt nothing, save the gnarled bark beneath. He
waited, and there was still nothing, not even the sensation
he remembered, as of a window closed upon him. With
slow care he shaped within his thoughts a clear memory,
a voice immense and commanding that seemed to be borne
from vast distances upon a gusty wind, yet fell upon his
mind rather than his ear. He shaped that voice a name, a
name of power and meaning. But still no answer came.
At last, impatient at the graying sky, he shrugged and
turned away. Just then a sudden flurry broke out within
the tree, and he snatched for his sword. Then he had to
stop himself laughing aloud, for a very small green bird
bounced out onto a limb level with his face, and peered
at him with bright fearless eyes. Two more fluttered down
from above and sat ruffling their feathers and preening.
Another hung upside down from a lower bough, peering
at him dubiously, cocking its head with such an absurd air
of wisdom that he had to grin. He whistled to them softly,
and in an instant he had a whole flock of them bouncing
and shrilling their cries around his head. He laughed and
cursed all at once; their row might alert somebody. He
glared impatiently at the graying sky. He must needs wait,

and try again when he could; he fought down the urge to beat on the trunk with his sword hilt.

That will not be necessary.

Elof jumped in fright, and whirled round. That voice came from no human throat. Nor was it in the least like that immense windblown voice, or any other he could imagine; it was weird, at once fluting and sharp, musical yet incisive, cold and clear as spring water. "Who are you?" he gasped. "How do you know my thoughts?"

Do you not know me, One Alone? Truly, men forget too soon, without my aid. Yet once I used you well when you were within my power, and gave you aid. I hear it served you.

"T-Tapiau?" whispered Elof. "It served me well, yes, and I have not forgotten. But I . . . your voice has changed . . ."

It has not. I have no voice, or I have all voices within my domain. When last we met I spoke in that which is nearest to me, the secret voice of trees. But there are many others, and not all can hear them, or understand. But you have tasted the blood of the worm. Look up.

Mutely Elof obeyed, squinting into the high branches. He found himself meeting the beady gaze of one of the little green birds, bobbing and twittering among the leaves just above his face. Elof returned the look incredulously; one tiny bird could hardly produce that vast voice. Then another chirruped, and another, and in the shifting harmony and discord of their voices he heard a higher music take shape, a clear ringing line, expressive as a song, that grew more distinct as more and more of the little flock took up the song. Then, like a chorus in sudden unison, they were forming words. *You touched the tree, as before, and your thoughts are strong. Well, would you know more?*

Elof felt the shiver of apprehension once again. Roc's sleeping giant had awoken, and turned a cold eye hither. It might be better if he appeared not unduly curious. "Whatever you see fit to tell, Lord of the Forest . . ."

There is nothing to conceal. Did you doubt the folk of Lys Arvalen? Yet as they name themselves, so in veriest truth they are. You see and speak with the very men and women of the ancient realm of Morvan, who fled it at its fall, a thousand winters past.

Elof felt coolness pass over him, a breath of great wonder and great fear. ''Then, Lord of Trees, since it is you who says this, my doubts are at an end. But how came this marvel to be?''

Through my will. In bitter distress I found them astray in my realms, and I gave them shelter. They honor me as the Preserver, and well they may. For all but alone among the ancient Powers am I, in holding true to my primal trust. I take the part of all that lives, of life itself. To the wasting Ice, to the renegade Powers whose domain and weapon it is, I am sworn and bitter foe. So long ago I gave thought to the survival of men, and set aside this land as a haven for them. Here they find a safe refuge not only from the Ice, but from disorder, from disease, even from death. And from all else that the fleeting years may bring. Here they may live wholly as they wish, free to do as they will, save where it would injure or endanger another. Though few would wish to, when they are relieved of their own needs and fears. What more could men wish for, than that?

Elof shook his head, barely able to take in what he was being told. ''Lord of the Forest, it is hard to imagine . . .''

Very well, then. I charge you, tell all I have told you to your companions, to your lord. You came seeking a new home for yourselves and your folk, a harbor and a refuge against the menaces the Powers of the Ice unleash in the world. Tell them they have found it! Tell them that they need search no further, least of all into the east, long dead and decayed. Within the wide realms of the Forest, greater even than your own lands, there will be room for all. I bid you stay among us, and in due time, when plans have been laid and preparations made, all your folk also. Tell the lord Kermorvan!

And with that, as suddenly as it had come, the voice was gone. The little birds bounced and chirped no less eagerly than before, hopping and squabbling like living emeralds among the leaves, shrill heralds of the growing dawn. But the unison note, the chime of meaning, had vanished from their cries. Elof, his head still ringing with what he had heard, sat down on a bench beneath the tree and watched them a moment, enjoying their antics. He was rising to return to his bed when he heard light footsteps come into the hall, and became acutely conscious of himself, half-naked, armed like some lurking outlaw; he did not want these proud lordlings to find him thus. He stepped over the bench and crouched down.

Two figures crossed the hall, but close entwined, a tall man and a woman speaking in soft voices. He recognized neither, though they might well have been among the crowd he had met. Gray forms in the gray light, they stopped before a door and there embraced and kissed, briefly, almost passionately. The woman leaned back in the man's embrace, and raised her arms above her head. He touched her fingertips with his own, and ran them very lightly down her arms to the shoulders of her robe. That he parted, laying bare her breasts, tracing their contours with his fingers which cupped and caressed in a smooth, slow gesture. She turned then, a door opened, golden light spilled out across the gray stones and they were gone.

So love still endured among immortals! Elof smiled. He had it in him to feel embarrassed at his intrusion, and yet he could not. In the embrace, in the caress, there had been something so detached, so formal, that it seemed almost ritual, symbolic, far removed from the intricacies of passion. It was beautiful, as a dance was beautiful; yet it held as little involvement. He could not caress any fair woman so dispassionately, let alone one he truly loved. To touch Kara thus . . . The idea ran molten silver through him, quickened his breath; it disturbed him bitterly as he clambered the weary stairs back to his room. But at least his mind was no longer churning over the marvels he had been told. And from the moment he cast himself down on his bed he slept long and deeply, and dreamed, so far as he remembered, not at all.

CHAPTER SIX

The Snow on the Forest

Kermorvan took what Elof had to tell him with great calm. "It could not have been otherwise. I should have trusted what my heart told me. They are too real, too alive, these great folk of old." His eyes shone bright as a child's. "And it is given to me to walk among them, to speak with them, to dwell with them . . ." He shook his head in sheer wonder.

"To dwell with them . . ." Elof echoed him, his voice even and quiet. "You trust Tapiau, then? You are determined to do as he wishes?"

"Hardly!" said Kermorvan hastily. "Not so soon! Many questions must yet be answered. But how will I do that, save by staying here awhile? I dare not neglect such a chance, I would be failing my folk if I did. And on the face of it, this place is truly fair."

Looking around, Elof had to agree. It was late afternoon, for all the travelers had slept far into the day, himself longest of all. The warm sun shone golden on the walls of stone and wood, and even he found himself admiring their noble symmetry, the graceful sweep of the shingled roofs above them, and the richly colored carvings and reliefs that covered so many of them, hitherto hidden by the darkness. High about the outer walls coursed carven tangles of foliage like petrified creepers, delicate yet strong, their intricate coils ensnaring graceful harts whose lifted heads strained forever after leaves that would never

172

bend. All around this tower's winding stair a dragon wound its coils and clasping wings, only to throw back its head in agony near the summit, where a warrior's sword had pierced it through; by contrast, about the balcony crowning the tower the heavenly bodies danced a graceful sarabande. Round the inner walls of the great court itself immense sweeps of painted waves arose in low relief. Across them silhouettes of proud ships glided, a fleet of great majesty with the sunrise behind their sails. But on the rear wall a gale seemed to sweep through the grain of the wood; the waters were storm-tossed, breaking against the very eaves, the sky dark with clouds. On all the angry ocean one shape alone was seen, a tall dark figure battling with the ragged sail of a small boat.

However unwillingly, Elof was in sympathy with Kermorvan. He of all men could not easily seek out evil among such evident craft and care and love of fair things. And his first fears had received a sharp setback, as a group of Guardians appeared to bring food. They no longer seemed so weird to him, so unnatural; their long limbs and strange hands and feet were simply different, shaped by and for their tree-borne lives as he would shape his tools. As well hate the sleekness of a seal because the sea shaped it, or the large wise eyes of the duegar in the shadows under stone. And among the Guardians he was startled to see their old folk, and their children. These were of all ages from infants to youth, and very fair in their fashion. The sun ran molten bronze in their hair and their freckled skins, and set green lights dancing in their wide eyes. They were livelier than their elders, and a merry word could often win a shy smile, as Tenvar soon found out. And through them the adults lost some of their reserve, and would talk. To Elof the childlike quality Korentyn had mentioned seemed more an alert but unformed intelligence, verging on the animal in its disregard of all but things immediate or imminent; even the oldest, with lined faces and graying hair, seemed no less casual and heedless than the young. The coming feast was all they cared about, at which they would be both servers and guests; they seemed to find equal delight in both, and would talk of little else in their harsh gusty voices. So ere long Elof left them, and went to lie in the shade and clear his troubled mind. That the Guardians should have children and grow old accorded very ill with his first wild guesses about this castle, and left him muddled and unsure.

All that day long the travelers rested, eating and drinking as they would. Korentyn came to see that they had all they wished, but otherwise left them to themselves. They slept as well once more, and on the morrow rose again as late as they pleased. The Guardians showed them sweet springs and pools around the hillside beneath the tower where they might bathe. Though the water was cold as the rock it flowed from, it cleansed them of the taints of travel, and brought a tingling life back to stiff limbs. On their return their old garments were gone; laid out in their place was rich garb of the fashion the castle folk wore. Elof was startled to see the black tunic and hose of a smith laid out for him, the more so as they were heavily woven with thread of silver and gold about wrist and collar, a pattern of characters and symbols he found strangely familiar. Yet it was not until he ran his fingers over the meshed bullion that he remembered. He fetched from his pack the ancient crook-tipped rod of bronze he had once used as a cattle goad, and which he guessed must once have been something more. He stared in astonishment at the semblance of the characters before him; they were the same as on that rod, and in the same order. Only the arrangement was different, the pattern laid out round the collar and repeated in two halves at the wrists. Black distrust welled up in him once more; had he not set some of these characters upon the mindsword itself, that dark distortion of his inborn craft? Those characters had channeled virtues of compulsion and command. With narrowed eyes he stared hard at the broideries, but could see no shimmer of living light deep within them, nor could his fingers trace out in them the thrill of presence that lay within the rod. Which was, after all, as it should be; the more potent the pattern, the more bound it was to the material and shape it was meant for, and if transferred or copied it should be meaningless. Tentatively he lifted the tunic and drew it slowly over his head; he relaxed as he felt no influence, no trace of difference come over him. But in smoothing the material down, his fingers told him one more truth; it was not new, it had been worn before, and trimmed to his stature. What smith had passed that way before him, wearing about him as a token that strange patterning? And where was he now?

One by one the others of the company appeared in their finery, some uneasy, some, like Tenvar, positively strutting. But every head turned when Ils appeared in a billowing gown of white kirtled with silver, for nothing could have contrasted more with her habitual black jerkin and breeches or kilt; its flowing line lessened the square duergar frame, and set off her curly black hair and her sparkling eyes. Tenvar went so far as attempting to kiss her hand, before he caught the dangerous gleam in her eye and thought better of it. Only Kermorvan was missing, and Elof was about to remark on that when footsteps sounded on the upper stair. Into the gallery stepped Korentyn, about his shoulders tunic and heavy mantle blue as dark seas, and with him Kermorvan, clad exactly as he, but in green; about their heads were fillets of gold set with gems, about their throats collars like ropes of rare metals wrought and twisted. To Elof's eye those jewels shimmered and flashed like sunlit water; strong virtues dwelt in them, that wove about their wearers an enhancement of their kingliness and power. The Guardians hid their eyes as from the sun and made obeisance; after a moment Elof and the other travelers bowed also. And when at that night's dinner the two lords led the travelers down the steps into the Hall of the Tree, a loud fanfare and music of instruments heralded their coming, and the whole lordly company bowed as reeds to the imperious wind.

All the travelers were seated at Korentyn's own table, set now upon a high dais beneath the tree; on the right of his tall chair he placed Kermorvan, beside him the lady Teris, and on the left side Elof and Ils. There was much

ceremonial about the dinner, but little solemnity; the talk
was soon flowing merrily enough, not least with Gise and
Merau Ladan holding forth on hunting. Only Elof was
silent, gazing around at the bright folk of the court, trying
to imagine the burden of a thousand years of memories in
his own mind; was there enough of any man to fill such a
space of lifetimes? It felt almost beyond his understanding, like so much else in this place, and that irked him.
He could not accept it as blindly as the others seemed to;
he must keep his distance from it, study it as dispassionately as some trial piece simmering at his forgefire. Then
he would judge it, not before. But his dark thoughts were
interrupted by Korentyn, pouring wine for him and smiling in his wise way which disarmed all ire. "Well, sir
smith? This is very old wine, will you not try it? Your
new garb becomes you well. I trust it is to your measure?"

"Very well, my lord. But if you will forgive the question, whose was it once?"

"Ah!" chuckled Korentyn. "So you noticed that? I
hope you were not offended. From what I hear of you, he
would have counted it an honor to have you wear it. Now
what was his name? A friend, and it escapes me, shame-
fully . . . Thyrve, that was it! Thyrve, a northerner as you
are by your speech, and a man commanding a boundless
craft and skill. Why, even Lord Vayde respected him, who
was himself a great smith. It was Thyrve's livery."

"Livery?" Elof had never heard of a smith wearing any
formal garb save his guild's.

"Aye! He was the king's chief smith. Did you not guess
that from the pattern?" For a moment the prince's kindly
vagueness fell from him, and his eyes glittered as he gazed
into infinite distance. "It lives in my mind, though long
it is since last I saw it. Long since Keryn gave it secretly
into the hand of Ase our sister, she whom we called the
Deep-Minded, to take westward and hold there for his
son. Is it not the symbol of the power the smith sets in
the hand of the king? Is it not the pattern on the Great
Scepter of Morvan itself?"

How that meal ended Elof never knew. He must have eaten, held converse, taken his leave in some kind of dazed trance, for it was like an awakening when he found himself alone in his bedchamber, the bronzen rod cool in his clutching fingers. In the keeping of Ase it had been; but Kerbryhaine had cast out Ase with the other northerners, who had then founded the realm of Nordeney. So what might Asenby mean, where he had had his rough raising, but the settlement of Ase? A remote place where such a treasure might be hidden, and in time even forgotten, till it found such use as a gaggle of peasants might have for an instrument of kingship and command. Small wonder the Ekwesh chieftain had kept it from the sack of Asenby; his shamans could not have failed to know it for a thing of ancient power. A greater mystery was how Elof himself could have been so blind. Yet even as he remembered with a shudder how casually he had used it to tug and prod the huge cattle about, he felt the shimmer and flux within it fade and shrink to a distant gleam; he thought of it in a king's hand, and to his inner eye it burned with a warm golden flame. Startled, he let it dim once more, overwhelmed by the strangeness of his destiny. For all he knew, the sole purpose of his whole existence might be to restore this heirloom of power to hands that owned it by right. But whose hands were those? He knew one with a good claim; but now he had found another. That was too good a recipe for strife. Decisively he wrapped the scepter in its soft leathers once again. Kermorvan was his friend, he would tell him before he told Korentyn; but he would tell neither yet.

The days of ease that followed held no more shocks for Elof. Indeed, they seemed to lessen the impact of all that had passed, making familiar what had felt so strange. Resolve as he might to keep apart from the court, he soon found it would not let him. In truth, as Roc and Ils delighted in pointing out, the fault was his own. In his way he was fair of face, and his withdrawn, thoughtful manner, together with the rank and power his new garb suggested, brought him into notice among the ladies of the court, and great demand. At every turn he was greeted with a mixture of awe and breathless interest that few men could ignore, fewer still fail to enjoy, especially as young as he. Nonetheless it made him impatient; somewhere was Kara, and all the fair of Lys Arvalen could not for a moment take her place. Their attentions he enjoyed, but he found the courtly company and manners exhausting, suffocating, as rich and heavy as the garments and the hangings on the walls, and as dulled with age. Even Korentyn's unfailing kindness and courtesy began to seem bland, almost sickly. Worse, Kermorvan, who greatly revered him, was taking on the same airs, and losing or curbing those flashes of spirit, even arrogance, which had seemed so much part of him.

"Ach, it's not so bad," protested Roc. "Might be this lass Teris that's taming him, and who's to blame him for that? You've just got a morning head on you, or it's stale you're getting."

"Stale?" laughed Elof bitterly, ducking his head beneath the chill spring waters to clear it. "Worse than that! That feeling is with me still, that my past is slipping away beneath these trees! As if there's always been Forest, nothing but Forest, no place, no time beyond the shadow of these boughs that weigh upon my soul. And it grows worse! Even my craft fades, all the mystery and the scholarship. Small wonder, perhaps; among this world of things that grow, the arts that dwell in metal are scant service! What can I shape or smelt there, cast or hammer?"

"Well, find yourself something else to do! Go hunting, like Gise; he's off already with that great lout Merau. Tomorrow I'm going myself, with Ils and the other lads, all save Arvhes and Tenvar who won't be budged from the court. Why not tag along?"

"Hunting? What else have I done since I came here? Fisher, forester, hunter, gatherer, till my mind rots like the leaf mold!"

Roc rolled on his back and kicked up water. "You've

turned fisher and gatherer before, have you not, upon the Marshlands? You almost liked the life!''

"Aye, but there I had my smithy to balance them, and a useful service to do. Here I've nothing."

"You've your tools, and mine; you could tinker up something. What you need's a spot of hard work! Sweat all this holidaying out of your bones with some good honest craft."

"Work?" sighed Elof. "What meaning has labor here? And what place for it? How could I begin it without furnace, forge or library?"

Those may be found.

Elof twisted round sharply in the water. It was a voice clear and unhuman as before, but of a wholly different timbre. And it had not come from any of the trees around the pool, but from the rocky source of the spring itself. "What is it?" barked Roc. "What d'you hear?"

"The spring! The falling water . . ."

What you need, you may have. Did I not say that in my realm men may live wholly as they wish? You have only to ask, and your needs shall be met. There are metals enough in these mountains, and the hall has many ancient books of lore. Some will treat of your craft; smiths have labored in Tapiau'la ere now. Build your forge where you will. May your work bring you peace of mind.

"I heard something," muttered Roc. "A ringing . . . almost like a song . . . water in my ears, maybe!" He shook his head to clear them.

"No," said Elof, swimming up to the base of the little fall, and listening to the water hammering upon the stone. He felt suddenly alive and excited, his mind flooding with thoughts of what precious books a smith of old might have carried with him as he fled. And below them stirred the germs of a venture deep and perilous. "Tapiau spoke. He suggested, as you did, that I can try my craft here; I may, indeed. He has many voices, as he said. But how many eyes, I wonder, and ears?" To that the waters made no answer. Yet in the weeks that followed he was to hear the voice of the Forest again.

It was a time in which he grew increasingly alone. Roc went off on his hunt, and with him Bure, Borhi and even Ils; Arvhes and Tenvar seemed happy to lose themselves in courtly pleasures. Kermorvan was with Korentyn, plying him with questions about Morvan and other ancient lore, or with Teris; how serious that attachment was Elof could not guess. But though Elof could have found company enough in the court, he shunned it. An idea had been set in his mind, a spark lit that would not go out; his craft would not leave him be. He had found his purpose, and till he achieved it he could not rest.

Korentyn gladly gave him leave to search through all the castle's store of books, but at first his search seemed likely to be fruitless. It was chiefly chronicles and romances of old that had been well tended, and in some cases recopied; fascinating as he found many of these, they were distractions he had no need of. Books on almost any skill or craft he found dirty, neglected, in some cases even crumbling to fragments, as leaves to mold upon the forest floor. But he cleaned and patched what he could with fine cloth or parchment scraps pared thin, and drew rich rewards. There were a few elementary books, but his capacious memory already held all they could offer. It was lost works he hoped for, texts as rare and arcane as those upon which the Mastersmith had mounted his most deadly guard. Elof was not disappointed. From beneath a disorderly pile of histories he recovered one full scroll of the *Ircas Elyn*, an exhaustive treatise on symbols the Mastersmith had known of, but could never find. He had not dared hope for the *Skolnhere-Book*, yet he found an excellent copy on fabric, with many interesting marginalia, lying forgotten atop dust-lined shelves. The rarest work of all he found was the minor but fascinating *Daybook of Ambrys*, an accomplished armorer of Morvannec a century or so before Korentyn's day; smiths valued it chiefly for its brief quotations from even more obscure tracts, and its illustrations, so finely drawn they were a copyist's nightmare, for they could not be copied with blocks. It was one of these that caught his eye, and set an idea dancing in his mind. But it danced with doubt and fear, and a chill of revulsion at the cruelty he could not now avoid.

Nevertheless, that same day he went to Korentyn and sought leave to build a forge. To lessen the risk of fire, it would be made all of stone, and well beyond the castle walls, in a clearing by a stream on the slopes above. As he had expected, leave was given gladly, and more; Almayn remembered that some equipment still remained from an old smithy, and Korentyn called upon the strongest among the *alfar* to labor for him. Under Elof's direction, in the weeks that followed, they willingly stripped a wide square of the clearing floor to the bedrock, while others hauled down great chunks of granite, raw and iridescent, hewn from the mountainflanks above. The walls they raised were crude, but thick and strong, fit to bear the single great slab he set across them as a roof, like some monument of old; he would have no wooden beams, he said, lest they scorch. The slatted shutters he made of slate for the same reason, hinged upon pins of iron he hammered out on a riverside rock. He hung more slate upon an iron frame to make a door, and stacked outside it the firewood the Guardians brought him. His high hearth was built of dry stone, and around it were set a quenching-tank of pitched slate, and stone slabs and benches to work at. Last of all, dragged up the slopes by a crowd of laughing *alfar*, came what he had salvaged from the old smithy: a bellows engine, much restored and given new leathers, and a great anvil of a shape strange to him. Ancient and rust-cloaked it was, yet when he smote it with his hammer it rang true, sharp and defiant against the Forest's infinite whisper.

With these they brought such tools, clamps and vises as were still usable, and also the store he had found there, a very hoard of metals and gems in all stages of working, many rare and precious. They told him cheerfully that the mountains held as much more of such toys as he could desire; if he would sooner hunt dull stones than quick beasts they would gladly take him. With that, laughing, they took their leave, not lingering for his thanks, leaping with startling strength for the pine boughs overhead. Elof looked after them, and nodded to himself, thoughtfully; such a hunt among the mountains might serve many ends.

He sat down then by the door that was his, and gazed out over the wooded hillside. It brought back to him the mountain woods of his youth, only a few years behind him yet an age away. In many ways he had been happiest then, but he could never forget that only lies and corruption had lain beneath. He could no longer take happiness as a gift, without price or obligation, or trust good fortune he did not wholly understand. If Kermorvan was learning to trust his heart more, then Elof had learned to trust his less. Idyllic as Lys Arvalen seemed, he would, he must, delve out the truth that lay at its root. And to that end he had shaped this forge.

He reached for Gorthawer, leaning against the wall, slid it halfway from the scabbard, and studied the shadow the black blade cast. Warm and deep and dark, it seemed to flow over the ground like viscous ink, merging with the thousand shadows of the wood; the talisman was strong here, as should be expected. Swiftly Elof rose and swung back the heavy door, its hinges creaking despite their grease. As he stepped over the threshold the shadow seemed to shrink and fade, falling pale upon the scoured stone at his feet. He nodded thoughtfully to himself, and played the blade carefully all around the little forge, and most carefully over the water in the trough, and over the least of the stone slabs, always watching the shadow intently. But nowhere did it grow the least trace darker. He sheathed Gorthawer then, and took it outside with him once more, and sat down in the sun with a sigh. Beneath that small slab lay the only wood within the walls, the cedar lining of the chest wherein he stored his precious books against damp and smoke; even that he had immured within pitch and stone. There would be no more, save what was already burned to charcoal. He had guessed aright.

Now he must look to his materials. He reached for the heavy hide sack that held the ancient hoard, and spilled it

out over the sun-warmed ground before him. It was dazzling wealth that glittered there, but a smith's eye measured potential more profound than mere value. And what
he saw he found strange indeed. Many pieces were so
advanced it was possible to deduce the cunning design
intended, the subtle virtue half set upon them. Yet all such
pieces had been left unfinished, even where no fault or
flaw could possibly have barred their completion. So en-
grossed was Elof that he scarcely noticed a fish rise to a
deerfly struggling on the stream. Yet in the splash and
spurt of bubbles the babbling music of the water was suddenly, subtly, altered.

*So, smith. Are you now content? Or do you doubt still
the warmth of your welcome here?*

Elof bowed his head courteously to the empty air. "I
would be ungrateful, Lord of the Forest, if I did not believe you wished me to stay and be happy. Yet when I
strayed into your domain in the Westlands far away, you
at first bade me and my companions begone. Why, then
. . . or do I give offense?"

The waters chuckled lightly over the pebbles in the shallows, where small birds bobbed and picked. *You do not.
The question is fair. I traced in you . . . something . . .
that made me believe you other than you are.*

How so, Lord of the Forest?

Is such sight to be fettered in the weak thoughts of men?
The stream ran on in quiet a moment, dead leaves whirling
on its surface. *Say, then, that most men . . . cast shadows
in my mind. Shadows that vary, some lighter, some blacker.
But you, you are no shadow, you are like some shifting
glimmer in the Forest depths. Very like, indeed; for the
Forest is my mind.*

"Then why fear to have me in it?" asked Elof boldly.
"It harbors many a blacker thought than I."

The tall trees stooped and bobbed, looming dark over
the forge. *It was for one such I took you. I did not know
you for a smith among men. Aware of forces within you, I
thought you an elemental, a minor Power, astray in my
land without my leave, and perhaps a danger to my folk.*

That I could not tolerate. You should understand; you have met some, the dwellers in river and lake, and the Hunt.

"Do you not tolerate them? Many of my companions they took, good men and bad alike. Why hedge your land about with such horrors, if all men are as welcome as you say?"

The water swirled and gurgled, and its note grew deeper. *You are bold, smith, so to bandy words with one of the Powers, and not the least. If I were as ill disposed as you suspect, would I need to answer you? I harbor such creatures out of two concerns, and the greater is pity.*

"Pity?"

Even so. Where else have they to dwell? Those creatures, and many others it is well you did not meet, they have needs and ways of life that would seem wholly strange to you. In the world outside, the world of men, their day is past; what parts and purposes they once had in the world's shaping they have outlived, but they have grown used to their existence, forgetting or fearing the changes for which the time has come. That I condone, for I know how hard such changes may be; once this was a world of forest, smith, before the days of men. So under my trees I afford them shelter, and they guard the borders of my realm. And guards I must have. For though I wish men well, I cannot allow them in their wasteful ignorance to devastate my land, which will one day be their surest refuge. The alfar love their children, yet will they let them play with flame? Had I no sentinels, the trees would be hewn down to feed fires or build shacks, the animals hunted to extinction, the whole ancient cycle of plenty torn asunder when it might have provided for all. For now I must endanger a few lives, that one day, when the works of men totter to their fall, I may receive them whence they should never have strayed, back into the embrace of nature. Then shall I throw open my borders, and welcome all. And that day may not be long removed. In it I shall need great leaders; Korentyn for one, your friend Kermorvan, the lady Ils for her folk. And, if I mistake you not, you also shall be among them. Reflect on that among your labors!

That evening, as Elof strode back down the hill to the castle, he saw trails of torches winding among the trees below. He guessed it must be the hunting parties returning for the following night's feast, and hastened to greet them as they set down their catch on the greens-ward before the gate. Roc and Ils greeted him in boisterous good spirits; he had to endure much chaffing for laziness till he managed to tell them of the forge. They in their turn had something to tell him, for they had fallen in with another party, among whom was Morhuen, the renowned bard, coming to the feast. "Though he was scarce willing, till I told him of Kermorvan!" added Roc. "And who'd blame him? That's a fine carefree life he's been leading out there with the *alfar*, Elof! Do you be sure and try it some day!"

Elof smiled. "Perhaps I will, and soon. Would you go hunting metals in the mountains once again, Roc, as we did in the old days? And you, Ils? I thought you might!"

She laughed. "Where'd you be without me? Humans lack the eye for how the stone lies. And we'll see if *alfar* can beat duergar after *that* game!"

Roc snorted. "I'll be along to pick up the pieces. As usual. But for the nonce, nothing comes 'twixt me and my dinner, save a good bathe. Let's go in!"

All that evening and the next day the court was awhirl with excited preparations for the coming feast. But Elof was beginning to suspect they looked forward to such celebrations not only to break the monotony, but to lay down for a while burdens which had grown intolerable, their own natures. And when at last Korentyn and Kermorvan led them in solemn procession into the great court, glittering now with the strange lamps that had been hung even among the mighty oak's leaves, it was not long before his suspicions were confirmed. As the night advanced, he found the wine and music and dancing flowing together into a single inexorable current of ritual revelry. In its constant shift and change these strange folk could truly lose themselves, subdue the pain of thought to the stiff intricacies of the dance, disperse the pain of feeling in brief flirtations, spinning from one partner to another as heedless as the least-lived mayfly by the stream. Korentyn took no active part, but he presided over the rout with amused indulgence.

Only one of his folk seemed to take little joy in it all, the bard Morhuen, though many songs of his making were played. He was a gangling creature with shaggy white hair and beard, although in face and bearing he seemed scarcely older than Korentyn by whose side he sat. He heeded that honor no more; he shifted uncomfortably in his robes and spoke few words to any save Korentyn and the Guardians who waited upon him. His light blue eyes stared vaguely into remoteness, and at the many compliments paid him his full lips worked nervously. At the height of the feast Korentyn ceremonially presented him to the travelers, and it was only when his eye lit upon Kermorvan that the look in it became bright and alert, his bow deep and reverent. "For I see that all I was told of you is true!" he said, and his voice rang clear and strong. "You might indeed be my dear lord Keryn come once again."

I see in you a promise, and a token
That hope dies not with one day's ending,
That by one winter summer is not broken,
That springs may follow which shall flower as fair.
So may the tower arise, once to the earth cast down,
And on the humbled brows, there shall be set a crown.

There was a sudden rattle of applause, as if a breath of mountain wind licked through the hall's heavy air. "May it be so!" barked Korentyn, and raised his glass in a fierce toast; then, as if ashamed of his outburst, he smiled and sat down, and the brief tremor of excitement faded.

"Ah, marvelous!" breathed Teris, who was seated between Elof and Kermorvan, and shook her auburn hair delightedly. "Oh, and so very long it has been since he managed a verse thus, all of a moment! Master Morhuen, Master Morhuen, won't you sing us something? With the harp, if it please you?"

The bard bowed. "Never have I been able to refuse you

aught, *a'Terisec*, even if there were not these new guests to honor. I wax old, but I will essay . . .'' He paused as he met Elof's interested gaze. ''What is this?'' he puzzled, aloud yet almost to himself. ''What is *this?*'' A feeble terror flickered in his eyes. ''Do all the faces of fallen Morvan arise and walk abroad this night?''

''Master Morhuen!'' cried Teris, shaken. ''This is discourtesy! Here sits Elof the Smith, to whom my lord Korentyn presented you only a moment since . . .''

Elof leaned forward. ''I am not offended, lady! Korentyn also saw some likeness in me, but to whom he could not say. Can you, master?''

But Morhuen glanced at him with a mixture of confusion and distrust, touched his long fingers to his forehead and mumbled a word or two. Suddenly he turned away to where Korentyn and Kermorvan were in lively dispute over what he should sing. Teris seized Elof's arm, and her hair tickled his ear. ''Now you see why Merau calls him an old fool!'' she whispered, stifling a giggle. ''But he's so sweet, truly, and the way he sang for us, in the old days . . .'' Elof hardly heard; he was too acutely aware of her touch, the quiver of her breast against his arm as she chattered, the sweet scent of her, like flowers warmed by the strong sun of the south. Probably she was unaware of the effect she was making; she had set her cap firmly at Kermorvan. But Elof found himself fighting for resolve; too easy, too natural to be tempted, the more so with the frustrations that knotted inside him, and the wine. To let himself be seduced, to linger, to delay a quest he had no real reason to believe could succeed. He was immensely relieved when Teris drew free of him to join the applause as Morhuen stepped out onto the open floor before the tree.

Elof, seeing him afoot for the first time, caught his breath; the bard was not merely gangling, he was grotesque, his flowing robes concealing an odd shambling gait, as on limbs sorely twisted. From among the many groups of musicians in the hall, harps were thrust out to him; he made great play of picking the best and having its owner tune it to a particular fineness. Then he swept to the center of the floor, bobbed a bow to the court and announced, "By the will of our chiefest guest Keryn, Lord Kermorvan . . ." He chuckled deferentially. "And counter to the wish of our modest Prince Korentyn, I will sing the Deeds of Korentyn Rhudri at Lastreby!"

Kermorvan leaned across Teris to whisper to the travelers, "A ballad in the ancient mode. Lastreby was a hill town in Morvan north of the Waters, whose heroic last defense Korentyn led, his first great deed." Morhuen tucked the harp into the crook of his long left arm, and poised his long fingers carefully. Then he swept them down to a single chord that shivered off the ancient stones, merging a voice of metal as clear and bright as the harpstrings, youthful and heroic.

Hark! Hold you silent! Heroes are sung of,
Such as dared strive with the stern powers of old.
Men who withstood them, who waged war against them,
Harried them back from the heights of the north fell,
Held there till Ice came, that no man may hinder
Cracking and crushing what it could not conquer.

The harp pulsed and sang under Morhuen's fingers, and though the music was strange to Elof, it struck shivering harmonies in the taut strings of his heart. Loud chords rang a tocsin of urgency and alarm on the stresses of the lines, while between them the strings rippled the rhythm of a cantering horse.

Korentyn Rhudri, fiery-haired princeling,
Outrode his escort though rough grew the hillroad,
Fierce in his longing to leap up to Lastreby,
There deal a blow to the armies of darkness,
Strew them like sowings of death on the felltops,
Melt the bleak Ice in the blood of its minions.

Lastreby walls lifted high over hilltops,
Gaunt garth of gray stone ancient and grim. . . .

The harp struck a sudden false note, an ugly dissonance. The bard's voice faltered; he glanced at the strings, striving desperately to regain his fingering, but all at once the tune collapsed, the sound dissolved into a jumble. Morhuen bent forward an instant as if catching breath, then sang on with fervor. But already the spell was broken.

> *White on its battlements weather untimely,*
> *Snow in high summer laid siege to . . .*

He faltered again, repeated *"laid siege to. . . ."* and then stopped altogether, shaking his head, took his trembling fingers from the harp and clenched them tight. When he looked up and around at his audience, distress and shame were so naked upon his countenance that Elof could not bear to look.

Korentyn's face was wrung with concern. "Are you well, old friend? Would you retire . . ."

"No, my lord . . ." The bard's voice was tremulous. "I am sorry . . . I wax old, as I said. The old songs, they fade from my memory. And my fingers grow wasted and weak; I cannot force them to the fingerings of the harp any more. My lords, ladies, old friends and new guests, sorrow is mine that I must withdraw. Never should I have come."

Korentyn raised a hand. "Yet if your fingers fail you," he said encouragingly, "may you not still set words to dance, as you did at the first? For my kinsman here has been through a great adventure in the Westlands, he and his friends, a quest and a mighty siege. No other but you could set the tale in the song it deserves!"

Morhuen's pale eyes seemed to stare almost through him. "Oh, my dear lord, the music is fled from me, the fire is gone out; what then remains? A verse, a line, a fragment; trifles, scraps of bark set afloat upon an endless stream. No great ballad, not even at your behest. Not even yours. One song more I may make, one short . . . but that for you . . ." And suddenly he struck the harp he carried

with the backs of his stiffened fingers, and a sudden lilting
tune flowed from it.

> *Your praise resound,*
> *Prince of the Halls of Summer!*
> *Lord of a court*
> *Whose like shall not return!*
> *At your behest*
> *My songs have brought the past again,*
> *And made to live*
> *All that we loved and lost!*
> *Yet ever more that elder music fails me,*
> *The past grows dim and dark as prison wall.*
> *And stronger now a newer music claims me,*
> *The endless woods bring healing to my soul.*
> *Now I am ever eaten up with yearning,*
> *For freedom in the wild woods I am burning,*
> *Within these walls I find no home,*
> *Free, unhindered I must roam!*
>
> *All praise to you,*
> *Lord of the line of Morvan!*
> *All that I owe*
> *I cannot now repay!*
> *Honor and fame*
> *Have ever been your gifts to me,*
> *No minstrelsy*
> *Has praised a kinder lord.*
> *Yet I am not the man that long has served you,*
> *Though faithful still, I hear another call,*
> *And I am drained of song to set against it,*
> *Bereft of joys that held me in your hall.*
> *Now it is torment to me to remain here,*
> *Save for your kindness, all I find is pain here,*
> *I beg you, loose your claim on me—*
> *My friend, my master, set me free!*

Even as the last long phrase sang from the harp it sagged
and fell, dangled limply from his fingers. He knelt and set

it down gently on the flagstones, its strings still faintly ringing. Elof was shocked to see dark stains upon them, and a heavy droplet fall upon the frame: in Morhuen's struggle to play true they had cut into his very flesh. A murmur ran through the court, a soft troubled sound, and then all was silent. When at last Korentyn spoke, there was a deep tremor in his voice. "For such songs as once you made, old friend, my favor is poor recompense; you owe me nothing. If I can give you no more than leave to go, you have it, and my blessing. But may it not be long before we meet again."

Morhuen made no reply, save to bow deeply ere he strode from the hall. As he reached the high door and flung it wide, he plucked the court robe from his shoulders and flung it to one of the *alfar* waiting there. Elof caught his breath, and a deep unease grew in him. The bard's limbs, left bare by his simple green tunic, were not malformed; they were simply long, terribly long, and he had been standing hunched and uncomfortable to hide them. Yet this was, or had been, a man. The door swung to behind him.

Silence gripped the court, in confusion or shame; Korentyn stared at the bare board before him, his face pale. Around his feet *alfar*, hair and harness thick with garlands, gathered and gazed up at him with wide worried eyes. At length Kermorvan and the lord Almayn, who sat by, exchanged glances; Almayn gestured to the musicians. A flourish sounded, and they struck up a slow stately music. Couples, Kermorvan and Teris among them, rose and glided out into the formal patterns of a dance, sweeping this way and that across the floor in shifting lines as ceaseless and repetitive as waves upon the shore. Korentyn glanced up, but seemed to find little power in it to soothe him. No more did Elof; to him it was a slow torment. But barely had it drifted to its end before an older *alfar*, a mane of white hair hanging to his shoulders, gestured to the musicians quite as airily as Almayn. A drum beat out a slow rhythm; bowed strings sang a livelier tune, deeper plucked strings sounded a stamping, loping beat. A shout arose, and the *alfar* bounded out into the court. Korentyn looked up, startled, then smiled indulgently. Grinning widely, they began to circle the hall, slowly at first then faster, in a loping, bouncing run, arms held high above their heads, flicking their wrists sideways and snapping their fingers in time to the beat. Others, men and women, sprang out to join them, whirling and tossing on their long limbs like storm-sprung saplings. In a great train they wove and gamboled about the tree, wheeling and careering with such abandon that their braided hair flew wild and flung out flowers and garlands which fell among the watchers.

The sudden outburst of vitality brought laughter to Elof's lips, and a spirit of mischief; it reminded him of festivities in his own village, clumsy but cheerful, in which he had often longed to take part. "Now there's a dance!" he cried. With a swift bow to Korentyn he sprang out among the dancers, and seized a pretty *alfar* girl as she went whirling by. He barely glimpsed Ils and Roc hopping out after him before strong arms spun him away into the dance. Tenvar bounded by him with a girl on each arm, his feet scarcely touching the ground, and as Elof came round the tree once more he was startled to see some of the castle folk hovering tentatively on the edge of the throng. He had thought they might be offended, but they seemed more intrigued than scornful at this sudden eruption. At last Svethan the Mariner actually seized a partner and plunged in with gusto; others moved hesitantly after him. Elof all but stumbled as Teris tripped lightly by him, long gown kilted into its golden girdle, pulling Kermorvan after her, laughing wildly; behind them Almayn bounced along with a tall lady of the court, dignity flung like flowers to the wind.

The whole court of immortals seemed to be reveling in its lost decorum. The dance whirled endlessly on, the musicians whisking from tune to tune, circles forming, breaking, re-forming, till many had to fall back to draw breath. Elof was among them; for all his strength, he was at a disadvantage among these longer legs. His partner brushed a kiss on his cheek and bounced back into the throng; he was content to slump down beneath the great tree and let his roaring pulse settle, his dizzy head clear. Round and round they swept, woodfolk and castle folk and his friends, and as he watched them hurtle by a strange thing happened. Half-formed thoughts he had held back took shape in his mind, became a vision. It was as if the dancers sped faster, ever faster, till they merged into a bright, painful blur with a single static figure at its heart, frozen at the crest of a leap. Before his eyes it changed, burgeoned like a tree; the outflung limbs grew longer, the trunk stretched and curved upward like a supple birch, the very feet and fingers stretched out like eagerly grasping roots and tendrils. Then the vision was gone, the dance clear before his eyes. But Elof felt a sickening chill swell up in him, a growing, uncontrollable shiver. He was looking at his vision made flesh, not in one body but in all that flashed by him, in a chain, a sequence, a progression from Kermorvan to Korentyn, from him to long-limbed Merau Ladan, from him to Morhuen. And from his drawn-out, unmanageable limbs to the graceful climbing bodies of the *alfar*. And what of their minds? At best from nobility and wisdom to kindly simplicity, at worst from man to beast? Was that the true dance in the Halls of Summer?

He cursed under his breath. It still made no sense, not as long as the *alfar* had children and knew old age. How could they then be linked to the castle folk, who knew neither? He slapped a hand furiously against the rough bark.

Abruptly the walls seemed to vanish around him, the windblown trees come rushing in on him. Deep in a distant pool, intent on a treasure of glittering scales, an otter plunged; high over the borderless carpet of treetops an eagle screamed and dived, clawing. *The woodfolk are their children.*

Elof swallowed, shook his head, scarcely able to speak. This was not the fluting of birds; it was the first voice he had heard, far off in the west. Only here it was no longer remote and dim; it was all around him, and it blew through his mind like a gusty wind. He should not have leaned against the tree; too much of his secret thought might already be betrayed. But it seemed that only his immediate thought was read.

You have clear sight, One Alone. The alfar *are their children, or children of their kin, and they love and revere their elders, and delight in their service. But can that sight not also show you the reason for the change? For I do not hide it. Here life unending is offered to all, here they may live as they think best. Only offspring must be denied them, for children are a mirror of mortality. Nonetheless, many come to find that gift a burden; often those who grasped it most eagerly at the first endure it least easily in the end. Heroes alone may bear immortality for long, to wrest its glories from its pain.*

Elof clutched at his chest, where it seemed that a sudden stab of pain pierced him. "So that is why so many of the great names of old are gathered here! Lesser men have long since . . . fallen by the wayside."

Deep in the mold beneath a rotting tree a nightsown spore took root and swelled. *No. Not fallen. The longer men live, the less willingly will they embrace the idea of their death. Do not many even in hideous torment cling to that fragile cord of life? And yet they could not return to their old lives in the world outside, when all they knew there has long slipped away. So it is that I smooth their path before them. The wearier they grow of their lives, the less they are aware of time, the more pleasure they find in the passing moments, in the simpler things, growing more like children, like animals, as you guessed. They hunt with the* alfar, *live with them, like them; and as time, which dictates growth and change, fixes its claims upon them once more, they become more like the* alfar *in shape. The past slips from them, and they move into step once more with the great dance of nature. In the end they go off with the* alfar, *and never return; they mate with them, and bear children who are wholly* alfar, *and forget all that once they were. The mantle of mortality settles about them once again; they lead free and happy lives, knowing no difference, and in the end they die in peace, and rejoin the River.*

"But . . ." began Elof sharply, and then stopped short. He could only say too much.

You need not fear such an ending, for yourself or your friends. You least of all, while you burn thus from within. But even if it were otherwise, what then? Is it not worth the venture, to live longer at least than the scant span of men, with naught to fear at its end but forgetfulness and peace? To have time to hone and perfect your craft, to fulfill it with all the resource of my realm at your disposal? Alone among the ancient Powers I truly care for men. I know what is best for them. Through the Forest floor, muffled among the rotten leaves, came the light sound of a footfall. A snake tensed its coppery flanks, its flicking tongue tasting the air for the scent of warm blood.

Elof bowed. "Not for nothing are you named the Preserver, lord. I will take heed of your bounty, and venture to stretch it further. I would go hunt metals in your mountains, with such of my friends as will come."

You have only to ask the alfar. *They will guide you and serve you. May you find what you seek!*

Elof bowed. "Thank you, lord. I believe I will."

But it was not until the third day of their hunt, high on the rocky slopes, that he did so. For though he found many rare substances he might have need of, it was a richer prize he truly sought, the minds of his companions. "It was for that reason I brought you here," he told them.

Kermorvan nodded. "Here where the *alfar* cannot hear us, where no birds perch, where nothing grows, away from the eyes and ears of the Forest. I guessed that much. Well? What more?"

Elof looked unobtrusively over the edge of the narrow rock shelf upon which such of the company as he could gather were huddled. Far below, the *alfar* were preparing a camp among a clump of bristlecone pines. One of them glanced up anxiously, but Elof waved back with a disarming good cheer he hardly felt. He had expected Kermorvan to be horrified at hearing of Tapiau's words, yet he was as calm as ever. "What more? Is that not enough?"

"Why, pray?" demanded Tenvar. "To live forever,

that's a wonder! And yet still be able to escape from it and live in peace, what's so terrible about that?''

"Aye!" laughed Bure. "Like owning land on both banks of the River!"

Kermorvan nodded, though he looked a little unhappy. "I will allow it seems strange. I would prefer to end, if end I must, as my own man, with my own mind; but perhaps that is obtuse, and I would not expect all men to feel likewise. But for others . . . Borhi, how would you choose? And you, Roc?''

'To live . . .'' whispered Borhi softly, without hesitation. "Never face dying no more . . .''

Roc hesitated. "It's a mighty temptation," he muttered. "I can see it might be a burden . . . it's a gamble . . . but then so's every breath you draw . . .''

"Well then," said Kermorvan. "You hear the voice of the citizen." He shrugged. "I see no great harm in it.''

"Do you not?" blazed Elof, so loud he feared the *alfar* below might hear. More quietly he added, "Then look at it as it has taken effect! That architect, Ils; that bard, Kermorvan. What became of them? A hall half built, songs half sung, is that not so?" Ils looked at him uneasily, making no reply, but Kermorvan only shrugged.

"There must be many who could not stay the course, even men worthy and gifted. What of that? Is it not better to fall in a venture, than never to have tried? The more so, when the fall is so merciful, the venture so worthwhile. Has it not saved for this day such as Svethan, as Korentyn?''

"Saved?" echoed Elof, very quietly. "And for this day? I wonder. What might they have achieved in the world outside, these folk, if they had not been prevented from reaching the west? King Keryn's son, your ancestor, would not have lacked support. Korentyn and Ase would have established his throne, as Keryn intended; they would have prevented the bitter sundering of north and south that has so weakened our folk. Instead, what have they done? They have survived; and that is all. Aye, they live. But as what? Shadows in a court of shadows, remote, ineffectual, powerless to help or harm. Korentyn is noble, aye, and kind; he could not be otherwise and still himself. But what else have all these centuries riven from him? Where is the fiery prince he once was, the strong warrior against the evils of the Ice? And Svethan, far from his seas, what meaning has he anymore? And the lady Teris, is she any more than once she was?'' Kermorvan's eye grew bleak and cold, but he held it. ''And what of you? How have you fared, since you came here? What plans have you laid to summon your folk hither, those who depend on you, little though they may know it? When will word be sent back to Ker-bryhaine?''

Kermorvan frowned. ''I cannot act in haste! Do you imagine Korentyn and I have not taken counsel over this, long and deep? This place must first be made ready to receive great numbers, folk must be summoned little by little, as Tapiau decrees, and their doubts resolved. We will need more than a few days to plan such matters, will we not?''

''A few days?'' asked Elof quietly, though chill fingers traced out his spine. ''How long do you imagine we have been here? Roc and the others have been away hunting, I have had a whole forge built for me; it did not take shape overnight!'' He saw the bewilderment in their faces, in Kermorvan's most of all, and he thought back to the night of their coming. ''I wonder how long it has seemed to Korentyn?''

''Ach, that's as Tapiau told you!'' Roc objected. ''No wonder his sense of time's a bit blurred, after all these centuries . . .''

''No?'' muttered Ils uneasily. ''When already it seems to be happening to us? Elof, how long were we gone? It seemed a night or two only.''

''Three weeks, perhaps. Maybe even four; how should I know, if you do not? The forge was three in the building.'' The travelers stared uneasily at each other, but Kermorvan shaded his eyes.

''Perhaps our sense of time fades as our bodies cease to age,'' said Ils quietly. ''Tapiau might not be aware of that, for it seems he takes no form, human or otherwise. But it makes it hard to trust him, now . . .''

"How am I to know?" Kermorvan burst out suddenly. "When you told me of Tapiau's words I believed we had found what we sought! That out of the horrors of the journey I had stumbled on something greater than I had ever dared hope, the past I dreamed of restoring come again . . .''

"Henceforth let none of us be deceived by phantoms of his vanished past!" quoted Elof, darkly. "Whose words were those?"

Kermorvan hammered fist against palm. "But how am I to tell? How can I delve for truth in this morass? What profit would Tapiau find in so ensnaring us, when he could sweep us from the earth with a gesture, or have his creatures tear us to shreds? It makes no sense, Elof! I must have proof! And even if he is our enemy, how shall we fight him, or escape him? How shall we raise hand or will against a living Power?"

Elof hesitated, but in the end, as all the others were silent, he dared to speak. "That will be hard, indeed. But it may be that I can help you. Now that I have my forge . . ." He did not look up, but he felt their eyes upon him.

"You would wield smithcraft against the Powers?" demanded Bure, in doubt and wonder.

"A man must use what he has! I would turn my craft against the Steerers of the Stars if they threatened . . . those things I care for!" The fervor in his own words startled him; speaking without thought, he had bared feelings he hardly knew he had. He was aware as never before of the craft within him, a roaring furnace flame hungry to be used; he bent his mind upon it, and it narrowed to a needle of devouring incandescence, precise, measured, irresistible. "But I had no thought of open battle. Guile is used against us, and is best repaid in the same coin." He turned then to Kermorvan, who had not answered him. "Well? It seems to me that we came upon this place at an evil time for you, when you had begun to doubt your own leadership, your own wisdom in making this journey; perhaps the Forest had already begun to work on you, as it had on me. But I am not of that mind! You are our leader yet. You ask for proof; I will try to find it, though the attempt may be perilous. So perilous that if you choose, if you deem we may trust the Forest so completely, I will pursue it no further. Say now! Which shall it be?''

Kermorvan stood up on the rock, and gazed out over the Forest in silence. But it was only a moment before he spoke, his voice crisp and calm. ''You may try what you will.''

They came down from the mountains laden under many a sack of ores and other stones, which they gladly left at Elof's forge on their way to the castle. But Ils lingered a moment, and Roc at once began to busy himself about the forge as he had so many times in the past. Elof looked at him. ''You need have no part in this, if you do not wish to. Nor you, Ils.''

Ils chuckled, and leaned against the workbench. Roc screwed up his florid features into a ferocious scowl. ''Yours are not the only hands can wield a hammer! Could be ours grow a trifle itchy again, at that. And you'll be needing a brace of good forgehands, if only to pin down the top of your skull now and again. Eh, lady?''

Elof looked at them both, and he smiled. A great weariness seemed to lift from him, a cloud from his spirits. He hooked an arm round Ils' broad shoulders, and rumpled Roc's thick hair down into his eyes. ''Ass! I'm blessed in the pair of you! But I doubt any such task will need many hands. Slow and subtle it will have to be . . .''

''Aye, and secret,'' said Roc quietly. ''You were wondering yourself about the Forest's eyes and ears. We might distract it somehow . . .''

''And share the peril, yes; I know your mind too well now, my lad! But that may not be necessary.'' And he took up Gorthawer, which he was careful to leave outside, and showed them the dwindling of its shadow. ''Tapiau said it would avail me little among the cold stonework of men, and indeed upon Kerbryhaine's walls it faded. There he betrayed a limit to the Forest's power! I guessed that was why Lys Arvalen was completed in wood, not stone; in stone his thoughts cannot dwell! And I guessed also that both he and the castle folk would be wary of fire. So for reasons innocent in themselves I shaped a place within which his power could not extend, a dark spot in his mind.'' He looked around the barren little hut with a feeling of grim satisfaction. ''Within the Forest I built my forge. But within my forge the Forest cannot come.''

Roc blew out an astonished breath. ''Whew! So you've dared turn your craft against a Power already!''

''And succeeded!'' said Ils quietly, her eyes shining.

''Only at the first step,'' cautioned Elof. ''I do not think he has guessed yet, for I have spent little time in here. When I begin my labors he will find out, sooner or later; he will not do anything at first, I guess. He seems more concerned to win me over, for now. But he will not hold his hand forever; I will have only one try at my work. And I do not yet know what that will be.''

Roc stared. ''No idea at all?''

''I did not say that. I know what I need, and I know how hard it will be to achieve, subtler even than the mindsword. For it will brook no compulsion, but seek rather to loosen chains . . .''

Ils drew breath. ''I begin to see. But the craft that would take! And the time! You could use pattern-welding again, or alloying, but the one might be too coarse, the other too fine; you must needs try over and over till you hit upon the balance . . . Elof, little short of mastership will suffice.''

''I know!'' he said, striving to steady the tremor of desperation. ''And how will I find it here? But I have to try!''

''Try indeed!'' said Roc, chewing idly at a grass stem. ''It's often enough you've surprised yourself in the past, let alone me. When you need us, here we are. For now, well, there's your fire lit, bread and meat by your books, your tools laid to hand. And us on our way down to the castle, I think.''

Ils nodded, a little sadly. ''Toward nightfall we'll be back. If only to see that you sleep. I know you, Elof!''

Elof smiled as he watched them trudge away through the trees. Somehow he felt strangely free once more, here in this crude cavern of a forge; he did not understand why until evening, when he looked up from his reading as shadows fell and birds trilled their twilight songs. In his mind's eye reeds hissed in the breeze, and mists rolled silently over them; it was very like his strange old marshland smithy here, that place where he had sought and found healing, and with it himself. He smiled; the memory was newly clear in his mind once more.

He laid down his book. Roc and Ils would have no need to come and fetch him, that night or any other. Haste and worry might lead him to miss something vital. So it was that every evening around nightfall he would walk down alone through the darkling woods, following the path of the stream. And it is told that often in those times he spoke again with Tapiau.

It made him nervous at first, that voice that was many voices, the more so as it seemed well aware of his misgivings. But still it sought to win him over, and he spoke and questioned freely as before, and was told of many wonders. As the late summer drew on toward autumn, he heard the voice among the rush and whistle of the wind in the pines, the solemn thunder of a cataract, and once, fearfully, in the devouring roar of a distant earthslide among the pines. It was then, angry at his fright, that he grew bold enough to ask of Tapiau why he took no single form to speak, if the lesser Powers that haunted his woods could do as much. The deep pools of the stream bubbled up the answer.

It is because they are lesser that they may do so with ease. Would you confine this stream within your trough, this pool within your cup? You would catch only as much as your vessel might hold. So it is with Powers of high order.

"Yet I heard that some may do so, on occasion. The one they call the Raven . . ."

Indeed. Such as we may take human shape, or any other we care to. But in so doing we become only a facet of ourselves. The greater we are, the less easy we find it; forming a body becomes a difficult concern, and its result less like us. More than a man he may be—or she, for gender goes beyond the body—but less, far less than the Power itself. And flesh hangs on us like fetters. There is so much of ourselves, our wisdom and knowledge, that we cannot draw on till we revert to our true shape. Worse, we fall victim to all the strange demands of flesh, and often cope less well than those born into it; many become too like human beings, and may turn strange and willful, pursuing their purposes in odd manner, or even delighting in pleasures perverse or evil along the way. I would not so lose my dignity. Nor would I become so vulnerable; to be injured or destroyed in body is pain and weakening to us, and a lasting drain on our strength, even permanent, in some cases. Few will gladly risk it. And that is as well for your petty races and nations, for the ills the Powers of the Ice now cause are as nothing to what they would do if they could walk freely among men. Vast is their power, singly or together, yet vastly is it bound up in the sheer effort of sustaining the Ice, their most potent weapon. So it is that they tend to shun any true form, remaining immanent around the Ice and their domains nearby. Such is Taoune, whose realm borders upon my own, my mocker, my shadow, my great enemy, Lord of the Withered Marches. At most, when they wish to meet mortal eyes they may take on some half-substantial mask of power and terror.

"I believe I have seen such, benighted once upon the Ice . . ."

I hear it by the shiver in your voice. But being bound thus may force human shape upon them. For where the Ice will not serve them, they must seek out new weapons, new agents apt to their thought.

Elof remembered his late master, and nodded. Then it was as if the Ice clenched a chill fist beneath his stomach, for he guessed at Tapiau's next words ere they were spoken.

Now only the greatest of those cold minds are strong enough to do this, to don the shape they abhor. Once, an

*age past, Taoune was their leader; sustained by his weaker
brethren, he roamed the world and sought to twist weak
men to his fell purpose. But I am the friend of men, and
had the service of many. I wrestled with him, and threw
him down, and drove him back, stripped of his body and
sunken to a shadow of the power that once he owned. In
these days another rules, a clutching, binding spinner of
intrigue who ofttimes walks the world in a fair form to
sway the hearts of men. Veiled so in flesh, she shows but
a small portion of her own great beauty and majesty and
terror; yet I have heard that to men it seems great indeed.*

"What is her name?" choked Elof.

*Taounehtar she is styled, Taoune's deadly consort. But
the creature she becomes among men names herself Louhi.*

Elof remembered little of his walk back that night. He
ate little and slept less, tossing and turning upon the furs
of his bed. Could Tapiau have heard of his own quest, and
seek to turn him aside from it? Perhaps; but while the
Master of Trees might slant a truth, he would not lie so
plainly.

*Louhi also has taken an apprentice . . . if she's Louhi's
she'll be nothing for you and I . . . for what that girl has,
Louhi has, be sure of that . . . no smith welded my chains,
and even if you were the greatest among men you could
not make them . . .* The words of many voices blurred and
burned in his mind, and became one, echoing away into
distances vast and chill. *Nothing . . . you could not . . .*
If Louhi was as Tapiau said, then what was Kara? What
had he dared to love? What had he set out to seek across
all the breadth of this vast land, across all the world if
need be? But then, as if in answer, he heard the dark
timbre of her own words, remembered her heart leap beneath his hand as she spoke. *I am of no common sort . . .
I will not change.* He lay still then, and a bitter calm settled across his thoughts. She would not change? Then no
more must he. What he loved, he loved. It was as simple
as that. He could only go on as he had done, seek with as
single a mind as he had sought to counter the mindsword,
as he had sought to reforge Gorthawer. . . .

It came to him then. From his long search through the remnants of the Mastersmith's library a memory surged up, a matter that had seemed of little moment at the time. So might it still, in itself; but if he could turn it about it would surely serve his will. He slept then, but excitement awoke him at first light. He rose and waited agog for Roc or Ils to stir.

"What do I know of what?" she growled sleepily. "Of iron and copper in corrosives? Many things, though I am not my folk's best scholar in such matters; chiefly that they corrode. How much, how fast, what they form . . ."

"What they create!" hissed Elof excitedly. "That's what I mean! No? But you'll see! Now, we'll need quantities of corrosives, sheet copper and iron as pure as we can make them. And some of that powdery black stone the Mastersmith used for marking parchment . . ."

"Ought to be plenty in the hills!" yawned Roc. "Comes from schist or the like, doesn't it? Won't lead do as well?"

"No! It's not for making marks that way! Come, bestir yourselves, we dare not waste the day! We've long weeks of work ahead!"

He spoke truly, save that the weeks extended into months. They toiled far into that night, and many that followed, preparing the forge for the long work to come; then they vanished for weeks on end with the Guardians, hunting out rare or precious minerals from the stone and the finest clays that could be gathered. Elof made it his business to sweep Roc and Ils along by sheer will, till he could almost see the lethargy of castle life fall from them. As the long summer faded and the heavy rains of autumn passed, he spent every hour of daylight in the forge, and by night its fires flared and shimmered among the gaunt evergreens, a defiant assertion of warmth and energy. Many asked of him what he labored on with such exertion, but all he would say was that it was to be a gift. And there came a night when the little forge shone like a beacon through the trees, so high did its fires burn; every gap and cranny in shutters and door blazed with light, as if the stone beneath had melted and let the earthfires through.

Later the shutters were opened to let a cloud of steam disperse, and Roc and Ils stumbled wearily away down the well-worn trail to the hall. Elof lingered long thereafter, and the hammering and cracking of clay molds echoed through the night. At last he made his way down to the castle in the small hours of a morning that sparkled with frost. So silent was the Forest that he was quite unprepared for the sudden change in the music of the stream.

Well, smith? Upon what do you labor such long hours?

Elof smiled tautly. "A casting in silver, Lord of the Forest. A jewel, a gift, for a great lord."

I do not doubt it will be worthy of him. Yet have a care, abroad in these woods so late without the Guardians. You are aware I have other subjects; for many the night is their province. Upon the path to the castle you will be safe. But never stray from it! There was a sudden rustle, and Elof ducked sharply as a wide shadow swooped down upon him. But it passed and settled with a flutter upon a branch ahead, a huge owl that stared at him with glittering eyes topped by feathery peaks like horns, a stare cold and unnerving. Elof caught his breath and swallowed, hard. He nodded.

"I hear you, Lord Tapiau. I will keep to the path. Good night!" But his smile was grim as he made his way through the last of the trees, grim as the satisfaction he felt. He would keep to the path, indeed, the one he had trodden since the beginning. Tapiau had at last dropped the mask a little; but though that was interesting for many reasons, it meant he must be swift now, swift as the work allowed. And as ruthless. He clutched his cloak around him; the frost seemed to settle on his heart. Somewhere within him that seam of iron still lay, that callous streak which had let him forge the mindsword at another's great cost. He hated it, yet now he must summon it up and turn it to a greater good. That also would be an achievement of mastery.

The next morning all stood ready; he could not hold back. The sheet copper had been rolled into cylinders, rods of iron set within and the whole set in small jars of sand-fused glass, into which Ils added a strong solution of corrosive. From these, pitch-coated threads of twisted copper led into a stone bath full of a foul-smelling solution; a heavy spearhead shape hung within, of the purest gold they could attain. On a bench sat a crucible of the gray mineral, powdered fine and mixed with eggwhite and other substances, and beside it a light and intricate framework of silver, polished to a mirror shine. Roc and Ils watched in astonishment as Elof took it up and, referring to the litter of scrolls and slates upon the next table, dipped a fine brush in the mineral powder and began to trace minute rows of intricate characters upon it. Then, donning a glove, he touched the remaining copper threads to it. Roc exclaimed as a shower of tiny blue sparks arose, but Ils' face brightened with sudden understanding, and she nodded sagely as Elof fastened the threads tight to the frame and with long tongs lowered it carefully into the bath. He watched a moment, motioning them to silence, until he saw a faint bubble rise and burst upon the greasy surface. Then he began to sing softly, under his breath at first, but rising now and again into words they could make out.

> Awaken! Wake!
> From nightbound depths
> What long lay hid
> Let it arise
> To blind the day!
>
> From tomb, a voice
> From time, an hour
> From pattern, form
> From weakness, power.
>
> To darkness, light,
> In embers, flame,
> From dust, a tree,
> Silence, a name.

The stillness stirs,
Its loss regains;
What was, returns
What is, remains.

At length he smiled at them and sat back. "It begins!" he said.

"And what, exactly, might *it* be?" inquired Roc sardonically.

Elof's eyes glowed darkly. "A thing our late master never dreamed of! A coating of gold finer than the thinnest foil or leaf, a blending of metals finer than pattern-welding, more precise than alloying. I read of it as a method of extracting difficult ores, but saw how it could be made to act for me. In these threads flows a force that bites as fiercely as the corrosive spawning it; do not touch them bare-handed! It seeks to pass through anything, but water and most metals especially. And in flowing through that bath, from point to frame, it will carry with it minute particles of the gold. Little by little they are settling on the frame, more thickly upon the characters I traced. And other layers will follow, gold, silver, copper, chrome and other rarer metals; and upon each I can set its particular virtue." He laughed. "On every particle, almost, if I so desired!"

Ils tapped her large teeth and nodded. "I should have remembered; the like method for ores is indeed known among us, and no doubt for work like this, if needed. But the virtues you set upon it, well, they baffle me . . ."

Elof stood abruptly, and peered down into the tank. "Only a part of it," he muttered. "A small part . . . Meanwhile there is more to be done. Roc, that wide mold-flask I made, and the fine clay; I have the wax armature ready here. We are not finished our casting yet!"

Ils stared at the delicate waxen shape he lifted from a high shelf. "But what living use could that be?"

Elof grinned wolfishly. "A strength against my fears that my will has found! When it is complete, and wields its power—then you will understand!"

In the weeks that followed the castle saw little of him. Ever more often he slept on the hard hearthside, seldom returning even for food. Yet when Ils or Roc brought it him, the only ones he would suffer, they most often found him huddled motionless over one of the bubbling stone baths, as if he could watch or will the invisible flow of matter within its depths. Only his lips moved, and the words he spoke came not to their ears. More than once Ils bade him sharply have a care, for many of the liquids were fell poisons, unsafe even to breathe. Certainly in this time he grew pale and ill to look at, his brow furrowed, his eyes and cheeks sunken. But all he would do was shrug, turn perhaps to his books awhile, and demand to be left alone. So the days passed, and ever more chill blew the Forest winds, till the frost lingered long into the morning. It was in the early hours of such a day that Elof watched the last coating, which was of silver, take shape upon his work. And though it was no more than a dull gleam deep in the brown liquid, he knew when it should be ready. He took the longest tongs he had, and lowered them delicately, very delicately, beneath its surface, for the bath of silver held the most deadly poison of all. Then, taking a firm grip, he stood a moment, and for the first time since the beginning he chanted aloud, harsh, yearning, defiant.

> *Dark is the moment, great our need,*
> *Fierce is the fire that bids me heed,*
> *Burning bright in my breast,*
> *Drives me from life, from death—*
> *Unbinder! Unchainer! Burn with that flame!*
> *Renewer! Restorer! Be that your name!*
> *Break you the bonds that hinder my quest!*
> *Arise from the shaping to me!*

Then with a single smooth effort he drew the metal forth, upward, straight up till the metal threads drew taut and snapped amid a rain of sparks, boiling the poison beads to vapor as they showered back into the tank. Though the work had grown heavier, he held it for long,

long minutes unmoving above the tank, until no more of the venom fell. Then he washed it carefully many times in water distilled and set aside for that purpose. Only then did he dare take it in his gloved hands and scrub it gently clean in the trough, running his eyes across the perfect surface, the smooth, even coating over the steel that showed no trace of the myriad layers of many metals, the thousands of characters, traced out beneath. He could have lingered over it, rejoicing in its beauty and smoothness, in the completion of long months of labor. But the flames blazed yet within him; he allowed himself one curt nod before he turned to his bench and the fine work of finishing.

Thus it was only that same afternoon that a message arrived at the court, to the effect that Elof would be honored if he could show Prince Korentyn, and with him Lord Kermorvan, his forge, and the first fruits of his labor. Ils, who had delivered the message, came puffing back up the hill to the forge, with Roc on her heels. "They're coming!" she gasped. "Any moment, with Roc!"

Elof nodded. "How did they take it?" he asked.

"They seemed amused. Kermorvan wondered why you couldn't just come down, but Korentyn said it was a courtesy he owed you. He likes you, I think, Elof."

Elof nodded again, somberly. "I know."

"Teris wanted to come, but I said it would be too crowded. Just as you ordered, Elof. Now would you mind giving me some warning what harebrained scheme it is you're planning?"

Elof rose, and shook his head dismissively. "Better you have no part in it, should it fail, you and Roc. And perhaps should it succeed, as well. Silence, now! They come."

Kermorvan's voice rang out across the clearing, and a moment later his tall outline, swollen by the fur cloak he wore, blotted the cold light from the doorway. Elof stepped out to greet his visitors, and Kermorvan stared. "Kerys' Gate! You've changed, these last few days."

"Since I saw you last? Weeks, rather, even months. And so have you." For he thought Kermorvan's face was fuller, the look in his eyes no longer intense but relaxed, amused, like a watcher at some entertainment, a spectator at the margins of life. "But enough of that for now! My lord Korentyn, you do me great honor."

Korentyn smiled. "Not so! You honor me, and if truth be told I welcome the distraction; winter is a dull time, and I am leaving on a hunt tomorrow. Kermorvan promises me you can work marvels."

"You must be the judge of that, lord. Enter, and excuse the discomfort." Korentyn ducked through the doorway, as Elof had never needed to, and stood looking around him at the disorder of equipment on every side.

"This is a strange place," he said softly. "Forces are at work here, I could sense them if I were blindfold. You are a smith of power and craft, Elof."

Elof bit his lip. "Then accept this, lord, as some earnest of your words!" He reached beneath the bench, and lifted an object wrapped in barkcloth. "For you are a great prince, and it is . . . fitting that this, my first work here, should be yours."

The barkcloth fell away, and the others gasped; Korentyn himself went momentarily very pale as the gleaming thing was lifted to his eyes. But it was Kermorvan who spoke first, astonished.

"That is an image of the Coronet of Morvannec!" he barked. "How did you know of such a thing, Elof?"

"I found it, drawn in one of the texts here."

Korentyn laughed, shaking his head in wonder. "But why then have you set this fair thing on so rich a warhelm, smith? For I am nothing if not a man of peace, now!"

"Thus it was shown in the text, lord. And it seemed to me right that you should have your crown so, who fought so valiantly in your youth for the right. But will you not don it, if only for the measure?"

Korentyn seemed genuinely much moved. He bowed deeply to Elof, and raised the work of bright silver, tall plated helm and manypeaked crown, high above his head. The sun was falling westward, an angry bronze globe in the gray waste of sky, its long rays streaming in through the open doorway. They caught helm and crown, mirror-bright, and set upon its patterned plates a glow of fire, tipped its peaks scarlet as they did the mountain snows, awoke white fire and rainbows from the cluster of pale gems at its brow. The light seemed to shine through Korentyn's fingers as, slowly and with grave dignity, he lowered the crown onto his head. There for an instant it rested, framing his face, noble and serene as some ancient statue. Then the eyes flew wide, a spasm crossed the features, and they twisted in anguish. Korentyn screamed aloud, once, hoarsely; his fingers knitted with fearful tension, tearing at each other, at his garments. His tall frame convulsed and crumpled, and the Prince of Morvannec collapsed amid his streaming robes onto the stony floor of the smithy.

Roc and Ils cried out and ran to him, but Elof spread his arms and thrust them back by main force. Kermorvan rounded on him. "You! This is your doing! To him, who has shown you so much kindness! *What have you done to him?"*

"The cruelest thing I could possibly have done," said Elof, and in his voice was utter blackness. "I have restored him to himself."

"What . . . Enough of your folly!" growled the warrior, and plunged forward to the prince. But now it was Ils who jerked him back, thrusting him down on a bench, and so startled was he that he suffered it a moment. Elof looked down at him, his face bloodless.

"With the virtues set within that crown, that helm, I have broken the holds of the Forest, the fetters Tapiau has set upon him."

Kermorvan stared up at him, lips moving before he could speak clear. "You . . . you measure yourself against one of the Powers? You claim . . ."

"In a small space. For a short span of time. His mind and memory are laid clear now, set free with no sweet songs to cloud them."

"Free to remember . . ." growled Roc hoarsely, kneeling slowly by the prince's side. He could not continue.

"Free to remember a thousand years," whispered Ils, and tears trickled down her plump cheeks. "To remember, all at once . . . Poor man! Poor lost man!"

Abruptly Kermorvan barged past Elof and knelt by Korentyn. Elof saw him raise a hand to draw off the helm, and nerved himself to intervene. But it was another hand that clutched Kermorvan's wrist, and thrust it sharply away. Korentyn's eyes were open wide, gray and desolate as the winter sky they mirrored. "My dear lord!" whispered Kermorvan. "Prince Korentyn . . ."

The tall man shook his head, slowly. "Prince no longer," he muttered, and his voice was a whisper, dry and unsteady. "Korentyn no more . . . Korentyn is dead. His shadow am I, nothing more; his mask, empty, eyeless, hollow within. So are we all, all this court, a play of shadows dancing on the wall, the dancers long since fled. Shadows of life, of love, of honor . . . All lost. All sped. His work, his doing, accursed be he . . ."

"You see, Elof?" hissed Kermorvan. "You torment him, and to what . . ."

"No!" croaked Korentyn, clutching again at Kermorvan's arm. "Not him! Not him, for this pain I would buy with my own heart's blood, if need be! It is Tapiau I curse, the Forest and its poisoned gift of years! So many years, so many, of seeing, understanding, yet being blind . . ."

"Seeing what?" Elof's voice grew strange in his own ears, harsh and imperious, tinged with night. "What have you understood?"

Korentyn stared up at him, wide-eyed. "I know that voice, I know it of old . . . Tapiau's will, that I have understood, his design for men. His grand design!" The long fingers clawed in the dust.

Kermorvan looked at him doubtfully. "We know something of that. To be immortals, or *alfar,* as suits men best, are there not worse choices than that?"

"Are there?" There was no kindness now in Korentyn's laughter; it was cold and bleak. "Do you not see that there is no choice at all? Save whether to linger, or fall swiftly. To preserve the aspect of a man awhile, or surrender it at once. A year, a thousand years, what does that matter? The burden of the years is too great for any man, and the Forest knows that well. In time the change must come to all, slowly, subtly, insidious as poison." He looked down at his long fingers; his fists clenched in sudden spasm, and blood started between the taut fingers. "Do I not see it at work? Even now, within me? Look at me! Look at any of us! Are we not, all of us, on the road to the *alfar* form? And that is Tapiau's will."

"But . . . He's not one of the evil Powers, is he?" spluttered Roc. "The ones of the Ice? I mean, if the Forest's not on the side of life, who is?"

"Of life, yes," said Korentyn bleakly. "But of men? Are we, as we are, on the side of life untrammeled, unbounded? Of any life save our own? One thing of worth these long years beneath the trees have taught me, and that is that all nature is one, that when we waste it we spill our own blood, we tear bread from our own lips. That lesson it is the lot of all men to learn in time, perhaps. But Tapiau would not have us learn; he sees in us the wasting of his domain, the taming of his power. He fears us, as the first Powers feared the coming of life into the lifeless perfection of their world. Yet he dare not rebel as they have, for what would become of the Forest then? He seeks instead to force men into the mold he thinks best. To strip us of what sets us most in conflict with all else that lives . . ."

"Our minds," said Elof heavily. "As I feared. He told me that unending life was only for the heroes among men. But I see now that no man cheats the River without a price. Such life is for nobody. In the world outside, with all its chances and perils, it could not be. Only here, in this womb of the Forest, can the bodies of ordinary men endure thus. And that robs endurance of all meaning! For what value had your life here, what purpose? To tread the same paths over again, to dance the same dances, say the same words, act the same pale acts of love sunken to ritual. And all the time his hand lay on your minds, told you this was perfection, the best you could hope to find. Perhaps he truly believes it is, so little does he comprehend men. Small wonder you have all grown weary in time, however hard you fought to remain yourselves. And as you grow weary your minds cloud, your bodies change. Until you are driven to lay aside your humanity as a relief from lingering pain. Small wonder.''

Silence fell. Korentyn drew himself painfully to his knees, gazing at Elof in growing puzzlement. But suddenly his eyes shifted, staring past the smith, out of the doorway into the mass of trees beyond. Elof moved to bar it, lest he should try to flee, but then he also saw what had caught Korentyn's eye.

''See!'' croaked the prince. ''See! Snow falls! The first snow . . . Snow on the Forest!''

Kermorvan blinked like a man awaking from deep sleep. ''Aye, my lord! A few flakes, only. And it cannot lie long, for spring is not far off. What of it? Let me . . .''

''What of it?'' Korentyn twisted toward him, seized his arm once more with a frightening urgency and scrambled to his feet. ''It comes every winter, now. But it did not fall, not then, not here, even this far north, ever . . . There was no snow when first I came here.''

Kermorvan's face grew suddenly grim. ''What is it you seek to tell me, my lord?''

Korentyn stared out into distances further than the trees. ''Can you not see?'' His voice grew clearer, edged now with a bitterness and a desolation that tore Elof's heart. ''Why, it means that even a great Power may be blind to what he does not wish to see! It means that even Tapiau may welter in his own self-deceiving. For all that he has done to us, he has done in the name of helping us, saving us, even if only as animals among other animals. But even in that he fails! Across his boundaries the dark trees of Taoune'la spread, and behind them the barrens, the tundra, that smooth the paths of the Ice.'' The prince laughed again, and Elof shuddered at the sound. ''There is snow on the Forest, where once there was none! And where the snow comes, the winters worsen, the icecaps lengthen, the snow line sinks ever lower, the cold creeps ever southward, southward . . . till glaciers spawn in the Meneth Aithen. Till down these very slopes they sweep, to meet their chill brethren of the north. And what of the Forest then?'' He laughed again, but in the taut furrows of his face tears glistened. ''Why did I endure, to come only to this?''

''You told me why,'' said Elof quietly. ''You told me, and I understood. To pass on the wisdom in your charge, that was your wish, and your purpose. For such a chance, if no other, you have fought to remain yourself throughout long centuries. Give us now what counsel you can!''

Korentyn turned to gaze at him. ''And that chance you have made possible. Hear me, then, what counsel I can give in pain and haste! You must flee, and soon. At the Forest margins its power is weakest. Join one of the hunts that is being readied, the hunt for onehorns, for that will turn near the Forest's northern margins.''

''Northern?'' asked Ils, alarmed. ''Is that not the most perilous way?''

''Aye; southward is less so, or was in my day. That is the way Lord Vayde took Ase and her followers, sailing southward from Morvannec into a great bay that opens there, and thence up a river and across the margins of Forest and Waste. A hard route, but with fewer great perils than these trees, or the haunted swamp and barren of Taoune'la. But from here the south is too far, near three times the distance, and through the Forest's heart; you could never escape the *alfar,* or worse sentinels. Seize what chance you have; flee north and follow your quest!''

''You must come with us,'' said Kermorvan quietly. In the dim firelight of the forge he seemed to have grown, almost to the equal of Korentyn's height. ''Morvan's scattered children, east or west, have need of Korentyn Rhudri to lead them once again.''

Korentyn shook his head slowly, and the crown flashed and sparkled among the shadows. ''Not so! Not when they have Keryn again! For you are more like him than I would have thought possible, save perhaps that you have not yet come to believe enough in yourself. Seeing you, I could believe in truth that the River does cast us up upon its shores once again; and so, perhaps, the fear of it, the avoiding of it, is a cheat and a deception after all. If that is so, then perhaps we may meet once again. But not now. For I am out of my time, and strangely altered, no longer fit to wrestle with the world. That I leave to you, kinsman, descendant, brother, worthy bearer of our name, to you and these friends who follow you, valiant and wise. Do you succeed where we have failed! And my blessing upon you!'' Kermorvan knelt before him, and Korentyn raised him, and embraced him.

In the turmoil of his heart Elof stepped forward, and he also bowed his head and knelt. ''I ask no blessing, my lord! Only your justice, and your forgiveness, if you can spare it! For the deception I wrought upon you, and the cruel pain I cost you. But you know why these things had to be.''

Then Elof looked up into Korentyn's eyes, and felt sick and faint at the torment he saw there, a mind rent asunder in its struggle to be free. ''I know none better,'' said the prince, and that same air that Kermorvan bore, of justice and judgment out of the deeps of time, seemed to settle about him. ''You are clear-sighted, young smith; you have wisdom and power beyond your years. You have done a deed few if any mastersmiths of my own time could have equaled. Do you yourself think it master's work?''

Unable to look away from those agonized eyes, Elof nodded. ''Aye, lord. For it was as I planned it, from the start, the virtues I set in it harnessed and controlled. But it cost me dear.''

''Then for that,'' said Korentyn sternly, ''as was a prince's right of old, I name you now a smith born, made and proven, a master of your guild and mystery! Arise, Mastersmith, and prosper!'' Elof stumbled up, startled, and felt Korentyn's hard hand on his shoulder. ''And for that deed I hold you quit of the ill you have done me. But hear the doom I lay upon you in requital! For you have also a gift for cunning and ruthlessness; already it has served you ill, and may do so again. As well that you and others should be warned. So from this day forth you shall bear the name of Elof Valantor, which may mean the Skilled Hand, but also the Hand Hidden. Bear it with honor, but do not forget shame! And bear it with my blessing.''

Elof swallowed, though his mouth was dry. "Lord, I will. And may I never value mastery greater than the mastery of myself, and the truest desire of my heart."

Korentyn nodded. "So be it!" Then he stepped back suddenly, and stared out at the forest, turned all to white beneath the rising moon, and spoke softly. "And farewell, all! To you, smith so wise, yet unknown even to yourself! You, strong craftsman, worthy citizen! You, princess of our elder kin! You, warrior who could be a king, in the full flower of your youth and strength! See how it ends! Think on me!" And with clawed hands he tore the helm from his head, and hurled the heavy thing the length of the forge, to crash and roll among the coals of the hearth-fire. Roc, with a cry, reached for the tongs. But Elof waved him back, and shook his head, and his voice was bitter with grief and disgust.

"Let it melt!"

When they looked back, Korentyn was gone. His long paces in the snow led back to the castle, but that night they saw him there no more, and in the dawning he was gone, departed as he had planned to with the westward hunt. And whether the prince ever came back to the Halls of Summer they never knew, for no mortal man looked upon Korentyn Rhudri again.

CHAPTER SEVEN

The River of Night

Shoulder-deep among the thick bushes the huge beast threw back its head, shaking its shaggy mane in the thin sunlight, its long horn gleaming. Elof and the *alfar* woman ducked hastily lower on their high branch, though they knew it could neither see nor smell them this far downwind. Strings of soil-caked roots hung from its mouth, tangling among the fringes of coarse cream-white fur as its champing jaws pulled them in, its breath steaming in the cold morning air. Its small ears flicked, its little wrinkled eyes blinked about, reddened by the new-risen sun: then it snorted thick clouds from its nostrils and went back to its rooting.

"Be he not a beauty?" whispered the *alfar* woman, half hugging Elof with the spidery arm she kept across his back, nervous he might fall. "And his winter white not yet shed. Long I am watching that one, hasty to have the chase of him, but only this year is he of a lawful age. Already the young males best him at the matings, so he forages alone; soon he will be too old to run far, and then the wolves will have him, or the daggerteeth. Or some nightwalkers. Better and quicker he falls to us!" White teeth flashed in her long brown face.

Elof smiled; though his muscles creaked from endless hours crouched among treelimbs. "Better indeed!" he whispered back. "And all the more honor to us that you share this hunt, Hafi!"

"Honor is ours, lord!" Hafi whispered, stabbing Elof still more keenly with shame at the deception he planned. And yet . . . That odd name Hafi was a diminutive of Halveth, an ancient and honored woman's name among the northern royal kin. What blood flowed in her veins? What great lord or lady of Morvan had let fall the shackles of their old life to become her parent? She looked around. "Ah, Gise comes! Do you watch with Lord Elof, Gise, I go to fetch the others." Silently she slithered along the branch and was gone. No less silently, Gise's massive frame, clad in an *alfar* tunic and harness, swung down in her place beside Elof.

Elof looked around, anxious, angry. Gise was at home here, so much so Elof still wondered whether it had been safe to trust him. "By all the powers, Gise!" he hissed as low as he could. "I tell you once more, you've got to come with us! We'll need you, you of all people!" But the big forester only looked away, and shook his head slightly. Elof grabbed him by the shoulder. "You joined this venture to aid the Northland fugitives! It's your duty!"

Gise shook his head again, firmly; more than ever he seemed to fumble for words. "No, Master Elof, no! You, where you will; me, I stay. Like I said to my lord 'fore now. A new home it was I came t'find, and that I have, and damned if I'll leave it!"

Elof sighed. "So you fail us, as well as Arvhes; nothing will detach him from the court."

"And why not?" whispered Gise, the accusation stinging words from him. "Him 'n' me, we're the oldest! We've not the summers left to build new lives, not like you younkers. What'll we find, us, that's better than this? They're gentle folk, these, though a mite slow in the head; take you in, not fuss you. Not jealous with their women, either. I've one among them already, maybe a little 'un on the way." He jabbed a blunt finger into Elof's chest. "You, wise master, don't you go prating to me of your long tomorrow! What's it to me, so far hence even my sons' sons won't see it? You tell me in the here and now what life's better for a forester like me!"

"A free one?"

But Gise shrugged. "Free's as free does, to a plain man like me. The Forest's not half the hard taskmaster your Headmen or town elders were back home; you should know that, master, from all I hear of your beginnings."

Elof grimaced; there was truth in what he said. Now, though, he had fewer doubts; Gise had not changed much, if only because little change had been needed. But that, oddly, made it harder to leave him behind. "If only it did not feel so much like abandoning you . . ."

Gise grunted. "The River for that! We choose with our eyes open, Arvhes and me. More open than yours, maybe. Hist now, lest he hears us, he below!" But it was to the heights he looked, for just then a soft rustle in the foliage announced the arrival of the other hunters. There was a slight springing of the branch beneath them and Kermorvan inched silently along it. Elof was glad to see him so limblithe after many months of inactivity; they would have need of all his skill and speed for this. Kermorvan's brows arched as he saw the beast their prey.

"Does the onehorn please you, lords?" demanded Hafi softly. "No easy quarry is he! Against his hide mere arrows from the treetops do not serve. Spear or halberd it must be, in belly or throat where he is softest, on the ground and close to! We stalk him through the leaves and of a sudden drop down, fft!"

Elof swallowed, and stole another look at the brute. The idea seemed impossible; the great horselike head was carried higher than any horse's, the horn on it alone almost as tall as himself. It was bulkier even than a dragon, and, save for that living wall the mammut, the largest beast he had ever seen on land. This was madness, and yet Kermorvan was taking it quite calmly, deciding with Hafi which trees would be best. Finally they waved to the others, and the *alfar* moved up to help the humans through the branches. Elof needed little help, even with the halberd slung across his back, and the clumsy pack the *alfar* had tried to persuade him to leave. He had grown used to this way of getting about; there was no denying the thrill of being at home so high up. It made the Forest seem a different place, less hostile, more fascinating in the richness and variety of the life that worked out its purposes below. It was like nothing he had ever experienced in the world outside . . .

And then he realized with a little tremor of shock that the world outside scarcely seemed real anymore. Once again, far from his shielding forge, he could hardly imagine a world beyond the trees. For the passing of two seasons he had been immured within them, more than half a year of travel and of rest. Or was that all? He seemed to have resisted the Forest's timeless thrall better than his fellows, but might not that be an illusion also? Might not a century have passed out there while he had shaped and schemed in the shadows? Kerbryhaine might be long since fallen and overrun, mere circles of overgrown ruins haunted by owl and wolf, or torn down piecemeal to surround the Ekwesh stockades . . . He shuddered. A sudden horror of the outside passed through him, of haste and peril and problems he could not solve with study and cunning and skilled labor; he did not want to face it, he wanted to lurk and lair among the trees, and forget. Then the touch of a hand jolted him alert, a silent signal passing among the shadowy shapes in the leaves. He peered down; he could see little save bushes, but he could hear the snort and grunt of the onehorn all too loudly. A bush jerked noisily aside, and a shoulder of tangled white hair came into view, too close for his comfort. Slowly, silently, he unslung the halberd, made sure his pack would not hitch upon the branches. To his left he heard a faint sound, and saw there Borhi, sweating and shaking, green with fear. The young corsair had balked violently at the idea of leaving the castle, but had decided he liked being left there rather less. Elof gestured reassuringly, but himself began to shiver. He would have been tense enough simply with the prospect of facing that beast. But far more than that was about to happen.

Another touch, a sharp one, and then a sudden fierce springing in the branch beneath him. There was no time to think, to hesitate; Elof simply kicked out his legs, the whipping branch jerked out from under him, as the trap below the gibbet, and into empty air he plunged. But the ground was nearer than it looked, his feet were ill prepared. It slammed into his soles with bruising force, he fell aside and rolled on his back, holding the halberd high. There was a snort and a crash and he sprang up to find the light before him blotted out by a wall of tangled whiteness that reared and plunged among a flurry of greenery, shaking the earth. A figure bounced past, caught his arm; Roc, and beside him Bure and Tenvar, jabbing with their halberds at the mountainous beast that wheeled and bellowed defiance, unable to find a clear path to charge. "This way!" screamed Roc. As they had planned, they were not attacking the beast, but keeping it between them and the startled *alfar*. Elof was only too ready to turn and bolt under the trees; he saw Ils and Kermorvan there, but where was Borhi? The corsair stood still where he had dropped, staring aghast at the travelers as they ducked past the plunging onehorn.

"Borhi!" yelled Elof. "This way! *Now!*"

The corsair seemed to hear, turned and ran a few steps, then halted, hesitated, shaking his head and gesticulating frantically. "No!" he wailed. "I can't, I won't! I'm safe, I'm safe here! Come back, you'll all die, all die—"

Cursing, Elof tore free of Roc's arm and whirled back after Borhi. Then he had only the fraction of a heartbeat to throw himself aside, as the maddened beast at last ducked down its immense head and charged. Borhi, unmoving, seemed not to see it, or to understand what he saw, the monstrous thing bearing down on him like the corsairs's own gallery with outthrust ram. The great conical horn, the length of his own body, struck into the center of him and hurled him torn and spilling through the air. A trampling hoof shattered the half-frozen earth a handbreadth from Elof's head, the great flank whirled past him, red-streaked from halberd thrusts, and then a huge hand was scooping him up; Gise's. "Run!" growled the tall forester. "While you can!" He all but hurled Elof into

the arms of his friends, and spun about to fling his halberd
at the beast. It whirled and charged again across the path
of the *alfar,* who had to dive for cover among the bushes.
Then Kermorvan's clear voice called and the travelers were
running, running with abraded throats and agony in their
sides, chests working like Elof's bellows, the fire of his
forge in their tortured lungs.

Behind them the uproar grew, trampling and smashing
in the brush and shouting they could hear even over the
roaring in their ears. The hunters would have to slay the
thing before they dared follow; Elof found himself hoping
it would not slay any of them. As Gise had said, in themselves they were gentle enough folk; it was the Forest's
power that made them shadows of malignity, woodsprites
working dark secrets within the tree-gloom. Better to evade
them thus if they could, than come to open fight. A stream
gleamed among the trees ahead, and Kermorvan gestured
to them; into the water they must go, and upstream. But
as they splashed into the icy shallows, he himself ran right
across and out onto the far bank, leaving a fine trail of
muddy footprints, then as the ground grew hard underfoot
he leaped for an overhanging branch and swung himself
back with the others, into the stream.

On and on they trotted, their feet soaking and numb,
their packs and weapons turning to lead about them, their
heads bowed down and staring at the water that seemed to
suck the heart out of them. At last it dawned on them that
they were walking, and slowly at that; Bure and Tenvar
were weaving as if about to fall down in the water, and
Ils, whose legs were shorter, suffered badly from the cold.
With wordless gasps Kermorvan drove them up the bank
among thorny bushes, and there they collapsed, numbed
to stab and scratch, deaf to anything save their own
whooping gasps. Elof heard somebody retching, and his
own stomach turned over; his feet turned slowly from
numbness to fire.

"So," wheezed Kermorvan at last. "We have some
small advantage of them. And we must not lose it! To the

Forest's edge, by Gise's guessing, was a good day and a half's march. Up, all, and to the north!''

There was a chorus of groans, but nobody failed to stagger to their feet, or to keep up with the brisk marching pace Kermorvan set. Indeed they seemed almost more enthusiastic now, weary as they were, as if some burden invisible and intangible were lifted from their shoulders. After a while, when he was sure enough of his breath, Elof mentioned this to Kermorvan, who nodded. ''I feel as much myself. We draw near the Forest's rim. May that shield us from Tapiau's sight!''

All that day the dwindled company marched at a relentless pace, until the sun, hidden hitherto beyond the leaden clouds, blazed angry orange behind the dark treetops around them. Mercifully the undergrowth grew thinner the further they went, for now it was chiefly a forest of pines, firs and spruces, with only a few hemlock and cedar and cypresses; their soft needles carpeted its floor, and few lesser things grew in their shadow. The brief spring of those climes was not yet come, to fill shrubs and grasses with a short spasm of life and growth ere the chill closed in once more. The air was still but raw, burning in their nostrils and on their cheeks, and, with their wet boots, draining the warmth from their bodies. As night fell they chose a dry spot to camp; fire would have been infinitely welcome, but they did not dare build one, lest it drew down the *alfar* or worse upon them. A shelter of pine branches was the best they could contrive, and they huddled together to keep warm. They ate little, for they had not been able to bring much food with them, and knew it might have to last some time; then, too weary to set a watch, they slept. But it was a poor night's sleep, for the Forest was full of strange noises, and many things unknown passed close by them. And some way past the middle hours dreams of conflict and tumult jolted Elof awake. Parting the branches, he peered out at the sky in the hope of seeing some trace of dawn, and caught his breath. For a faint light shone through the treetops, but it was cold and constant, and it paled not the eastward but the northward stars. So once again, after many years and many other perils, he beheld the sign and banner of their fountainhead, the eerie glow of the Ice.

Morning, gray-bleak as ever, found them chilled and aching and uneasy, eager only to be gone from there. Walking loosened their muscles but brought them little warmth and less comfort, save that there was no sound of pursuit. "So they have not found our trail," muttered Kermorvan. "I hardly dared hope it . . ."

"Maybe they search the wrong way," suggested Ils, "eastward or south. They might not guess we'd take the way north, that they fear."

Kermorvan nodded. "That must be it. But when Tapiau's eye turns this way . . . Still, we should be within an hour or two of the margins, and those they will not cross." So the travelers cast nervous glances at the trees about them, expecting every moment to be shot at from the branches, or fallen upon like the onehorn. That nothing came only made them the more uncertain. The borders of the Forest might be minutes away, or hours, and all manner of ambushes set between. But suddenly, as they came out into the bank of a dank little streamlet, Kermorvan stopped and pointed. "See! The far bank, beyond the trees!"

That there should be anything beyond trees, save more trees, was a hard thing to realize. Yet they did indeed seem thinner, further apart; light as cold as the sky above shone pale upon their trunks, unhindered. It must be a wide clearing, for the trees of the far side were an indistinct black line; the Forest was growing thin indeed. Down the bank they hurried, splashing through the water without seeking a drier crossing. Elof stopped short, gasping; it was as if some chill weight had suddenly settled on his heart. Bure, limping along last, missed his footing on the bank and all but fell back in; Roc and Elof, turning to haul him in, looked back, saw the pines bend and sway, and heard the rushing as of a great wind, that they knew was no wind. *"Kermorvan!"* they yelled.

"I hear!" he cried, and sweeping out his sword he urged

the others past him. "Now for it! Run, and stop for nothing! Run to the light!"

Only when Bure went crashing by him, with Roc and Elof on his heels, did Kermorvan turn and run with them, leaping and bounding. The way was further than it looked, and there was more undergrowth here, frost-browned grasses and low tangled bushes that grew in the lee of fallen trunks; it seemed almost to rise up and snag them as they went, and the branches whipped and lashed across their faces. Kermorvan hewed at them furiously, and Elof drew sword also. It was like fighting some live enemy, some beast with a thousand entangling arms above and below. And at their very heels now was the windrush, all but overhead. Elof winced, expecting arrows in his back any moment. But all the time the light grew stronger, the open space seemed wider, the other side more distant. Then suddenly, staggering from one tree to another, Elof realized there were no branches overhead, nothing but the gray sky, and that the trees beyond were even further apart, a gap wider than the longest arms. Ahead of him he saw a root snag Ils' ankle, tipping her into his path, and Kermorvan scoop her up almost without breaking stride. A jagged stump snagged Elof's cloak, and in one whirling movement the black blade hewed flying splinters from it, and he was sprinting after the others. Ahead of them was open space, and they were slowing, staring, almost stopping. "Too near!" he yelled. "Still within bowshot!" Then he also slowed, and stared. It was no clearing they were in.

Trees ahead there were, as line of them tall and dark, impenetrable as the densest Forest. But to left and right, where the line should have curved back to surround them, there was only open space. Near at hand it was flat grassland streaked with half-thawed snow, sparse stands of scrub, wiry and stunted, poking up here and there. Beyond it was grayness, with a glimmer that might be water. There were other lines of trees, but none more than stands, clumps, scarcely linked to one another across the snowy scrubland and dismal pools, and nowhere to the trees of

the Forest. Elof, turning to look back, saw the outermost
trees bend and tremble, yielding tall figures that stalked
and paced within the bounds of the treeshadow, like menacing specters afraid of day. They would not step beyond
the fortress of the Forest, the immense wall of trees outflung to either side, set like vast uneven ramparts against
this chill open land. He knew then that they had reached
the bounds of Tapiau's power. They were out of the Forest
at last, free as he had fought to make them. What was this
heaviness upon his heart, then, this faint nagging ache
within him which was no pang of honest weariness? Why
could he not rejoice?

By him Kermorvan stood, his face as gray and grim as
this land they had come to, and as desolate. *"Genhyas,
a'Teris!"* he was muttering. *"Genhyas, a'Korentyn!"*
Then he lifted up his sword, as a salute. But from the
Forest a single arrow came curving, to plunge into the icy
soil some way short of them and there shiver to pieces, as
against a stone.

"Come!" said Ils hastily, drawing them both away.
"That may have been a ranging shot. Let us not await a
volley!" But in a lower voice she added, "I am sorry
about Teris. Could she not have come with us?"

Kermorvan's face was set, but Elof was shocked by the
deep unhappiness in his voice. "I did not dare ask her.
She who had dwelt so long in Tapiau's thrall, she might
have betrayed us. I could not risk us all for her alone,
when there was no certainty she would come, or be happy
if she did."

Elof swallowed. "Believe me, I am sorry. I . . . was
never sure how much she meant to you."

The tall man's mouth twisted. "No more was I. And I
to her? Something new, perhaps, to be tempted, teased
out, made to last as long as might be lest it grow stale.
To be lured ever within the hand, yet kept from the
heart . . ." He shook his head. "No more was I. Matters
are better as they are, lesser now than greater to come.
Day advances, and we must go." And swiftly he turned
his back upon the Forest, and strode out at a fierce pace

across the gray ground. Elof and Ils looked at their companions, and fell in behind him. Thus it was that they entered Taoune'la-an-Arathans, Taoune'la the Wastes, the gray and shadowy marchlands of the Ice.

Certainly it was no hospitable land they saw stretching out before them. Kermorvan stamped on the snow-spattered earth as he walked, and it rang and crunched beneath his boots. "This will be a swamp soon, when the thaw comes," he remarked, his voice more normal now. "As well we left our flight no later; we would surely have been mired here, and taken."

Elof gazed around him uncomfortably. "Save for the trees, it reminds me of the saltmarshes. The worst parts."

"Small wonder in that!" said Ils. "For both that land and this are shaped and sustained by the outflowing meltwater of the Ice. The same shadow lies over both."

"It is less flat than the marshes," said Elof thoughtfully, "though the rise and fall is very slight. But if anything it is wetter, and that means the water has pooled in the valleys and dips, and cuts channels between them."

"A land of pools and rivulets and little lakes," agreed Kermorvan, "of mists and mires and quags. All bitterly chill, and hard to cross. There will be no fixed paths in such a place, not even animal tracks. We will have to go around and about so much it will be hard to keep to anything like a straight route."

"Let us not be drawn too far northward, all the same," warned Ils. "Remember the evil name of this land!"

Nevertheless, even on that first night they found themselves with little choice. For in their way they came upon a wide swampy area that ended only under the eaves of the Forest itself, and was already more than half thawed. When they climbed to the top of a low slope to spy out its extent, Elof, whose eyes were keenest in the ashen dimness of afternoon, exclaimed in dismay. "A river flows through it!" he cried. "Down from the north, in among the trees!"

"Aye!" said Tenvar. "A vast river, twice as wide as the Forest River! There is no fording it here, even if we dared go back among the trees! That water flows fast, and it is very dark.''

Ils squinted into the grayness. ''Dark indeed!'' she muttered. ''There are tales among my folk of such a river, that flows from the Black Lakes in the northern Wastes down through the Forest, and they are darker yet. The Kalmajozkhe it is to us, River of the Dead.''

''Yet the living must cross somewhere,'' muttered Kermorvan. ''Or they will not long remain so; there is little to eat in this land. What is that, upriver there? An island?''

''It seems so,'' admitted Elof, straining his eyes. ''A large one, covered with trees; there are more along the banks. We might try there for rocks or shallows.''

Kermorvan nodded. ''We might, though the current may be faster.'' He saw the others looking to him expectantly, and shrugged. ''You wish me to choose? I see no choice. We may at least find somewhere more sheltered than this to sleep.''

They turned northward then, skirting the margins of the cold swamp, and plodded wearily on into the barren lands. Even over the short distance they could make out ahead they saw the lines of trees grow fewer and shorter, the land flatter and more desolate. Only coarse grass covered the soil, and a few bushes that cowered low to avoid the searing wind, their tough strands running through the grass like entangling tentacles; it was a miracle no ankle or leg was broken in the gathering gloom. They feared lest it might grow too dark to go on, even with Ils to guide them, but around sunset there came a fierce gusty wind that drove the clouds like sheep to the horizon and there tore them to bloody shreds. It gave the keen air an edge like jagged glass, and for all their warm hunting garb it cut the travelers to the bone. The rough ground leached their strength away as they stumbled and faltered over it. In the clear sky the stars appeared like frost-flecks upon cold stone, the full moon rising rained down its sterile light upon the bleak lands. And all across the sky to the north, in answer or in mockery, there arose the shimmering curtain of the Iceglow.

But when they lifted their streaming eyes against the blast, they saw tossing black against it the tops of a thick-meshed wood, upon which the moonlight fell without lightening its solid gloom. "The island!" cried Tenvar. "The island's thick with trees! Shelter, and fuel!"

"Would you light a fire in this place?" cried Ils.

"I would!" barked Roc. "We'll need shelter and more to stay living this night!"

"There is a rapids!" cried Bure. "See the white water about the rocks? And past the island as well! It goes right over! There's our crossing!"

"If anywhere!" agreed Kermorvan. "But go with great care! The rocks will be icy, and death swift in those black waters. I will lead."

Of that crossing Elof remembered little save weariness and terror, the cold rocks and the roar and swirl of the river around their feet as they clambered between them. The moonlight was clear, or they would never have managed some of the wider leaps; Bure and Ils were at a terrible disadvantage, and had often to be swung across on the single length of rope they had. But even longer legs were aching before they came beneath the first overhanging branches, and saw the island rise stark above them. "Find a hollow," gasped Elof as they clambered up the steep bank. "Screen fire . . . with branches . . ."

Ils shook her head fiercely, and he caught the glint of fear in her look; but even she, stronger and hardier than most men, was too chilled and weary to argue. Elof and Kermorvan were little better, and Roc, Tenvar and Bure staggering as if drunk. Bure had fallen at least once, and leaned on Kermorvan's arm for support. Nevertheless they waited on the bank, slumped against the lichen-encrusted trunks of the black spruces, while Ils with her night eyes searched the gloom. The wind whined through the branches overhead, their hard needles rattling and whispering horribly; it reminded Elof of gibbets he had seen outside the ruined farms of Bryhaine. But at last she grudgingly admitted she could see nothing amiss, and the travelers hobbled gladly into shelter. As Elof had suggested, they found a hollow, a deep gully carved by some flood long ago and now well screened by the wiry undergrowth, taller here than in the open. Kermorvan kindled flame in a hastily dug pit, and while the others cut branches to screen the little camp Elof decided to fetch water for a hot broth. Very slowly and carefully, keeping low and rustling the bushes as little as he could he slid out from among the trees and along the bank to a spot where he might fill a waterskin without falling in. He lay down at a place where the water had cut away the bank, shuddering at the freezing touch of the soil, and lowered the skin into the dark water. The cold river bit agonizingly at fingers just recovering from their numbness, and he leaned down further to make sure he could hold the full skin. A gleam caught his eye, and he stared in horror. The water had sliced a section through the bank, and the face of it glimmered graywhite in the river's reflection. Under a hand's depth, little more, of brown grass and peaty soil there lurked a layer of some whitish substance. He reached down to touch it, and jumped at the chill throb in his fingers; it was a deep layer of solid ice. He looked up and down the bank opposite and saw many such gleams, always at the same shallow depth, though in some places it seemed to have forced the ground upward. Suddenly the whole wide land seemed to him no more than shriveling skin atop a cold empty skull. This far, within a day's march of the Forest, the distant Ice had already its hidden vanguard beneath the surface.

The full skin tugged at his hand, and he reached down to put in its stopper. But as he did so he saw a brief flicker of movement mirrored in the water, a swift dark shadow sweeping over moon and star. In one movement he heaved up the skin and sprang back to cover; then he saw it clear, a shape of sable wings out-swept, arcing down the sky onto the moonlit blackness of the river. He heard the fierce wingbeat as it settled, and then the graceful folding, the curving of the delicate neck into its shape. Down the flow of the flood it drifted, a huge swan gliding upon its own shadow over the glittering waters; but which the swan, which the shadow, was hard to tell, for in every feather it was black. And as Elof stood there, beyond movement, beyond understanding, he heard a low music drift across the waters, a haunting, somber singing of dark things. For the music was a voice, low and mellow as that of a human woman, and its words of deep lamentation came clearly to him over the relentless lapping of the flood.

> *Birds of the night sky! Sorrow pursues me,*
> *Far as I have flown over the land!*
> *Gather! Hear me!*
> *Far flew I! Grief sought I! Found I my fill!*
>
> *Of unstilled yearning I sing,*
> *Of unquiet waters*
> *Of loss, of wandering I sing*
> *By seas endless, tides ceaseless*
> *Under the empty sky*
> *Alas! Alas for sorrow!*
> *I sing of living.*
>
> *Far flew I! Grief sought I! Found I my fill!*
>
> *Of hope past hoping I sing*
> *Of wounds unhealed*
> *Of rue, of suffering I sing*
> *Of mouth on mouth, breast on breast*
> *All that may never be.*
> *Alas! Alas for sorrow!*
> *I sing of loving.*
>
> *Far flew I! Grief sought I! Found I my fill!*
>
> *Of last despairing I sing*
> *Of the dark River*
> *Of pain, of lamenting I sing,*
> *A brand quenched, a flame swallowed,*

The stream flows silently.
Alas! Alas for sorrow!
I sing of parting.
Far flew I! Grief sought I! Found I my fill!

Elof stood astounded as the creature glided slowly toward the bank. What he saw, what he hoped, was a whirling in his mind; the song was sorrow and terror, and it gripped him fast. Not far along the bank arose a stand of reeds, dry and half withered, whispering and creaking, and into these swept the dark swan. But even as it slid among them it seemed to rear up, its immense wings beat as if in fury, then shuddered closed across its breast. Upward rose the shadow, taller, more erect than any swan, and with sudden grace the wings swept open and back to reveal a breast of gleaming black mail. A human breast, a woman's breast; for below the mailcoat bare legs gleamed, and above it lifted a woman's delicate throat, strong chin and full lips. The rest of her face, her hair, all was hidden by the eyemask of a shining helm. But from her shoulders sprang not arms, but the same wide wings held open to their fullest, blotting out the moon, shadowing her beyond recognition. Yet among the feathers it seemed to Elof that he saw a gleam of gold.

Suddenly she cried out, in a voice grown so harsh, so terrible, that Elof dropped to one knee, shivering. "Rash wanderer! Man astray, in realms men dare not dream of, hear me and beware! Already for some the lot is cast! Doom approaches, doom no mortal turns aside! Flee, if flee you may! Or what is owed you, call for it! Seize it!"

The wings whipped closed, beat once, powerfully, sending the reeds hissing low to the water. A great black swan lifted from the river and went wheeling high off across the water, over the island, out of sight. Elof's eyes followed it till it vanished behind the crests of the trees.

"What have I seen?" he asked himself aloud, and heard his voice tremble. "Like . . . so like, and yet so terrible . . . What land of visions is this?" Terror clawed at him; he scrambled up, seized the waterskin and bolted back up the slope toward the trees and the faint glimmer of the fire. As he stumbled and tripped through the wood, he heard Kermorvan's low voice, and Roc's; they seemed like the finest and most comforting sounds he had ever heard.

"Something might be made of that southward way poor Korentyn told us of. If Vayde followed it to take his folk west, it might also be a safe route back east . . ."

"Maybe, if it hasn't grown worse in all this time . . . Elof! What's the matter? Look as if you've seen a ghost!"

"I have seen . . ." he muttered. "A warning, perhaps . . . I know not . . ."

"You sit down and get warm!" ordered Ils sharply. "Here, give me that water! Don't drop it in the flames! Now, what was it you saw?"

But Elof could not shape words around what he had seen. "A warning . . ." he gasped. "A judgment . . . We are in peril!"

Kermorvan sat up straight, and swung the gray-gold blade across his knees. He looked at Elof intently, his face set, brows drawn tight. "I need no vision to tell me that. Is it near?"

"It approaches . . ." gasped Elof. "She . . . It . . . said that . . ." He stopped, because Kermorvan's intense gray eyes had widened abruptly. He was no longer looking at Elof, but was staring over his shoulder, brows arched, lips parted in amazement. In the same instant Elof's skin crawled with the icy awareness of some presence at his back. He knew better than to look round; he was about to hurl himself forward, away, when out of the corner of his eye he saw a figure, somehow familiar, step forward and slouch casually down by the fire, holding out his hands and rubbing them hungrily. Steam rose from his clothes, which clung damply. The travelers stared, aghast. Then, just as Elof realized who it was he was looking at, Roc found his voice.

"Stehan! By all the halls of Hella! How'd you come to escape those . . . those water-things? How'd you . . . ?"

The corsair made no reply, but suddenly looked up with such a look of cold contempt on his face, dull and gray in

the firelight, that Roc stopped short, opened his mouth as
if to say something more, and then slowly closed it. Kermorvan seemed not to move, yet suddenly all the tension
of a drawn bow was in his body, drawn and ready to loose;
his knuckles gleamed white on his sword hilt. Across the
little hollow, at the far edge of the firelight, other shapes
were moving, approaching slowly, unhurriedly through the
freezing night. Down through the encircling bushes they
came in an uneven file, and the icicles that festooned the
meager branches chimed and rang and shattered like glass
at their passing. And as he saw the first of them Elof sought
to cry out, to spring up, but his limbs would not obey
him, his tongue clove to the roof of his mouth as if the
chill air froze it there. For the first was Holvar, and he
paid no heed to any, but came and sat by the fire as easily
as if he had but left them a moment before. Bure hid his
face in his plump hands, and the blood drained from the
brown skin; Tenvar sat rigidly immobile among the capering shadows, but a faint moan of horror broke half-
voiced from his lips. The wind screeched and flailed the
branches overhead, the fire blew flat and roared like a
trapped beast, light and shadow flickering faster than the
eye could mark. Into the hollow they drifted, one by one,
just as quietly, still without speaking, those members of
the company whose quest had ended, who should be walking in the world no more by night or day. Behind Holvar
strode tall figures that were Eysdan, and Maille the bosun,
and Dervhas, who walked easily on a leg Elof had seen
stripped to a tangle of raw sinew about the bone. Close
behind Dervhas moved Borhi, hunched up and clutching
his arms tight around himself, as a man might to close his
cloak against the chill. But he too, like the others, quietly
took a place by the fire, with neither look nor word for
those already there, and sat silently staring into the beating
flames. And though his face was fixed in a grimace of
fear, he spared not even a glance for what shambled in his
steps. Kasse the huntsman, eyes glittering malevolence
where empty sockets had been, took his place by the fire,
and within that firelit hollow, with the black pines sighing

and rattling above them, the living were outnumbered by the dead.

No word was said, no figure stirred; like silent statues they sat, the fire's smoke eddying this way and that about them, and it seemed to Elof that the chill which gripped this land, the ice below its soil, had flowed up and into his veins, and set the fire's warmth at nothing. He was shivering violently, too violently to speak, even to form the words in his mind. The dead had joined them, but their eyes were not dead; a living will dwelt in them, and a glare of menace and accusation he could read as clearly as words. Then a thick branch toppled and rolled in the fire, unstopping a vent of flame blown blue by the wind. In the waft of smoky scent Elof was suddenly reminded of his smithy on the Marshlands, of lying by the forge during his long illness there, and of the tormenting phantoms that had gathered around him; those horrors he had faced, and in facing overcome. The log split with an explosive crack, spattering sparks; a pulsing fire traced out the grain in its bared heart, and a like flame surged up within him, a bitter anger at the silence around him. It was mockery, contempt, and that unearned. Whatever the outcome, he could at least voice a challenge and a defiance. He clenched his jaws to quell their shivering, and he spat out the words as if he hammered them hot from his anvil.

"What do you want with us? Our friends you once were, but you do not come as friends should. Speak, or be gone! Leave what no longer concerns you!"

"Leave?" whispered a voice suddenly, and a cold breath of laughter coursed across the hollow like an echo of the wind. The voice was Stehan's, but might have been any; the same meaning burned in all those faces. "Good smith, it was you left us. All of us! In ambush, in fight, in flight you left us!"

"Pulled me down . . ."

"Shot in the throat!"

"Spitted like a fowl!"

"Hunted like vermin!"

"Broken and drowned!"

"Stripped the flesh from me like the bark off a willow twig, while you played tug o' war . . ."

"Said, promised, you'd keep me safe—left me to that beast . . ."

"You left us! Left us! Us! Us! *Us!*" The voices came together, blurred into a hissing chant almost void of human meaning, a wordless litany of hungry menace that battered at Elof's mind. He quailed for a moment under the weight of it, numbing, drowning, as under the impact of a waterfall. Then another voice sheared across it with the clean force of a swordcut.

"Enough!" barked Kermorvan, and his voice rang clearer and harder than Elof had heard it for many a day. "Enough, I say! Have I not laid such charges against myself, and worse, in all the long hours of these our wanderings? There are worse trials than you can put me to, worse terrors than you can inflict!" For a moment his voice lowered, his gaze dropped. "And did I not all but break myself in answering them, all but resign myself to inaction, to stagnation, where at least I need lead no others into harm?" Then he lifted his eyes again, and a fierce glare, a stormlight, shone in their grayness. "Bitterly did I regret your loss! Aye, even you, Kasse, trothbreaker who would have sacrificed a sworn comrade for a catch of meat! Craven who ran blindly to his own doom, out of the mercy of those who would have shielded him! I would have saved you, all of you, if I could, and risked my own life to do so; you at least should know that, Eysdan! But I could not. And the burden of regret ground me down. But by the help of Elof I was shown my answer!" He stood, and the long gray sword he rested point down upon the ground before him, leaning his crossed hands upon its hilt. Weary as he seemed, it was as if strength flowed into him from the very horror he confronted, for his shoulders straightened and his voice grew stern as stone. "I was shown that to live eternally shielded from all the chances of life is to live shielded from life itself, from good as well as evil. It is to do no good, to receive no good, merely to exist, and

in existing inevitably diminish. That the perils of life should be lessened, is good; but that all risk should be avoided, even when great good may come of it, that way lies a path of foolishness. You knew there would be perils on our quest, you knew you risked your lives; but also you knew great good might come to pass. The only amends I may offer you is to fulfill that quest, to give value and meaning to the sacrifice you made by saving lives that would otherwise be lost, and ensuring that your names live on in honor. That is as much as I myself would wish. If you yet keep some aspect, some part of the true heart and mind of the men that once you were, then you will understand. And if you are not . . .'' The tall man laughed suddenly, though in his voice there was no mirth, and he slapped one hand hard on the hilt of the sword. "Then I bid you begone! For among the living you have no place!''

The last defiant words rang out into silence so absolute that Elof caught his breath. Even the wind had died; not a leaf stirred, the fire sank down to a flameless glow that spilled no color into the night. It was as if the whole scene were carved in blackened silver, with a great red stone at its heart.

It is you who have no place here.

The voice jolted them all to their feet. Whose lips it came from Elof did not know, nor was he sure such a sound could come from human mouth at all, so bloodless, so hollow, so vast. It was like the stark echo of some greater sound, greater and more terrible, though what he could hardly imagine.

You have no place here. From the moment you passed the treewall, the lands you have walked in, the Gray Lands, are mine. And it is to the Island of the Dead you have come. Elof heard Ils give an involuntary cry of alarm, and as quickly stifle it; evidently the name was known to her. *They have no place here who are yet weak prisoners of the flesh, and here they spy and trespass at their most deadly peril.*

It was all the dead who spoke. Their heads were lifted now, their eyes fixed upon the travelers with an intensity

that made them even less human. And the voice seemed
to course at random from one mouth to another, sounding
always the same, hollow and terrible. But Elof was as
much angered as daunted, to see those who had been his
friends and companions so grievously abused, and though
Kermorvan, guessing his mind, flashed him a glance of
caution, he spoke boldly in reply. ''You, whoever you are!
If we have no place in your domain, then equally you've
no sway over us! Let us pass, and have done—''

*One day I shall hold this whole circle of the world in
my hand. None are beyond my sway. I am the Keeper. I
am Taoune.*

The name fell upon Elof's ears like a blow, dizzying,
sickening. This was disaster, this was ruin. He had spoken
with Powers before, grown reckless, almost, in confront-
ing them. But Raven seemed to be benign, and Tapiau
believed himself to be. Not so this presence, this appalling
sound of waste and desolation given voice. This was what
he had been warned against, what he had striven against,
what he had most feared. Perhaps they had strayed too far
north; or perhaps, since the land was so underlaid with
ice, they had been foolish ever to enter it. But whatever
the truth of that, they had come directly under the eye of
Tapiau's great adversary, one of the primal foes of life,
betrayers of their trust, lords of the world's worst ills. In
his arrogance he had dared to bandy words with one of
the ancient Powers of the Ice.

But he remembered what Tapiau had told him, that this
Taoune was a defeated Power, reduced to a shadow of his
former majesty, a mere marchwarden for the greater Powers that had succeeded him. The greatest of these was
Louhi, and had he not spoken to her, aye, and outfaced
her in defeating the Mastersmith her servant? And as he
had started, so he must go on; there was no turning aside.
So, though every hair on his head bristled and lifted, he
steadied his voice, and strove to copy in his deeper tones
Kermorvan's proud ring. ''Keeper? What have such as you
ever kept, save a vigil over the woes of men?''

To his astonishment the voice sounded almost hurt. *I?*

*I wish men well, for they have minds. Am I not one of the
loyal Powers, loyal to that which was first and has been
corrupted, the rule of pure mind? It is only the delusions,
the distractions, the wastefulness of the flesh we seek to
counter. So it is that here in the Gray Lands I seek to
preserve thought, to save all that is best in men. I gather
the minds of men about me as they are purged of their
gross bodies, their thoughts freed from the foolish lust for
growth, for change.*

Elof swallowed. His mouth was dry, but he could feel
the sweat trickling down and pooling in the folds of his
shirt. But anger triumphed, and hotter than caution it
flared, hotter than fear, a new rage added to the old as he
looked upon the emptiness in the eyes of those who had
been his comrades. He had had enough of the lies of Powers, that were as self-serving as those of men. "Then you
gather nothing!" he shouted. "What is real in men, if it
survives at all, has slipped through your grasp! Any live
human can see that! These are toys you show us, cunningly contrived to copy the actions of life! No more!
Nothing!"

"Nothing!" cried Ils, fired by his outrage. "Husks,
shells, shadows, no more!"

The same anger kindled among all the travelers, sparking from one to another as a forest fire leaps from tree to
tree, and made the fiercer by the terror they felt. "Did you
not hear me, Taoune?" cried Kermorvan, shaking his hard
fist in the empty faces of the dead. "Without the power to
live, to grow, men are no more than the sum of their memories! That is all you capture! That is all we see in these
miserable, hungry things you show us! Emptiness and
falsehood, that is your domain!"

"Aye!" bellowed Roc harshly. "They've the shapes of
folk, but where's the folk? Gone, anyone can see it!
They're like empty gloves, these shapes!"

"Like toys!" spat Bure. "Toys, that's all you make of
men!"

"Puppets to dance to your will!" yelled Tenvar. "Call

yourself Keeper? Waster, despoiler, grave-defiler, bird of carrion, so I name you—''

With fearful speed, without any warning, the shape of Holvar launched itself upward from where it sat, seized Tenvar in its arms and bearing him backward to the ground it lunged open-mouthed at his neck. Even as Kermorvan, with a great cry, swung up his sword and sprang right across the fire, Holvar's shade sank its teeth into Tenvar's throat, tore and worried like a wolf. Kermorvan's blade, a fire-lit streak of gold, slashed once, twice, about the thing, and in the same heartbeat Bure's sword hewed its arm and Ils' axe rang against its skull. It rolled back, but Tenvar lay still, his hands outthrust, rigid, clawing at nothing, his wide eyes still and unseeing. Elof, frozen with horror, saw the other shapes rise up as one, and he seized Gorthawer singing from the scabbard. The giant shape of Eysdan loomed over him; half-sobbing, Elof slashed wildly, Gorthawer sang a great dark note and the creature was hurled back among the advance of the rest. They halted, stumbling, and the black blade snarled in the chill air as he wove it back and forth before them. Back they swayed as it passed, like dark reeds upon the marshes, but inched forward when it was furthest from them. Then he heard Roc cry out as if in disbelief, and could not help looking. The creature that was Holvar, hewn and slashed as it was, was on its feet once more and clawing out with its good arm at Kermorvan's throat.

"Run!" yelled Elof. "They fear my sword, it will hold them! Run to the far crossing while you can!" Then he whipped back to his own adversaries, and it was as well he did; he had the fraction of a heartbeat to duck aside as a long arm hooked at the air where he had been. In that instant's inattention Taoune's creatures had almost reached him. Gorthawer hissed out in their faces, and they dropped back, but only a little way. Elof heard crashing among the trees; at least the others were getting clear. As if in a dream, he noticed for the first time that his panting breath hung in silvered clouds before him, but that before these nightwalkers there was none. Another shape bounded up beside him, and in panic he almost cut at it before seeing Kermorvan. "I told you to run!" he shouted.

"The others have a start now! Come!"

Even as they glanced aside to speak, the wave of dark creatures leaped silently forward. Elof struck down the clutching thing that looked like Borhi, and Kermorvan, with a hoarse yell of fury, slashed at the thing that was Kasse, sending it crashing backward into the dying fire. "Run now!" he shouted, and seizing Elof by the arm he all but dragged him up the far side of the hollow. Out among the pines they charged, over the barren carpet of dead needles and out, out again into the open air, so cold now in the latter hours of the night that it was like breathing the starlight raining down on them; it turned to cold fire in their straining lungs.

They overtook Ils, Roc and Bure as they neared the crossing. They were the shortest of limb; Kermorvan had been right to win them a start.

"Should we stop again?" wheezed Elof. "Hold the pursuit back once more?"

"No!" gasped the tall man as they drew level with the others. "In the open they would only run past us . . . At the crossing-stones we may hold them . . ." But even as he spoke they saw dark shapes thrashing through the harsh bushes ahead, hastening to cut them off from the crossing. He set a faster pace, to take Elof and himself into the lead. "We may manage to cut our way through! There are not many . . ."

He was cut off by a sudden strangled shriek. A tall lean figure had come bounding up behind Bure, clawing and clutching at his trailing cloak, and even as they turned they saw it catch hold and spring upon him as he stumbled, sending them both sprawling among the thorny scrub. Kermorvan spat a curse, whirled about and sprang back with all his lithe speed. He struck out once, tearing the creature loose; it folded its limbs as it fell and sprang at him. His sword scythed in the air, and clove the figure in half as it leaped. At once Kermorvan stooped to Bure, but stood abruptly, shaking his head, and came running back to the others, swinging a pack in his hand.

"Run!" he shouted, and there was a wilder horror in his voice than they had yet heard. "That was Tenvar took him! Run, ere Bure comes after us in his turn! Run, for the last stretch!"

The horror of that thought, of being pursued by the friends they had seen slain a moment since, stampeded them all. But as they charged down the last slope Elof's heart sank in his breast; the instant's delay had cost them the crossing. Dark figures were massed there now, and some were already streaming up the slope toward them. But he saw Kermorvan raise his sword with set face, and copied him; here there was no retreating, and if they fought well enough, some at least might win through. He read the same knowledge on Roc's face, and on Ils', and wondered crazily if in minutes to come he might not be fighting her semblance, or she his. Together, without shout or war cry, they plunged into the last stand of bushes.

Then he almost fell over, as something huge and black shot up flapping before his face. A harsh scream tore his ears, and from far downriver he heard it answered. He looked wildly that way, toward the distant Forest where heavy rainclouds swept over the horizon, rising to envelop the sinking moon. Like winged daggers against the clouds he saw two black silhouettes rise to meet, wheeling, cawing and squawking in idiotic triumph at what they had found. The bushes blew and riffled into his path, snaring him, holding him; all through him there coursed a sudden thrill, an awareness of some vital change, and a thought that was almost too great for his mind to contain. Then he cupped his free hand skyward, and shouted to burst his lungs.

"You there! You searching sentinels! Tell your master! Tell him, ravens, with all speed! I call in my debt! *What is owed, I reclaim!*"

It was as if the world had stopped, a moment of breathless, prickling hush so profound that Elof held his breath, though his lungs labored with the effort. It seemed he must listen, listen hard. The wind was changing. That was what he had felt! From the southwest came a stirring in the air; the light flickered as a vanguard of the cloudbank touched the chill moon and passed across it, blotting it out. A cold droplet, heavy and wet, stung his upturned face, another, two more . . . But for a moment more the moonlight broke through, and in its brief gleam he was appalled to see the dead leap forward.

Then the moon might have come crashing down upon the earth, so great was the blast of white-violet light that shattered the night. Into the ground before them it struck. Elof reeled from the impact, and the downpour that crashed to the ground like a curtain of steel chain almost knocked the travelers off their feet. Elof recovered, staggering, soaked in an instant, and then, as abruptly as the lightning, something huge plunged out of the rain into the midst of them, and he and Kermorvan had to leap for their lives. It was a horse, an immense beast and white, and its shrill neighing rang louder than the wind, the stamp and trampling of its huge hooves louder than the thunder and the roaring rain which danced smoking from its flank. A rider it bore, Elof could see boots in the black stirrups, but all above was hidden by the blinding torrent. Across their path charged the beast, then it wheeled and reared up against the rain and came thundering back, so close to Elof that he had to jump once more, lost his balance and crashed down onto the hard wet earth, almost losing hold of Gorthawer. Strong hands seized him and dragged him up.

"Run!" screamed Ils in his ear, and Roc's voice echoed it.

"Run!"

"Run!" cried Kermorvan. *"They come!"*

His legs obeyed faster than his mind; he was running before he knew it, running blindly into the sheeting rain, his only guide Ils' hand on his arm. He glanced back, and saw shapes in the grayness bounding hard on their heels. Ils' grip slipped from him, and he whirled round, ready to fight. But then the great horse was among them again, plunging, snorting, wheeling about as if to trample them all. Its huge flank slammed into him, sending him reeling off backward in the mud till he plowed into Roc, who had fallen to his knees. Elof hauled him up, and they staggered on after Ils' voice. The next few minutes were sheerest nightmare, of icy mud and drumming, stinging rain, of falling and being helped up, of helping others up, of losing hold of someone and screaming frantically to stay together, and, most of all, of fighting to stay out from under those maddening, terrifying hooves that came charging out of the storm at every turn or step, whenever they were least expected, making the travelers jump aside or be knocked off their feet. There might have been a thousand horses around them, yet Elof knew that there was only one. And always there was the rain, roaring in his ears, hammering on his head till his mind seemed malleable as any metal, his thoughts struck shapeless. Time lost its meaning. How long he had been running, or where to, he had no idea. There was only the mud, the endless ache of exhausted limbs, the hands that dragged him on, the others he dragged in turn, and always, always the white horse plunging, the cascading rain. But suddenly, as abruptly as it had begun, it stopped.

In the sudden blackness Elof tripped; he had no choice but to stop running. He risked a hesitant step forward, stumbled and barked his shin on some sharp straight edge of stone. Then he cried out in surprise as he was himself rammed in the back by a small but solid weight. "Ils?" he gasped.

"Here!" came her voice from behind him. "The others?"

"Here!" said Kermorvan, so close beside them that they both started. "And Roc?"

"Here!" they heard him say, but he was not so close, and his voice sounded strange, as if there was a faint echo behind it. "What in Hel's halls was that all about? And where are we now?"

"I guess," said Kermorvan carefully, "that on some trifling debt our mastersmith has been given full repayment, and an excellent rate of use! And that more than one Power found us when we quit the Forest. But to answer your second question, I fear we must stand quiet and await the dawn. Do not move till you can see! Who knows now where we might be . . .''

Silence fell, broken only by heavy breathing. But despite their fierce run, nobody was panting, and Elof felt no more tired than he had before; his limbs had been aching just as badly then. Very slowly he stooped to touch the stone at his foot, and the contact sent a shiver of excitement through him. Cold and bleak it felt, covered with lichen, but its shape, its sharp edges, were regular, formed, made. Then he looked up, and saw that the blackness had turned to gray, but it was the gray of evening, not dawn. Beside him stood Kermorvan and Ils, staring wildly at the immense heap of rocks that loomed up before them, high enough to blot out all else, spreading out like arms on either side to form a small bay or cleft. In a narrow gap at the base of the wall stood Roc, and he was gaping idiotically, not at them but past them. They looked at each other, and as they turned Ils gave a little shriek, and Kermorvan swallowed visibly. The end of the bay was open. Before them, clearcut in the cold air, a vast plain stretched out unbroken to the far horizon, flat and barren save for the frost-twisted remnants of grass and bush. The cold was devastating, the light clear but thin, as if here the sun were forever veiled. In all that chilly emptiness no bird sang, no beast moved, no figure stirred. And of island, of river there was never a trace. They were utterly alone.

CHAPTER EIGHT

Dry Grasses

"So!" said Kermorvan stiffly, as if surprised to find he could speak. He smiled thinly. "I am glad I never doubted your earlier experience, Elof. Here we are, still together, and it seems none the worse for . . . whatever has become of us."

"So, indeed!" said Ils sharply, fixing Elof and the barren lands beyond in a single impartial glare. "Here we are, and where's here? It still looks like part of Taoune'la to me, and no better than the one we left, with the night drawing in. What've we gained?"

"Wherever we are," said Elof absently, gazing around him, "I am sure there is some purpose in it, though we may have to search for it. Perhaps the rocks would offer us some refuge . . ."

"A perilous one!" snorted Ils. "This whole hill is some huge ancient fall of scree and boulders, with barely enough earth about it to hold stable. It must've hit something, some standing rock or outcrop maybe, to fan out into this little notch."

Elof shook his head. "No outcrop." He tapped the stone he had touched in the darkness, and others strewn about. "This one, that, those over there; weathered, but the shapes are still visible. Something of dressed stone, something manmade . . . or made, anyhow."

Ils shook her head incredulously. "Strong enough to break that fall?"

"So it would seem," said Kermorvan quietly. "Some of the boulders were shaped also."

Once he had pointed it out, the fact was inescapable. Many of those immense bulks, looming against the cloud-roof, had once been subdued to a shaping hand, and this evidence of its strength held them in awe a moment. Then the rough excitement in Roc's voice broke the spell. "To Hella with those pebbles! Come see what I've found!" They saw him still standing in the gap between two tall stones, staring down as if at something on the ground and beckoning them urgently. He climbed up a little, to squeeze his rounded frame further in; then, with a sudden outraged howl and a deep bouncing, echoing rumble, he vanished. Elof and the others ran to his aid, Ils for once in the lead despite her shorter legs, bounding over the loose rock with sure-footed ease. "Hold on!" she shouted, and flung herself down on the edge of a protruding stone. "See? There's loose rubble everywhere . . ." But even as she spoke the edge where she knelt collapsed, the stone pulled free and tipped her down into the darkness in a flurry of rock and dust. Kermorvan, leaping up, made a futile grab at her disappearing ankles. A rumble and rattle echoed out of the dark, and a jolting shriek.

"There's rubble indeed!" Roc's sardonic tones echoed eerily out of the dark, and the sound of Ils coughing and swearing, sounding more angry than hurt. "A whole loose slide of it!"

"Are you all right?" Elof yelled.

"Aye, considering!"

"Don't move, we'll pull you up . . ."

A ghoulish chuckle floated up to them; Ils was evidently undaunted by her fall. "No! Do you come down! There's something you should see. But your eyes will need some light. And mind your head, long man!"

"Come down?" demanded Kermorvan. "To what purpose?" Elof tapped him on the shoulder, and indicated the stones flanking the gap, that had kept it from collapsing or being blocked with debris. Very worn and weather-scoured they were, those massive tilted slabs, but upon their inner surfaces the remains of neat edging and beveling still showed clear. Kermorvan raised his eyebrows, and nodded.

"Very well! But what can we use for light? We have only our tinderboxes, and what little oil and kindling is in them . . ."

Elof smiled. "I may be able to do something about that. Wait now!" From within his tunic he pulled his gauntlet of mail, and drew it on in one smooth movement. "One could wish for more sun or brighter, but still . . . Now where is the west?" Kermorvan pointed, and Elof swung round and extended his hand, as if he would capture in the gem at the center of the gauntlet's palm all the pearled radiance of the westward sky.

"There indeed the sun sinks," said Kermorvan grimly, as he stood waiting, wrapping his cloak round him against the intense cold. "Over Bryhaine, over Nordeney, over all that we have left. All that now depends on us, little though it knows it, upon our quest. And there remain only four of us to fulfill it!"

"The four who threw down the Mastersmith," said Elof quietly, not looking at the tall man.

"I know," Kermorvan answered. "And I think it no accident. Perhaps we were simply the hardiest, the most alert, most accustomed to long and perilous wanderings, most inured to frightening encounters. Perhaps there was something more; who am I to say? But sorely though I regret the others, I could ill have spared any of you. So, since we have come this far together, let us not be parted ere the end!" He stood straighter then, and his gray eyes shone, bleak and grim as the skies, yet as lasting, as untouchable. It was Kermorvan as he had been, and yet not so; it was as if his determination had indeed lost some of its fire, but become thereby all the harder. He had not lost his doubts; but in that awful moment by the fire he had confronted them, defeated them, made good use of them to grow stronger. It was a path Elof knew only too well, a journey he himself had made.

At last, at the end of a long cold half hour, he clamped

his fingers tight across the jewel. "Will that suffice?" Kermorvan asked, as he turned to climb back to the gap.

"Even this weak sunlight is far stronger than torch or candle. If I let it out little by little it will last us many hours."

"As long as you can maintain your grip," said Kermorvan, peering doubtfully down into the darkness, and swinging himself into the gap. "I go first, to be sure you do not slip!"

"Very well, but first let us light our way!" He stepped up, and checked as he felt his feet slide out from under him. But in the same instant Kermorvan's steely grip closed on his arm, and he was able to lean forward into the darkness and stretch out his fist.

Slowly, carefully, he relaxed one finger a fraction. Light pooled in his palm, glinting on the metal of the gauntlet, so that it seemed to float disembodied in the blackness. Then the glow began to spread slowly, spilling down the slope of loose rubble to where Roc and Ils, scratched and dishevelled, were awaiting them. Kermorvan swung himself nimbly onto the treacherous slope and moved down it with ease, Elof scuffling one-handed after him and trying not to dislodge too many stones. The air underground seemed fresh and cold as outside, with none of the odors of damp and niter he would have expected; perhaps it was too cold for that.

"Now, Ils," called the warrior as the last of the slope crunched under his boots, "what is in this darksome cavern that you are so eager to show us?"

"For one, what you're standing on!" she said. "Look well!"

Kermorvan scraped idly at the layers of dust and dirt with his boot, then dropped suddenly to one knee. A plain pattern of concentric circles had appeared, in shades of red that shone startlingly rich against the dim dust. "A mosaic floor!" he exclaimed.

"And as fine as any you've trodden, I'll warrant," said Ils. "Save perhaps among my folk. But this is no work of ours I recognize."

Kermorvan rose suddenly and seized Elof by the arm, lifting it high. "And this no cavern, indeed!" A wave of pale light flooded across high smooth walls, glanced upon the angles of vaulting in the roof high overhead. Elof gazed around in astonishment; this was an intact chamber in a building, and of no mean size, at least twenty paces square. And it stood still, under the immense weight of the rock-fall that had shattered its upper levels. For how long had it endured thus? A hundred years? A thousand?

Kermorvan nodded. "A strong building, Elof, as you said. But whose, I wonder, was the strength?"

Elof looked around in astonishment. "I cannot say. But at least it offers some shelter for the night, this place."

"A damned chilly one!" Roc grunted. "At least there's no damp, though, and no nasty things crawling about. Nothing live at all!"

"Not even lichens and molds," muttered Ils. Her wide nostrils flared, and she sniffed. "And I smell no bats, which is odd; they love such places as these. The lands about must be too hostile for them. But as for us," she added, "there's just one little thing more . . ." She pointed to the darkness at the rear, and Elof, retrieving his arm from Kermorvan, sent light in the path of her gesture. The sudden flooding glow revealed a wide gap between floor's end and far wall, a well of blackness beneath.

"Stairs," said Ils laconically. "Used to be covered by slabs of this mosaic; see their fragments strewn about it now. And as for where they lead, well, it's too black even for my eyes down there. But the air's fresh enough, in fact it's flowing this way. What'd that suggest to you, now?"

"A tunnel . . ." said Elof, and whistled softly.

"You thinking what I am?" demanded Roc.

Kermorvan thumped fist into palm. "Kerys! This is the purpose in bringing us here! This is what we are meant to find!"

Elof frowned. "Perhaps. But where can it lead? Around us there is only the Waste, and this hill of stones."

"They must have fallen from somewhere," Roc pointed

out. "A high place we were too deep down in that cleft to see . . ."

"So sudden a rise in this flat land?" mused Kermorvan. "Elof is right to doubt. A tunnel it may be, but how long? Will we have light enough? We should go back outside, and scout . . ." His voice tailed off. Beyond the gap the glimmer of sky had vanished, and there was now only blackness. Night had come again to the Withered Marches, and it brought them deep unease.

"Looks like we'd better camp down here, then, and wait for morning," muttered Roc. But he sounded less than happy with the prospect, and cast a suspicious glance at the sliver of darkness above. "Doesn't seem much shelter now, though . . ."

Elof agreed. "Not open thus to the night, and with a second unknown darkness beneath us. And we cannot even build a fire here."

Kermorvan nodded feelingly. "A tunnel may lead down or up! I think before we decide to rest, we should at least have some idea what lies below. We may find some corner there that is safer, or at least more easily watched."

Ils shrugged. "I'm ready enough. And I confess, the further I am from that black sky, the happier I'll be."

"Then we will take a morsel of food, and explore it ere we rest," said Kermorvan. "But Elof, hoard that light of yours, and warn us when it grows dim! Its last glimmer is our lifeline!"

When they had eaten a little and rested, it was with drawn sword that Kermorvan led them down the stairs. Behind him, as he commanded, came Elof, arm outstretched and already beginning to ache, and with him, her large eyes peering eagerly into the darkness, was Ils, whose duergar strength could best support him if he lost his footing on the rubble-strewn surfaces. Roc brought up the rear, casting many a nervous glance back at the shadows that rushed in as the light passed on. It was no easy descent, for though cut into hard stone the steps were narrow and steep and hollowed with wear, and at the top they were strewn with rubble that had spilled down. Very deep

that stair led them, angling this way and that, so that the
travelers never knew what to expect round the next corner.
But for long there were only more stairs, till at last it came
as a jolt to find the next step as level as the last, and hear
the faint echoes of their footfalls go fluttering away into
air grown suddenly wider, cooler. The stair had become a
level corridor, its rounded roof supported by arches whose
plainness gave no clues to their builders. Through other
arches other descending stairs opened into it, but at its
end, only a few paces away, there was a wall of blackness.
Elof's light reached no further into it than the fringe of an
enormous flagstone, and yet somehow, perhaps through a
change in air or sound, the impact of space and emptiness
beyond was as tangible as a wall. Involuntarily Elof
clenched his fingers, and the light vanished. Quickly he
held up the gauntlet again, and as he did so it clinked
against metal; something creaked, slow and harsh, startlingly loud in the corridor.

"What was that?" hissed Kermorvan. Hastily Elof
turned the light that way, and saw the warrior's tense
shoulders relax a little; heavy hinge sockets protruded from
the wall, and dangling from them the sorry fragments of
what must once have been a strong gate. But as he stepped
out into the space beyond, Kermorvan's manner was still
watchful, and Elof, following him, saw why.

It was no mere cavern or tunnel. On either side of the
gate the walls stretched out as far as the light would reach.
Their stonework was immense, yet somehow rougher and
more ancient than in the chamber above. The flagstones
too were larger, and laid without pattern or ornament.
Kermorvan gestured to Elof, who very gradually un-
clenched his fingers a little further. Light welled and
spread over the dusty stones, but the blackness seemed to
swallow it, and he had to loosen his grip still further. Then
he sprang back and caught Gorthawer ringing from its
sheath; Roc growled and snatched his mace, Kermorvan
dropped into fighting stance and his blade hissed and flickered in the still air, defying the tall and sinister bulk that
seemed to burst in among them through the leaping shad-

ows. But Ils only laughed, caught Elof by the arm and held it steady, and they breathed more easily. The shape no longer seemed to move; it was so close they had almost blundered into it. It was only a pillar, squat and un-adorned, first of long ranks that stretched out glimmering into shadow, supporting the wide low vaultings of the roof. If it had only been higher this place would have seemed like some great hall, or even the square of a prosperous town, for its walls were pierced with gaps of deeper black-ness, doorways and alleys leading away into night. Roc clicked his tongue in wordless astonishment.

"Well!" whispered Ils. "Whatever this place is, at least it is not small. But clearly it was built more for strength than beauty."

"Couldn't be some old warren of your folks, could it?" suggested Roc.

Ils shook her head. "The masonry is excellent, but we have seldom built in such a fashion; we favor the living rock. Well, stair and corridor are bare enough, and poor places to linger; we might fare better here. Let us look!"

They spoke still in whispers, because the slightest sound echoed and carried so clearly in the still air, and because the hall was that kind of place. It reminded Elof of the great tombs and shrines of Bryhaine, but with an air of power about it that all their decorations and stained glass could not match. Even when they found many of the pil-lars cracked or broken like diseased teeth in a healthy mouth, and that a great part of the ceiling had collapsed, burying a good quarter of the square, it did not diminish the aura of strength; rather it increased their wonder that so much more of this ancient stonework still held firm, without sag or cracking that Ils' keen gaze could detect. Somehow they felt no less safe beneath it, and sensed that strange atmosphere enhanced.

"Yet it seems wholly empty," Kermorvan muttered, stirring the rubble in one of the doorways with the toe of his boot. "And unmarked, undecorated, as if it were not in everyday use . . ."

"Not wholly!" hissed Roc. "There is something here . . . Elof! Do you let me have more light! But be careful!"

Rubble from the fallen roof had piled up like a landslide against one wall, and he was clambering eagerly up onto the heap, scrabbling away at debris covering what appeared to be a plaque of carved stone. Elof, straining to hold his hand higher, could make out some design on it in relief, but not what it represented. Kermorvan hoisted himself up on long limbs to look closer, and a frown settled on his face.

"A crest of some kind . . . A design like a flame, with something behind it, something beneath . . . But it cannot be . . ." And he too fell to digging away the rubble. Then he paused, and sat back on his haunches. "A beacon," he said softly. "A cresset, such as is burned on the tops of our tall towers to guide ships at sea. And behind it is shown the outline of a wide-sailed ship . . . Kerys! I have never seen it drawn thus, but I know the sign well. Past all error, it is the emblem of our Mariners' Guild." He looked around, and shook his head in sheer disbelief. "Then . . . it was *my* people who built this place?"

"Aye," breathed Roc. "Must've been . . . But why? And where are . . ."

The sound that stopped his words was all the more sudden in rising out of such utter silence, the more frightening in being, in this sterile place, the voice of something alive. But it was not human. It was a deep coughing growl that came echoing out of the darkness. That it was far distant did not diminish the menace of it, and it jolted them back to the dangers of the realm they were in. Heads turned, bodies tensed, hands caught at weapons, too suddenly; the disturbed rubble shifted beneath them. Whose foot it was that first slipped, whose balance that was lost, did not matter, for none could have avoided it. Elof certainly was not to blame, for it was down upon him that the others slid and tumbled among a landslide of loose stone and stinging, choking dust. He had no time to resist, nor any hope of it; the slide landed with a thunderous, torrential crash, his legs were whipped from under him, and he fell backward, arms flailing. His head hit the paving with a stunning ring, his fingers clutched convulsively and sagged open. For a moment it seemed that lightning struck in the chamber, so bright was the glare that filled it, showing every nook, every corner in stark relief and jagged shadow, setting every mote in the billowing dustcloud agleam and dancing like iridescent jewels. It showed the travelers to each other, sprawled in grotesque attitudes, wide-eyed, dishevelled, dustsmeared, blood-streaked from cuts and scratches. Then it was gone.

Utter blackness rushed in on them, a darkness so absolute it seemed solid, more stifling even than the dust. Elof, struggling feebly to rise, found himself seized by strong hands and dragged swiftly free of the rubble. "No bones are broken?" hissed Kermorvan in his ear. "Good! Get back to the wall, that way! Stay silent!" Elof blundered into the cold stone and leaned there, fighting to quieten his breath, to listen in the absolute darkness; it was all too easy to imagine something, drawn by the noise, rushing toward them. But after a moment he heard Kermorvan's urgent whisper again. "Nothing stirs! So we have a few minutes, at least! Is all the light gone, Elof?"

"Yes!" he choked. "I am sorry . . ."

"No fault of yours! Ils, if you can see anything . . ."

"Nothing!" she gasped, her voice shaken.

"Look back!" whispered Kermorvan harshly. "Do you press your back flat to the wall here, so, and you will be looking back the way we came, to the stairs! Some faint glimmer of light might yet filter down . . ."

"Still nothing!" Her voice was shaking, and that was a rare thing. "It will still be night out there . . ."

"There might be moonlight!" insisted Kermorvan with savage urgency. "Move your head about, there may be a pillar in the way! Come, girl, you are our only hope!"

"No!" she sobbed. "I have walked too long by day . . . If we wait till dawn . . . Ah!"

"What?"

"Light . . . very faint, but true light . . . but that cannot be the way we came down!"

"We have no choice!" muttered the warrior grimly. "Even if it leads us onto that beast, that way we must take! To linger is to court the same fate, for surely it will be able to hunt us by scent and sound!"

"And if there are more stairs on the way? Or worse obstacles?" demanded Ils.

Metal tapped softly on stone. "I will feel the way with my sword. But the nearer we come to the light, the better you should see such things! Take my hand, and Roc yours, and Elof, do you bring up the rear this time!"

"I don't mind!" grunted Roc, barging into Elof as they shuffled along the wall like a troop of blind beggars.

"Kermorvan is right!" Elof whispered. "Gorthawer is sharper than your mace for anything to run onto in the dark!"

"Quiet, and follow!" said Kermorvan, and his voice had his sword's edge. "Now comes the worst of it!"

And indeed it is recorded that, although there were dangers as great, few hours in all that long journey seemed worse to Elof than that travail in the dark. For in the blackness he could do little but find one footfall after the next, sliding and scraping across the stones, and listen, and think: he lost the sense of the passing moments, and the fires of his fancy burned high. It brought back to him the stairs of Vayde's Tower, and the black emptiness he had sensed there, the wrath and regret that churned the very dark. Here too the dark seemed full, but of no single feeling; it was empty, yet filled with complex patterns, like the molds for some intricate jewel. It pressed in on him like a vast crowd, insistent, demanding. Were they the builders of this place, these thronging phantoms? He sought to separate them, to bring some distinct image of them into his mind's eye now that his outward sight was made useless. But what rose up before him was a single face, a startling image that faded even as it became clear, yet seemed burned into his memory. Haggard it looked, hardened, yet in its way handsome, the jaw firm under a short white beard, the nose straight and strong but flanked by eyes that burned like coals out of deep sockets, belying the lines of age about them, the forehead deeply furrowed beneath thick white brows and hair. It was a commanding countenance, strong and wise, yet holding an alarming ferocity. And somehow it was known to him. He felt a great need to recognize it, and he wrestled with it in the blackness. He thought of Korentyn, or Kermorvan at his most lordly and ageless, but this man they resembled only in stern kingliness and strength; there was no likeness of feature. And this face wholly lacked the calm kindness native to them both; he felt that even its compassion would be fierce. It puzzled and haunted him all through that dark time, and for long thereafter, ere he came at last to the truth of it.

How long they walked thus in the blackness they never knew. Elof could gauge it only by hunger and thirst, and lack of sleep; he was not hungry when they set out, but he was ravenous ere the end. He thought it foolish to dwell on that; time enough for food when they had light. They had their packs, at least, and Kermorvan Bure's also. There was food enough for a few days, if they were careful; though by then they had better be under the sun once more, and among living things. But where their way was taking them, that they never knew. They went a good way round the walls of that deep hall, across the mouths of many doorways and corridors that led off from it, whither they knew not. Every moment they awaited that dreadful growl once more, or a sudden silent rush out of the shadows; Elof clutched Gorthawer tight, leaving the hammer at his belt, for it was little use if he could not see its target.

At last Ils found the opening that was the source of the light, and they turned to follow it. Kermorvan sought to blaze the wall with his knife at this point and others, to mark the way should they need to return, but he could seldom be sure whether he was marking an alcove or a corridor, or even whether he made any visible mark on the unyielding stone, and he soon gave up. Ils tried to count her steps, but the way was too long, and there were too many stumbles. That they passed through at least one other hallway they were sure, for they touched more pillars. But it was far from there to the light.

Deep into those winding ways it led them, from open space to narrow way, till Elof began to fear it might be some wisp of foul air, like the marshfires that led travelers astray. But Ils insisted that it was growing brighter as they drew nearer, and Kermorvan pointed out that they seemed to be following the flow of the air, raising hopes that it might be another way out. They heard no more of the terrible growls, and that, too, heartened them. At last, as they made their way down a wide lane, it seemed to Elof that he could see something more than the shifting colors of the eye in blackness, and a moment later he was sure: he could make out the shapes of the walls at the end, silhouettes against a faint greenish glow. It was not long before Kermorvan also saw it, and Roc, and they hastened to find its source. The lane ended in another open space, this time round in shape, its upholding pillars arranged in circles. But as before, some were damaged or altogether broken, so that the stone roof had cracked in many places. Between those cracks some stone had fallen away and left a wider gap; it was through this that the light came, a long streak in the roof. Kermorvan blinked. "I had not thought us so close to the surface," he remarked. "We may indeed find a way out here! Let us look closer, but this time take more care!" The air here grew very cold. They edged closer, clambering more carefully over the heaps of debris, gathering under the precious glow. Kermorvan was the first to reach it, and look up. But all he did was stand there on the rubble, saying no word even when Elof staggered up beside him. He saw why at once.

The roof was not open, and there was no sky beyond it. It was a pallid greenish radiance that filtered down, such as he guessed might be found in the depths of the sea, too dim for any eyes of men save those long deprived of better. The crack laid bare a solid surface like a seam of quartz, a soiled translucent white in hue. Elof, his brain numbed, reached up to touch it, but Kermorvan seized his wrist. "No! No need to risk that!" he said, in a strange half-choked voice. "I know what it is. And so also I know now what this place must be." He stared around at them, wild-eyed, his face and voice a weird blend of feelings. "It is far that Raven has borne us, very far. Beyond Taoune'la we have come, to the margins of the Ice. And beneath; for there we see it, above our heads. That is the Ice itself."

A cry of disbelief rose to Elof's lips, and died there unvoiced. He saw as much on the faces of the others; they stared up at the riven roof, shocked, unbelieving, yet unable to deny that pallid whiteness shining through the rock.

"But it can't be!" he heard Roc whisper in protest. "I mean, if there's a whole great thick glacier up there, then how's so much light getting through here?"

"It might be the bottom of a crevasse," muttered Ils. "Cracked deeper, perhaps, by the collapse of the roof . . ." She hugged herself, and shivered. "The Ice! I have seen it before, but never so close . . ."

Elof nodded. "I have trodden it, crossed a narrow stretch of it. Evil is that memory! But never did I dream of passing *beneath* it . . ." Indeed he hardly dared imagine it, the glaciers that scoured the earth in their advance, the ice-sheet that enshrouded tall mountains and left only their summits protruding, stark and bare as fleshless skulls; that incalculable, implacable weight of Ice, crushing, malevolent, hung now only a few feet above his head, held at bay only by the flawed and transient works of men. . . .

The works of men. A sudden suspicion grew in him, a revelation brighter than this pool of light in the grim dark, a shock of understanding, coming so close upon the other that it gripped him and shook him hard. He knew now what else Kermorvan had seen: only dimly could he conceive all that it must mean to him, warrior lord, prince in exile, last of a dispossessed line of kings. Even in Elof, of no lineage that he knew, awareness of where he stood awoke great awe, smoldering anger, deep regret, and a wild coursing wonder. In Kermorvan he read all of these, and more. The warrior quivered as if a storm raged within him, and yet his face was calm, transcendent, uplifted. That also Elof understood. Kermorvan stood where he stood, and not even death could snatch this moment from him. His voice resounded in bright music against the ancient stones.

"Aye, my friends. Elof knows. Do you? Do you guess whither we have come? These are the underground ways at this land's heart, lost home of our folk, lost realm of my line. We tread where no man has trodden since the flight of Korentyn a thousand years past. We walk in all that remains of the City by the Waters, the vaults and cellars and storehouses of Kermorvan the City, the mighty Catacombs of Morvan. And out of time, beyond hope, a lord of Morvan sets foot in these vaults once again. I have come *back*!"

He stepped stiff-legged down the rubble, staring around him as if afraid it was a vision he saw, that might melt away at any moment. When he came to the nearest pillar he pressed his hands against it, savoring the solidity of the stone. And he rested his head against it, and closed his eyes, and spoke no word for a long time.

Roc too gazed about him a while, and cocked his head approvingly. "So this is home! Or what's left of it. Solid bit of work, is this, to hold up with such a dead weight atop it! And it has a fine feeling about it, for all the dark and the chill. If this is the cellars, the city must've been a grand place." He rummaged in his pack. "High time we had a bite, to celebrate! Hard bread, smoked flesh, dried fruit and a swallow of wine. Fit for a king! And I feel like one, coming back here!"

Elof glanced at him in surprise. "You say *back*, as Kermorvan did. Yet neither of you has ever been here, any more than I."

"Ah, but we have! In spirit, like. These are the Lost Lands, that were snatched away from us, and that we never thought anyone could see anymore. I can just remember when I was a little lad, marveling at all the old tales of it: to set foot here, that's a marvel rarer yet. Don't you feel any of that? You're one of the old northerners by your looks, after all; this was where your folks sprang from, too.''

"I have felt something here," Elof admitted. "But not that." Roc passed his handfuls of food, and while they ate, sitting with their backs to a pillar, Elof told him of his vision. Roc nodded vigorously, his shaggy red hair flopping over his face: he knew Elof well enough not to undervalue his feelings.

"That would be of the last years, maybe," he mused. "When there was mayhem and panic and even bare-faced treason, by all accounts; Kermorvan could tell you more. That face you describe might belong in such a time. The ending was noble enough, aye, but the last throes were savage. They gave Kerbryhaine that bad beginning, come back to haunt it now. Still, it's the nobility that lasted here, I reckon."

Elof nodded. "It is noble, true enough. But it is dead, and a place of great danger for us still." He stared up in dismay. "How will I ever gather enough of this dim glow to light us out of here? It would take a day in itself!"

A plump finger jabbed him in the ribs. "No need for that, boy! Leave it to the Elder Folk to flog their wits for you, as usual! Though I'll admit that the builders of this place were not unpractical, either, in keeping a good store of these ready to hand!" And she dangled before them two long handles of rough stoneware, topped by cages of light metal, and from a bag she tipped lumps of some grayish substance. "What we should have looked for in the first place! Pitch and tow and sweet resin, and many other substances too, I've no doubt. The city folk might have cleared their cellars when they fled, but they'd not bother taking their torches with them!"

"True enough!" acknowledged Kermorvan, coming to join them. To their utter astonishment he laughed aloud, and hugged Ils so boisterously he swung her from the ground. "I should have thought of that myself! The more so, as the Catacombs were intended also as a refuge in time of war, with great store of all necessaries. Little did the builders foresee the coming of that enemy before whom no refuge stands!''

Elof chuckled. ''You had much on your mind, just then . . .''

''True again,'' said Kermorvan wryly, slumping down beside Elof and accepting some food. ''Even yet I am amazed! That the Catacombs endured I could never have dreamed, let alone that it was to them we had come. Your friend the Raven! I am torn between the urge to fall down and revere him, and to wring his neck!''

''And do I not know that urge!'' said Elof with deep feeling, and they chuckled. Hemmed in by darkness as they had been, the promise of light made a vast difference to their mood. But when they had eaten and rested a few minutes, Kermorvan swiftly grew serious.

''These Catacombs . . .'' he said quietly, glancing around him. ''It is good, very good to have trodden here. To have sat at ease beneath the very citadel and strength of our enemy only adds spice to the drink! But let us not forget that is where we are. Great as it once was, it has become dark and perilous, and even I have neither wish nor cause to linger.'' He caught up one of the link-holders and thrust a torch onto the spike at its heart. ''Let us see how well this burns, after a thousand years!''

Roc was already flicking the wheel of his tinderbox. A fragment of smoldering kindling laid upon the dust-grayed pitch sank and smoked a moment, then blossomed to a flare of bright orange fire that set the shadows capering and dimmed the pallid Icesheen to nothing. The other torch flared as easily in its flame, and that one Kermorvan took. ''And when you feel able, Elof, do you capture a little of the torchfire, and give us one safeguard more. Now, let us be gone from here!''

At once, though, it became clear that this would be no easy task. For from this circular hall many ways opened, and they could not agree on which one they had entered by. But at length Kermorvan said, ''Do not despair!'' and lifted the torch he carried high, almost to the roof. The shadows raced across the stone and capered in the open ways, and he marked the way the flame fluttered. "There is still the flow of the air to follow. It leads us that way, I guess."

"Better than no guide at all!" said Roc cheerfully. "And at least we'll not be stubbing our toes so often now!"

So it proved; for in the bright warm light they passed quickly over the cold flagstones of the ways, past many doorways dark and mysterious. Glancing into some of these side chambers, they found many empty, and some still stacked with bales and boxes they did not stay to examine; in this chill dry air their wood had not decayed. But in others box and bale had been torn asunder and their remains and contents strewn violently about, sometimes right across the corridor, making a considerable obstacle.

"Surely we never passed this!" grumbled Roc, wading awkwardly through a mess of shriveled debris. "We are off our path!"

"If you know another way, take it!" Ils snapped, kicking the rubbish from her boots.

"The air is still with us," said Kermorvan calmly. "It should lead us to some way out, even if not the one by which we came."

"Aye!" retorted Roc, looking behind him into the blackness. "But how soon?"

To that Kermorvan made no reply. He was weary, as the sag of his shoulders betrayed, bone-achingly weary as they all were now that their flush of excitement had worn off, and sorely in need of sleep. Whether it was day or night now in the world above they had no way of knowing; the only hour they cared for was that of their escape from this unhappy place. Roc's tread grew leaden, his head bowed; Elof found his feet dragging, his heart chill. Only Ils, invigorated by being below ground, seemed to keep her strength, her wide eyes gleaming, her heavy boots skipping lightly over the flagstones with scarcely a sound. "Yet this is not my world," she muttered. "We live among soft light and even winds beneath the living stone. And if not those, then sooner harsh sun and bitter weather upon the stark surface than this lifeless shell. Here death alone reigns!'' How truly she spoke they were soon to find out.

It was some hours later that the corridor again opened out before them, into the curved wall of a small hall shaped like the halfmoon. Three other ways joined it, but the airflow led them to the straight wall opposite and the great double gateway of steel bars set in it, most skillfully wrought and ornamented. But both outer and inner gates had long ago been twisted and half torn from their deep runners, leaving a gap through which even Kermorvan could pass without ducking. Ils sniffed the new air disdainfully. ''Do you not smell it? A faint rankness in it, like an animal odor . . . It might be bats! And that would bode well, since they must live within reach of a way out.''

''Can't be too soon for me!'' grunted Roc.

Behind the gate lay a single corridor, wider than any so far, and as they held up their torches the walls seemed to spring to life around them. Carvings covered them from floor to ceiling, delicately detailed but vivid and forceful, figures in low relief of men, women, beasts familiar and strange, tall ships and high towers, wide lands and mysterious horizons. And every now and again, as they moved down the long walls, the strangest figures of all appeared, human in aspect but so eerie and vast, so idealized in their setting, that Elof knew he must be seeing images of the Powers.

''That is so!'' said Kermorvan, gazing about him in delight. ''This looks to be some private fane, or other place of reverence. For here are depicted tales from the early days of the world, before the coming of men or duergar or any living thing, when it was given over to the Elder Powers for its shaping, and then to the New for the coming of life. Then it was, say the tales, that the Elder Powers rebelled, refusing to hand over the custody of what they had shaped and grown to love, to be used and drastically changed by mere growing things, plants and beasts and men.''

Roc snorted. "More fool they. A barren love, that, for a lifeless world; what was there in it worth their interest?"

"More than you might think!" Elof told him. "For there is beauty and order in the patterns of matter that does not live. Think of the slow change and flowering of crystals; might not a snowflake or spar or gemstone be to them as a flower to us? Or at the other extreme, might they not find beauty in the roaring energy of a volcano, the thunder and lightning of great storms, the ceaseless motion of the waves? We can, at times. Even the Ice can be fair, very fair." He looked at one tall image, of a woman, unclad, stately in her beauty, standing amid what seemed to be the waters of a waterfall, save that it hung above mountains, and its flow and billows were all of stars. Kermorvan looked at him and nodded somberly, sharing a memory of majesty and terror. He pointed to the frieze around the image, within which in archaic characters a name was set. Ils lowered her torch and spelled it out.

"T . . . A . . . OU . . . Taounehtar! Brr!" She tilted the torch away hastily. "There's beauty you may have, for my money, and well rid! Why put her on your walls? You neglect the best and greatest of the Elder Powers, the one who never rebelled, him we most revere."

"Ilmarinen," nodded Kermorvan. He lifted his torch, so that the flames spilled and smoked along the roof, and waved a hand at the wall opposite. From floor to ceiling a single vertical slab was set in it, graven with a single vast image. "He was neither forgotten nor neglected. See him there, much as your folk portray him, Ils."

Ils sniffed. "You make him too tall, like a long human, with huge shoulders and spindled legs, not fair and square proportions. And what is he hammering out on his anvil there?"

Elof peered down at the slab. "It is hard to tell . . . The image seems worn, or defaced . . ."

Kermorvan held his torch lower. "Mmmn. Yes, there are some gouges and chips out of the edge here, and many deep scratches. By the color of the stone beneath they were done more recently; certainly since the destruction of Morvan. As if something had been clawing at the slab . . .''

''There's a keyhole here!'' barked Roc. ''This whole slab's a door!''

''And a solid one, for it has never been opened or broken,'' said Kermorvan thoughtfully.

Roc groaned. ''That'd be safe to sleep behind, if we could only get it open . . . Elof, you're a sharp lad with locks—''

''Not ones a thousand years old!'' protested Elof. ''Time alone can weld metal, even without much corrosion. And how am I likely to succeed, when hostile hands have not?''

''Their approach was less subtle,'' Kermorvan said. ''They would not have battered at the door thus if they knew anything of locks. So why not set your hand to it?''

Elof sighed, took his bag of tools from his pack, and extracted a light hammer and some long shapes of bright metal strangely wrought and twisted. ''There will probably be ten open doors further down the corridor . . .''

''Something open that suddenly becomes shut may attract a certain attention!'' countered Kermorvan dryly, watching Elof tap all round the lock, feeling the vibration with his fingertips, then pass the long probes into the keyhole and tap on them. ''Well, do you think you can do it?''

Elof shrugged, produced a little bottle of fine oil from the toolpack and dipped a probe into it. ''Who can tell? If it is as simple as it appears . . . But I doubt that. Morvan the City was a great center of our craft, and much wisdom was scattered to the winds at its fall.''

''Yet it had to start somewhere. If that lock was old even at Morvan's fall . . .''

Elof's irritation flared. ''Then the accursed thing really will be set solid! Quiet, and let me work!''

Kermorvan smiled tolerantly, and strolled a little way up the corridor, gazing watchfully into the dark. Roc and Ils joined him, peering at the carvings and talking in low voices. ''What d'you reckon that place might be behind there, anyway?'' muttered Roc, suppressed excitement in his voice. ''Some secret hideaway?''

Kermorvan shrugged. ''It is hard to say. For people, you mean, or treasure? That is less likely. The lock is not well concealed, and the folk of Morvan must have known there was no hope of rescue or recovery in their lifetime or their descendants'. But many old houses of Kerbryhaine have some kind of hidden entrance or stair . . .''

''You mean . . . that could be the lower end of some such thing?'' Ils demanded. ''Leading to an escape, perhaps?''

''Perhaps. But do not build up your hopes. For now I will be content with some place to rest.''

Elof pursed his lips, and went on probing at the lock. He had sprung its levers free, oil was spread liberally over the channels where the key should travel, and he had traced their shape; it did indeed seem simple, too simple to deter any save the most casual attempt to open it. Perhaps they had thought the great gate protection enough. Next, he must twist and tap a scrap of stiff wire into the shape of the wards; held in grippers, that should shift the bolt, if it could still be moved. He maneuvered the wire into place, and began to twist it, squeaking and scraping, through the channels. Up it went, up, up, and he became aware without turning that the others were breathing down his neck, tense and silent. Slowly, with all the delicate strength he could muster, he twisted it to the very top of the lock. Then it was as if fire and ice flowed into his arm, a convulsive, tingling shock that must have showed in his face.

''What is it?'' Kermorvan hissed. ''Are you all right? Can you not . . .''

''I am a fool!'' snapped Elof between clenched teeth. ''Who would place so strong a virtue upon so simple a thing? But there it is, a force of stern authority such as I have seldom encountered . . .''

''To what effect?'' Ils whispered.

''I don't know,'' muttered Elof. ''It was too quick, I wasn't ready. I must . . .'' Gritting his teeth, he twisted the wire once more, hard. Again that pain surged into

him, but this time he met it, endured it, opened himself
to it and sought to read the resonances it awoke within
him. A feeling grew in him, which became a note, a
phrase, a line, a complex net of surging music. And in
that music he heard words of stern command.

> *Look to the lock! The wards are of fire!*
> *Of ice the bolt!*
> *It stings,*
> *It burns*
> *The hand that turns*
> *That lacks the right,*
> *That serves the ill!*
> *It scorches,*
> *It freezes,*
> *Its strength shall consume you!*
> *Fall back then, false that you are!*

"Ah!" he murmured. Never before had he been so
clearly aware of the virtue within a work; it was as if
words were reinterpreted, remade within his mind, as if
the voice of that unknown smith of elder days spoke to
him, self to self, through the power of their common craft.
Eerie he found that, and daunting, and yet at the same
time its sheer clarity aided him. "It says only one with
authority may open this door! Ancient and arrogant and
strong it feels, older than the metal of the lock itself . . ."

"Is that possible?" demanded Roc.

"If the lock were repaired piecemeal, over many, many
years, yes . . . and if the virtue were made strong enough
in the beginning. Which it surely was."

Kermorvan growled with impatience. "Then you cannot open it?"

"Not directly! But let me think . . ."

"It would be a strong force indeed," he heard Ils murmur, "that could resist what is in him . . . if only he can
bring it to bear . . ."

Elof searched his mind with growing impatience. In

what would the lock recognize authority? A key, set with a matching virtue? But keys may easily be lost in the course of time, and that spell was meant to last. Was that why the lock was made deliberately simple? So new keys could easily be cut . . . and used with some greater authority, less likely to be lost. Any number of locks could be secured thus. Most men would need some outward emblem of authority, imbued by smithcraft with virtues of command, but a smith might manage with a simple form of words, if only they were the right words . . .

Or strong ones. The arrogant sting of the spell, the shock of pain and the contemptuous dismissal in the words, these had roused a great impatience in him, and it swelled now to danger. Kermorvan had bidden him open this door, and who now was lord of these ruins, if not he? Elof bitterly resented being so daunted by this ancient force; he would meet its demand for authority with his own. He would create a counterpoint to that wild music, an answer to those challenging words, as surely as he had shaped wire to ward. And with that thought his impatience turned to a harsh insistent rhythm, a chant of authority no less imperious than that upon the lock. He leaned his head against the cold stone and though he muttered the words he seemed to feel them batter against that guardian thought like a forging hammer, like that of Ilmarinen in his image.

> By the self that hears your singing,
> And the craft that burns within me,
> By the strength I turned to evil
> And the evil that I withered,
> By the skill that I have nurtured
> And the knowledge I have gathered,
> By the courage of the seeker
> And the quest that now I further
> These the rights you shall acknowledge
> These the strengths you shall bow down to,
> You, a singing of the Old World,
> You shall hearken to a Master
> As the Shaping to the Shaper

In the image you are set in!
As a rightful lord has willed it,
By that will I bid you—open!

On the last word he gripped the wire and twisted, this time
with all his strength, ignoring the pain that lifted before
him like a forbidding barrier. Then suddenly, astonishingly, it was no longer there; the lock was turning softly,
silently, the bolt sliding smoothly back from the socket it
had lain in a thousand years or more. Elof let out a great
sigh, and sagged down on his knees, still clasping the
grippers. Under his weight the slab creaked out a little
way from the wall, and stopped.

"Bravely done, my smith!" said Kermorvan admir-
ingly, as Roc helped Elof to his feet. "Do you rest now!
For since your skill has freed the lock, let mere thews do
what remains!" And he leaned forward, clenched his long
fingers round the lip of stone, braced a foot against the
wall and hauled. Slowly, ever so slowly, the great door
yielded to his careful strength, a finger's width, a handspan; the faint protest of hinges could be heard, but no
more. Ils ducked under his arms to add her own unhuman
strength; her shoulders tensed, the muscles stood out on
her shapely limbs, tracing the shape of the heavy bones
beneath. The slab advanced a handspan more, and in its
exposed edge metal glinted, a diamond-shaped plate of
tarnished bronze that could only be the lock. Upon it were
incised many characters, but it was the cartouche upon the
square face of the bolt that caught Elof's eye, that sowed
within him a sudden unease. So fierce a challenge, on a
lock so simple . . . Those characters, that pattern, he had
seen them on other bronze; his hand flew to his pack, to
the wrapped shape of the scepter, and he saw at last what
crooked shape it must be that Ilmarinen forged. That
carven door must symbolize royal command, the power
those characters embodied; and so he had misread that
challenge. Not arrogance, but a stern decree of state . . .
"Kermorvan, hold! This may be no common hiding
place . . ."

But he was already too late. Under the unison of strong
arms the stone was swinging outward with a momentum
of its own, sending Ils hopping out of its path, Kermorvan
striving to halt it lest it be torn from its protesting hinges.
The torches fluttered, and from the open doorway the
darkness billowed out like curtains in the wind. A slight
rush of air swirled out after it, a waft of odors strange to
the cold corridors, a heavy, stifling weight of dust and
must, a strange scent tinged with a thin spiciness, with
aromatic resins and pungent balsam. It was such a smell
as antiquity might have, the dust of withered summers, of
faded years.

Kermorvan, releasing the door, swept up the guttering
torches and stepped over the low sill into the chamber
beyond, holding them high. They flamed up and flared,
the blackness cowered away at their fire and fled down the
long chamber before them. For a moment Kermorvan's
tall shape hid it from the others; but then he seemed to
crumple as if struck. His cloak billowed about him and he
sank down to his knees, the torches sagging in his hands;
red light and long shadows surged up the walls. Strange
shadows they were, from the high slabs and pedestals of
stone ranged along those walls, from the still shapes upon
them. Kermorvan bowed his head low in the somber glow.

"What ails you, man?" Elof whispered, hardly able to
speak aloud. Kermorvan made no reply, nor showed that
he had heard. "What is it?" persisted Elof, ever more
unnerved. "What place is this?"

To those who knew him less well, Kermorvan might
have lacked expression, have looked like the graven image
of a man painted into life yet tinged with the stone that
lay beneath. And they might have asked, those who did
not know him, into what unimaginable depth or distance
his gray eyes stared. His companions, each in their way,
knew better, saw the play of feelings inside him like cloud
shadows going across a hill, like breath upon glass, heat
through iron. His stony lips stirred, but it was not to them
he spoke.

"*All that we were . . .*" he murmured, and shook his

head, almost in disbelief. Roc, hearing the words, looked around him quickly.

"It can't be!" he burst out. "We've not . . ." He bit his lip, and to Elof's astonishment he looked ready to turn and run. Kermorvan repeated the words softly.

> *All that we were, passes;*
> *A sheaf of dry grasses*
> *That late in green meads blew,*
> *To this end are we come.*
> *Passed on, scepter and crown,*
> *Justice and rule, laid down,*
> *As least man must, we rest*
> *Silent, in our long home.*

"Ils and Elof, you would not know that," he said gravely. "It is the opening of the rhymes of lore that are called *Arel Arhlayn*. Few in Bryhaine now learn them, but that first line has become proverbial."

A dreadful understanding cut through Elof's confusion. "But *Arel Arhlayn*, in the old words that would mean . . ."

"The Tale of Lords, the tally of kings. Exactly so. And you could say you stand among it here, its living self, or that once lived. For as you feared, this is no common hiding place. We have strayed into the crypts of the ancient King's House, and by your craft laid open the place called Dorghael Arhlannen, vault and tomb of the Kings of the realm of Morvan, the deepest hallow of all that land. And all around us they lie."

Elof could have wished the cold stone to open then and swallow him. For in his haste, his old ruthless haste, had he not seen that stern barrier only as a thing to be broken down, without thought or respect? Even thus an Ekwesh pirate might shatter a casket of fine crystal to get at the gold within. The Kings of Morvan! Kermorvan's own line, his forefathers whom he most revered . . . Like Korentyn. Elof thought then of the brand that ancient lord had set upon him, of open honor and hidden shame. Had he not now earned it doubly?

"Elof Valantor . . ." said Kermorvan, and Elof sickened at the name. The warrior's voice was hushed, but the same cold strength was in it that the smith had heard first among the duergar, and never forgotten. "Well may you bear that title! For by the cunning of your hand you have brought an era to an end, a long era of division, of separation, that should never have taken place. To this place of old it was the custom that every prince must come ere he took the kingship, to revere his ancestors, to take counsel among them, to reflect upon the end to which even such power as his must come, and so use it more worthily. And because the son King Keryn sent east was too young to have done this, it was the pretext his enemies chose to deny him the throne, and all of us of his line following. Now let them regret it! For they have laid so much weight on that one custom, that it shall turn as heavily against them. You have done me greater honor than I deserve, my friend." He looked round, met the astonishment on Elof's face and smiled gravely. "Did you fear otherwise? Why? It was at my behest you broke the enchantment on the lock; what followed was mine to bear, for weal or ill. And bear it I shall! Share this with me, my friends; look around you, imagine, wonder! Here lie in state the remains of the Kings of Morvan since the first founding of that kingdom upon the then unknown shores of Brasayhal, a good four thousand years ago."

The shadows shivered suddenly; the torches were smoking, dying in Kermorvan's hand, yet he paid them no heed. A deep awe had settled upon them all as he spoke, upon Roc, upon Elof and even upon Ils to whom the realms of men were slight and transient; and that same sense of presence which had troubled Elof in the outside blackness now returned. He looked from bier to bier, at the shapes that lay beneath dulled armor and the ragged remains of rich robes, mere webs now held together only by dust and the rich metal threads of their ornament; fit warning indeed for any aspiring prince, but a source of deep pride also. Elof thought he might find it in himself to envy such a lineage, yet in truth he did not; he cared little for his ancestry, there being so many other things he yearned to know. He could guess, though, what they must mean to Kermorvan, these rows of shapes stretching out into the shadowy depths of the tomb, and to Roc also. Their silent majesty told strongly upon Elof, and all that they stood for; the weight of years, the building of a mighty realm of men, the long sustaining and last defense of it against the relentless, ageless enemy, and within all those the high events, war and peace, battle and building, the myriad lives of men they had once both ruled and served. And they served them yet, bearing mute witness to the life of their kingdom when all other traces had been erased. Then the torches guttered again, and the thrall was broken; Ils snorted impatiently, plucked the linklights from Kermorvan's fingers and waved them about to rekindle them.

"Aren't all here, are they?" she demanded. "Didn't some die away from home, or at sea?"

"Few," answered Kermorvan, rising stiffly, "and we always strove to bring their bodies back. Those few are here in effigy, with arms or armor that were theirs. You see those arches, spanning the vault? They were once its rear walls, and mark the many times Dorghael Arhlannen was extended. At the last the number of biers was increased to two hundred, and one hundred and sixty-four kings lie here in state."

Ils chuckled sardonically. "A grave matter as you might say, then, that with all the spare accommodation some should lie on the cold floor!"

"What?" cried Kermorvan, seizing back a torch. "If some enemy has defiled this place . . ."

As he sprang forward Elof saw what Ils' sight had picked out of the shadows. Far down the tomb, to either side of the last arch, two shapes lay like a child's stick drawing marked in the dust of the floor. But the lines stood proud of it, and most so at the heads, for they were skulls. It was by the bones of two men that Kermorvan knelt. "These were not thrown down!" he murmured. "Surely they lie as they died, helms on their heads, harness about them . . ." Gently he lifted the remains of a mailshirt, and a long halberd, still intact. "By the look of it, harness of the old Royal Guard . . ." Then he gasped, and stood up suddenly. "The two guardsmen! Korentyn said it! He took with him only two old men of his guard!" Slowly, almost unwillingly, he stepped through the last arch, and stopped there. The others crowded behind him, and saw as he did.

The long rows of biers here were empty, save for a few near the arch. The dark shapes upon them were covered, as all the rest had been, by robe and mail and helm, all save the last. Like the guardsmen, he lay uncovered, save by a great black shield, a sunken shape within his mail. But above it was no common helm, for even through the layers of dust the torchlight drew an answer from it, a glancing sparkle of brighter fires, glittering there in many colors about the head of death.

"So this is where he came." Kermorvan's voice was somber, deepened by sorrow, and yet within it the triumphant ring still sounded. "He and his comrades, to the heart of the city they would not surrender. Here they stood, as the Ice ground and thundered overhead and laid Waste all that they had known and loved, all that those around them here had built up. This place at least they could die defending. And when the ruin was complete, and this vault still stood, they chose to perish here, of thirst or hunger or by their own hands, rather than risk opening that door to despoilment and desecration. And they are proven right!" He darted forward suddenly, and knelt by the side of that last bier a moment, while the others watched in silence. Then, slowly, he rose, and reached out with hands that shook to the figure that lay before him. Gently, reverently, he detached the helm, and set it down on the bier's end. Then from his own pack he drew the helm he had carried through so many adventures, and, lifting from it its linings of soft leather, he set it upon the fleshless head. Only then did he lift the other from the bier, and drew his long cloak across it in a flourish. Dust flew from it like banished time, and in the torchlight it flared and dazzled as he raised it high. In fashion it was like his own, or the other that Elof had crafted, jet black, high-crowned, with a facemask whose aspect was all hawkish ferocity and dire rage. But the slanted eyes of that mask were picked out in bright gems, the sculpted brows were shapes of silver and gold, and above them rode a circlet of gold in which a great white stone blazed among a setting of green gems, white as clear water, green as spring grasslands, golden as the kindly sun.

"Behold the Great Crown of Morvan!" said Kermorvan softly. His gray eyes shone with the light of the sun over the infinite oceans. "Against all chance I have spoken with my kin, the last alive who walked here. Here I have come to what remains, to Kermorvan itself, Morvan the City, to him who sleeps here, its last king. From him I receive what was to him entrusted, and that he faithfully preserved to the end. And that trust I take upon myself! The chain that was sundered is made whole, the line that was severed is restored in me. No longer is he the last King of Morvan! For another shall follow him." And he raised the helm above his head.

Then, to the surprise of his friends, he lowered it, and cradled it in his arm, and smiled. "But not yet. I must give meaning to that name, before I claim it." And he picked up the linings, and began to fasten them within it. "Strange, are they not, the workings of destiny? And foolish our wish to guide them. For Keryn my ancestor sent the Great Scepter of Morvan westward, that his son might have regalia of royalty in his new kingdom, but kept the crown for himself, that it might remain in Morvan as a symbol, I guess, of continuing resistance to the Ice. Yet in the chances of time it was the scepter that was lost, and it is the crown that now passes into the hands of his kin."

Then a great lightness came within Elof's heart, warm as a wind from the living south. And beyond all doubt, all danger, his laughter rang in that solemn place like the laughter of the Powers in the morning of the world. "Strange are those ways indeed, lord! Stranger even than you can imagine! Yet do not call them chance! For is it chance that you met and befriended a boy from Asenby, and helped him, among many greater causes and concerns, to recover a thing that had been his to use since childhood, in a humble labor? A thing so worn, so aged that even you could not guess what it was. That I could not, till Korentyn himself gave me the key!" And he drew from his pack the rod that had been a cattle goad, and held it out before Kermorvan's astonished eyes. "By the craft within me, which brooks no gainsaying, I tell you now that this is the scepter of Morvan. From Asenby it came, the home that Ase who took the scepter made for herself; it bears that pattern which only the scepter ever bore, and within it are set craft and virtues which even I cannot yet fathom. Receive it now, and read it as I do—a sign. For chance it cannot be."

Kermorvan looked at the rod, but made no move to take it; instead he looked, more keenly yet, at Elof. "Who are you?" he murmured. "Korentyn knew you, Morhuen knew you . . . If Asenby was indeed Ase's home, then you may be a descendant of someone from that time, and bear their face, as do I of my ancestors."

Elof shrugged. "I was not born in Asenby. As to who I am, you have named me yourself; and I have told you what little else I know."

Kermorvan inclined his head, sternly. "Well then! Whoever you may be, the scepter was given into your hands, and has been well guarded there. Do you hold it for me still! And if ever I come to any kingdom, you shall receive it from me again, as counselor and prince, next after me in all my realm."

"Well spoken!" said Roc quietly, and Ils nodded. But Elof dropped to one knee.

"My lord, I am not worthy of . . ."

"Will you question the judgment of a king?" demanded Kermorvan, in tones that smoldered.

Elof raised his head defiantly. "Aye! Or what use else is a counselor?" Then he noticed the faint twitch at the corner of Kermorvan's thin mouth, and they all grinned.

"Mind you," chuckled Kermorvan, "I could as easily name you ruler of the stars, for I own them as much or as little as any other realm! And I will hardly better my estate by lingering here!'' He gazed once more at the blazing crown, shook his head in amazement and wrapped it lovingly in the oiled cloth that protected his own mail. ''Come, friends! I have paid my respects to what has gone by; now let us look to the times to come.'' He hesitated. ''We could rest here, if you wish; those who already slumber here would take no exception, I am sure . . .''

''No thanks!'' said Roc hastily. ''I've learned some lore of the past also, and one or two of these noble gentlemen weren't quite as accommodating as you!''

''And the air is too dusty,'' added Ils, ''with this reek of embalming. I would not sleep here.''

''Nor I,'' muttered Elof. ''I might see that face again.''

''Well then, let us seek somewhere else,'' sighed Kermorvan, sliding the bundle of mail back into his pack. ''Come!'' But as they stepped back through the arch, he hesitated, looking to either side. Then he stooped, and began to gather up the bones that lay there. It was the same humane instinct in him that had served them so well in their first encounter with Tapiau's Children, that balanced the fearsome manslayer he could become. With the others helping him, he bore them back beneath the arch, and with swift care arranged them on two empty slabs. And he spoke to them, saying, ''On the biers there lie by your lord! Living, you did not presume to, but his heir awards you that, the only honor he can. You shall be the last to lie in Dorghael Arhlannen, and in no less worth than all the rest. Guard it well, until the changing of the world!'' Then he bowed to them, to the rest of the darksome hall, and last of all to the silent shape that bore his helm. And Elof and the others bowed also, ere they turned their faces to the distant door.

But as they moved out beyond the arch, Ils sniffed suddenly. ''That rankness again . . . and stronger than the dust . . .''

''I smell it also!'' said Kermorvan. ''Too strong for bats . . .'' Then suddenly Roc, who was leading them, cursed and swung his torch high, and they stopped dead, stood for two heartbeats unmoving, the very breath stilled in their throats. In the darkness ahead of them, on a level with Kermorvan's head, two points of red fire shone with liquid brightness. They hung there an instant, glittering like the jewels on the helm, and Elof felt a sudden flood of the same cold terror he had felt at the tombs' opening, for he knew that they were eyes. But they were too wide apart to be human eyes, and below them he made out a glint of white, glimpsed jaws, long and narrow, floating in the dark as if disembodied, yellowed fangs linked by streaks of saliva. Then the same coughing growl they had heard before filled the vault, and a waft of breath, hot and foul.

So much Elof saw in that unmoving moment; then he felt a sharper wind whistle by, like the sweep of a sword-cut. But it was no sword; Kermorvan had flicked down his linklight so fast it flung out the ball of blazing pitch, as from a catapult. Straight at those ghastly jaws it sped like a starstone, and the thing reared up in a wall of whiteness with a shrieking yell that seemed to split their ears. Elof grabbed for his sword, but Kermorvan had been faster yet, stooping as he threw to snatch up the ancient halberd from the floor. He sprang forward and struck; the old blade bounced and skipped across the tangled whiteness, but scarlet sprang up in its path. Again the shriek, and the beast tumbled back between the rows of biers. Kermorvan sidled forward, slashing, thrusting, leaping, harrying it; a huge foreleg lashed at him with a paw the size of his body, but Gorthawer was in Elof's hand, the black claws met a blacker and flinched at its bite. Ils bounded up, her axe hacked at the limb with severing force but passed only through the billowing fur; she slipped and fell, her torch rolled aside, the paw descended, and then Kermorvan had flung himself across her and the blow fell upon the up-raised halberd. The white muzzle snapped forward, Roc's mace struck and bounced, and a yellowed fang cracked in bloody ruin. The beast reeled and fell on its sloping back, howling and clawing at its jaw with its long forelegs, its shorter hindlegs beating at the air.

Kermorvan scrambled up, helping Ils, while Roc caught up the torch and ducked back. "Light another!" yelled Elof. "We dare not be left in the dark now!" Then the thing made another blundering rush, and he thrust Gorthawer to meet it. But the halberd hewed out in front, slashed a bloody streak below the eyes, and the beast jerked away, snarling, its claws scrabbling and clicking on the stone. Ils stumbled to join them, and together they advanced on it, weapons swinging, forcing it back till its haunches met the door. It reared up as if to spring, but new light flared in the tomb; Roc leaped forward with the fresh torch blazing and thrust it straight at the bloody muzzle. The creature, caught off balance, tumbled back in a scrabbling mass and fell out through the narrow opening into the corridor beyond. After it leaped Kermorvan, blade poised, and the others behind him. The halberd arced upward, flung like a spear, but the beast sprang while the haft was still in Kermorvan's hand, and in the air they met. Right in the angle of its massive neck the point took it, and deep into the fur it sank with all Kermorvan's strength and the beast's own weight to drive it. Down on the stones crashed the creature, snapping and shrieking at the tormenting shaft.

"Is everyone out?" cried Kermorvan, thrown against the wall by the force of the blow. "Have we all our gear? Then, Elof, shut that door!"

Elof turned and seized the grippers protruding from the keyhole, and thrust all his weight hard against the rim. The great slab swung before him, ground forward on screaming hinges, and smashed into its socket with a reverberating crash that drowned even the screams of the wounded beast; the floor shook, stones and dust fell from the ceiling, and to his horror Elof saw a crack race and radiate across it like the root of some dark plant. He twisted his makeshift key in the lock, and sprang back as a wide chunk of the ceiling crashed down where he had been standing. Above the dustcloud he saw Kermorvan, sword in hand, hacking and slashing at the writhing heap of white before him. "Get back!" Elof shouted, hearing his voice crack. "The roof gives!"

Kermorvan sprang back. Then Elof cried out in horror as the creature threshed and struggled back to its feet. Blood poured from its panting muzzle, dripped from the deep slashes on its side, the shattered truncheon of the spear drooped from its neck, and yet with ferocious fires unquenched it reared again to spring.

But it was not to have the chance. One massive paw, upthrust, slammed into the sagging center of the vaulting, with more than enough force to dislodge it. The whole center of the ceiling fell in, and with it a cascade of broken stone from above. Down upon the snarling head it fell, and the creature vanished in a thundering slide of rubble.

"Run!" bellowed Roc, as he and Ils scuttled back. "For your lives!" Elof, ducking frantically, grabbed Kermorvan's arm, and together they fled down the passage, racing the cracks that spread along the roof. Glancing back, Elof glimpsed briefly the upraised hammer of Ilmarinen on the door, beneath it a white-furred leg kicking above the rubble, and then all was thunder and collapse.

How long they ran they could not guess, the torch flames trailing out behind them like starstones in the dusty air. The corridor was straight and level, else the ruin might have overtaken them. Only when they came to a stout arch did they pause, hearing the rumble and crash of stone subside behind them, and there they slumped down against the wall, panting and choking from the dust.

"That was neatly done, long man!" Ils told Kermorvan, between coughs.

He shrugged, and shook dust from his shaggy hair. "The halberd was to hand, and much better in such a fight; a sword would have been too short to get past those great limbs."

Ils eyed him. "It was not only that I meant, and well you know it."

Kermorvan shrugged again, in great confusion. "Dorghael Arhlannen is well shielded now, at all events!" he coughed. "And with a fierce spirit to watch at its gate!"

"A stinking brute!" Roc wheezed. "Stalking us like that! Slinking up all quiet! If I hadn't heard a claw click on the stone . . . And vicious with it! What was it, anyhow? One of those big white snowbears?"

Kermorvan shook his head wearily. "I think not. They live chiefly by the sea."

"I've seen 'em," added Ils. "They're not so weighty, specially in the head. This was something different, something I've never seen. And yet . . ."

"I know," Elof said. "It did look familiar. The jaws . . ." He thought of others with such teeth, swift and savage little hunters, serpentine scuttlers across the snowfields, bane of hare and bird. "More like ermine or marten . . . or that one they call the glutton!"

"Aye! And it was ferocious enough!" said Roc. "But big as a bear?"

"The Ice can breed such monsters, it seems," said Kermorvan darkly, "or preserve them from Elder days. Such were its main armies once; it found fewer men to serve it, ere the Ekwesh came!" He stood up, painfully. "Well, we should not linger here; the roof may yet fall further. What lies before us now?"

Roc raised his torch, and the dust-blown air sparkled and swirled before their stinging eyes. Elof blinked, and saw that they had come to a division in the corridor, no open hall as before, but a chamber whose other three walls each held an arch like the one they stood in, each with the remains of a gate. "Some crossroads in the secret ways of the King's House, no doubt," said Kermorvan. "The way opposite is a corridor like this, the one to the left is a stair, leading down . . ." They peered cautiously into it, and recoiled in disgust.

"The stench of the brute!" grunted Roc. "Must be its lair down there! You smelled that, Ils, not bats!"

Kermorvan swung round. "No doubt! But the same is true for both. It could hardly have lived by hunting down here, so . . ." He held up the torch to the third arch; it flared and fluttered suddenly, and by the uncertain light they saw a narrow stair curving upward into shadow. "One more effort!'' he grated. He swung his precious pack closer to his side, gazed back down the dark corridor once more, and strode to the stair. Roc also looked back; Ils did not. Elof lingered a moment, for now the torches were gone it seemed to him that he saw something there in the blackness, a faint gleam and glimmer, pale, sterile, cold. He knew only too well what it must be; there also the Ice now gleamed through the riven roof, like bone laid bare by a mortal wound. He shuddered, and hurried after the others.

The stairs were steep, and fouled by the beast that had used them; generations of beasts, perhaps, by the claw-marks on the stone. Only the strong draft of clean air made them bearable. The steps led to a tunnel, still sloping steeply upward; at its end lay another stair, and at its foot the air stirred with promise of the open. Here they had to rest, though the foulness still denied them the food they desperately needed; their gorges rose at the thought.

''And where could this be leading?'' groaned Elof, as they staggered up the worn steps once more.

''I guess at that,'' said Kermorvan, his voice calm and encouraging. ''At the margins of Morvan the City there was a high hill, the King's Hill, that was left green and wooded for the folk to enjoy, with many fair walks and parks at its foot, open to all. But its summit was the king's own park, whence he could escape for a while the cares of his high office. It was said that a secret way led there from his palace, and this is surely it.''

''But what a way!'' complained Roc. ''We must've walked twice the width of Kerbryhaine by now . . .''

''And only crossed the southern side of the City by the Waters,'' said Kermorvan with weary pride, ''for the King's House, as I recall the old accounts, was in the south quarter of the city, which was the first built. By so much was what we had mightier than what we have made. By so much are we lessened.'' The brand he carried flared suddenly, and it was as if his voice caught its flame. ''But it shall not always be so!'' And then he laughed, and sprang up the stairs with the lightness of an eager child. The others scrambled after him no less wildly, guessing what he had seen. And as Elof, still lastcomer, rounded the curve of the stair he also laughed aloud, for there before them was a narrow little landing, an arch much cracked and worn, with empty sockets in the stone of it, empty of hinges corroded to nothingness—corroded by the open air that flowed around them, dark and cold and clean as a mountain stream, infinitely refreshing. Upon the landing, Kermorvan seized the others as they came puffing along, swinging them up with casual strength to join him. When Elof arrived, they linked arms and staggered out through the arch.

But even as they emerged their smiles and laughter died, and a weight settled on their hearts, a clutching hand as bitter and sharp as the air that stabbed their lungs like blades of adamant. In the open indeed they stood, and upon a hillside, but it was a hillside scoured bare, utterly barren even of soil, as by a thousand flaying winters. Above them, very close, was the summit, stark and shelterless against the chill sky of new night, cloudless, moonless, naked to the searching stars. And not far below them the hill of stone vanished, engulfed as by a sea. But the sea was calm, its waves unmoving, solid, their flanks faint streaks of gray against the enveloping whiteness. Elof remembered his first sight of it, this dazzling mockery of a living ocean, and the summits that thrust up from it like short-lived islands, their resistance pathetic, meaningless to a foe that could wait upon the leisure of time and wield the weapon of erosion. The King's Hill was such a summit now, and a low one. All around it, without breach or break, there blazed the eerie majesty of the Ice.

CHAPTER NINE

The Raven's Shadow

Kermorvan knew better than to linger in a place so exposed. He cast one quick glance around that blasted land, wrapping his cloak more tightly round him, and then ushered the others back into the mouth of the arch. "A poor return for all your perseverance!" he said darkly. "I should have known the hill would be immured in the Ice . . ." He made as if to strike his fist upon the stone, but Ils intercepted it and drew it gently down.

"Still too full of yourself!" she said, but her tone was unusually mild. "Where else was there to go?"

Kermorvan shook his head wearily. "Nowhere, I suppose. I hoped that the open air meant the Ice might have missed this corner of the city. An idle hope! Why should it?"

Roc raised an eyebrow. "Well, how'd that building escape, the one beneath the rockfall?"

"Perhaps because it was beyond the walls, a guardhouse on the road outside the southern gates, maybe. That would explain the strength of its building, and the secret stair, a retreat into or out of the walls . . ."

"But did it escape?" Elof asked. "Where did the rockfall come from? We never did climb it to find out, remember? The Raven saw to it that we would find the chamber first. Ils, the Elder Folk are wise in the ways of the Ice; what halted the spearhead it sent out to destroy Morvan? Why did it not strike further south yet?"

Ils thought a moment. "It was not halted, not as such. The Ice is forever advancing, fed by snow and rime nearer its center; as it moves into the warmer south, though, the outermost rim begins to melt, and so extends no further. But neither does it retreat, being replenished by the Ice coming from behind. Its masters must have concentrated that renewing force in one narrow area, to drive the Ice further south than it would otherwise have gone. For at the point where the clime balances the advance against the melting, there the Ice appears to halt. But in truth, it never does. That is why, when a great enough cold comes, it can advance so suddenly; it simply ceases to melt."

Elof nodded. "And in that melting, what would happen to those?" He gestured out at the frozen waves of moraines. "Great mountain weights of shattered stone, borne along in waves by the Ice to spread ruin and mayhem at its foot. That is what the rockfall was! Without knowing it we stood then in the very shadow of the southernmost Ice."

"As well we did not know!" said Kermorvan. "Or we would hardly have dared venture down those stairs!" His hand strayed to his pack then, and his smile was as bleak as the world outside. "Though I cannot complain, can I? It is you others I worry for."

Elof found it in himself to smile. "We struggle in the same net, do we not? But console yourself. If this hill was in the south of Kermorvan the City, we cannot be far from the margins of the Ice. We should be able to cross it, as you and I have done."

"But not by night!" said Ils with a shudder.

"No indeed!" agreed Kermorvan feelingly. "I have had enough of that little game, and Elof also, I do not doubt. Which means we must contrive to rest here till dawn as best we can, and without freezing to death! Ils, how many torchlights remain?"

She rummaged in her pack. "Nine . . . no, eleven. And those two half burned in the holders . . ."

"Then we will build a fire of them! The burning ones,

and two more, to begin. But not up here, where the light can be seen; it must be further down the steps.''

''Ah well,'' said Roc lugubriously, ''perhaps the smoke will clear enough of the stench. The brute is slain, but it has its vengeance yet!''

By common consent they ate their meager fare in the cleaner chill of the archway before they built their fire. It burned bright but gave them scarce warmth enough to balance what the cold stone sucked out through their cloaks as they sought some comfortable posture to sleep in, huddled together on the narrow stairs. ''Here of all places we should set a watch,'' said Kermorvan painfully. ''I will take the first span of the night . . .''

''No, I,'' sighed Elof. ''The nearness of the Ice makes me restless, weary as I am. I shall sleep the better for growing used to it.''

''As you will! I am past all argument.'' The warrior pulled his hood over his face, and pillowed his head on his arm. Roc and Ils were already asleep. Elof felt suddenly dreadfully alone. He warmed his hands once more at the meager blaze, rose and clambered out into the archway and the Iceglow. Two nights without sleep, as he reckoned it, and with only a little food, had made him weaker than he realized; his legs wobbled beneath him, and a deep ache burned in his bones. At least that would help him keep awake, and should grow less as he sat awhile. But time passed, and it did not; indeed, it worsened a little, or he felt it more clearly, and found in it a shade of the pain his first steps on the living Ice had cost him.

High up over the curve of the world glided a cold sliver of moon, like the sail of some unseen bark. Even to that faint radiance the Ice awoke, and Elof, who had been sitting numb and heedless in misery, sat up with a gasp. A greater spectacle it was than ever he had seen before, even in the Northlands. Here there were no mountains to hedge in that dazzling desolation, few outcroppings above it save this. The Ice shone out clear, unbroken, boundless from one edge of the world to the other and beyond, one vast

sweeping sea of shimmering splendor, one enormous jewel
that made the petty majesties of men seem minute, mean,
transient.

But even as that feeling came to him, he thought back
upon Morvan, upon the mighty dead of Dorghael Arhlannen, and he cast it back, rejecting it utterly. Small wonder
that the Ice provoked such thoughts; they were enshrined
in it, spawned by the minds that made it. But slight and
flawed as living things might be, at least they lived; they
grew, they strove, and in their several ways they loved.
And all those things men did, and had minds also. They
could love the diverse riches of life, but still savor this
sterile glory; theirs was the world in both its aspects. And
by that much were the kindred of men richer, stronger,
greater than those rebel Powers. Looking out over this,
the embodiment of their narrowed vision, he almost found
it in himself to pity them.

As the moon climbed higher he found that the Ice grew
tiring to watch, that his eyes seemed to be playing tricks
upon him. Every so often in the distance northward he
would see a sheen or flicker of light, but whether in Ice
or sky he could not be certain; it would play slowly across
the brightness for a moment, then vanish and reappear
somewhere else, sometimes nearer, sometimes more distant. It began to disturb him, and he reminded himself he
should be watching every way. He stood up stiffly and,
staying in the shadow of the arch, turned southward. To
his surprise, in this clearer light it looked as if the Ice
there did not extend quite so far, as if it might end before
the horizon. But as he could see nothing beyond it but sky,
he could not be sure. Then something in the distance flickered: he groaned, rubbed his eyes and blinked. But when
he looked again he saw it still, and more distinctly. This
was no trick of his sight: it was on the Ice and moving,
moving very fast, straight toward this hill. He turned to
wake the others, but a sudden wailing wind ruffled his hair
and plucked at his cloak, strongly enough in his weakened
state to make him stumble. Then the shape was already,
incredibly, almost at the hill's foot. And when he saw what

it was, he stood in gaping amazement one moment too long. For the figure in the heavy mantle of midnight blue had already swung himself from the huge horse, and was striding up the rocky slope at as fierce a pace as if it was some trifling hummock.

Elof gathered his wits. This time he would confront this weird wanderer, this time he would demand straight answers from this Raven who pecked and plucked so lightly at his destiny. Grateful as he was for the good things done him, he had a right to be angered at the play that was made of him, as if he were only some mindless piece on a gaming board. He was not; he knew he was not; and before much longer, come what may, the Raven would know it too. Elof ducked back into shadow, and as the heavy footfall passed he stepped out with all the grace he could muster, his hand held out to greet and to command.

As well might he have sought to bar the wind in its course. The mantled figure swept up unheeding, and only its shadow touched him. But that touch struck him dumb, appalled, terrified. As from heights unguessable it fell upon him, and for an instant the swirling mantle seemed a thunderhead of cloud cresting the summit of the hill, the staff taller than the tallest trees of Tapiau. As immense as the Powers carved on the corridors of Dorghael Arhlannen he saw that shape, a towering shadowy vastness against the stars. Then it passed by him, and it was no taller than a tall man; but still its shadow swallowed up the arch, and Elof within it. He could only stand still and stare as the figure bestrode the hillcrest, and brandished its staff as if to strike down the wheeling stars. He could only listen, as it cried out in that same voice he had first heard upon the wind outside his marshland smithy, that rang out now above the gusts that wailed about the hilltop.

> *Hearken, Louhi! Taounehtar, hark!*
> *From deepest Ice heed my behest!*
> *I call you up,*
> *I summon you*

From your bleak caves.
From your stark caverns, arise!
Louhi!
Louhi!
Mistress of Ice!
From shimmering stillness
Rise to the heights!
Strong songs compel you!
Hearken and answer!
Wisdom within you
I would awake!
Louhi! Louhi!
Lady of Death!
Hearken and heed me.
Hear me, and come!

Silence fell as the song ended, fell like a blade. The breeze sank, the chill grew stronger, biting into Elof's trembling flesh. The tall figure stood unmoving as if it had taken root in the bare stone, its staff outthrust at the sky. But suddenly at the staff's head, wavering, crackling, sparking, a great column of green balefire burst out. Slowly the hooded head turned to the northwest. Elof followed its gaze, and sank down, shivering. Intense, vivid, closer far, that shimmer he had seen coursed through the Ice, and the whiteness darkened and grew transparent as if melted all in a moment to a deep pool. And within that depth stars awoke, mirroring the blazing skies overhead. Yet the stars above were still, while their images leaped suddenly, darted and swirled in the deeps like small fish around one single point of blue light that did not move. Brighter it waxed, broader, clearer it grew, until he saw in it a shape arising, floating upward as one drowned; a woman's form, unclad, her limbs outstretched and drifting, her pale hair billowing about her in some unseen current. He could see her face clearly, waxen and still, the eyes closed, the pale lips unmoving. But from the depths sang a voice, a voice clear and fair that he could not easily forget.

Strong calls the song,
Mighty the craft that should shield you!
I do not sleep,
And I am come
Only to see who would dare . . .

Deep-throated laughter echoed out across the Ice.

A wanderer am I, and craft I called on
To summon you far from your lair!
A world-wide roamer,
Thinker, Reflecter, delver of wisdom
That lies at the roots of the world.
Thus have I called you
That you may answer,
Thus am I free from your will!

The staff swung downward in his hand, and in the swirl of its passage the green fire guttered into nothing. A black blade glittered in its place, that struck the stone of the hilltop into leaping, dazzling sparks. Elof blinked, and when his eyes opened the Ice stretched out unbroken, white and bleak as before; but another figure stood atop the hill. Slender and fair she was as the Wanderer was massive, and very straight she stood, haughty pride in the angle of her head, in the blazing sapphire of her eyes. Exactly as last he had seen her, years past, did she look, her pale fine hair gathered back from her brow but spilling in cascades about the shoulders of the soft white robes she wore, through which the starlight shone. And the quiet chime of her voice still set him ashiver, even with cool anger in its tone.

"You are not what you would seem! Why summon me thus? Have you sunk to the level of the witless things you shield, that you must don their shape to speak with me?"

The dark voice was calm. "You are not what you wish to believe! For though you deem yourself a conqueror, lady, yet to your own impatience are you still a slave. I came to save you some trouble, that is all. To tell you where he is, that you most seek."

"To tell me . . . Where, then, Lord of Deceptions?"

The tall figure shifted his mantle a little, settling its shadow more thoroughly over the archway. "Why, where you cannot see him, lady. So save yourself the trouble of searching, as you have done so frantically since you sensed his presence. He is free now, and will not easily be tamed again. Spring comes, even to Taoune'la, and that dark power declines. Your consort also can hinder him no more."

The woman who was Louhi whirled sharply about, her eyes questing out across the southward Ice, her full lips working in fury. She rounded on the tall figure. "You! Though you skulk among the heights, and seek to shield your doings from my eyes, I know of them, believe you me! You give him too much aid. He is no free champion, such as you must have, but only a shadow, a thrall, a powerless puppet of your will!"

The suspicion of a chuckle lay under the words that the Wanderer gave in reply. "What men have from me shall only balance what other Powers set against them. So it is with him. At most, perhaps, I have shown him a few truths he might otherwise have come upon more slowly, perhaps not even in time. But he has had to earn them, and what use he makes of them is his affair entirely. When he was under the hand of the Forest, could I help him, or you hinder? Yet he escaped. Without his free courage, and that of his friends, none of this could have come about. Lady, it is you and yours, fettered in yourselves, who deal in thralls. Powers that are free, only free heroes can serve!"

The stamp of her foot split stone. "So is it all over, then, with the Powers? What is left to you or any of us? Why need you exist, if those who should serve you must be free to make sport and scorn of you at every turn of their feeble will?"

"Lady, lady, will you always be what you were? Will you not learn, as I have had to, and thereby grow? Change and reshaping are the rule. They brought you into being as much as they did men, and that you cannot alter. Nor should you seek to restore what was, solely and selfishly because it pleased you! Deep in himself even grim old Taoune knows that! Or why else should he seek to pretend he preserves the minds of men, when he is only snatching at their shadows, wearing the sum of their memories like a mask of dead skin!''

Louhi turned away angrily, still searching the Ice. To Elof's astonished eyes the falling moon seemed to settle behind her head, like a jagged crown. ''And what of Tapiau?'' she demanded, her voice taut and troubled. ''He embraced life, yet even he abhors men, and seeks to subdue them!''

The mantled shoulders shrugged. ''Once he escaped your error, only to fall into it again. As if life and men were separable! Sooner or later must life lead to mind, in some form, just as your lifeless world had sooner or later to bear that life. Of us all, I among us, perhaps only Ilmarinen understood from the first; all things go their way appointed, and in their own time. Our hindrance or help may mean less than we think. So, there is more to come—but that you must find out for yourself!''

The mantle shook like a shifting hill; a gigantic cawing laughter echoed through the stillness, deriding its barren majesty, stripping away its pretensions with the merry warmth of a spring breeze. Louhi's face twisted in fury. A pale flame beat down upon the hill, a curtain of light, green and scarlet, flickered and lashed about the mantled shape. Then like the echo of an angry cry it sprang away northward and faded. Below its passage the Ice heaved and shattered explosively, flinging bright shards, jagged as lightning, high into the empty sky.

The Wanderer stood alone upon the hill a moment and then, without a glance at Elof the tall figure turned and retraced his steps down the steep slope. Behind the hill's shoulder he vanished, and a moment later the great horse sprang away across the Ice, westward after the sinking moon. Trembling, Elof lowered his brow to the cool stone, and when he lifted it again, though it seemed but a second, the stars were already paling in the eastern sky.

On limbs first numbed, then aching, he heaved himself

wearily up, brushing off gravel that had bitten into the flesh of his face, and hobbled down into the archway. There lay the others as he had left them, around a fire which had burned away unfed to a black stain upon the stone. Anxiously he started down, but at the first scrape of his foot there was a whirl of dark cloak, and Kermorvan was on his feet. The warrior blinked at the faint gleam upon the wall above, and frowned. "What, man, have you watched the night through?" Then he glanced from Elof's bruised cheek to the dead fire, and smiled wryly. "Ah, you fell asleep, did you? A mercy you did not freeze, and we also! Well, we were all of us weary . . ."

"It was more than that . . ." mumbled Elof, as Roc and Ils began to yawn and stir. "I saw . . . I scarcely know what I saw, whether it was a dream or . . ."

"Well, have a stab at telling," yawned Roc, "while we rekindle the fire."

"No!" said Elof, though he yearned for the warmth and the comfort that fire gives. "We dare waste no hour of day. We are hunted, and must be off the Ice as soon as we can!"

Kermorvan cast one swift look at him, and snatched up his pack. "Then tell us on the way! We will climb down to the very edge of the Ice, and at first light make what speed we can across it."

"And what then?" sighed Roc gloomily, as they plodded out onto the hillside. "Back into merry Taoune'la?"

Kermorvan glanced at the graying sky. "I cannot say. But I think you do not realize how much farther east we were taken. I am hardly certain myself; even the duergar maps do not extend this far. But by the stars we could be as far from where we fled the Forest as that place was from the Shieldrange."

The others stared at him. "That far?" asked Ils.

"Very possibly. Perhaps here Taoune's dead hand will hold less sway. We can only hope." He set his face to the weather-scoured stone and began to clamber down the uncertain slope, the way the Wanderer had taken.

"We have some reason to hope," said Elof, and as they climbed, he told them of the meeting on the bare hilltop.

"You actually heard them talk?" marveled Ils. "Talking as we do?"

"I don't know what I heard!" confessed Elof. "Whether it was true speech, or . . . I don't know. But the meaning, that I am sure of. Louhi took it as an insult that he addressed her in human form. But I think, I am sure, somehow, that it was so I could hear and understand."

"Couldn't all have been just you dreaming, could it?" Roc asked. "Had some funny ones myself, on an empty gut . . ."

Elof smiled ruefully. "Dream, or vision, or whatever, how can I tell? But something happened, of that I am sure; a search, an encounter. And that we were shielded, and she misled into thinking we had already quit the Ice . . ." Then he fell silent, gazing at the rubble beneath his feet. "Aye, I am sure. See here, here in all this deathly Waste!" There, and all the way downhill to the very edges of the Ice, wherever there was a scrap of shelter among the barren soil, tiny stars of bright hue had sprung up. Where the Wanderer had trodden, the King's Hill was carpeted with flowers.

"Spring comes!" said Elof. "As he promised, even to this ruined place. It is not wholly conquered!"

"Not yet!" said Ils. "Not yet!"

They rested for a few precious moments at the foot of the hill, watching light climb up behind the gray clouds eastward, and they ate the last of their provision to fortify themselves for the coming dash. Elof sat silent, for a thought had come to him in the middle of his tale, the memory of words he had hardly taken in. "Kermorvan," he said suddenly, "if what you said is true, then this is about as far as we might have come, if we had had no hindrance! If we had been traveling for all those months we lingered in the Forest!"

Kermorvan frowned. "You would say that he repaid the time the Forest took from us? It could be, I suppose . . ."

"Yes! As he cleared our way through the western Forest, because Niarad had forced us ashore too early."

Ils nodded. *'What men have from me . . .* That must be what he meant, mustn't it?"

"Some of it, at any rate," said Kermorvan thoughtfully. "He may also have been warning us we could expect no more help for now."

"That was my thought also," said Elof.

"Might be a relief!" growled Roc. "His brand of help's a whit hard to handle; I'd sooner fend for myself. Short of any more spooks at my shirttails, that is!" he added hastily.

"I am inclined to agree with you," said Kermorvan, very gravely. "Given that small exception!" They laughed, and it was as if that living sound was answered. Molten gold spilled suddenly across the rims of the charcoal clouds, and then burst between them as a river through a crumbling wall. Long beams lanced out across the lifeless landscape, playing over the curve of the hill as a hand might caress a cheek, warming and gladdening. And from the south came a breeze that was not yet turned cutting and cold, and carried still some faint benison from warmer lands. Kermorvan sprang up, and threw back his cloak. "That is our sign! Let us not waste a second of it!" He strode out onto the Ice, and Ils after him. Elof hesitated, and Roc watched him keenly.

"Something the matter?"

Elof stretched out a foot, like a hesitant swimmer, half believing he would have grown immune to the pain by now. But at the first touch of the Ice agony lanced up his leg, and he stumbled. Roc ran to help, but Elof shook him off and staggered on, probing within himself for the source of that pain as a surgeon might search a wound. Like a thin blade it flickered and stabbed at him, striking in one place and then another as he sought to guard it; he was like a swordsman set against an opponent who could toy with him, as Kermorvan once had. But against it, as against Kermorvan, he set the smith's strength in him, and looked through the pain, past it, as he might look past the sting of forge-sparks in the finishing of some fine work. When Ils and Kermorvan looked back in concern, he stiffened his back, swung his pack about him casually, and even managed to force a smile.

He was not alone in his troubles. The rising sun struck fierce reflections off the Ice, light that seared streaks of color across their sight, and troubled Ils worst of all: she pulled her hood low to shadow her eyes, but ere long she was all but blind. Her folk, as she remembered, were accustomed to wear a kind of visor or eyemask with thin slits when they crossed such bright places. But they had none, nor anything to make one save a thin silken scarf; with that bound about her eyes she could see enough to guide her own steps. Despite all, though, they made better time than they had feared, for the Ice proved less arduous than they remembered. Here at its southern border it did not press hard up against a mountain wall, as in the north; it lay thinner upon the land, and the moraines and crevasses were further apart, shallower and more eroded, easier to cross and climb. The spring sun gave the travelers warmth and softened the glassy compacted snow of the glacier's surface, but not to deep dangerous slush as it would in the brief days of high summer. They had meltwater to drink, flowing by them in fast rills and streamlets, though they had to warm it in their flasks awhile. Nonetheless it was a wearying land to cross, and Elof and Ils could hardly enjoy even the scant rest Kermorvan allowed them. At length, as the sun fell away into afternoon, he called out and pointed. The white Wastes ahead had suddenly ceased to seem infinite. At the boundary between bright Ice and sullen sky a thread of darkness had appeared, thin and wavering, and with even a few steps forward it thickened and grew more distinct.

"Land!" cried Roc. "Open land! That's the end of the Ice!"

Elof had to fight down the urge to run; in his excitement he lost the reins of his pain, and felt it all the more keenly anew. They could not hurry, as it turned out, for even with the scarf across her eyes Ils' sight was failing rapidly and she could scarcely keep up their former pace; it was some hours before they came to their goal.

All this time the land opened out before them. At first they saw only a flat country, dark and indistinct, spattered and threaded here and there with gleaming surfaces, snow or water or mire, there was no telling which. It seemed all too like the heart of Taoune'la to the west, though still infinitely more inviting than the Ice. But as they drew nearer the rim of the glaciers, they saw the first distant signs of the transformation the changing season would bring. Plaintive cries echoed down the wind; arrows of gray geese beat across the glistening clouds, settling in great flocks upon the bright waters southward. "But no nearer," Kermorvan sighed hungrily. "So close to the rim the meltwaters must be too cold. Still, we may find hardier creatures to hunt. On now to the end!"

But when at last they neared the margins of the surface Ice, they halted in bafflement and dismay. Thin though the Ice was, its shattered margin stood still a tower and fortress above the lands; beneath their feet it fell away in an unclimbable precipice. Its few breaches led down to perilous-looking slopes of snow-clad rocks and scree such as the Raven had set them down in. Elof tipped down a small stone, and almost at once they had the doubtful pleasure of seeing a whole segment of the slope go bounding and thundering away into shadow. Silently they looked at one another, and at the rapidly sinking sun, and turned to search elsewhere.

Strangely enough, it was Ils, blinded as she was, who found their way down. As they passed across a wide promontory in the cliffs she exclaimed that the Ice sounded hollower beneath her feet, and then that she could hear running water echoing up from beneath. She insisted they follow it. The sound of the water led them some little way along the cliff to the edge of a deep fissure, almost invisible from the Ice behind. And when they peered over, they knew they had found their climb.

It was as if some great worm had gone burrowing through the Ice, leaving behind it a wide round tunnel with sides as smooth as green glass, which now spilled a small stream out into the fissure. This had evidently once been part of the tunnel, but had worn so wide that the roof had collapsed. Now the floor was eaten away into a fantastic labyrinthine set of falls that wove away down the steep slope toward its shadowy foot, and made a passable stair.

"But what did the eating?" puzzled Roc, as they lowered themselves gingerly down the glassy surface; he had elected to take the lead, to hammer out handholds with his mace. "Not that piddling little trickle, surely?"

"Hardly!" said Elof, forgetting the new pain each handhold cost him as he gazed in deep wonder at the weird fluted shapes in the cleft, columns and stairs and baths through which the brown streamlet leaped and chuckled like some merry child, mocking greater waterfalls. "If this much water comes through in the first days of sun, it must be a great cascade by high summer."

"You don't know the half of it, young human!" said Ils wryly from above his head. "So much ice melts that the sheer weight of its flow can drive tunnels like these uphill, or dam up behind rockfalls and send them spilling out across the land ahead, to shatter and flood and finally to freeze. But to the glacier that much water's nothing, less than the sweat on our brows. To the Ice as a whole it's less still, because as much or more will come back in the winter as rime and snow. Three great rivers we've seen since we left my mountains, and it's the meltwater that feeds them all."

Kermorvan, who was guiding her down, shook his head in dismayed wonder. "We know too little of this. If the last Kings of Morvan had had the counsel of the duergar, they would not have reckoned too little of the menace of the Ice, and so saved more from the ruin. Great evil indeed has come from the sundering of our folk!"

"From the sundering of all kindreds," said Elof thoughtfully. "The Elder Folk from the Younger, north from south, dying Morvan from newborn Bryhaine. The Powers, even, from men. Wisdom is not passed on, and must be bought anew, and ever more dearly."

"There speaks as true a wisdom as any!" said Ils force-fully. "But who shall bring it to an end?"

"Who indeed?" said Elof, guiding Ils across from one steep icewall to another, and becoming thoroughly entangled as he sought to lead her limbs to Roc's footholds.

"Well, that is hardly the way!" she protested darkly. "Have a care where you lay your hands!" Roc and Kermorvan chuckled.

"Bear up!" said Roc, clambering down onto the rim of an ice basin. He peered over the edge, and added, "If you'll forgive the words! There's not so far to go now!"

"All the more reason to make haste!" said Kermorvan, swinging himself after Ils.

So they slipped and scrambled down the last stages of the fall, only to find that its foot tumbled down over an ice-sheathed boulder in which Roc could cut no proper holds. Bracing himself, Elof pressed flat to the Ice and fought to keep his limbs steady as its bitter flame burned into him and knotted his muscles. He climbed jerkily, like some cunning automaton of lever and cog, and indeed agony was stripping him of thought and feeling. He hardly noticed when the icy fallwater splashed across him, when his feet and fingers began to slip, when at last they slid free and he fell into air. A moment free from pain was almost as agonizing in its suddenness, then came the kiss of soft snow and the jarring slam of the stone beneath. But it was mild, bearable, compared to what had passed, and he lay there laughing weakly until Roc and Kermorvan had made Ils safe and hurried to help him up. "At least you'd only a step or two to go!" said Roc, as they dusted him off: Elof did not tell him that for all he had known then, or cared, it could have been one or a hundred.

He had been at the end of his strength, but the moment he was free of the Ice it returned to him very quickly. They had come down upon a rockfall like the rest, but less steep and unstable. The stream chattered away among the heaps of snow-clad rock, and they decided to follow its course downward. Across the snowfield it led them, and at last out of the lowering shadow of the icecliffs above.

It was only then, on the brink of a long slope, they turned and looked back. Ils tore the bandage from her bloodshot eyes, and gazed with the rest upon the bulwark and rampart of their foe.

In looming heights of strength, dazzling as gilded steel in the light of the sinking sun, those cliffs arose across the skies of the ruined land of Morvan from east to west unbroken, unbreached, buttressed by immense ridges of fallen rock, whole ranges of rubble hills. A strength and fortress, it seemed, that mere men should not dream of resisting, could not hope to challenge. "Yet we passed beneath you, over you, through you!" said Kermorvan softly. "We came back to Morvan. And we won free. Free, and with a prize of infinite worth!" Then he drew the sword Elof had made him, and cried in a great voice in the two tongues of his folk, *"Morvan Morlanhal! Morvan shall arise!"*

Word and blade together sparkled defiance in the free air before those sullen faces of ice and shattered stone. As the last echoes died he turned the sword gracefully in his hand and slid it back into its scabbard. "It is a lord of Morvan tells you!" he muttered. Then he turned his face from his lost domain, and strode down the slope. The others followed quietly, and let him be, and it was not until much later that he spoke again.

By that time they had reached the end of the slope. Their little stream joined with another and larger, a black seam of meltwater wavering away through thinner, softer snow, down toward the more level lands below. They followed the larger stream, which was joined by others and itself flowed into a river of some width. This was still partly frozen over, but now the meltwater below and sun above were swelling it, straining the Ice and cracking it into great loose floes that ground and splintered against each other with creaks and crashes and the musical splintering of glass. Along its bank the snow was turning soft and patchy; here and there plant stems protruded through it, chiefly gnarled patches of willow scrub. On some of these the first soft catkins were appearing, and as the travelers came to one wide thicket they were startled when a stout white bird flew up almost in their faces with a sharp chattering cackle of rebuke. To their surprise it did not fly off altogether, but flapped heavily to the far side of the thicket and scuttled for cover. Roc cursed. Elof stooped readily for a stone as he had learned to do on the Marshlands, but it was already vanishing into the bushes. Ils blinked and squinted after it. "A snow-grouse, losing its winter plumage; they never fly far. Good to eat, for they live on willow, not pine which taints the flesh."

"That wouldn't have stopped me!" said Roc.

"Courage!" said Kermorvan. "Where there is one, even so close to the Ice, there will be others. The more so, as the snow is failing. Next time we shall be ready!" And indeed, at the next large clump of willow, in the shadow of a high boulder, they flushed some four or five of the birds. Into the midst of them hissed Elof's stone, and one dropped in a flurry of feathers. "Bravely cast!" Kermorvan cried, and the others echoed him. He clambered up the boulder and looked downriver. "And only a thousand paces or so southward there are trees!" he announced, springing lightly down. "Shelter and fuel! We have just enough time to reach them ere the light fades." The others groaned, but they knew he was right.

The march seemed endless, the twilight long and dreary, with the slushy snow caking around their boots, and when they came at last to the trees, a stand of windswept evergreens hunched above the snow, they found little enough comfort there. But it was something to be among life after so long in a dead realm, to squat in a snowless hollow of the riverbank and warm hands at the smoky little flames of a clay oven well hidden in the bank. And never, never, had anything tasted so good as broiled strips of grouse, and the broth they boiled from its tough meat for the morning. "Let us hope it foreshadows better times!" said Kermorvan, as they curled up against the warmth of the oven. "Sleep now, and I will take the first watch!" He smiled grimly at Elof. "May it be briefer than yours, and less disturbed!"

And indeed nothing worse came about them that night than a northwest wind whining among the trees, and brief flurries of sleet that were uncomfortable but not unendurable. When Roc, who had the last watch, woke them, they found the snow already melting in the rising sun. The day that followed was one of sunshine and showers, which seemed hardly any hindrance to them now, and though the land around was often marshy, they came among many more trees. Elof and Kermorvan cut themselves saplings and made crude birdbows which won them two more grouse, and, later, a large white hare; they smoked some of each as a reserve. Elof, too, discovered some of the marshland roots he remembered, swollen with the stored food that had let them live out the long winter and sprout again, and they carried some of these also. Desolate as it was, this land was kindlier than the eastern marches of the Ice. "Which should be no surprise," Kermorvan reflected over the next day's breakfast, "for it must all once have been the richest grainlands of southern Morvan."

"Hard to imagine!" said Roc. "This stark plain carpeted from east to west in green shoots, all yellow come harvest! How far south'd they stretch?"

"I do not know. So little lore of Morvan was preserved. I have seen rough views of Kermorvan the City, drawn from a failing memory and many times recopied, but the rest of the realm I know less of. I do know that the eastern boundary of the king's own lands was a range of mountains, less high than the Meneth Scahas; they marked the boundary with the lands of Morvannec, Morvan the Lesser, which was Korentyn's princedom. Over those mountains, if anywhere, the outcome of our quest should become clear."

Elof looked at the horizon, south and east. There were signs of the land rising a little, turning into rolling country, perhaps, which might eventually give way to low hills. But sight or sign of mountains there was none. He grinned at Kermorvan. "A long step, then. I'd no idea your ancestors were so mighty. We'd best be on our way."

A long step it was indeed, as the Chronicles record it,

but a peaceful one. For though the lands they moved through bore the imprint of a cold hand, it seemed to be less strong this far south, as if the Ice had overreached itself in the drive to shatter Morvan. The earth was not as frozen in these lands as it was in Taoune'la, nor did that air of death and decay spread across them as it had in the Northland mountains. Spring here was a muted thing, but life flourished nonetheless, and it was life the travelers knew well, much like that of northern Nordeney; they were never again short of food for long. The snow-grouse were seldom far away, their plumage changing from pure white to black around the neck, behind their eyes two absurd tufts of bright scarlet with which they made much play in their spring rivalries. Great flights of geese and ducks settled upon every river and lakelet, and hares were common enough. And it was only a few days later that they came across a herd of large deer moving out onto the plain, of exactly the same kind that flourished in the Northlands; their coats were still in winter gray, and their antlers half grown and still in velvet.

"I wondered what that white brute preyed on," said Kermorvan thoughtfully. "Probably it had slept out the winter in its deep lair, and awakened to await their return. Other hunters will no doubt be doing the same; we had best be on our guard when the herds are near." At first, though, they encountered nothing save a pack of wolves, scrawny after the long winter, who were more interested in lame deer, hare and small rodents than men. When Kermorvan's bow brought down a young deer they circled and scurried about, but seemed glad enough to squabble over the stripped carcass and leave the travelers in peace by their fire some way off.

But just after dark, as the first of the Iceglow climbed up the sky, there came a mighty outcry of yelping and snarling, and a deep gurgling growl that no wolf ever made. The travelers sprang up and drew their weapons, lest whatever had appeared should turn on them. Silence fell, was as suddenly broken by the pop and crunch of bones, and then a strange beating, swishing sound, the thud of something falling nearer them. Kermorvan caught up a blazing brand from the fire and strode forward, the others close behind; then he stopped so suddenly they barged into him. A patch of bloodsoaked mud showed where the deer's carcass had lain, but it was there no longer. Neither were the wolves. There were drag marks in the mud, but they went only a few feet and the grass around was unbent. Kermorvan moved the flame about, and they saw in the mud, still oozing, a single imprint longer than a man's foot, a great tridentine talon.

"There, by the bank!" cried Ils. Kermorvan cursed and swung the torch high, and they all saw what she had glimpsed in the darkness. The remains of the deer, much mangled, lay by the riverbank, at the foot of a low rocky outcrop. Atop this, hissing like quenched iron from gaping jaws, perched a dragon. It flared its wings and reared up at them, short legs tucked in against the serpentine body, the long head outthrust and spitting. But it was a young beast, quarter the size of the ones Elof had first seen, and not yet come to its flame. When Kermorvan advanced on it menacingly it spat at him again, then ducked its head to seize the ragged remains of the deer, threshed clumsily aloft and wavered away into the night to find some quieter place to enjoy its scavenging.

"A good thing it was no larger!" said Kermorvan, shaken. He tossed the brand back on the fire, and glared at the cold glow in the northern sky. "A fond farewell from the Ice!"

In that he spoke more truly than he knew. From that night on they were no more troubled by strange creatures. As night followed night, and the lands grew warmer, the pale light of those bitter ramparts sank and dwindled beneath the horizon, growing ever fainter until they saw it no more. And it is set down in the Chronicles that many long years were yet to pass ere any of them set eyes on their great adversary once more.

The deer, and another they took the next day, gave them a good store of meat, which was as well; they encountered no more herds as they walked further to the southeast, following the rivers that ran like dark veins through the rising land. On the seventh day of their journey they drew at last into higher ground, a hilly country with many long stretches of evergreen forest. Though they viewed it at first with deep suspicion, it seemed younger and more sparse than Tapiau'la-an-Aithen, and like the Northland forests it wholly lacked that oppressive air of watchfulness. Larger creatures were still scarce here, but there were more birds. Jays screamed, black woodpeckers drummed, swifts shrilled over the treetops and swooped so low over clear ground that their wingtips hissed among the weeds; a thousand small flashes of life bounced and chirruped in spring feather through the woods. The sun shone more often now, and the rain, though often hard, released rich scents into the crisp air. Bare though the land was, after the desolations they had been through they felt they could wish for no better garden.

Food had given them back their strength, and only the cold remained to plague them. Yet though they strode ever higher among the hills it did not greatly increase, save when the wind blasted down upon them from the north, bringing sleet and stinging hail to send them leaping for the nearest large tree. They were content enough to find no worse adversary. Fire warmed them at evening, and they met the next day, the next hill, as they came to it. So it was that they were surprised one bright morning as they left a large area of woodland flanking a chain of broad waterfalls to find that they were already high among the lower slopes of the mountains they sought, and that the peaks stood clear above them now.

"Such as they are!" said Roc scornfully. "Hardly mountains at all, are they?"

"Lower than our western ranges," agreed Kermorvan unhappily. "And they run northwest from here; they must meet the Ice eventually. A poor barrier!"

Roc shook his head dolefully. "Might've just flowed down around the far side!"

"I doubt that," observed Elof. "It had to make a great effort to swallow Morvan; nowhere in the Westlands did it come so far south. And to pass round these mountains might be a greater effort yet. They are older than our mountains, I think, and more worn, blunt as old teeth. But they may well be wider.'' As they climbed higher, finding peak behind peak, and came at last to the mouth of a likely pass, they saw that he was right. Broad as that pass was, with a river at its heart, they could not make out its end; it snaked away among the peaks into the blue distance.

"They gain from being lower," said Ils. "There is snow here, but it is melting as summer comes. There are fewer snowcaps for the Ice to seize on."

"That is some hope, at least," said Kermorvan. "But Korentyn did not speak idly. Morvannec was small, its lands thinly peopled and half wild; it could not long withstand any determined onslaught. Still, something may yet endure. And so must we!"

The snowy grassland that flanked the river grew sparse as it climbed the flanks of the pass, and still thinner till at last it dwindled to bare earth. For the first three days they saw no life at all, beyond small birds. The snows that had faded on the plains still fell at times, not heavily, but enough to make them use the firewood they had carried from the hills more rapidly than they wished. Elof wondered if their food would last; it was little enough they had now, yet among their other hardships it made the vital difference. He could hardly bear the thought of going hungry again. On the morning of the fourth day, when the opening of the pass had vanished behind them and a low crest limited the view before them, they were surprised to see movement on the riverbank ahead, black specks drifting through the snow-speckled grass. At once they dropped from sight behind stones and scrub; whatever was about up here should be approached with caution. As Elof and the others sidled closer, keeping behind a huge boulder entangled in willow scrub, he saw that they were beasts, large and four-legged in shape, not unlike small wisants with immensely shaggy black coats; but their short horns, curving low and close to the sides of the blunt heads, suggested sheep or goats.

Kermorvan smiled to Ils. "Some old friends of ours, I think, lady? Among your folk I had occasion to guard a herd or two. Worthy beasts, save to the nose."

She exclaimed in surprise. *"Velek Ilmarinen!* Musk-oxen! Now why . . ." She glanced quickly around the barren slopes above, and along the pass to the crest.

Kermorvan was still watching the herd. "There is little point in stalking them, I fear; they are cunning and quick, and would not fall easily to two mere birdbows. Elof's hammer might do, but it would be hard to get close enough. Ils, what say you?" Then he sensed her unease. "My lady?" At once he too was scanning the heights, alert and tense.

She shook her head grimly. "There is nothing there for you to read, Lord of Men."

Kermorvan evidently noticed the unusual title she gave him, and the dark tones in which she spoke it. His own were guarded, but alert. "Yet there is for you, lady?"

"For what it matters, yes; such signs as we place upon our mountain paths and pastures, that our eyes alone can read, even in what is darkness to you. None clearer, though, than those beasts; where they are, so also were the duergar. They are descended from our herds."

"Here? Your folk dwell here?" Elof looked around him with wonder; Roc also, but with more of apprehension.

Ils shrugged. "The signs are ancient. Only traces remain. And the herds are gone wild. See!" She stood up from behind the rock. A long muzzle lifted, lip curled and nostrils flared to taste the air; another looked up, its shaggy coat twitching nervously, and then long horns tossed in warning. Ils went stumping quite slowly and casually toward the herd, and suddenly they were wheeling about in bellowing disorder and bounding off across the meager grass with a goatish skip that belied their bulk. Out of reach they halted, by a wider patch of willow, snorting, suspicious, pawing the ground in threat. "You see?" Ils tossed back over her shoulder to the others. "These have not seen my folk in many a generation. Why do you linger back there? You may walk these lands without fear, now, and forget whose they once were." And without another word she stalked on.

Elof and the others exchanged startled glances, and hurried after her. Rarely had he heard anything to match the bitterness in her voice. "My lady," demanded Kermorvan, "are you all right? Or how have we distressed you?"

But he had no answer. She was slow to follow their path, and when Kermorvan laid a hand on her shoulder to draw her away she writhed and slapped it off. She walked with them then, but wreathed in a silence that spoke, black fury upon her brow. The others too were silent, for despite her words they found themselves constantly scanning the skyline for unfriendly eyes. Though they saw nothing, they were glad when near sunset they rounded a sharp bend in the river and saw that the peaks ahead, reddening in the last rays, were much lower; the end of the pass was near. The river they had followed up from the forests came tumbling down here from its sources among the heights; they quitted its cold company for a smaller stream that led them downward a long and winding way between the lower peaks. They camped some way down, in a pocket of rock that would be easy to defend, and built a good fire of scrub. But Ils curtly refused food, and slumped down in a corner; the others gazed at her in some concern. A look Elof could not read had closed over her face like a visor. It reminded him forcibly of how strange she could be, of how alien her stock. He thought of the cold countenances of the duergar court, of the harshness of old King Andvar, hater of men; he had never seen her look so like them.

"Ils," he ventured. "I am sorry that your folk dwell here no longer, truly sorry. But why should that lead you to shun us so, your friends? When you have come so long a road with us . . ."

She raised dark eyes to him, glittering through the dusk. "And should I have? Should I not have fled you, as my folk have ever done, you who live and breed so much faster than we? Around half the wide world we have fled, and those who would not, they have stayed and . . . dwindled." Her eyes narrowed, as if some new and chilly light shone upon her. "Those signs, they were rough, crude, scrawls that had all but lost their meaning. The work of near-savages! Yet there was a time when no duergar lived thus; it was newmade savages who drew them, children of wealth tumbled to the gutter." She gave a bitter little laugh. "Aye, now I have seen whither that road of yours leads! I have seen what we can come to, how great will be our fall, when it comes! Aye, when! We cannot flee forever. Before us there is only the Western Ocean, and beyond it the Ekwesh lands. So why do I walk with you, why do I dream of bringing our peoples closer?" There was a dull flame now in her eyes, burning like a low fever. "Will that not simply hasten our last and losing conflict? I think I understand old Andvar a little better now. If we can come to . . . to that, should we not indeed shut you out with gulf and stone, and slay all who intrude? If we are doomed in the end, why should I seek to speed it?" She turned away furiously, and flung her cloak about her. Elof would have put an arm about her shoulders, but Kermorvan drew him back. Concern furrowed his brows, but he shook his head.

"Better to leave her be," he said quietly, turning the strips of venison that toasted among the ashes. "She is angry, afraid, as who would not be? But in all she said I heard only questions. Doubt wracks her, not certainty. We shall try to find answers when she is ready to listen. For now, do you let her rest. And when you have eaten, rest yourselves, you and Roc. I shall watch, for now."

So Elof sought sleep. But the unease of the day seeped into his dreams which beat and fluttered like great birds caged, or stalked with menace around the margins of waking. It seemed to him that he heard voices speaking of dark things, of war and death and decay, and then turning to higher yet hardly more hopeful matters, and he knew suddenly that he was awake, although his limbs and body seemed too heavy to move. It was Ils' crisp voice he heard, and Kermorvan's clear answer.

"And will it not happen again, wherever men are? More than our shape divides us. The tides of our thoughts flow apart. We can think and live as you do, upon the surface, but into deeper waters few may follow us. Elof, perhaps, and yourself. Roc, no, though at least he would see and respect. But there would always be many others, lesser men who would not see, only resent.''

"And among the duergar also, I do not doubt! I have met only too many of both races. But if enough of each are willing, it would take scarcely two generations . . ."

"If? That is the greatest gulf of all, one that reason is too weak to bridge. A greater force is needed, and you humans are not equal to it. You could not feel as deeply as we. You cannot comprehend our thoughts, still less the passions that speed us on. You would ground on the shallows of your souls."

"Would we? There are some whose thoughts flow deep as your dark mountain streams, aye, and passions also! Look at *him.* Within him embers are quietly smoldering, ready to burst into flame at a touch of his thought. All this long road they have driven him for love of a girl he has seen in all his life for barely an hour together!"

There was a silence, and Ils' voice changed when she spoke again. "He is more like us, indeed."

"So, not all men are as cold in heart as I . . ."

Ils snorted in surprise. "You? You're no blindfish!" Her voice was tinged with gleeful malice. "You love, all right. The lady Teris might have had something to say on the matter, had you but the wit to ask it!"

"I? I was raised to treat women properly! With respect, with reverence, with . . ."

"Spare me! And you love him . . ."

It was all too obvious whom she meant. Elof almost sat up in astonished outrage, then struggled to stifle a smile at the strangled sound Kermorvan emitted. "Not like that!" For a moment his voice was a model of stately outrage, and then he collapsed into a rare rueful chuckle. Elof guessed Ils had prodded him in the ribs. "Oh, I know, the more I struggle the deeper sinks the barb! I suppose I am fond of him, yes. As I am of Roc. And of you, though Amicac knows why!" His voice took on a mild edge of its own. "He is a fine fellow, after all; it is not hard to be fond of him, in one way or another. It seemed to me, lady, that even you . . ."

"Even I!" She spat the words out with a force that startled Elof. "What would you know of that? As well he does not so much as notice me, him and his damned embers! And you're the man who'd have our races mingle! Can you not see, fool, blindworm, sluggard, how slow either will be to do that? Do you not understand what alone can drive them to such an unheard-of act? We look odd to each other, we even smell odd . . ."

"To men you could not look less than fair, lady . . ."

"Aye, thank you kindly, sir, but fair as one of your own, all willowy and wispy? Golden or red, aye, or auburn about the hair, like a certain lady of Lys Arvalen? I take leave to doubt that. To us, long man, you look stretched out like a shadow, weak as a hank of straw, thin as a dribble . . ."

"No doubt," interrupted Kermorvan calmly. "So, to awaken feelings we must look past that, to what is common in us. It can be done. Have we not come to that, in some degree?"

Ils' voice was grudging. "Perhaps we have, thrown together in strange circumstance. But others will need some motive to try. In such matters rulers cannot rule. But leaders may lead . . . if they can."

So long now was the silence ere Kermorvan replied that Elof almost lost the fine tether of attention that held him awake. "Neither leader nor ruler am I, as I have said ere now. But should things change, princess of the Elder folk, shall we not speak more of this?"

"Aye, if I can hold back from laughing. But at least you lighten my mood, long man, you and he. Look at him, sleeping like the child he is! And within him a force to break the will of a Power! Perhaps we should ask his aid, have him weld races as finely as he does metals, mix an alloy of hearts, an amalgam of minds . . ."

"Perhaps we should," said Kermorvan, with no mockery in his voice. Elof heard him shift position, and sigh.

"For now, this child also would sleep, and leave you the remainder of your watch. But think on this night! Remember it well!"

All that Elof heard then was the faint crackling of the dead embers. Was that truly how they saw him? He had never felt less ready to take flame. And yet . . . He sought to open his eyes, to search the sky above. But the effort was too great; he felt his mind whirl away into a cavern of blackness. Like foam upon the deep waters of Ils' own realm it swallowed him. But his last fading thought was that there were deeper waters around him yet.

Next morning he awoke in a pool of spring sun, much refreshed, and all things seemed so much as usual that Elof viewed his memories with deep suspicion; he could not tell whether or not he had dreamed all or part of what he had heard. Kermorvan was his customary calm self; more significantly, perhaps, Ils was also hers, and of yesterday's horrors there was no trace. In the warmer air it was possible to bear washing in the chill stream, and she even sang a merry little song to herself as she splashed about. And though that needed no better explanation, Elof had to fight down a sudden twinge of doubt and confusion. Her feelings for him, his for Kara, Kara's for him, how much did he truly know of any of these? What did he want of any of them? Unreasonable, ridiculous, to wish Ils at his heels like a dog, while he pursued . . . what? A shadow, a girl of a single hour. What did he know of her, save the cold and dangerous chains about her, the creature that held her bound? Why chase after her, when right at hand . . . He could not finish the thought. But nor, in the days to come, could he throw off a haunting sense of loss, not even in thoughts of Kara.

The warmth of day as the travelers set out lent a new zest to the air and a spring to their steps, and they scrambled down the rocky way as lightly as mountain goats. Not far below, the stream pooled beneath a low ridge between two rounded hills, and spilled over its edge with a noise of muted drums. Up the poolside rocks to the crest the travelers clambered, onto the level shelf beside the low falls, and realized that their view was no longer barred by peak or slope or standing rocks. It was from that ridge that they looked their first upon what they had come so far to reach, the ancient Eastlands of the land of Brasay-hal.

Elof's first thought was of jewels, emerald and sapphire. For all the land below him, from the steep slopes that seemed almost to fall away from his feet to the wide expanses of forest beyond them, to the hint of softer hillsides on the northward horizon and lower, flatter grasslands to the south, all blazed with every shade of green, shifting, changing, glowing in the soft light. Sapphire was the water that flashed and winked among them, deepening the blues it plucked from the sky of lapis behind white clouds; and these also had their reflection upon the land. In the tree-girt basin far beneath the last of the morning mist was gathered, a whiteness purer than the Ice, a pool of gleaming milk whipped up by the first breezes into a towering wash of cloud that hung almost level with their eyes, like a sea wave frozen in the moment of breaking.

"Or like a hand that beckons!" breathed Kermorvan, poised tense and eager upon the very brink of the rock as if impatient to follow its behest. His gaze soared like a questing eagle across the verdant land outspread before them; its rivers sparkled in his eyes, its vibrant life in his voice. "See the richness of it! The Ice has never touched this place in many a long year. From where it now is, it could send little more than bad weather across these mountains. And near the sea the climes must be warmer, as they are in the west . . ."

"Aye, but see also the wildness!" chimed in Roc. "If the Ice hasn't touched it, no more has man. Doesn't look like we'll be finding many easterners!"

"There never were many," answered Kermorvan calmly. "Morvannec was small, and upon the seacoast, which must still be beyond our sight. Thither is our goal, to see what if anything still remains of it, and if these lands may be lived in."

Elof felt a warm bare arm slip through his and cling

tight; it was Ils, who had no great love of heights and open spaces, and he felt obscurely pleased that she had come to him for support. "And after that we've only to get back home, without ending up stiff or daft by the way!" she growled. "No small order. But this I can say, we'll not hasten the search by perching on a cliff edge, gawking!"

They laughed, and admitted the justice of that. Yet to Elof, after lush forest and bleak realms of Ice the fair balance and harmony of the view refreshed both eye and spirit; he was loath to leave it so suddenly, as if quitting some spectacle before its climax. He lingered a moment after handing Ils down, and gazed due eastward, to where the sun shook off the clouds and poured down richness upon the mellow country. A faint flicker held his eye, a black speck amid those streams of molten gold, a shape that swooped against the dazzling distant clouds. Straight into the path of the rising sun he stared, shading his eyes, squinting till dots of color danced and blinded him and he could see no more. Now Ils had to help him down, while his sight cleared. "What'd you expect, idiot?" she demanded.

"Black wings," he muttered. "In the path of the sunrise, as I was bidden. Let us go down now."

Their descent led them by the lower slopes of the falls, where already grasses and flowers were burgeoning among the stones, and out at last onto steep slopes where the land's bared bones still thrust up through the thin skin of soil. Yet even here the grass grew ever thicker and lusher, most of all along the leaping streams; they came to a mountain meadow whose grass itself, breast-high to Ils, seemed like some deep pool of greenness where fish might swim among the waving stalks. They looked down its slopes to stands of tall trees, and although those around them were almost all evergreens still, they could see the crowns of seasonal trees spreading below, bright with new leaf. Before day's end they were among those trees, a woodland with light and air and running waters, all full of life. Among white pines and balsam firs, gray birch and tall beeches they walked, and found track and trail, heard scurrying and dashing among the mold; birds fluttered among the trees, fish rose in the deep pools of the streams. There was no need to fear hunger, at least; in so rich a country they could expect to hunt and fish and snare enough for their needs with little effort and delay.

So indeed it proved, over the days that followed, while they made their way down through the woods to the lower lands beyond. They passed among paper birches, hickories and elms; they camped one night under massive oaks with green leaves, the next under chestnuts that loomed like stepped towers in the morning mists. Elof could not help missing the great redwoods of his northern woods, Kermorvan the tall alders he knew, for those grew here only as large streamside shrubs under the willows and the poplars and quaking aspens which seemed more common than in the west. It was a long avenue of these poplars that caught Elof's eye some mornings later, silhouetted by sunrise upon the crest of the next hill. He called to the others, and they saw, as he had, that the trees grew strangely regular and separate. After a bolted breakfast they hurried to investigate, but long before the hill's crest they could see that something lay there. When at last they struggled through the tangled bushes at its edge, the road came as no surprise, save perhaps for its width and its state of preservation. The stone slabs that surfaced it were cracked in many places, with grass and other plants thrusting up through the crevices, but so large were they to begin with, and so smooth, that save at the edges, where the poplar roots had been at work, little of the paving was wholly overgrown. "I've seen parts of our High Roads in less good repair!" exclaimed Elof. "Have men kept it this clear? Or has it lasted . . ."

"No man has passed this way for many long years," said Kermorvan, gesturing downhill to where thornbush and bramble overhung the path. "This must have been maintained since the fall of Morvan, yes. But I would guess it is a beast's track now. Still, it seems to lead eastward, and we have no better guide. Let us follow it!"

The road proved a good guide indeed. Often they had

to hack aside overgrowth with sword and axe, but hardened as they were to rougher country this bothered them little. They made swift progress along its kindly path, and strayed from it only to gather food, or bathe in the rivers. Out of the woods it led them at last, winding like a gray stream among grassy hills that might once have been rich pastureland, and out onto a raised bank across a wide plain. It seemed as if only spring grasses grew and tossed here now, but Kermorvan, plucking the heads from many, found that they were grains grown once by men. ''And now sunk back among grasses and tares!'' he muttered, kicking at a weathered hummock by the roadside. ''See, here sat the boundary stone of a field. And somewhere nearby there would have been a farmhouse, a village even. Over there, perhaps, that low mound where the road turns for no reason.''

They gazed at it in silence as they passed. ''How long'd such a place lie forgotten, to come to that?'' Roc wondered.

''Five hundred years, maybe,'' said Ils, ''or twice that. It must have been left long before the fields ceased to be cultivated.''

''It was indeed,'' said Kermorvan darkly. ''For this must have been land farmed by the sothrans who fled west to found Kerbryhaine. Those who stayed must have kept up the land . . .'' His words tailed off, but Elof had read his thought, and could not help but voice it.

''Kept it up, until there were so few that they could not, or they no longer needed its produce. And they maintained the road, which must have led over the mountains to Morvan, till it was clear that none would return that way . . .''

''Till now!'' Kermorvan barked, his face gone all to edged flint. ''We have come back! And few or many, they will know that we are the heralds of a new time!''

For many more peaceful days the road led them on. Into woodland it wound again, sparser now and with few evergreens, and the air grew warmer, milder, with every day that passed. The woods straggled out through low hilly country where among good but empty pastureland the ruined stone circles of cot and fold gaped like empty eyes, and still no man stirred. As the days went by Elof began to believe that he could smell the sea upon the breezes, and soon Kermorvan was agreeing with him. They found that the road seemed in better repair, and beside it they came upon ruins that still stood, a lone wall, three walls and a gable, four walls and half a roof sunken askew between them. On a night of rain they sought shelter in one such ruin, displacing only owl and bat from its hollow rooms. "Here, remember the places we camped in, by the High Roads?" chuckled Roc. "Seems a lifetime past, yet it could just about be the same . . ."

"Not quite," said Kermorvan seriously. "Whatever reduced this and the others, it was not war as such; they have not been sacked or burned, simply . . . left. Neglected. And not for very long, to be still standing thus; fifty, sixty years, perhaps, certainly less than a hundred."

"So recent?" asked Ils. "And . . . all of them? All abandoned at once?"

Kermorvan's mouth twisted. "They look about the same age. Not a comforting thought, is it? That there were folk here until so few years ago, and then . . . none. There could be many reasons for it, few good, most ill. But the sea cannot be so very distant. And there we will find at least part of our answer." He turned over then on his bed of cut brushwood, and went peacefully to sleep.

"Aye," muttered Roc. "Always providing it doesn't find us first!"

It was no more than a day or two later, as the tales are told, that the road led the travelers up a steep slope of the land and into a patch of thick woodland that Kermorvan guessed had been cultivated as a windbreak for fields beyond. They found the truth of his words in the lively breeze that set the boughs to dancing and whipped at their cloaks. And as toward noon they emerged into the open once more it stung their wide eyes, and yet hardly did they know or care, for the gleam of wide waters under the sun was in them, and more than that. They looked with awe upon the end of their perilous journey which had lasted from one spring's beginning to another's end, and from one shore to another of all the vast land. Boundless before them, unbroken to the horizon, stretched out now the waters of the Eastern Ocean.

These were the Seas of the Sunrise, over which the fathers of men, founders of the realm of Morvan, had first sailed to this land. Far below the horizon, beyond the very curve of the world, these same waters lapped upon the fabled strand from which they had sailed, the shores of Kerys. The sight of them in itself was a mighty wonder. Elof's heart leaped to behold again great waters, and to hear, borne faintly over the long miles, the play of their waves like a vast breath upon the shore. Yet it gripped the travelers for a few moments only, as long as it took their sight to resolve out of the dazzling light the lands below and the great hilly promontory, stark against the glittering sea, that so dominated them. Such a sight Elof had beheld from afar once before, and it stirred in him now an even greater awe. That ordered landscape, fair and fertile, the checkered pattern of field and orchard and well-tended woodland, these were the mark of the children of Kerys upon their new homelands, nature mastered but not plundered, tamed but not ravaged. But whereas around Kerbryhaine the fields had been scarred with fire, enshrouded with the smoke of siege and sack, they stretched out here unmarred from hill to sea, from north to south as far as his eyes would pierce the hazy air, at least twice as great in their extent. And as greatly as they overmatched the lands around Kerbryhaine, so also in the same proportion did the city at their heart. Kerbryhaine had seemed to Elof a jewel, a brooch or boss upon that blazon of fields, but this, laid out along that wide ness like some ark of the Powers come to shore, this distant city was a towering coronet. And it held the eyes of Kermorvan as no lesser jewel could have done.

It was Ils who spoke first. "Kermorvan! You did not say that your people had another great city to the east! Or is this the work of some other folk?"

The tall warrior shook his head. "From the site of it

there is only one place this could be. Does it not sit like a crown upon the cliffs of a long ness? Does it not thrust like a spearhead out into the sea, a mighty seawall to shield its own fair harbor? On that same shore that lord of Kerys set foot who was the first king of all my line, and there he made his first town, from whence his sons were to found Morvan the Great. Did we dream ourselves mighty, we of the west? Did we dream we had revived and kept alive the glories of old?'' His voice shook, but it was a wonder that he could form his words at all. ''Behold then, a dreamer has journeyed long to awakening and found how tawdry was his vision beside the glory that is true, and lives! For do you look now upon Morvannec, Morvan the Lesser! In your minds mirror from it the much greater splendor that has passed—and mock our child's pretense.''

''I would not make compare,'' said Elof softly. ''Kerbryhaine is the greatest city of the west, but the west is a realm divided, two lands that should be one. I would rather see in this what Kerbryhaine might have been, had your wise line been its lords. A city of one kin, one blood.''

The others looked at him and smiled, and only then did he realize how apt was that title. For a city of one blood it might well have been. In the noontide sun the sand-red stone of its far-off walls gleamed warm and ruddy as if living blood did indeed course through them. ''That's the right of it,'' said Roc. ''And the sooner it turns that way again, the happier we'll be. A right marvel is this place!''

''It is!'' breathed Ils. ''Mighty are men, if Morvan was greater!''

Kermorvan nodded gravely, and placed an arm about her shoulder. ''But mightier still they will be, if their Elders will but stand by their side! Come, it is still a good four leagues away, at the least. If we hope to reach its gates before nightfall, we must not delay!''

It was as well they had a smooth road before them, for none of them could long bear to take their eyes from the miraculous city, lest like some deceiving vision in the Wastes of the south it rippled and vanished into the haze.

But as they drew nearer it grew only clearer and sharper in their eyes, yet still more marvelous.

Elof saw now that like Kerbryhaine it had grown and spread gradually outward from the crests of its hills. Many walls that had once been outer walls wove between them, overwhelmed and overtaken by waves of new building in their shadow, until these were walled around in their turn. But this Morvannec had not the look of Kerbryhaine, with that city's chill walls of ivory stone and circles of rooftops in cold grays and greens, its looming citadel, a diadem of gold-crowned towers, as a cold heart. Here all the defenses were toward the outside, walls wider and thicker, smooth and seamless, with a very roadway for their parapet and at every turn and corner a vast round tower, massive and broad-based, smooth-flanked and windowless save for a gallery with firing slots just beneath the high conical roof; turrets and gatehouses of the same pattern lined the walls between. "They are strongly shaped, those towers," said Ils. "Built less for vainglory, and more for use."

"Looks friendlier, all the same," was Roc's view.

Ils arched her brows. "But of course! Squat and solid like duergar, not tall and weedy like men. They are bound to look kinder than those haughty towers of Kerbryhaine."

"The whole city has a warmth to it," said Elof.

"A lack of order, you mean," grinned Kermorvan. "But I can forgive it that, for what it holds at its heart." He gestured at the crest of its highest hill. There the stone of the cliffs surged up through the circles of the city like the back of some vast seabeast breaking surface, and out of it a vast plinth had been hewn. Great stairs flanked it, and raised above them was a high straight-walled tower of immediate strength and majesty, that bespoke immense age. Yet this was no grim fortress, blind and commanding, but rather a great hall of many galleries and wide windows, which bore its light fortifications as might a king a crowned helm, chiefly for ceremony, but serviceable at need. "It was said of the City by the Waters that you could not walk its width between two sunsets," mused Kermorvan. "You could cross Kerbryhaine in half a day. And this place?"

Elof squinted to judge the distance. "Midway between, I guess. We see it so clearly only because we are nearer the end of the ness here than its beginning. Happily there are gates on this side, or we should have a long walk!"

So much the travelers must then have seen: but there is much more here recorded of that city's aspect that could not have been visible from so far off. Some, no doubt, they saw as they made their way down out of the hills and in among the inland farms, and some, perhaps, was added later, as is the way of chronicles. But of the immediate impression it made upon them there is no doubt, and the palace most of all. It looked to be of the same red-gold stone as the outer walls, but darkened almost to blackness by weather and the smokes of the town beneath. So also were the walls of the inner circle and its lesser buildings; they were of a type, tall and stately with high-peaked gables under gray slate and columned frontage, built in long rows and facing outward around the hill, outward to sea and sky and land. Many in the circle below were of the same lordly fashion, but some among them glowed in stone of a lighter gold, some in a dark stone with a greenish gloss to it that winked and glittered in the sunlight. And these, where the hill permitted, were laid out in squares or circles with small splashes of greenery at their hearts, and like slender ladies or impudent children, other smaller buildings danced around them; these were not uniform and austere as in the west, but of a merry variety. Gray slates clad the taller rooftops, but the lesser were a cheerful riot of tiles in all colors, red and yellow and blue the commonest, and all manners of glaze and pattern. Their walls were of colored stones, or bricks in many earthen hues. Some were faced with glazed brick, or rendered in dazzling white, or simply painted in many colors.

But it was the gaggle of houses in the notch where cliff and wall dipped down together toward the wide harbor that caught Elof's eye. Many of them seemed to be built boat-like in wood after the fashion of his own home village, their roofs of scaly wooden tiles tar-blackened over high crested gables. Their walls were painted in many colors faded to lightness, and it seemed to him, straining his eyes over the distance, that some bore bright designs, leaping and curling shapes that could be very like the waterbeast patterns he remembered.

"It seems there are seamen here," said Kermorvan. "Probably of northern stock . . . But where are their boats?"

Roe shaded his eyes. "There's some masts in the harbor . . ."

Kermorvan frowned at the small dark streaks within the great breakwater. "Indeed, but only a few, and small; light fishing boats, they could be. A city this size should have greater ships than that, if only to bring in produce from fields that stretch as far as these. It would be far cheaper and faster than drawing it by road . . ."

"But are all these fields in use?" Ils gestured to the ones nearest her, and Elof saw that though they were still clearly hedged off, they had not been cultivated at all for some time; the hedges contained a tangled riot of growth, chiefly weeds.

"Strange," muttered Kermorvan. "And no beasts in any field I can see, no sound or movement from the farms, no smoke from their chimneys . . ."

"This is all too like what we found before Kerbryhaine," said Elof uneasily.

"Yet there was a siege, and here, as we can see, is none. Nor any other cause. Could it be that their stock has failed, their people dwindled? If so . . . But the sooner we come there, the sooner we will learn. Make haste!"

Ancient and noble as Kerbryhaine was, to Elof now it seemed young against the venerable crag that rose before them, frail and slight against those strong walls scarred by an age of wind and weather. And though the city below might seem more jumbled and less august, it spoke more truly to him of long ages of life and growth than did the unchanging face of the west.

"Perhaps that is so," Kermorvan admitted. "In the

thousand years since its foundation we have striven to keep Kerbryhaine fair, and so built more or less strictly in the fashion of what has gone before. But this city was where man first dwelt in all these lands. Few buildings, even the palace, could have stood so long. You look upon a city that grew like a living body, that was built and rebuilt over and over again down all the long years. Why do you shiver?''

Elof smiled, somewhat shamefacedly. "You spoke of years, of the first coming of men to this land. I cannot take them so lightly, seeing them embodied before me. I am a smith, well used to looking deep into the past, delving for ancient learning. Yet even I am awed by the passage of five thousand years.''

Kermorvan's eyes gleamed. "And the last thousand wholly apart, alone, as we were. I believe these last strong walls could be no older than that, and many of these buildings also; as if the city was swelled then by refugees . . . Will they have changed, I wonder? Do men of southern and northern kindred dwell together still as they did in Morvan? Who rules here, since Korentyn was lost to them and had no heir? A thousand questions await answer!''

Roc shook his head. "But the first one's got to be whether or not they shoot at strangers! Even ones that might be kin. Or king.''

"I had considered that. Best we make ourselves known at first only as men of the west. Call me Kermorvan still, but not by my given name—''

A rush and whistle cut the air. He had already dropped to a fighting crouch, his sword half-drawn in a single fluid move, before the arrow struck into the ground at his feet; but then he stood, and moved no more. Ils cursed and snatched her axe, then like Kermorvan she stopped, frozen, as she was. Elof's hand was on his sword, but he too made no move to draw; he also had seen the hedges stirring along the other side from whence the arrow had come. They were outflanked by a band of unknown number, and they might all have bows. Behind he heard Roc breathing heavily, and his muttered words. "Rush 'em! Fight 'em, like we did before!"

"No!" breathed Elof. "Hold your hand, Kermorvan is right! We have not come all this way to our lost kin only to slay or be slain by them, have we?"

Roc snapped his fingers. "Aye, well . . ." But there he stopped, for he too had heard Ils' strangled cry. He stared with the others at that arrow, and saw that the fletches it bore were striped in black and white. And out from behind the hedge, that perfect ambush, there arose a dozen tall warriors of the Ekwesh, bows in hand.

Elof's fingers convulsed upon his hilt, but there was nothing he could do save think this a bad dream. Yet there they were as he had first struggled against them when they took his village, as he had last seen them at the ambush in the wood; tall men in armor of stiffened black leather, faces writhing with cicatrized serpent markings and the scars of war. The bows were very steady in their hands; they would not miss.

There was a sudden hiss and a whirl above, and next moment Elof was enveloped in damp rope, foul with fish-scales and salt. A net had been cast over them all, and even as Elof struggled to draw and slash at it, dark shapes rushed up and seized his arms. From then on the tussle was without hope, though he fought and struggled for his pride's sake; at last he was bound and tied and lay threshing, hearing other sounds of struggle only a foot or two away, unable to see or help. A ghastly gargling shriek chilled him, and the sound of threshing in the dust. But at last the net was plucked from him, and a hard brown hand hauled him to his knees. He looked up, and had a terrible shock, for the face above him was too much like the old chieftain who had so nearly had him slaughtered. The likeness was of type; this was quite a young man, grinning through filed teeth.

"*Ora!* We have you!" He slapped one of their great copper-edged clubs into his palm. "Obey, march, you live! For now. To the city, go! *Kianhnu nat'deh!*"

Their packs and weapons were plucked from them,

given no more than a perfunctory glance and passed to others to carry. With spearhead and dagger at their kidneys, arms bound, legs hobbled, they were pushed forward along the road as they had been going, toward the sunlit walls ahead. The young warrior caressed the patterns painted upon his breastplate, and grinned again. "You think we fools, not to watch road? Word come, we watch all ways." He jerked a thumb at the city of Morvannec. "This ours now."

CHAPTER TEN

The Flames Mount

The travelers were driven along at a brisk trot, too dazed at first to take in what was happening. Elof could hardly make sense of it: it had come about with the suddenness and utter unreality of nightmare. The Ekwesh had barely conquered half the west, and that chiefly by their overwhelming strength upon the sea; how could they have reached the east? How could they have overcome so massive a burg, so much greater than Kerbryhaine, without leaving any scars of siege and strife?

For a moment he wondered crazily if time in the Forest had deceived them more thoroughly than they thought, and decades, even centuries had passed during their few brief months there; but that he could not credit. In his bewilderment he stumbled, and at once felt a sharp sting in his back, a trickle of warm blood ran down beneath his tunic. The pain jerked him back to cold awareness of the immediate danger. He was being goaded along as once he had goaded cattle, and to much the same end, perhaps. He smiled thinly to himself. Once he had refused life as an Ekwesh thrall, knowing it might lead only to being ritually slaughtered and eaten. What else could he expect, now? But the time between had been worth it, come what may; and if he could not hope to find Kara, what else was there for him? It was for his friends he was most anxious. If he had managed to slay one of the ambushers, as had Kermorvan, might it have tipped the balance, given them a chance to fight? No; they were too many, too well-armed, and there was also the net. A fight would have earned them nothing but the finality of a quicker death; he was not ready to embrace that yet. While he breathed he must hope, and be alert for any careless move by his foes, any chance the others might take.

He risked a glance at Kermorvan, and was dismayed. The tall man also walked as if in a dream, his hands bound at his back, torn and bloody from the net. Roc was behind him, out of sight, but Elof could just see Ils at the corner of his eye; she too was bound, and rage boiled up in him at the grinning Ekwesh who drove her along, for every so often he would crack the rope's end across her broad thigh. When he tired of that he began to rummage in one of their packs that he was carrying; Elof's heart sank at the thought of all they might find in his. And what Kermorvan's held . . .

But then the young chieftain turned, barking a command that wiped the grin from the warrior's face, and hit him a ringing blow on the arm with his white baton, another on the ear when he answered sullenly. The warrior cringed, muttered something in their guttural tongue, and let go of the pack. Kermorvan laughed coldly. "Stiff discipline, if naught else! Booty goes untouched to the chieftains for due division, is that not so?" His neckrope was jerked, and he fell silent.

The reproved warrior subsided into sullenness, and then, to Elof's horror, he began to work out his anger in a crueler game. Every so often he would jerk Ils' rope, so that she stumbled back against the blade in his hand. She did not cry out, only caught her breath and bit her lip, but within a few minutes the back of her jerkin was cut and bloody. Elof was ready to kick out at him, whatever the cost, when the chieftain looked around again and growled a few words: the warrior swallowed, and passed her rope to another.

"What's this then?" jeered Roc. "Manners 'mong the maneaters?"

"You mistake him," said Kermorvan dryly, ignoring

the tugs on the rope. "It is not we who concern him, but discipline; now is not the time for such games. Also . . ." He fell silent suddenly, but his blue-gray eyes flashed a look of startling intensity to the others. Elof gave a curt nod of understanding, for the same thought had occurred to him. He had assumed they were being kept alive as thralls; but it looked very much as if there was some command to deliver them unharmed, perhaps to be questioned. The flick of a rope would not matter, but a stray stab might go too deep, or loss of blood weaken. The reluctance to slay might prove a valuable weakness, should some chance of escape appear.

But none did. The vigilance was unwavering, the pace unrelenting, rope and blade ready to punish the slightest hesitation or stumble. And stumble they did, weary and dismayed in the growing twilight. After what seemed like a limping eternity there came a harsh command, and the company halted so suddenly that the captives were caught by their ropes; Elof fell to his knees, and was driven aside with blows and kicks. Looking up, he saw the outer walls of the city looming in the darkening sky ahead, startlingly near; the Ekwesh had set a murderous pace. Yet now they were squatting by the roadside, talking softly among themselves, as if waiting for something. He raised tired eyes to the city, and saw that the road they had taken led to an arch in the wall, a small side gate compared to those he had seen from afar. There they waited while darkness advanced and the first stars appeared; he was surprised how few lights showed above the walls. Even in the palace only a few windows glowed. When the last daylight was gone the chieftain sprang up, and the weary prisoners were hauled to their feet and herded down toward the darkened gate.

Ahead they heard a booming blow, a curt exchange of words, and the creak of a port opening. Torchlight glowed on the red-brown skins, set fire in the dark eyes that surrounded the travelers, fierce and pitiless. Elof felt that there was something out of the ordinary about these men; they were as hard as any Ekwesh he had ever seen, but they

seemed quieter, more formidable, than the yelling clans-
men of the raider ships or that first ambush in the west.
Also, few save some with chieftain's markings were young.
These were picked men, veterans, and something else also.
It came to him as he and the others were bundled through
the little port and into a darkened, empty street flanked
by featureless silhouettes of tall buildings: the inner calm
of these Ekwesh was the calm of fanaticism. Old warriors,
young leaders—that fitted both only too well. It reminded
him of the Mastersmith.

More Ekwesh formed up around them now, a whole
column, and at the chieftain's word the ropes were jerked
violently. The travelers found themselves dragged forward
now over a road of smooth cobbles, and swiftly. Around
them their guards broke into a trot, but Elof quickly realized they were more concerned with watching the sides
of the street than the captives. Sweat stung his eyes, and
he could make out no more there than high walls and
looming shapes, dark against darkness. Suddenly the column swerved sharply, sandals slapping on the cobbles,
and turned off the broad street into a bewildering succession of winding lanes and alleys. They were dark, without
even a spill from lit windows; one or two Ekwesh slipped
on loose stones and fell cursing while the runners poured
over them. With the stupidity of fatigue Elof wondered
why they did not carry linklights. Could it be that they did
not want to be seen? Or was it him and the others they
wished to conceal? But from whom? And why?

The moon came out from behind the clouds then, and
by its light Elof looked his first upon the face of the city.
The lane they ran in was bounded by two tall buildings,
joined by a curious arched bridge, roofed in and win-
dowed. Beyond these ran walls of some light stone, only
a head or so higher than a man, topped by spikes that
seemed more decorative than effective and broken by many
arches and gates. Behind these walls on either side rose
remarkable buildings of the same stone, with between them
spaces of what seemed to be greenery and garden, with
trees that were tall and fair. One edifice rose to their right,

many times higher than the wall; arched windows, very tall and graceful with leaded panes, filled its frontage from the wall to the roof, and atop the great bay in the center a carved eagle spread its weatherstained wings. Opposite it, almost against the wall, stood a lower building with many small windows between which ran bands of carving, startling and very skillful, images of animals and flowers mingled with grotesque human caricatures. Harried as he was, he strove to take it in; its sheer exuberance captivated him. It was civilized craft, worlds away from the grim vitality of the black and white Ekwesh emblems, yet it seemed quite recent, clean-edged and unweathered. His suspicions were confirmed. If this city did now belong to the sea-raiders, it had not done so for long.

After many turns the lane broadened and opened into a wide thoroughfare, its skyline jagged with buildings of many shapes, from tall towers to wide halls and lower houses, yet as a whole fair and well proportioned. Across this the column hurried, and there the moonlight showed a grimmer truth. From a stout linkbracket upon a house wall a corpse dangled by a rope round its neck; it was not garbed as an Ekwesh, but no more could be said. It had been there some days by the look of it and the taint in the air. Atop the bracket, perched on one leg in glutted sleep, sat a fat gray gull. Elof found his own horror and anger mirrored in the faces of his friends, but the Ekwesh paid no heed to the sight, and bundled them up a narrow alley beside an inn.

All through the city they climbed thus, a long and weary way worsened by the devious routes. Long before they reached their destination, not far short of the middle hour of night, Elof had guessed it would be the palace. For all its darkened stone it seemed a fair and noble building, with warm light from within to gild gallery and buttress; it put him less in mind of Kerbryhaine than of the Halls of Summer, its grandeur more graceful than proud. But he was left little time to look; there were many Ekwesh on guard, and the arrival of the column started them stirring like ants. The chieftain wasted little time on words; in moments a side door creaked open, and the travelers were dragged into the smoky red light within. Stairs led downward, worn and winding, low-roofed and echoing; Kermorvan and the tall Ekwesh stood alike in danger here, and in fact as they turned into a level tunnel the chieftain managed to strike his head a heavy blow on a keystone. But he saw his captives hurried down and through a stout wooden door into a dark cellar, and he stood over them, cursing softly and flicking blood from his eyes, while they were unbound and thrust down at spear's point against the cool wall. Then stout manacles were fastened on them at wrist and ankle, and through these they were chained to wall rings at their backs, so tightly they could barely stir. The chieftain stayed long enough to test the fastenings, and order Elof's tightened; then he swept out, and all the rest in his wake, taking all the torches. The door slammed, a key grated in the lock; blackness and silence settled upon them. None spoke, none stirred, for they felt stifled. The nightmare was made absolute.

But at length Kermorvan moved; they heard the clink of his ankle chain. "What has happened?" he asked, in a low voice, dull and incomprehending. "Kerys, what has *happened*?" None of the others answered; they had been about to ask him the same.

"They hurried us here after dark," Elof mused, "as if they did not want us seen . . ." Then suddenly the words stuck in his throat. Very slowly, very quietly, the key was turning once more in the lock. It drew back, and for an endless moment silence fell again. Then, very cautiously, the door was pushed open a crack, and a feeble glint of yellow light shone in. Above it a face appeared and Elof choked. It seemed deathly, spectral, floating in darkness like one of the faces of Dorghael Arhlannen dust-whitened to a semblance of life. He saw with a shiver that it had their look indeed, of strong bones beneath stretched skin, sunken at cheek and temple, crowned with wisps of colorless hair. But as it glided closer he saw that the hair was thick and silvery, the nose firm and straight, the lips thin but with a trace of color in them; dim blue eyes shone in the sockets. Yet still it might have been one of those faces living, or some other he could not place. It was a very old face, yet noble and fair with the fragile grace of age; in youth it must have been handsome as . . . Kermorvan. It did not mirror him as Korentyn had; the likeness was of cast alone, but strong, not least in the glitter of cold vitality that rose in those eyes as the light fell upon Elof. He strove to return the old man's gaze, but it was not an easy face to look upon, grown to age, and aged by suffering. The voice bore witness to both.

"Will you say, sirs, who you are?" The voice was fair, the speech was southern, strangely inflected but as clear as any Kerbryhaine, save that it trembled. Instinctively Elof waited for Kermorvan to answer.

"Wayfarers from the west," he said at last. "From the western shores, that men of Morvan settled after its fall."

"Ahhh . . ." It was a sound of understanding, yet almost a gasp of pain. "How can this be? We did not know that the west had come to anything. And it is a fantastic, a terrible distance to have journeyed . . ."

"We knew no more of the east," said Kermorvan quietly. "And it was indeed terrible, and cost many lives. But most terrible of all is its ending! What has happened here, that these barbarians who menace us also hold this city?"

The face turned away sharply. "So they hold the west also? Then perish, what you awakened . . ."

"They've not got it yet," growled Roc. "Those you speak to had some say in that, even myself. Sent 'em running with their shirts on fire!"

"Then hope lives!" said the old man urgently, and then grew flustered. "B-but have you need of meat or drink? I have brought you what I could, poor as it is. I have no better myself."

"That is kindness indeed!" said Elof fervently, for his tongue was swelling with thirst. "But can you free our hands to eat, good jailer?"

"No, good sir, for I am no jailer, not even a turnkey; only for the most menial tasks of a prison am I tolerated.

They do not trust me with any keys save the doors. And rightly so!'' For a moment metal rang in the tired voice. ''You are a northerner, by your speech? It is good to know they thrive in the west also. I must feed you; do you forgive me if I am clumsy, my sight fades fast. But hearken, if you will, to the tally of our woes!'' His hand, long and strong as Kermorvan's, raised a flask to Elof's mouth. Watered wine, cool and fresh, flowed against his lips, and he gulped gratefully. ''Where did they begin? They have many beginnings. As long past as the fall of Morvan, perhaps, and the deaths in its defense of king and prince both, Keryn and Korentyn.'' Kermorvan seemed to choke, on the wine as it might have been. ''Morvannec they had committed to the care of Karouen the Lord Warden, their cousin, and when the last fugitives fled across the mountains with the sad news, the people took him and his line as their lord. And worthy lords they were, for the most part, being of the line of Kermorvan. Only its fiercest fires they lacked, perhaps, and many thought that no bad thing. Once it was clear that the mountains and the clime held the Ice well at bay, they became more concerned to build new life and prosperity for Morvannec, which had languished so long in the shade of Morvan. And that they found, and enjoyed through many long lifetimes, content for the most part to settle their own immediate problems and forget the past.'' A bitter note in the old man's voice awoke an echo.

''So also it was with us!'' said Kermorvan fiercely. ''But go on. How long did it last, this complacency?''

''Till the days of my age,'' said the old man bleakly. ''And I lived as complacent as any. Would I had died so, and rotted in illusion still! About four years past it was that the plague came, if plague it was; some say that our wells were poisoned, though they cannot tell who might have done such a thing. Then in one swift summer a full two-third parts of our folk perished, and those left alive were hard put even to burn their bodies. My family perished; children and close kin; yet I hold it a worse evil that our Lord Koren died, and his lady, without issue, and left us lordless.''

"Had he no brothers?" asked Roc, champing at the scraps of bread and meat he was being fed.

"All too many! And some of not the worthiest stamp. They declared their rivalry, and somehow strife and riot broke out around them. Though to do them credit they none of them fostered it; yet it followed them. Lesser men gained influence over the crowds, and one most of all, a roving merchant from our lesser towns as he claimed to be. I doubt that now! For he brought with him as servants many brown-skinned men from lands far southward, as he said, and hired them out to help us, in town and in field. They were hard and tireless workers, and a great assistance to us. We grew used to seeing them, and could not tell how many there were in the city. Then, only last spring, this merchant returned from some voyage. And that same night these servants cast off their guises and took up arms and armor they had concealed, and fell upon the few guards at our gates. Others hastened down out of the wild lands to the north and were given entry. Our other towns they took in like manner, but with ships they stole from our harbor. Many wished to fight them—aye! even I—but we were leaderless and weakened, and from the first they acted as unquestioned conquerors, as if resistance were unthinkable; that counted for much. In a week our whole land was overrun, and for more than a year now we have borne their heavy yoke; we labor ten times harder for them, than ever they for us."

Kermorvan looked at the old man. "Even to serving as their jailer?"

"Aye, even so, in cellars that once held no worse than good wine, and where I was chamberlain and master. Resistance of any kind, even slight and passive, they quell at once and brutally. If you have fought them, you must know the cruelty that is in them, how little of good save in bravery and order, and what manner of evil they practice as worship and kin-rite. That men could sink to such horrors I never dreamed! Their hearts are as dark as their skins!"

"They are a people corrupted," said Elof quietly. "But the skin is no mark of that. Many such have mingled with the old northern kindred, and have suffered as cruelly from the Ekwesh, and hate them as bitterly as do you.''

The old man offered Ils bread with elaborate grace, and sighed. ''I am sorry for them. But it restores my faith in humanity. I could almost have thought we dealt with some other breed, as legendary as duergar.''

Ils snorted, and her eyes took on an evil glint, her voice sardonic menace. ''Beware lest a legend snaps off your finger-ends, old human!'' The old man gasped, and peered at her so closely their noses almost touched.

''Are you then . . .'' he stammered, and then smiled in sheer wonder. ''Oh, my lady, forgive me! I did not mean to match the Elder folk with these brutes, save as being reputed as far above common men as they are below. Still less did I expect ever to meet one of them! Would that you had graced our city in happier circumstances—''

Ils blossomed, but Kermorvan cut urgently across her reply. ''Sir, you say the Ekwesh have lingered here a year. Why? Have they brought in their families and thralls, to settle as is their practice?''

The old man shook his head. ''No, that they have not. And they waste this city as if they do not mean to stay, herding in the country folk and letting the fields go untended while they waste our store. We have wondered what is their purpose. Almost it might seem they were waiting . . . Though who can say for what?''

''This merchant,'' put in Elof. ''What is he doing? He is not one of them, you say, yet he rules them?''

''Aye, he does. Him, or his women.''

''His women?''

''I have seen them. One has dwelt with him since his first appearance here, and departed on his voyages with him. The other . . . I cannot say. But they do not carry themselves like wife or daughter, either of them.''

The chill at Elof's back was deeper than chain or cold wall could set in him, and he shuddered in apprehension. Yet it had to be asked. ''Are they . . . is one tall, blue-eyed, very fair of hair and skin? And the other . . . not quite so tall and very slender, with dark locks cut close?''

"These are they, indeed!" burst out the old man. "But how come you to . . . ah. They have been in the west also."

"And this merchant, what of him? Has he a name?"

"Aye, though what right to it I know not. For once it was honorable of its kind, one of the families that have opposed the line of kings since the ancient days of Morvan. A Bryheren he is. And Bryhon by name."

A sudden spilling of redness across the floor looked more like blood than light. "That's so, old man. But what business have you saying it, that's the damned question, eh?" The torch was held low, the figure behind it all but unrecognizable between shimmering light and shadow. But that bluff orator's voice there was no mistaking.

The old man stood up stiffly, painfully unbending bowed shoulders, and met the accusation calmly. "Sir, it is my given task to feed prisoners."

"Aye, those you've had orders to! And not to wag your doddering tongue! Be thankful that nothing you've said will matter, soon enough. Be off out of the palace, and be damned to you!" The old man was thrust violently up the steps, and the door slammed to behind him. "Stinking rathole!" muttered the voice, and quick steps crossed the room. There was a creaking crash, and a shutter dropped down. The light of a full moon flooded over the dusty earthen floor, and cool air flowed in, bearing the sound and scent of the sea.

"Thank you, Bryhon," murmured Kermorvan calmly.

"Not at all," answered Bryhon Bryheren with equal calm, as he hooked his torch into a wall bracket and came to stand before them, leaning against a pillar and folding his arms.

"You!" raged Roc, straining at his chains. "You spawn of Amicac, how'd you come here? What're you about, you traitor filth?"

Bryhon shrugged. "I don't know what you mean. I am no traitor, and never have been. What I serve, I serve faithfully."

"But solemn oaths you have broken," said Kermorvan, his voice level and cool as edged iron.

"None I meant. None I was not bound to break by earlier, sterner oaths, bound both to take and to break."

Kermorvan sighed deeply. "So it is true, then."

"It is," answered Bryhon.

"What's true, you damned doubletalking loons?" hissed Ils, an instant ahead of Elof.

Kermorvan shifted on the stone. "That there is, and has long been, an . . . say, an undercurrent within our folk. A mirror image of all we believe and stand for, a hater of all we revere, a worshiper of what we shun the most. A secret reverence of the ancient Powers. A hereditary cult of the Ice."

Bryhon nodded. "A fair summation. Save that we despise, rather than hate. And we do not merely revere." His voice became suddenly smooth, and yet beneath it, like quicksand beneath a firm crust, was the tremor of a growing excitement. "We *worship*. As we have done ever since the first days of men, among the former, lesser, Winters of the World, before even the rise of Kerys the Accursed. From Kerys we came to Morvan, and from Morvan westward, though by ill chance here in the east our line failed also. And in all that time we have striven against the spreading, corrupting filth that is mankind. Whithersoever men flee, so shall our faith flee with them, to the utmost corners of the Earth, to the last breath drawn. It is mind we worship, bold and independent, freed from the stinking cesspool of the body. We seek the utter cleansing of the world, the cooling of that corruption, the frenzied, thoughtless ferment that is life. We atone for our flesh by subduing it to the service of the purest mind, we seek its mortification and the suppression of its demands . . ."

"And meanwhile you lust after power and possessions," said Elof dryly. "Spare me sermons I have heard before, Bryhon. I know their worth."

"Do not judge me by your late master!" snapped Bryhon urgently; a nerve had been touched. "That he was something of a hypocrite, I allow, though he thought himself a strong believer. But is this hypocrisy?'' With savage energy he thrust back his right sleeve almost to the shoulder. ''Or this?'' He pulled apart his jerkin to bare his barrel chest.

Kermorvan exclaimed in horror. Roc cursed. Ils turned away, looking sick, and Elof felt his own gorge rise. The wide skin of the upper arm was a lacework of scars and weals, some old and faded almost to whiteness, one or two new and angry half-healed scabs. The chest was the same, save that there were also thinner weals curling right round his body, as if lashed with a whip of hot wires. ''To this exercise of faith I have devoted my life, as my father and his fathers of our line before me! And you, boy, you dare name me traitor!''

Roc spat at him. ''Aye, and all your cracked forefathers! Hella fry the pack of them in their own mad filth!''

Kermorvan gave a sigh of astonishment and even pity. ''I can guess now why you have never taken a wife, last of the Bryherens.''

Bryhon tilted his head. ''We are bound to wed only in later years, and solely for the engendering of heirs, of course, not for mere pleasure.''

''Of course. But I meant . . . other things.''

''Small wonder he got here safely!'' muttered Ils. ''Not even the Hunt would soil their claws with him! He might enjoy it!''

Bryhon's eyes widened at the mention of the Hunt, but he regained his composure at once. ''So that's the company you've been keeping all this while, is it? But do you think it much to have crossed this land just once? These last few years I have crossed and recrossed it many times.''

''Over the Ice, of course,'' said Elof.

''Only at first,'' Bryhon answered. ''The Ekwesh we had to bring that way, though it meant losing a good few. But they are brothers in blood of the Hidden Clan, and took that as they should. No, I tread a faster way, and a darker. How, you of all men should know; the means was of your making, after all.''

Elof snapped rigid in his chains. "The Tarnhelm!" he cried.

"Indeed. Lady Louhi had it of your master. But she has honored me with its use, many times, in preparing the taking of this place and the assault on Kerbryhaine. I was concerned lest you had seen me appear with it, that night on the battlements, but your wits were fortunately slower than I expected. Your late master had only then finished giving me an exaggerated idea of them."

"So it was you betrayed us to the Mastersmith!" said Ils, in tones as silken as Bryhon's own.

He shrugged. "Naturally. By the helm's aid I could take frequent counsel with him, to ensure that I and those few followers I would still need should be safe when Kerbryhaine fell; the smith and I were kin from afar, but that made us more rivals than allies. And of course I summoned the Ekwesh to waylay your expedition when you set out. If there had been more of the Hidden among them it would not have been so mishandled."

"Strange," said Kermorvan quietly. "To think I almost believed you meant your wish, that we would reach our goal . . ."

"I did!" said the dark man, as if mildly surprised. "It was my duty to prevent you, but I hoped you would manage nonetheless. Because here I would be free to settle with you myself, as I could not without sacrificing my influence in Bryhaine. Here I could fight you openly, and end you and your decayed line at a stroke."

"Well then!" blazed Kermorvan suddenly. "Here you see me! You have only to speak the word. Unbind me, return my sword! Then let us see which way the stroke falls, which line is ended!"

Bryhon shook his head. "Pain it is to me, but I cannot. I came chiefly to tell you as much, and add my regret. That grace is denied me, and your lives allotted to another. A matter of discipline, I believe, a certain stiffening of the will, and a fit requital for many strayings. And on your part, reward enough for the trouble you have caused us. Madness and despair await you before your death, for such is the gift of the one who is sent you." He looked round quickly at the open shutter, and when he turned back fine beads of sweat glistened upon his high forehead. "I must not be here. I have lingered too long as it is. Tomorrow I return to the west, to set in motion again that cleansing strife you have hindered, and the assault that shall follow. Do not delude yourself that any shall halt it. The raven is a carrion bird, and cares not whose bones he picks. Farewell!" The low steps were taken in one stride, the door slammed, the key twisted sharply, metal squealing upon metal. Then there was no sound save the quiet harmony of wind and sea, far below.

Elof sought to speak, and could not. Nor could the others; the terror they had read in Bryhon had infected them all. The man had been deadly afraid of being caught up in what was about to happen, even of witnessing it, though his strange shadow-life must have acquainted him with horror enough. A sudden clink of metal made Elof start and tremble, till a sobbing breath of effort told him it was Kermorvan straining furiously against his bonds, and vainly. Elof too tried, till the very seams of his jerkin were ready to burst, or the threads of the muscles beneath. But the steel of chain and manacle held firm, and he toppled on his side in the dust, gasping. Fear settled on that darkened cell as slowly, as thickly, as the disturbed dustmotes that drifted down through the bright moonbeams. Suddenly they leaped up, those dustmotes, as a blast of chill air whistled in the cell, and another, another, a pulsing beat like great wings. The motes sprang and swirled and sparkled like metal, ever more thickly, more brightly, till it seemed that the dust swirled into shadow, into solidity, into a slender shape of light and shade. There in the moonlight it took form, and out of the moonlight it seemed made, a thing of silvery brightness and blackest night. Brightness it wore as mail, night as a cloak outspread like black wings, one with the outer darkness of the cell. Bright was the helm it bore, black the fierce bird-eyes of its visor, black the long spearshaft, bright the gauntlet that brandished it high above their heads. But brighter than any, blacker than all, were the spearblade at its tip and the swirl of patterns set thereon. They caught at the eye and held it, yet Elof stared past them as if they were not there, at the fair face half hidden beneath the visor, the lips that moved, that voiced his name.

"Alv! Elof! Look upon me!"

In awe and terror, in sick apprehension, he could scarcely find voice. "Say, then, who you are, so fair, so grave! Show me your face!"

Like distant chimes on a chill night rang the answer. "When I am armed for war, who meets my gaze thus leaves life and light behind. They alone may look upon me now, who are marked for death at my hand."

A deadly shudder shook Elof, a qualm of chill like the onset of some bitter fever. A grim laughter rose unbidden to his lips, for that voice, changed as it was, he knew. "So will you slay us here, bound and helpless as we are? Speak then, bold one! Set your name to the deed!"

"Of the Morghannen am I, the Valkyrior, Givers of Life, Choosers of Death. A Warrior of the Powers am I, and from them is your death my charge. My name is Kara."

"Kara!" It was if the name was wrenched out of him, though he had known it from the first. He gazed up at her, his thoughts awhirl like the dust, unable to take in what he saw, what he had been told. He could not accept her as the girl he had first spoken to, lost and unhappy as any daughter of men might be, as the slender form he had held and kissed in an hour of dark danger. Yet, just as surely, he knew this was her, that this was the truth of her, and the consummation of the fears that Tapiau's words had sowed in him. And he remembered also how afraid of Kara the Mastersmith had seemed; his heightened awareness must have sensed some peril in her. Elof could not fly from the truth. He had dared to love one of the Powers; how foolish she must have thought him! His heart seemed to wither within him, as once he had seen a man wither and known it for his own work.

It was like drowning, like being back in the Forest lake

with dark claws dragging him down. Sickness, emptiness, loss welled up over his head. The world, the act of living, seemed suddenly alien things, beyond his understanding, and he pulled darkness about him like a shroud. For him nothing remained . . . Yet even as that thought came to him, he knew it was not true. His very desperation came to aid him. His friends, bound beside him, they remained, they would suffer if he could not help them. So that was left him . . . and a memory of whispered words. *"Kara!* Is this then what you are? Then you choose also between truth and falsehood. For once you swore to me that you were of no common sort. And true is that! But you swore also that you would not change!"*

The mouth twisted, the helm flinched, yet haft and blade did not. And grave, implacable came the reply. "What I am, I am. The sentence given I must execute. That pain is mine to bear without ending. Make ready, and be still."

Elof swallowed desperately, and fixed his eyes upon the blank mask of the helm. "Hear me! Are you then a Warrior of the Powers? But which Powers? A Giver of Life. Are you a Chooser of Death? Then why do you serve those who admit no choice? By whose will do you deal out death?"

The upraised blade wavered. "By the will . . . that binds me! Seek not to change its working, nor delay. No fear, no weakness has it that you or I could challenge. Seek not to worsen your agony, and mine! Even now . . ."

"Even now?" He heard himself shouting, his voice echoing in the vault. He strove to force strength into his words, to drive them upon metal at his forge. "Even now you are tormented, Kara! Even now you are torn! Torn between your will, and that which is set upon you! Between what you are, and what holds you in thrall! Be what you name yourself! Choose freely!"

A shiver rippled through the mailed flank. The spear faltered, fell away. Then she jerked violently, her head thrown back as if some sudden hand had seized her at the neck. Her voice rose to a cry. *"Upon me you look! I have no choice left me!"* Back flew the cloak, scattering shadows. High rose the spear, madness shivering at its tip, and at his heart it drove.

The patterns on the spearblade seemed to writhe and uncoil like a nest of snakes, and strike full into his eyes. Darkness and cell wall vanished, he was hurled and buffeted amid a torrent of boiling blood that softened his flesh like wax and washed it from his bones, while shrilling voices shrieked wordless taunts in his ears. "Kara!" he screamed, over the voices, over the torrent's thunder. He struggled to hold on to his thoughts as they were broken and scattered, his memory as it dissolved and leached away; to one perception he clung, one sudden rock in the torrent, the sight of her arm upraised as the cloak fell back, and upon it, leaping like understanding to his eyes, a sudden flash of gold. "Kara!" he cried out. "By what you took upon yourself I conjure you! By the virtues I set within it I command you! For by my armring also you are bound!" Abruptly he was sprawled on the cellar floor, every muscle clenched and cramped in shrieking rictus, and above him the birdmask stooping. He drew a tortured breath. "Yet in those bonds . . . lies only freedom. Kara, by what you are you have sworn! Be yourself, then! Be free! And as ever you loved me, aid us! They do have fears, we are their fears! From the city they hid us . . . and so you may thwart them! Do what they feared! Rouse the city! Summon—" The arm flashed forward. The blow fell.

He screamed something, he convulsed against the immovable chains even as the blade chilled his neck and struck downwards. The cell lit with a flash of white fire; he felt the blasting force of the blow, and it was as if it rebounded on Kara. Her head snapped back, her spine arched, and behind him the stone wall splintered, the taut chains shattered and flew ringing apart. His hands sprang free. Kara shrieked aloud, the dreadful shrilling cry of a wounded falcon; vast wings beat once in the narrow space, the open shutter smashed to splinters, and with wrenching suddenness she was gone. Elof fell face down upon the earth.

A voice was calling into vast depths, and slowly, effortfully, he swam upward, struggling to understand and answer. He could scarcely make the effort, he wanted to cut free, to rest. But then a hand touched his shoulder, and he was suddenly wide awake. The old man was stooping over him, his eyes wide, his silver hair awry as if from some great wind. "Sir! Sir! What is happening? What has passed?" Elof shook his head, unable to answer, and in sudden panic looked to the others. They sat there, still chained, their faces pale with shock but alive and alert. "Has it come to you, sir? The whole city is astir!"

"Has what come?" snapped Kermorvan.

"I . . . I cannot say . . . A v-vision, a visitation. A terrible sight, upon rooftop after rooftop. In mail, barelegged, slender as a young girl, yet . . . Like a bird. Crying out, chanting . . ."

"Like a bird? Her helm, you mean, and her feather-cloak?"

The jailer shook his head. "No! No cloak . . . All over the city she is seen, on one rooftop she appears, then vanishes and takes shape on another. And each time, sir, each time wilder, each time more like a bird! The way she cried out, the shrieks! And then the words, a chant, a summons, a warning . . . that there were those come to . . . to deliver us . . . a lord in danger of being slain in secret . . . that we should free them, heed them, that we might all win free! And I thought at once of you, how secretly they brought you in and Bryhon came to you. And under cover of the uproar I crept back . . ." He stopped. "Listen! Do you listen, now!"

Faintly they heard it, a shrieking incantation, a clarion cry that rang and echoed across the city below. And though wordless with distance, yet it set the hair bristling upon their heads, the blood surging in their hearts. And under it, even as it cut short, another sound arose that might have been the sea rising yet was not, was the distant slam of shutter and door, of voices raised and feet running, and here and there the first angry shouts of conflict, screams and turmoil and the thin clink of arms. The old man winced. "Sirs, lady, she's rousing all the quarter around, men, women, children! The man-eaters will cut them to pieces! Is it you? Is the one she promised among you?"

"We must get free!" cried Kermorvan. "Elof, she broke your chains—"

"Aye, but my feet are still fastened!"

"Hold, sir!" The old man picked up a stout bar of steel. "I could find naught else, and doubted its strength and mine. But you . . ." Elof snatched the bar out of his hand, thrust it through chain and staple, and gave a single sharp heave. The bar quivered, the staple rose, bent, and then with a crack bar and chain shivered as one, and Elof rolled free. He snatched up the larger piece of bar, but it would not shift the heavy ring fastening Kermorvan's manacles.

"Your hammer, man!" wheezed Roc. "Your tools!"

"They took them with the packs and the swords!"

"Two great swords, sir? And packs of green hide? They lie in the guardchamber, sir, at the stairhead. I might . . . if the guards are occupied . . . I might . . ." The old voice trembled.

"Show me!" hissed Elof, and together they plunged for the door. The corridor beyond was empty, but from up the stairs voices echoed, and the slam of doors. Motioning the old man to stay behind him, Elof sidled up, striving to be silent, hastily gathering up the lengths of clinking chain still hanging from his manacles. He felt no fear; that moment of insanity, that shattering spearthrust, had blasted fear from him. He moved as if in a daze of concentration, taut, ready, intent as beast upon its prey.

The door at the stairhead stood open, and in it two Ekwesh, staring out into the restless night. The old man touched his arm, pointing to the firelit archway beyond them; the guardroom. Elof nodded, and as he did so the clumsy manacle scraped against stone. The Ekwesh whirled around, but Elof had already launched himself across the floor. One hefted a spear, but Elof dashed his manacled wrist into the man's face, and he fell. The other sprang aside, drawing a long dagger, but Elof whipped at him with the loose chain, once, twice, and caught him in the throat. He also fell, and Elof snatched up the spear from the floor as a third warrior ran out of the guardroom. The stout targe on his arm turned the awkward thrust Elof aimed, but the force of it overbalanced his own stroke; he stumbled past, Elof sprang aside and drove the broad spear through his back. But the first man was up now, drawing his short sword, and Elof could not free the spear. He let go, gathering up his chain, but the Ekwesh jerked suddenly, gurgled, and collapsed. Behind him stood the old man, long dagger bloody in his hand. "There are only these three! The rest must be outside somewhere. Quickly!" Elof thrust closed the outer door; there was no key, but he shot the heavy bolt, and turned to search.

Within the guardroom, laid carelessly upon a table, lay Gorthawer and the other weapons, and beside them their precious packs, apparently untouched. "If only the chieftains were too busy to look at these yet!" muttered Elof, thrusting them at the old man. "I need my hands free!" In his right he took Gorthawer, in his left the hammer, and one of the torches from the wall. "Now, down again!"

The hallway was empty, the stairs also, though raised voices and heavy feet echoed elsewhere in the building. They plunged back into the cell, and Elof locked the door behind them. "That wins us minutes, at least! Now, all of you, lean away from the wall!" Three great strokes smote chains and hasps out of the stone, another three the staples from their feet. Then, heedless of gasped thanks, Elof delved among his tools and found grippers to unfasten the bolted manacles.

Kermorvan stood up, swaying only slightly from his cramped confinement, and seized his pack. His breath shuddered a moment, and he shut his eyes. "It is here!" he gasped. "They have not taken it!" And he spilled the bundle of mail from the pack, and began tearing at his tattered traveling clothes. "Do you others don your war gear! We may need mail to win free of here!" Swiftly he pulled the black mailcoat over his head, donned belt, mailed leggings and boots, and buckled on plates at shoulder, arm and knee. Only the jeweled helm he did not don, but returned carefully to the pack which he hung beneath his cloak. Last of all he took up the small breastplate, and beckoned to the old man. "Now, sir, I may answer your question! Bring here the torch, and look well upon me." The damascened tracery on the breastplate gleamed redly as he buckled it on; the dim eyes squinted at it, widened in shock and lifted at once to his face. Kermorvan nodded curtly, and they filled with sudden tears. "Aye, chamberlain. The raven spreads its wings in the east once more. And one named Keryn bears it."

The old chamberlain bowed his head, unable to speak, and then he glanced at the others, Ils in her bright mailshirt and Roc in breastplate and steel helm, and stared in amazement at Elof. He alone bore no armor, but after shedding his tatters he had donned the smith's garb given him by Korentyn, and over it his swordbelt and the long mail gauntlet. "Sirs and lady, as noble and fell a company are you as fits this hour! If we can win through to the streets, I will guide you as far as old legs may bear me. Say no more to me, but to the people!"

Kermorvan drew his sword, unlocked the door and threw it wide. Out into the passage he sprang, the others behind him. There he hesitated, looking at the other cell doors, but Elof, knowing how impulsive his humanity could be, and how perilous, barged him forward. "You cannot help them yet!"

Kermorvan turned reluctantly to the stairs, and sprang up them with Roc on his heels, Elof and Ils helping the old chamberlain. The slain guards lay undiscovered in the few minutes that had passed, the door still closed. At Kermorvan's behest they flattened themselves against the wall while he spied out through the doorway. "Everywhere Ekwesh!" he whispered, tense as a bowstring. "But no solid line, and their gaze is turned outward to the city. Best we burst through from behind and bolt ere they recover!"

"Then you must leave me!" gasped the old man. "I will delay you . . ."

"Enough!" said Kermorvan crisply. "We leave together! Ready? Now!" With a swift heave he sent the weighty door wide on its hinges, and charged through. Elof, right behind him, had a brief confused image of firelight, smoke and disorder, and the black silhouettes of tall men only a few paces ahead, pointing out into the blackness and shouting. Not until Kermorvan was almost upon the nearest ones did they seem to hear, and glance back; one was fast enough to whirl round and raise his spear, and by a flicker of the fire Elof knew him for the young chieftain who had captured them. But before his spear left his hand Kermorvan's sword reaped the smoky air, the spearshaft shivered and the chieftain seemed to spring backward in a glittering spray of blood. Kermorvan leaped over him and hewed the head from another, while Roc smashed his mace down on the shoulder of one still drawing sword. With that they were through to the outside steps, and clattering down them into thicker wreaths of smoke; Elof saw with a dreadful sinking feeling that they were drifting up from the town, and that the firelight was burning roofs. Shouts came from behind them, and on the steps below startled brown faces loomed suddenly out of the murk; Elof struck at one and it vanished in a clatter, Ils another, then for a moment it was hard hewing, shouts and shrieks, before a way was clear and they could run. Elof lagged a step, his bootsole greasy with another's blood. Suddenly a ghost plucked hard at his cloak, another hissed savagely by his ear. He called a warning to the others as the arrows whined in the blackness and rattled across the worn stone of the stairs, but through the smoke now only chance could have found them a target. Behind, though, Elof heard the heavy tread of pursuing feet, and further off the sound of hooves. Abruptly there were no more stairs underfoot, but ringing cobbles, and the chamberlain was gasping out directions. Down a steep winding street they ran, into a narrow alley and through to another winding street. But round the corner of that, doubling up the slope from the city below, came a file of some fifteen Ekwesh, alert and watchful with their spears readied. Without a break in stride Kermorvan swung up his sword, yelled "Morvan morlanhal!" and flung himself at them.

The sheer speed of his attack carried him down the line, and three fell almost before they could counter him. But by then he had burst through the file, while Ils and Elof fell on its leaders. It might have been a sore skirmish, but the Ekwesh broke away the moment they could and ran off up the slope.

"Cravens!" jeered Roc.

"Not these!" panted Kermorvan. "They must have orders. Orders not to risk engagements . . . That is it! Patrols have been mobbed, and they are pulling in the rest. No more policing; they regroup for an attack. Sir, we must come fast among men of the city!"

"To where folk would most likely think of mustering, then," the chamberlain croaked. "To the Landfall Square!" Across the street he led them, and to a gap between buildings so slight that few would think of squeezing through it; Roc, slimmed as he was by hardship, had some trouble. Into a courtyard it led them, by the boarded windows of an inn, and out under a low doorway in the inn buildings into a wide straight street of tall towers and dwellings that sloped away down the hill and into the distance. Sounds of pursuit were left behind, but they hurried along as fast as the old man could bear. "If I fail," he gasped, "do you go straight that way, follow that road and the sound of the sea to . . . by Kerys' Gate!"

He pointed with trembling hand, but there was no need. The others also had seen and heard, the sudden flash of light atop the tallest tower at the hill's foot, the eerie cry that rang so loud the deepest sleeper would be blasted awake and shivering. But more shattering to them was the sight they saw clearly, being almost on a level with the tower top. A figure stood there, and instead of arms it had vast black wings, which smote at the stars. Atop those wings was no helm but the living head of a giant bird, a bright-eyed raptor with sickle bill agape, shrieking alarm as if each breath cost bitter agony. But beneath head and wing, mail clung to the heaving breasts and body of a woman, bare legs below were fastened by a gleaming chain and shackle. And from moment to moment it was as if the wings faded to a drape of shadow over slender arms.

Folk of Morvannec! Harken and hear me!
Start from your sleep now, wake to the watchcry!
Strike off your shackles, shatter your slavery!
Free and at hand is your destined deliverer!
Into the streets with you! Out at the summons!
Sweep out as streams in the surge of the stormrains,
Strike as the waves at the walls of the harbors,
Burst with your bright blood through bond and through
    barrier!
Look to your lord for the light of your liberty,
Heed him that through him you all shall be free!
Harden your courage!
Harden your courage!
Harden your courage, and hew at your foe!

And it is told that a mighty wind did then seize the bells of that tower, and many others, and shake them like so much chaff cast up from the winnowing. Across the city a great clangor of chimes arose, and the voices of men answered them. But atop the tower the voice wavered, the figure tottered as if seized and pulled off balance; the vast wings threshed, and with a last ear-splitting shriek of pain it vanished.

"They have her!" said Kermorvan grimly. "She was sorely torn, but she has done your bidding, Elof, and that is much!" He looked up at the dwellings around, where startled faces peered out from behind door and shutter, staring from the empty tower top to the armed figures in the street. *"Out!"* he cried, the clear metal of his voice mingling with the wild bell music. "Out at the call! The city is risen! Freedom and death hang in the balance! Find weapons and follow! Follow to the Landfall!"

"Follow to the Landfall!" cried Roc, and Elof with him. But the city folk needed no further summons. The cry from the tower had done its work, here as elsewhere, with the bells for confirmation, and the sight of armed

men abroad who were not their Ekwesh oppressors. Out of doors they streamed, men and women and even young children as the chamberlain had said. They took up the cry with a force that drowned the bells, and after Kermorvan and his company they streamed, all the way down to the sea. Many ran from other streets to join them, some newly arisen who had scarely heard the summons, others from the streets near the citadel which had risen first, who had already seen battle and their houses burn, and were now in fell mood. "Who is it summons us?" growled one in northern tones, hefting a bloodied sword.

"One who was spoken of," answered Elof shortly, for Kermorvan was silent. "At the Landfall more will be said."

Hearing the northern speech the man looked sharply at Elof. "I thought to know all of our kindred within this city, and most within the land, for I have traveled widely. Yet though your face is somehow familiar, you I know not, nor your garb."

"Nor should you. For from the utmost shores of the west I have come. At the Landfall all will hear. Wait till then!"

But his words were heard, and a whisper raced through the crowd. "The west! The west lives! It awakens, and comes to war!"

A sudden scent he knew and loved, a reek of sea and ships and all that went with them, reached Elof's nostrils and he smiled.

"Aye, it is as I thought," croaked the chamberlain. "Here they have gathered, where first men set foot in all this wide land, beneath the images of our vanished glory." And indeed, all around the square a ring of tall shadows towered silent and grim upon their pedestals above the heads of the milling crowds, dwarfing the hotheads who clambered there to harangue them. All kinds, all ages were gathered, with every sign of disorder and haste; many were half clad and wild, but none without some kind of weapon. The Ekwesh in their confidence, or design to appear so, had made no great effort to confiscate weapons save the armories of the City Guard. Many others had weapons and even some armor in their homes—merchants who had once had wealth to guard at home or abroad, and others who had kept older weapons as trophy or ornament; there were many of these, chased pike or polished sword, worn but serviceable. For the rest Elof saw hunting bows and short falchions, slaughterers' poleaxes and heavy butchers' cleavers, boathooks and spikes stripped from the quayside, carpenters' hatchets and fearsome rakes and bills that must have come in from the fields, or tended the green gardens of the city. Where those were wanting, even the ordinary tools of the household had been turned to use, maul and meat knife, chain and weaving-sword, or simply stout wood for staff and cudgel. Anger and fear broke over the crowd like surf, and made these homely things deadly in the hands that held them.

Into this mêlée plunged the newcomers and their following, at the chamberlain's direction making for the raised platform that began the seawall, flanked by two tall statues that he named the Watchers. A few would-be leaders stood there and shouted conflicting commands that few heard, let alone heeded; all eyes were turned upon the travelers, for their armor and their air of purpose. Many also recognized the old man they bore with them, half fainting from the race through the city. "It is you who must speak, if you can," said Kermorvan urgently. "You they may believe sooner than an outsider!"

"Then set me upon the base of the lefthand Watcher, and give me a torch!" Ils and Kermorvan boosted him up easily, and many following began to call for silence. The other speakers were drowned and fell back abashed, slow to argue with armed men. The crowd's roar gradually sank to an uneasy murmur, and the old man, catching his breath, hauled himself up against the legs of the statue and cried out, "People of Morvannec! Heirs of Morvan, Morvanniannen all! You know me, Erouel, late chamberlain to Koren our lord, and like you downtrodden into the very dust!" His dry, dignified voice was better than the loudest herald, for the true passion that alone sustained it could be heard. "But this night I have beheld a great wonder, men of might such as we heard of in olden time! All the way from the west they have come! The Powers herald them, as many have seen, and the Elder folk are their allies! Hear them! And above all him who . . ." He gasped and swayed, as if he would fall. "No more words do you need! Only behold!"

Kermorvan sprang forward, lifting his arms to catch the old man. But he fell not, only lifted high his torch to spread flaring light over both statue and man below. And the crowd swayed as one, and gasped, for one might have been the other. Elof read off the stiff characters upon the pedestal. *"Kaer.. Yn! Keryn! Keryn the Fifth!"*

"Small wonder old Korentyn mistook!" breathed Roc. Armed alike were Kermorvan and the statue, closer still in countenance, and life seemed to leap between them. The golden stone took on the tint of living skin, the sculpted hair a tinge of torchfire, the armor of black marble glistened brighter than the dulled steel, and from both their breasts shone in gold the Raven and Sun.

Kermorvan swung to face the crowd, shrugging back his cloak. "Words you are owed!" He spoke without effort, yet his voice carried over the crowd's excited chatter and stilled it. Elof remembered his quiet command of the crowd in Kerbryhaine, and how he had bound them to his will; he was leaving no time now for any ebb of doubt. "The likeness is no chance; I am Keryn, Lord Kermorvan, last of that line in the west. But in proof of my name I show you its tokens! For through the ruins of Morvan itself have I passed, beneath the devouring Ice; in Dorghael Arhlannen itself have I stood, and borne away a great prize." And from his pack he lifted the crowned helm.

A sighing shudder ran through the crowd as the torchlight flamed upon its gems, a louder stir as Elof stepped forward and drew from his own deep pack the worn bronze rod. "Here you stand where your ancestors first stood," he said in a low voice. "If here is not your kingdom, then nowhere is. Receive the scepter!" Kermorvan's mouth twisted in a quick smile. He took the rod, balanced it on his palm as if savoring the moment, and then with swift decision he held crown and scepter high above his head. Like a retreating wave the crowd of thousands drew a single breath, and then as surf that broke in thunder they cheered, a sound that must have shaken the very shutters of the distant palace. Torch guttered and brazier flared as if a sudden storm blast swept across the square.

Yet Kermorvan did not don the helm, as it seemed he might, but instead quickly handed both to Erouel, as if eager to free his hands. "Enough!" he cried, and there was an instant hush. He spoke swiftly, quietly, but his tone was grim. "Now is your time of need. Above us there the barbarians muster. You have taught them a dangerous lesson, shown them that they cannot any longer act like guards over beaten thralls! They gather as an army, for that is the only way they dare meet you now! And if they defeat you they will not be content to keep down heads with a few patrols, and here and there a sharp example; they will slay you every last one, for they can never again feel safe. Perhaps they are already on their way. You have no lord now, no marshal, and you need one. I have seen something of war. But only by your will would I wish to lead you. Say . . ."

He got no further. The crowd swayed like a cornfield scoured by a storm of hail, and the torrential roar of acclaim was deafening. It did not stop until Kermorvan gestured furiously for silence, and then only by degrees. "So be it, then. Let any who held high rank in your guard come to us now, and merchants, captains of the sea and other men accustomed to command. But do you remember! For this time only are you bound! When peace is restored we shall take counsel once again. Meanwhile I ask only that you receive also my companions, without whom I could not have come to you, or won free of the enemy's snares. Skilled they are in fighting, but stronger yet in the ways of peace. Of both our kindreds in the west they come, and of an older yet. Learn that we men do not stand alone against the Ice and its minions! An emissary

of the Elder folk fights beside us, the lady Ils!'' An astonished hush greeted her, a ripple of curious whispers, none
of the hostility of Kerbryhaine. "For the sothran folk
stands Roc, worthy citizen and soldier!'' It was a genial
roar that greeted him, for if Kermorvan's face looked down
from the statue, Roc's grinned back at him from the crowd,
many times over. "And for the northern kin, a smith of
surpassing craft and wisdom, by name Elof!''

But when Elof stepped forward in his smith's garb, the
cheering faltered among those closest to him. Then suddenly a woman on the steps below him pointed, and
screamed. Other arms shot up, words raced through the
excited crowd, then so deathly a hush fell that only the
calm sea's lapping at the wall below was heard. Alarmed,
astonished, Elof looked to his friends, only to see them
also staring, not at him, but at the second Watcher above
him.

Though to the same scale as its fellow, it seemed gigantic by comparison. An image it was of a towering man,
sturdy in body and limb, a shape of strength and grandeur
that seemed better clad in bronze and stone than flesh.
Not landward did it gaze, but out to the boundless sea,
whence came a breeze that set torch and brazier aflare.
And in the sudden light Elof also gasped, as the Watcher's
countenance became clear. Well formed in its grim way,
yet stern pride and anger seamed it, a marred and ferocious mask. It was the countenance he had glimpsed in
Morvan, that had haunted his mind ever since. But why
should that so affect the others? Ils moved to his side, and
took his arm tightly. "Do you not see? But you would not.
An old troll, whoever he was, large even among men, old
and bearded and cruel of countenance; all these things you
are not. But for the rest, the face . . .'' She shook her
head. "You are the stamp of it.''

Elof's voice stuck in his dry throat. For his looks he
cared little; it was the impact of that face that unnerved
him. All that he read in it seemed alien to him, and horribly disturbing. He wagged his head in protest, yet he
could almost feel the mold of his own features betray him.

He looked desperately to Kermorvan, and found only astonished confirmation. "But how is it possible?"

"Amazing!" murmured Kermorvan. "Small wonder that I resemble my forebears, being of a close-bred line. But you, ignorant even of your own parents, let alone ancestors? Yet it seems you have found one." He turned to Erouel. "Could it be an accident? Is that a true likeness of its original?"

"But do you not know?" demanded the astonished chamberlain. "It is said he went westward, and for all we know died there. But here he landed, and here he would ever look back across the ocean, as does the image, made by one who knew him. Do you not know the lastcomer from Kerys, the lord Vayde?"

"Vayde!" breathed Kermorvan. "Elof, that is Vayde! Vayde the Great, whose tower we scaled, on whose roof you forged your sword . . . Aye, we know him indeed!" He looked from the statue to Elof, and back, and grinned. "Yes, I could well believe that fiery blood runs somehow in your veins. Does that dismay you? It should not. No better friend had the kings than grim old Vayde!" He laughed aloud. "Keryn and Vayde!"

The gathering guardsmen, merchants and other leaders, hanging on his every word, took up the cry, and through the excited crowd it raced amain. "Keryn and Vayde! The Watchers are come down among us! Keryrn and Vayde are arisen! The Watchers come back to war!"

Kermorvan rounded on them. "Well then! Let us order our fight!"

Of the swift preparations for the Battle of Morvannec the Chronicles tell little, and scarce more of the first fighting itself. It is likely enough that the preparations were few and simple. Against warriors hardened and fanatical Kermorvan could oppose only an ill-armed citizenry, but one driven as hard by wrath at its sufferings, and now also by a wild exultation at what seemed the sudden resurgence in their midst of a mighty past. He could not deploy his people in subtle tactics, or rely on them to defend a strongpoint; he could only hope to hurl them against the foe in great waves, and bear them down by sheer weight of numbers. So he laid his plans, and so the outcome was determined.

It appears, though, that Elof was scarely aware of all this, and played little part in its shaping. A great misery and sickness had settled upon him, a reaction perhaps to the terrors of the past hours, the impact of too many shocks, the burden of harsh discoveries not easily borne. He sat slumped against the base of the stern statue that so resembled him, and the world grew bleak and hopeless. It seemed to him that Kara, for whom he had come so far and through so many hardships, was now eternally beyond his reach. As well might he seek to love the stars that wheeled above him! They appeared as she had, almost close enough to touch; yet how infinitely distant they truly were. And without her, what did anything else mean? His life had fallen inward suddenly, as logs heaped upon a fire burned out at the heart, leaving only a cloud of bitter embers. His long guilt, his sojourn in the saltmarshes, his long quest against the Mastersmith mattered nothing now, and still less all the hazards of the way east. The sport and toy of destiny he had been, a gaming piece in the strife of the Powers, lured on by false hopes and foolish dreams; lured on to do some good, perhaps, but little enough for himself. He looked up at the statue. What was it to him whose blood flowed in his veins? He had heard little of Vayde, still less that he liked. But he too could have looked out at the ocean thus; he listened to it, rising now as the wind freshened, and felt a deep wish to cast himself down into those infinite waters, and there at last, perhaps, find peace.

The tide of blackness arose again, and overwhelmed him. Chill and nausea crept upon him; he shivered ceaselessly till he could almost imagine his marsh fever was returning. Lack of food and sleep made all worse; a harrowing night was wearing toward its end. Ils or Roc might have cheered him, but they were already away, leading small bands of such experienced soldiers as could be found into the nearby streets, to give warning of any sudden assault by the Ekwesh. But it was typical of Kermorvan that he, the center of so much activity and excitement, should have found time to consider what ailed his friend. When the hard hand was clapped upon his shoulder Elof looked up with dull eyes, and met a look that blazed. "Take courage!" hissed Kermorvan. "Only take courage! Men have dared ere now to love the Powers, and great good has come of it. Did you not know? It is said my own line, the royal line of Kerys itself, sprang from such a union in the lost deeps of time, and so that great nation was born! And she, she also loves! Think only what she did for you, when bonds we cannot imagine were tearing her heart and spirit! For that alone you must fight on!"

Among the ashes choking body and mind Elof felt a trace of returning warmth; he nodded, jerkily. He could still fight. If he could do nothing else for her, there was always that. And against those who had so misused her he had a long score to settle. "Good!" said Kermorvan, sharply. "An ill thing when a cool heart like mine must rekindle the fire of a smith! Come, there is a morsel or two of food; eat while you can, for there are stirrings in the upper streets! I wonder they have not already attacked."

"Could it be Kara?" breathed Elof.

"The girl! Of course! She has put the fear of Hella into them, appearing thus. And well she might! They fear to venture far beyond their stronghold. Time it is that we gave them cause!" He turned away, shouting orders, and Elof saw the crowded square begin to stir like a great whirlpool. The smell of cooking meat drew him, but he had barely time to gulp down some of the savory scraps toasted over a hastily built bonfire before Kermorvan reappeared, and with him Erouel. "Into your hands, old man, I commit crown and scepter. If I return not to claim them of you, do as you will with them; they will no longer mean anything. But better the sea should have them, to my mind, than the Ekwesh. Now, Elof, are you ready?

Your place is beside me, if you will, for it is our column must strike the hardest.''

"I am ready," said Elof, and he plucked a brand from the fire. To Erovel's horror he drew his mailed hand down it, and at once it sank to charred blackness; even the smoke rolled leadenly groundward. But between Elof's clenched fingers a gleam awoke. "We may need light; would we had a dragon to give it! But this will serve."

Fanfare and drumbeat there was none as they filed out of the square, not even a warcry or a lighted torch; Kermorvan had ordered silence, and it suited the mood of his followers. Their first wrath had cooled, and they knew there was no going back. Many no doubt thought themselves as good as dead already, but fell rather than fearful it made them. Some still wore only the nightrobes they had rushed out in, but to Elof they seemed not comical but eerie, an army of shrouded forms gliding over the dark cobbles, Kermorvan and the dark-cloaked goblins at their head.

They were well into the city, climbing the broad street that rose in stepped terraces toward the palace, when the night ahead roared into sudden life, to shouting and the clink and hammer of weapons, the hum and spit of bows, the rattle of running feet upon the cobbles. Against a burning building up the hill silhouettes appeared in furious combat, and the column made as if to surge forward. Furiously Kermorvan ordered them back. "A feint!" he hissed. "That is their advance guard meeting ours. If only . . . aye, here come the first of them!"

Sure enough, Ils and her party came flying down through the back streets, with Roc's not far behind. "As you ordered!" she gasped, when she had regained her breath. "We broke and ran in disorder, as they thought it. Will it tempt out their main force?"

"It has!" panted Roc, arriving with his force. "Soon as they saw us scatter and thought they'd only mobs to deal with, out they swarmed like bees from a byke! They're less scared than you thought!"

"Or harder driven!" said Kermorvan, and raised his

voice. "Now, as we ordered! Into the side streets with you, and remember—await the word!"

The great column split and swiftly melted aside. Kermorvan lingered to urge the last of them into cover, and barely had time to draw Elof aside before the vanguard of the enemy burst over the edge of the terrace above and poured down the slope. In a taut spearhead they ran, light-armed runners with spears and small targes, their hard faces set in fierce grinning masks; a few mounted men cantered at their flanks and in files behind them, some with bows as well as lances. Then behind them the main ranks came down in wave after wave like flood over waterfall, spearhaft and swordhilt rasping a sinister song against the painted shields held as a wall before them. So swiftly ran the vanguard that they were already past the first side streets before they noticed the throng in the shadows. Before they could halt, Kermorvan barked a single order. A gust of arrows wafted up and rattled down among the vanguard, and scarce slower surged out the people of Morvannec. Up against the disordered vanguard they thundered, and past it, leaving it to those who were coming up from below. Up the street they charged, Kermorvan at their head, and as flood meets flood in boiling turmoil, they came up against the main force of the Ekwesh.

To Elof it was a time of thunder and madness, as if he had been caught between his own hammer and anvil, and bitterly he hated it. He fought often at need, but never before had he been caught up in the whirling fury of a battle, where survival lay in hewing men before him as brush in a forest, stumbling over limbs that still twitched, slipping in blood still flowing or fresh-spilled entrails. He saw men and women hurled down at his side, yet he himself was untouched by the weapons that raked at him, always that shade too slow. Gorthawer met them in the red-tinged night, and they bowed before the blade and the strength of his arm, and fell away broken upon the bodies of their wielders. He swiftly lost sight of his friends; Ils reappeared briefly, toppling a tall warrior by main force and sinking her broad axe into his breastbone, and now and again he caught brief glimpses of Kermorvan, always ahead of him, his warcry on his lips and his gray-gold blade sweeping in intricate patterns among the hedge of spears and shields. At length Elof dared to hope the intensity of the fighting might be slackening, only to find it redouble suddenly as a new wave of foes swept forward over the corpses of the first. And with it, in armor as bright as Kermorvan's was black and marked with the emblem of the broken chain, the tall shape of Bryhon Bryheren came plunging through the fray. The sword he swung was long and heavy, a huge two-handed thing with a scalloped edge to the upper blade, but he wielded it with the same liquid grace as Kermorvan his, and cut a deep swathe of bloody panic among the city folk. Then into his path Kermorvan sprang, and in a ringing flurry of blows they met, flowing around each other with the deadly grace of a dance. Never before had Elof seen a warrior to match Kermorvan, but for the first time he realized that Bryhon's confidence was no mere bluster, that he was indeed of the same order and schooling. And he was fresh, and bore a visored helm where Kermorvan was bareheaded. If Bryhon's gangling frame moved with less fluid ease, there was a vicious power in the sweeping strokes he favored, which could suddenly switch direction without slackening. Such a stroke, aimed at Kermorvan's body, leaped aside in the very instant he parried it and slashed down upon his unprotected head. But Kermorvan sprang aside and ducked in the same swift movement, the point grazed his face, glanced off his shoulderplate and struck the cobbles. With a suddenness that startled even Elof, Kermorvan's steel-shod boot crashed down on the blade and tore the hilt from Bryhon's grasp. Bryhon sprang back, tugging something from his shoulder, a broad-bladed battleaxe half his own height. But the fighting swirled into the gap, and Elof, battering frantically at a new shieldwall, saw the adversaries borne apart on its tides.

Then, as suddenly as it had come, the shieldwall fell back, fragmented, melted away before his eyes, and he found himself striking giddily at empty air. He lowered his sword and strained for breath, deafened by the roaring in his ears. His head ached terribly, though he could find no wound; the blood spattered on his mailed arm was not his own. He looked around, and was startled. Though he had not been conscious of moving, the battle had borne him ever higher up the hill, till now he stood in the square below the palace whence so recently they had fled. He looked back, and winced; the street behind was a very carpet of bodies, some moving feebly, some still. It was hardly possible to tell which were Ekwesh, which not, for the same wash of blood boltered them all as they lay. Steam and stench tainted the night air.

"So!" said Kermorvan's voice beside him. "We are not yet parted, then, we four!" He stood there, calm as ever despite his tangled hair and the broad slash that skipped from forehead to cheek. Roc was with him, and Ils not far off, helping to tend a woman who lay wounded and shrieking. Indeed, the air was filled with groans and cries, and the sound of them raised the hair at Elof's neck.

"Have we won?" he asked, and cursed the stupidity of the words. But it seemed that Kermorvan understood.

"Not yet!" he croaked. "We beat them back to the palace, but at terrible cost. Then out sallied a rearguard under that creature Bryhon, and covered their retreat within. Some five or seven hundred we slew out of their two thousand-odd, but the rearguard was easily that large, and more would remain. I guess they still dispose of well-nigh two and a half thousand men, fighting men at that. And our losses . . ." He closed his eyes a moment, then gestured at the ragged force he had led, standing shocked and bewildered among the carnage or searching desperately among the maimed and dead. "Arm yourselves from the Ekwesh!" he shouted. "Spear and shield and armor, if you can! And form up then, for soon we attack again!" He ground his teeth, and added, almost under his breath, "We must. We have no choice. So many Ekwesh crowded into the palace, they will know they cannot withstand a siege. Any moment now they will sally out—and what then? Will the people endure another such slaughter?"

Other columns that had seen little fighting were swaggering into the square, only to halt in horror at the butchery. "Look near ready to drift away now, some of 'em," muttered Roc, "whatever the cost."

Kermorvan frowned. "This is hard for tried soldiers to endure, let alone peaceful citizens. I had hoped their anger would give them an edge in strength, but there is something else, some inner will that spurs on the Ekwesh no whit less hard, nearly to madness . . ." The same idea came at once to all three.

"If she could raise the city so swiftly—"

"She could be turned against us—"

"But where is she? She could be deep within the palace . . ."

"No," muttered Elof. "She would need to see . . ." Between finger and thumb of his gauntlet a thin white flame arose, and its light danced along the darkened windows of the palace. A murmur of wonder arose from the folk behind, and they pressed closer to see, only to fall back as Ekwesh archers tried for the mark. But Elof ignored the arrows skipping around him; he could see none but Ekwesh at the windows. He swept the light swiftly along the galleried roof.

"There!" cried Ils.

"There's nothing but statues . . ."

"See there! In the middle! There's one too many . . ."

When Elof looked again he saw it. Impassive, unmoving behind helm and shield, she might indeed have been a statue like the rest, save that one corner of her long cloak fluttered in the restless breeze. Elof looked around desperately. "I must get to the roof! Those windows there, do they not light a stair? It must begin somewhere near the main doors. If I could only get through the lowest window . . ."

Kermorvan raised his eyebrows. "Then we could turn our assault on the main doors. But be swift, if you would save lives! And weigh them well against . . . other claims."

Elof nodded, for words he could not find, and Kermorvan turned to bark out orders. A great beam was lifted from one of the ruined houses and borne forward, still smoldering, in the arms of the strongest, Roc and Ils and Elof among them; along it and over them were raised Ekwesh shields to guard against arrows. Kermorvan cast an eye over his motley force, gave a curt nod of encouragement and waved them forward with his sword. Over the cobbles trotted the bearers of the beam, gathering speed, and up the worn steps without a single slip. As they reached the top, arrows rattled and thudded into the shields, and the bearers began to run, gathering speed. One man fell, the others skipped over him and hurtled on toward the high bronzed doors, the tarnished figures on them shining strangely in the faint starlight. Then they were under the galleries, and in the last moment ere they struck Elof hurled himself aside. From behind him he heard a mighty creak and clangor of bronze, and another as the rebounding ram was swung back and dashed against the doors once more, and a loud wolfish cheer. Then with a rumbling crash the doors swung apart, tore free of their hinges and toppled; the rammers sprang aside, but Elof, turning to the window, was caught. One buckled bronze mass loomed over him and crashed down. It was instinct that raised his gauntlet to it; it stopped short in a rush of escaping flame, poised on his palm, all the force of that heavy fall drawn into his gauntlet and captured. It was still dead weight, but without the impetus he could thrust it aside, and dodge. It crashed down among the rising roar of battle renewed. He dared not look back; he swung himself up to the carven sill and punched his mailed fist through the tiny lenticular leads. The high window creaked open; he flung himself through the gap, and down into the hallway beyond.

Coming in from that reddened night it was dazzling, a place of white walls and mirrors and lamps and candles burning behind bright crystal; even the empty floor was a mirror of black marble. But striding onto it from a dark archway was a tall figure in sweeping robes of white, and at the sight of her, great wrath and chilling fright warred within him.

"Louhi!" he cried out. *"Stay!"* She was turning toward the great staircase that ringed the hall, and she was arranging something that glittered about her head. At the sound of his voice she turned, and he saw her clearly, as fair as ever he had thought her, blue eyes wide with astonishment. Then they blazed furiously; she took a step toward him, hesitated, then whirled and ran up the stair. She was swift, past the first flight before he was anywhere near the foot; he could guess whither she hastened, and she would be there long before him. "Stay, lady!" he shouted again, and in desperation he drew the hammer from his belt and slapped it down between his clenched fingers. It felt then as if he held an earthquake in his palm. He swung his arm in a great wheel and threw. With all the strength of his body behind it, and all the pent-up impact of the falling door, the hammer hurtled high into the air, a blur of movement, and, with a crash like the lightning it had forged, it smote into the side of the stair only a few steps beyond Louhi's hastening feet.

The stonework cracked across, sagged, and cracked sharply once again; dust puffed outward, and a great chunk of the stair tore free from the wall and went crashing down in ruin upon the gleaming marble below. On the very brink of the gap Louhi tottered, her dress and robe billowing around her; the glittering thing flew from her head and tumbled jingling down the stairs, coming to rest on a step near Elof as he came running up. He knew it at once, a thing of hooped bronze and ringmail, ornate in copper and gold; he had already guessed, or perhaps his own work called to him. For it was the Tarnhelm.

He raised his eyes to Louhi, pacing down the steps toward him with the measured intensity of a great cat poised to spring, and lunged for the helm at the moment she did. Their hands struck it but did not grasp, it jingled down a few steps and their faces all but collided; for a moment they were as close as lovers, he felt the warmth of her satin skin, he tasted her breath on his lips and found it fragrant as spring. Then she recoiled, eyes blazing, and put a hand to her thigh as if hurt. "My fair young smith! Such a fool I never thought you! Do you not by now know who I am? Would you, fragile as fine works are, go up against a Power?"

The shriek and clamor of battle echoed through the hall, and Elof felt his grin go horribly lopsided. "You are not the first, lady," he croaked, and drew Gorthawer, and leveled it menacingly at her breast.

Louhi stared incredulously at the black blade, and then at his face. "So!" she said. The hand at her thigh suddenly clasped a hilt; from among the folds of her dress a bright broadsword sprang and struck down at his head. So swift was the blow that the black blade barely turned it in time, so hard that he staggered. Then she was at him in a flurry of cuts and slashes, as thick and fast as the first falls of a cloudburst, and the vicious strength behind them startled him. Yet though it seemed too great for those slender arms, it was only human strength, and the skill behind it no greater than his own. The first hail of blows he countered, and then himself sought the attack. But he felt something amiss with his sword arm, and at every blow he struck it worsened, as if the ringing impact numbed his muscles. He cut hard at her, and his point slashed the billowing fabric of her robe; she hurled herself forward, their blades met and locked before their distorted faces, their panting breath clouded their blades. And before Elof's appalled eyes it froze on both surfaces to a skin of rime.

Now he knew what that numbness was! With a shudder he sprang back, feeling his arm bones ache with the spreading cold, and Louhi hewed at him with both hands. But now, instead of Gorthawer, he caught the blow on the palm of his gauntlet, and closed the fingers round the bright blade. To his horror, where blade met mail a faint greenish flame sprang up, sputtering and crackling, such as he had seen upon the Ice, and he yelled in agony as his own mail sucked the heat from his skin. "You would gather up my strength in your clever little toy, would you?" breathed Louhi, and her breath smoked like the first airs of winter. "Well, young apprentice, Master Mylio taught you ill, who forged my blade to my design. Or do you not remember that cold cannot be so contained? It is no force, child, but the absence of force, the negation of it in all things, that brings to all stirrings stillness. And peace."

Then a fearful seam of chill shot down his left arm, and stabbed like a skewer at his heart. It leaped, convulsed, skipped beat after beat; the breath wheezed out of him, his legs sagged and he shuddered. He could stand no longer; but he could choose his fall. With all his weight he slumped upon the blade. Unprepared, Louhi staggered, the edge was turned away from him, and he tore free his fingers.

The bright blade leaped out of Louhi's grasp. High it sprang, glittering in the brightness, and over the gap in the stair. A loud clatter sounded from the floor far below. Louhi recoiled with a gasp of pain, clutching at her hand; Elof sagged weakly against the balustrade. Then, recovering, she sought to push past him and seize the helm from the step. But she recoiled abruptly as Gorthawer's edge hissed a finger's breadth from her throat. "The cold, no," grated Elof. "But you struck too hard, Louhi. *That* force it could capture, indeed." He clambered to his feet, Gorthawer leveled again at her breast, and caught up the Tarnhelm. "And now, woman, in this body of yours you can be hurt. So either you will release K—"

He got no further. With a horrible shriek she sprang upon him, striking and clawing even with her broken fingers. But by the sheer force of her spring she ran Gorthawer through her left shoulder.

Louhi's lips parted in a soundless gasp. She wrenched violently free of the blade; a single spurt of blood drenched her robe, and stopped. Fury shrieked out of her, an endless wailing cry of wrath and frustration that rang with deafening force in Elof's ears, that shook the very walls, that overrode the battle's clamor and brought the fighting for a moment to a frozen halt. Elof let fall Gorthawer and clapped hands to ears as mirrors and crystals all cracked and shattered and rained down in glistening shards. Louder, stronger swelled the cry, like a rushing wind in the hall, like a blast of bitterest winter that whipped the air full of flying splinters. Asunder flew lead and bar upon the windows, they blasted outward in an explosion of wood and glass and through them streamed the wailing wind. Elof, shielding his eyes, saw Louhi's ripped and blood-stained robe billow violently about her and suddenly float free, rippling and gliding out into emptiness like some eerie creature of the seas, wafting slowly downward. Out of the hall shrieked the sudden wind, and all across the northward rim of the city bells jangled as it passed, tower tops were toppled and rooftops torn; the wreckage below sparkled suddenly beneath a crust of white rime, and so also the empty stair.

Elof, rising, forced down all thoughts save one. In shattering the stair he had barred that way to the roof; he could find another, or . . . He retrieved Gorthawer and with clumsy fingers set the Tarnhelm upon his head, feeling the metal of the mask icy on his skin, as if from Louhi's touch. He pulled the mail closed across his face, and thought hard, thought of the palace roof, of the gallery round its rim and the rows of statues. *There! Among them!* He felt something stir; the few lights left seemed to grow dimmer, the shadows stronger, the sounds of conflict more remote. Yet he was still upon the stair. He cursed; he had made this thing, all save the mask. Could he not now control it? It bore his very name, in both its meanings, in the couplet he had set upon it.

> *Eynhere elof hallns styrmer*
> *Stallans imars olnere elof . . .*

Aloud he murmured the words, while in his mind he summoned up in the same archaic tongue the words for shadow and roof, to add to the cantrip a final line.

> *Istans nethel, erand alt!*

"Darkness and shadow, to the height! It is Elof calls you!" Blackness slid so suddenly across the eyeslits of the helm that he stumbled, fearing himself blinded. His hand found a balustrade of cool stone; a brisk seabreeze rippled the fine-knit rings of mail. As well he had left Louhi no time to use the helm! For he stood upon a walkway of worn stones sloped for drainage, in the shadow of a tall statue. In the blink of an eye he had been carried to the roof, and not four strides from him, spear held high as if to strike, stood the figure of Kara.

CHAPTER ELEVEN

The Mold is Broken

But now the spearpoint was not turned against him. Over the balustrade it pointed, down into the square below, where the bloody surf of battle raged and roared against the palace wall. What he saw looked ill; the bulk of the fighting was outside the palace now, which meant the assault was being driven back. There indeed was Kermorvan, mustering a ragged line for another charge against the uneven shieldwall commanded by a tall man in bright armor, but all around the heart of the battle smaller struggles raged, little knots of fighters swirling this way and that in a mad crush. Forward surged the line; the shieldwall broke at its center, where Kermorvan led the charge, but Bryhon was there at once, the great axe flashing as it cut a terrible swathe through Kermorvan's men. The edges of the shieldwall had held, and now they curved round across the square to trap the front lines of city folk; Kermorvan was falling back hastily, attempting to regroup once more.

It could not last; even Elof, unversed in war, saw that. In the end the iron discipline of the Ekwesh would be the deciding factor, and that flowed from the fanatical strength of will Kara was pouring into them, as he might into some work of his forge to give it unity and strength. With every moment that passed the appalling slaughter grew worse. Elof knew he had no choice. He looked at the slender shape, dim against the last of the dark, swallowed and reached for his hammer. But that lay somewhere under the rubble of the stairway below. So much the worse . . . He raised Gorthawer and sprang forward.

She became aware of him even as he leaped, and swung round with unhuman speed. He had aimed for the spear; the shield was suddenly there to take the blow, and he half expected it to be immovable as a mountain, the black blade to shatter against it like obsidian. But it was the shield that broke; it split, slid down and went clattering over the balustrade. Off balance, as startled as he was, Kara half-stumbled from the rail and down upon the walkway, and Elof flung himself against her. The arm that held the spear stiffened to strike, and, dropping Gorthawer, he seized that wrist in both hands and forced it down against the edge of the roof.

"Kara!" he gasped. "It's me! Elof! Stop this, Kara, stop the slaughter now!" The spear wedged against the balustrade and would move no further; the strain on the hand grasping it must be terrible now. The mailed figure threshed against him, and it took all his strength to hold her. "Louhi compels you no more! I've driven her off! She's wounded and fled! If you ever truly . . . Kara, *please* . . ."

The fingers slipped from the spear. He seized it, was about to toss it aside when her legs doubled up under him, caught him in the stomach and catapulted him back against the sloping roof behind. The spear flew from his hand and rattled off down the leads. Kara sprang to her feet. She could dash past him and reach it—

But she limped, hobbling against the silver fetters on her ankles, and the spear rolled out into emptiness. With a shrilling cry she seemed to fall forward, her cloak spreading out along her arms. Then they were slender arms no longer, but wide black wings, and a huge swan with gloss-black plumage sprang from the roof and swooped after the spear. What then? Who would she serve, when she caught it? Elof clapped both hands to the helm. He was terrified, but there was nothing else he could do. *Let him think of a shape, and it masks his own* . . .

The wings he thought of were black also, and wider yet. The shudder that ran through him was fiery, climactic to the point of pain; again night descended upon his eyes, and when they cleared he was sweeping down the wind. Like the times he had ridden fast it felt, with his cloak streaming out around him, but here the cloak was part of him, and his steed the rushing airs of dawn. How often he had seen the great condors wheel about the upper airs, and madly envied them their serenity and freedom! Now it was his, and he gloried in it, forgetting for a moment all human concerns. But then below him, out over the harbor, he saw a black swan wheel with a shining spear clutched tight in its claws. With a cry of sheer joy he kicked his clawed feet forward, curved his wing closer to his side and swooped down upon her.

She was not expecting him, that was clear, she saw nothing till his shadow enveloped her. His cruel talons raked the spearshaft and dashed it from her, seized her by the wingroot and bore her downward. Struggling, they fell as one, and below them the bright spearpoint twisted and dwindled till a pale splash sprang up from the dark harbor waters. The wing in his claws gave a convulsive leap, and suddenly it was no longer there; something sleek and narrow shot from his grasp, and slid into the water after it. So startled was he that he had no time to brake his dive, the water rushed up to meet him, gray as stone and little less hard. In one last instant of panic an image leaped into his mind, and he felt no impact as that surge of fire again passed over him.

The green gloom opened before his eyes, and he saw the gleaming flanks of the shape that dived down, down away from him. But his body was long and lithe now, ribbon-lithe, and he sped after it, the bubbles of his breath streaming past his nose. This shape was more natural to him, more of a size with his own, and it brought back memories of sitting on rocks above the bay of his home village, watching the long sleek sea otters sporting and feeding in the shallow swell. As they had sought shells, so his eyes sought the spear, a point of brightness in the miry bottom. But over it shot a shape larger than the one that had tumbled from his grasp, caught it up and surged away from him at a speed even he could not match. Like a spear itself it seemed, or the broad head of a crossbow bolt. And yet he had no doubt it was her; its flanks still gleamed like the mail she had worn, with air bubbles trapped in the fur. Strange, how appearances were preserved; was there something about him, clad in long body and blunt head, that she also could know? But he had to stop her; she was heading for the surface too fast. He thought back to his childhood once again, and to the high leaping shapes painted in black and white upon the walls of the Headman's house . . .

This time there was scant pleasure, great pain. This was the hardest of all. His muscles clenched in cramps, his back arched, and suddenly he felt himself break surface, streaming water, and the breath blast out of him and roar inward with explosive force in the instant before he surged under once more. His eye was dimmed, but the rising gleam caught it clearly; he kicked out with his powerful tail, feeling the water fountain behind him and eddy around the high thin fin on his back, and saw the seal break surface just ahead of him. It saw him also, twisted in terror and kicked out with a tailfin around which silver gleamed, turning for the shallows. But it could no more avoid him in this predatory form than a man outrun a landslide. He kicked out again, heaving his sleek bulk upward, and like a toppling hill indeed he slid down upon his quarry. He felt the gape of his great-toothed jaws close neatly round the spearshaft and pluck it free, felt it bend and distort in their inexorable grasp, and at last splinter and snap like a green stick. He spat it out, and saw the ruined thing sink down into the deeper waters of the harbor channel. A shadow passed over his eyes, wide wings of blackness, and with a mighty thrust he rose from the water as if to pluck her down. But the swan wheeled away from him in the air, and he toppled clumsily back. This time he was scarcely aware of thought; again the fire passed over him, and suddenly, he was beating up from the water's surface on black swan's pinions of his own, gliding toward her in the air. Would she understand? Would she believe? *By different roads we reach the same end; what is in your nature I have made mine by my craft. We are alike, you and I . . .*

Out to sea she might have flown, northward perhaps, or even eastward, out into the trackless ocean. But he turned her away from there, the wind chill on damp plumage, and back, back down toward the palace once again, down to the roof whence they had come. She might have struggled longer; did she come now of her own will, or did she seek to trick him again? In among the statues they flew, he close behind her, right to the spot whence they had come. It was a close landing, confusion and a clumsy impact, and a flare of fever played over him. But by then he was already himself, dazed and winded, sprawled there upon the roof a few paces from Kara. Gorthawer lay at his fingertips, as if he had simply fallen there in springing after her and no weird change had ever come upon him. But he could feel the sting of salt drying upon his cheek, and the light of dawn was now stealing swiftly up the sky.

The roar of battle burst up from below, and in dire dread he hauled himself up against the rail, clinging to some ancient's sculpted robe. But when he saw what passed below him, though the square was a place of carnage, his heart filled with a flaming joy. For even as he watched a sweeping assault of city folk burst against the shieldwall of the Ekwesh, with a cry like the angry sea, and now like the sea they washed over it. The painted shields toppled before them, and were borne down. In scant moments the black-clad ranks dissolved, hewn and beaten down by the sheer force of a wrathful folk whose fettered hearts had at last been set free, whose foes had lost the force that underpinned their belief. Men they were still, brave men, but they knew themselves deserted by all that they had served. From iron order they became a milling, desperate mass fighting only to escape from the square, and so being scoured from it piecemeal. Only around Bryhon Bryheren, last symbol of that service left them, did they gather and rally, and stave off the doom that closed around. His armor shone cold in the first gray light, bright as a fragment of the very Ice itself, and the fall of his axe clove those foolhardy enough to challenge him as the Ice the land it passed over. But into the very center of those diehard Ekwesh struck a charge of their foes as arrow into target, and at that arrow's tip were three before whom no Ekwesh stood. The knot broke, and this way and that they fled, crazed with despair, and cast themselves over the steep sides of the square, or stood at bay with screams of meaningless defiance and were struck down with ease by the citizens. And in an open space upon the steps, Kermorvan and Bryhon came face to face at last, and Bryhon had his true wish.

Though both were weary, like men fresh and young they fought, the great axe whistling in the air as it chopped and cut at Kermorvan, seeking ever to force him to a false footing upon the worn stair. But his sword was light in his hand, and as Bryhon's strokes passed, it bit and stabbed at him so fast he was forced to parry with the long axehaft. Showers of sparks flew up, for it was bound all in rings of steel, but Elof knew well the strength of the gray-gold sword and the arm behind it, and guessed what must soon happen. So evidently did Bryhon, for as Kermorvan thrust hard at him he changed the way of his stroke with amazing swiftness, and let its own impetus whirl him round. Abruptly he was no longer in the path of the thrust; Kermorvan lost his balance, stumbled to his knee on a lower step, and Bryhon whirled right about and hewed down with fearsome speed at the back of his unprotected neck. Kermorvan could not throw himself out of the path of that terrible blow; he threw himself under it instead, straight against Bryhon's feet. The axe hissed past Kermorvan, and at the same moment his legs kicked straight, carrying him to his feet. The axe crashed into the stone and shattered in flying splinters; Bryhon toppled over Kermorvan's rising shoulders and crashed down beside it in a jangle of metal. The gray sword flashed skyward, and with the first rays of the risen sun it fell upon that bright armor. And deep as the sun into clear ice, it struck it through. Metal clashed and screamed; Bryhon convulsed, his limbs jerked at that impaling stroke, and the chain was broken indeed. Kermorvan plucked free his sword, and Bryhon in agony rolled over onto his back. In the silence that had fallen, Elof heard him mouthing, snarling, but could make out no words, if words there were. He folded suddenly, clutched at himself, then his hand came free with a broad dagger and he rose on his knees and lunged at Kermorvan's midriff. Kermorvan's sword crashed down once again, and passed point down between Bryhon's armored collar and his neck. He fell back, head downward upon the steps, shuddering. A great rush of scarlet stained the tangled beard, spread out in a wide pool upon the steps, and he was still. A deafening cheer arose from the square around, and the crowd rushed forward. Slowly, shakily, Kermorvan sat down upon the steps and put his head in his hands.

Elof turned slowly away, at once glad and sickened, and in a sudden flood of horror realized he had forgotten Kara. He looked up, and was startled to see her only a pace or two from him, her brown eyes wide beneath her salt-straggled hair. What had she lingered to watch—the battle, or him? Clumsily he put out a hand to her, and like a wild creature she started back. "Kara!" he croaked, and she sprang back another pace. He stepped forward and tripped over Gorthawer; the helm slipped over his eyes, and he heard her halting footsteps stumble back further. He wrenched off the helm and stuffed it in his tunic, picked up the sword and sheathed it. But still Kara backed away, her full lips trembling, and suddenly, coming to a low doorway, she whirled and sprang down it. In panic Elof dashed after her; if once she got out of his sight she could assume any shape, and how would he ever find her then?

The door led down a short stair into an upper corridor of the palace, richly appointed but with an air of neglect in recent years; the rich hangings on the walls had a faint smell of mildew about them. Kara was hobbling along ahead of him, staggering along the walls in desperate flight; the sight plucked at his heart. Why had she changed so from the brief moments they had shared before, when she had seemed to return his love? Now she seemed to fear him, the last thing he would have. His heart felt empty as these unhappy halls, and he cried out her name as she fled, as he saw her turn a corner and vanish through a wide doorway. Round its heavy pillar he whirled, and found himself in a wide and airy room, a bedchamber with an open balcony beyond. A tall brazier still burned there, that had warded off the night's chill. Beyond it, on that balcony with her back to the balustrade, bedraggled in her mail, stood Kara, gazing at him with the same fierce feral look.

"Don't go, Kara! Don't flee! Did I not do as you bade me? I followed the dawn, Kara. And dawn is here."

"And I did as I promised," she said quietly. "Though many a time I had to break away in pain to do it, and endure punishment after. Did you not see my wings?"

"Often," he said. "And grateful I am, and grieved at your pain. But could you not have come closer? That fleeting vision brought me as much foreboding and fear as comfort."

"Fear and foreboding is the lot of mortals who mingle with Powers," she said. "That I would spare you."

"Why? Because you love me?"

"Because I too have been caged so long!" She was shivering now. "I would have no more bonds, nor wish them upon others . . ."

"If I have learned one thing in all this long year's journeying, Kara, it is that we all must bear the bonds of our own selves. In that men and the Powers are alike."

"Come no closer!" she gasped. "You know me for a Warrior of the Powers, and you would dare match yourself against me? You would still dare speak of loving me?"

A breathless laugh bubbled in Elof's breast. "I would! I have loved you since first I looked upon you. And if you are of no common sort, nor, it seems, am I! For you would not be the first of your kind I have matched myself against. Have I not broken the will of one great Power, in the heart of his domain? And gone up against another in body, and bested her also? And by the craft that burns within me have I not won for myself arts scarce short of your own, strength that outmatched you at the test? Though I saw well that you never sought in any shape to harm me, Kara. You love me, as I you. And none of these deeds I dare boast of, not even the blood of Vayde that may run in my veins, nothing would make me worthy of you if that simple truth did not! I am told that men have loved the Powers before, Kara; but those Powers must also have loved men.'' He stepped closer, came up to her upon that bright balcony, and she stiffened, her body tautened, but she made no move to flee. The silver chain clinked at her ankles, and he stared at it with hatred. ''I have no forge nor hammer to hand! But let us see—'' And he caught up his gauntlet, and thrust his mailed hand into the brazier. The dancing flames sank, the coals crackled and dimmed, the glowing metal blackened and dewed the cold. ''He who made this bond I cast down! She who willed it has fled me! Shall mere metal stand against my will? I have seen the sun's warmth melt the Ice itself!'' He clamped his gauntlet hard about the fetters. For an instant they seemed to drink in the intensity of heat, and then suddenly they shattered. Kara's legs quivered, and he caught her as he rose. He stripped off the gauntlet, and reached out with hands that trembled to clasp the cold mail at her shoulders.

''Would you destroy me?'' she whispered desperately. ''Would you shatter my fair reflection upon the dark stream?''

He shook his head gently. ''I would only drink of its waters, Kara, and slake a thirst ere it consumes me. I am wreathed about in fires! But if I were to drown in it, I could ask no more.'' He bent his head and kissed her, and smiled inwardly as he tasted salt upon her lips. Then he did indeed start, as at a sudden burning, and he clutched her close, slid his hands from shoulder down across the smooth mail of her back, felt her firm breasts flatten against him, and leap as she gasped.

''Here also there is flame!'' she breathed, her eyes

wider, wilder than ever, an abyss of darkness beneath him.
"With all the force of my being I could crush you in my
arms, drink of you, burn you, consume you! Elof, would
you? Dare you? Do you not fear the madness that comes
upon me?"

He threw back his head and laughed. "Ah! Since when
did a smith fear a flame?"

Then suddenly his laughter turned to a cry of shock.
For the mail he caressed caved inward, and fell away to
emptiness in his grasp. Dazed, he let it fall and jingle
upon the polished stone, and stepped back from it, bewildered. Of her feather cloak there was no sign. The sky
above was empty, the room . . . There was the cloak,
draped flat like counterpane across the bed. With a tingle
of anticipation he threw it back. But beneath it there was
nothing save a sheet of creamy silk. For a moment he
stared at it, and then he saw the gleam that flowed within
it, as through true smithcraft, and he laughed again, and
shed his own soiled tunic and hose, and lay down upon
it. Under his hands it squirmed and surged, and was Kara
again, her own laughter warm in his ear.

"You wrong yourself in silk," he told her. "You are
smoother far to the touch . . ." She gasped deeply then,
and he kissed her from throat to pulsing breast, and pulled
her to him.

"But if it were purest folly," he whispered, as his hands
flowed over her, "if I were unworthy of you; if it meant
death for me, and everlasting doom, still I would venture
it, and go rejoicing down into the dark!"

"Rejoicing!" she whispered, guiding his fingertips,
matching touch for touch. "Rejoicing, into the dark!"
Then she closed his lips with her own, and came to him.

It was full day when they went together down through
the stairs and corridors of the palace, and out of the broken doors. The dead had been moved from the square and
the streets below, although the stones were still dark with
blood. Thus darkened, as later chroniclers have related,
they were ever to remain; for so deep into the stone had

the stain sunk that a century of rains could scarely lessen
it, and as Plen Curau, the Square of Shed Blood, it was
evermore known. "But it is a blazon of honor!" said Kermorvan. "For though a thousand and more have fallen
today, yet by that sacrifice they have saved many thousands
more. And of the Ekwesh not one alive remains, and their
masters are dead or vanished." It was a great crowd he
addressed, for almost the whole folk of the city had come
swarming now into the square, and it was the sound of his
voice that had summoned Elof down. Roc and Ils were
beside him, and Erouel the chamberlain, and they would
have run in joy to greet Elof, save that they saw Kara on
his arm, and halted in astonishment. But Kermorvan
smiled, and such a look of relief settled on his hard and
wounded features as was seldom seen there. Calmly he
nodded to Elof, as one who sees his confidence confirmed,
and turned back to the crowd. "A new day dawns for
Morvannec! And you must take counsel, that it be a day
of growth and healing . . ."

"We need no counsel!" called a voice out of the far
ranks of the crowd, a deep voice that Elof seemed almost
to know. "Lord of the West, you have proven your right,
and taken already what is yours! *You are the rightful lord!*"
And the crowd echoed him in a joyous chant that seemed
to spread all across the city, till it rang in the very peal of
the bells.

"*A king!*"
"*The lord Kermorvan from the west, he is our king!*"
"*King Keryn, he lives!*"
"*We have a lord once again, a rightful king!*"
"*Keryn the King, hail! All hail!*"

But although the words had been in all their hearts,
nobody remembered which man it was spoke first, and
none there present would ever admit to it. So it is set
down; but the chronicler adds that Elof had his suspicions.

But Kermorvan's face remained stern and unyielding
under the dried blood that had flowed down one side of
his long nose and matted the stubble on his jaw. "A proper
prize, stood it in the gift of the Powers of Life themselves!

Yet surely you offer it too lightly; little do you know of me, as yet. Therefore learn now my will! Last lord of the line of Morvan am I; and that I shall remain. Let its name lie quiet with its ruins, and so also the division and strife that marred its end! Of a realm so torn, I could never be king.''

The crowd murmured, and gazed at one another in dismay. Kermorvan smiled faintly. ''But, if you so wish, I might be the first lord of the line of Morvanhal, Morvan Arisen! For so I would see this city now named, and the country and realm in which it stands. And I would have us work together with all folk of good will, of whatever race and kin, that it shall rise indeed, to be a lasting bastion against the evils of the Ice!''

The wash of sound rolled over him once more, and a tide of feeling that did not draw back. He paused a moment, and his face grew grim once more. ''Aye, you cheer, and that is well! But to cheer a fair hope is little effort! Will you also endure as gladly the pangs of bringing it to birth? For pangs there must be. From the west that is doomed through folly I shall summon those wise enough to come, and from kindreds of men that you can scarely guess at as yet. All these strangers you shall receive to dwell among you, greet them as gladly as if the kin you have lost this night and in the sorrows of the last years are returned. So shall the dwindling of your numbers be halted, so something of your loss be restored. And so ancient follies shall be buried, timeworn sundering healed!'' The crowd was silent now, yet the air quivered as it might in the first breathless advent of a storm. Kermorvan surveyed them calmly, his blue-gray eyes lofty and remote. ''Thus far my word is as steel. I shall brook no lessening of it. Here and now I will hear you swear to obey it always, in hard times as in good; and should you turn against that oath, even only once, city and land shall see me no more, and you may fend for yourselves thenceforth. To me you shall swear, and to these my companions, and Erouel the chamberlain; for they shall be my lords and counselors, and you shall hearken to their words as I do.

On these terms only shall I accept . . . this,'' he touched the crown gently, ''and all that goes with it. Well, do I have your oath?''

With many words, but one voice, the crowd roared, a thunder of affirmation that started the very gulls from the distant shore. Erouel, his white cloak blowing, stood contemplating the uproar with an air of kindly detachment. ''My lord,'' he said mildly, ''you were wounded in the face, I see. Better that you had taken care, and worn your helm.'' Before Kermorvan could move the old chamberlain had clapped the bright thing upon his head, the scepter in his palm, and now the crowd erupted.

''A fine coronation!'' laughed Kermorvan, when he could be heard again. ''To take a man unawares, indeed! For my ancestors' sake, we will have to have something more formal one day. But for now . . .'' Kermorvan nodded, and a great tension drained out of him. ''It is well. And for that, may the Powers of Life gaze with favor upon our city.'' He looked then at Elof and Kara, and smiled. ''For surely they move among us this day!''

He raised the scepter, and pointed. Over the harbor two great ravens flew up, circling in the eye of the risen sun. And as the free folk of Morvanhal watched them, they wheeled away far out across the gilded ocean, as if they would seek out its easternmost shores.

Coda

At the end of the Book of the Helm is set down only that many a long year of happiness lay ahead for him and his love, and for their friends. Yet the years may not be as neatly closed as a chronicle; for during this very time the snows were massing upon other summits far away, and sundering and suffering were to follow. But also to come, as the Book of the Armring recounts, were the deeds which won Elof Valantor final renown as the mightiest of all magesmiths amid the dark days of the ancient Winter of the World.

Appendix

Of the land of Brasayhal, its form, nature and climate, and of its peoples and their several histories, such as are set forth in that volume of the Winter Chronicles called the Book of the Helm.

The Book of the Helm, being the account of a single immense journey, is more easily rendered into a coherent tale than its predecessor the Book of the Sword: no less living a voice sounds from its pages. Yet as before there remain many instances where much of interest is omitted, and much included that, however fascinating, is irrelevant: for the tale's sake a balance must be found. A brief account of the most important aspects is therefore included here. Though it can do no more than sketch in some details and guess at others, it may at least drive back a little the shadows cast by time upon the great deeds of an age that is gone.

THE LAND

In the years of the Long Winter the extent of the land of Brasayhal was very great, a vast continent that stretched some thousand leagues from ocean to ocean across the northern world. The journey of Elof Valantor and his companions took them from the southwestern to the northeastern coasts, an even greater distance, and through a range of the diverse lands and climes it then held. For the most part, of course, it was Forest; yet within that Forest there were as many variations as in the lands about its boundaries.

THE LAND OF TAOUNE'LA

The first of these beyond the Meneth Scahas, the Shield-range which marked the border of the Westlands, was the sinister realm of Taoune'la. For the most part it seems to have consisted of three regions; the northernmost of these appears to have resembled today's Arctic desert, and was seen by the travelers only briefly, at the entrance of Morvan in the Withered Marches, and in a much narrower region at their eastern escape from the Ice. Below this opened up a region of *tundra*, bleak grassland underlaid with thick layers of frozen water known as "permafrost," whose expansion can often cause the hummocky deformations of the land mentioned. Between this and the Forest, and perhaps extending into it, was a region of *taiga*, a slightly warmer, often swampy country in which patches of woodland can often still grow; permafrost may still occur in *taiga* regions, but more sporadically. To judge by the state of the ground the travelers found in springtime, however, the climate was swiftly worsening, and the tundra gradually encroaching on the *taiga*, which would bear out Korentyn's gloomy prediction. The land they came into after their escape from the Ice was some leagues further south, and save for the immediate area around the Ice a much more usual form of southern *tundra* or *taiga* landscape; its sudden burgeoning in spring is characteristic. However, the land there may have been unusually rich; for desert, *tundra* and *taiga* were all relatively recent arrivals. Before the coming of the Ice all the east of Taoune'la had been the *mor guerower*, the "greengold sea," the infinite southern grainfields of Morvan.

THE OPEN LANDS

Beyond the western margins of Taoune'la the river Gorlafros flowed down from the Ice into the Open Lands. In the north these were a bleak and empty country of hill and moor, much the same on both banks: it was as if the chill of the meltwater that fed the river tainted and impoverished the soil, and it may be that there also the permafrost was spreading. But the worst of the taint, perhaps, was carried by outflows westward through the Shieldbreach into the Marshlands, and thence to the cleansing ocean. For south of the Breach the western bank of the Open Lands grew more fertile, until they gave way to the wooded country which the duergar claimed as their own. And on the eastern bank the true Forest flourished.

THE FOREST

Here, growing in temperate, hilly country, it was much like its lesser western arm, Aithennec; but eastward, as one approached the Meneth Aithen, the land grew somewhat lower, the climate warmer and moister, and the Forest ever taller and more dense as plant and tree struggled and competed toward the life-giving light, as they do in the *selva,* or tropical rain forest. However, the types of tree described clearly belong to cool temperate forests; it seems, therefore, that the ecology of the whole central Forest must have been of a kind almost extinct in the world today, the temperate rain forest. It may be significant that it was within this ceaseless ferment of growth, fed by a constant cycle of rain and mist, that Tapiau was at his strongest, and that it was an ill clime for civilized men. It was no accident that Lys Arvalen was sited on higher ground, the foothills of the Meneth Aithen.

These mountains were the only break in the rain forest, supporting a drier and sparser coniferous woodland that continued high up into the slopes of the range, yet their effect on rainfall patterns may have helped sustain it. Then as now, they must have been the tallest mountains in that land and a terrible obstacle to travelers, though one would not guess it from the brief account of the crossing the Chronicles supply, or from the extent to which the Forest is shown to dominate them. Evidently the Forest served the travelers as guide, for where it could grow unbroken the easiest passes must be, and spared them the dangers of the greater peaks. But their worries about food are no exaggeration; even for such hardened wanderers the crossing must have lasted many long days. Beyond the Meneth Aithen the land once again grew flatter, and in the central and southern regions the rain forest returned to dominance. In the far south the Forest is said to have become more like the complex tropical *selva*, but if the travelers ever went into that region it must have been in hunting parties from Lys Arvalen, for nothing is recorded. It is known that this jungle very soon thinned out into the Wastes; these began as arid scrubland, not unlike the utmost south of Bryhaine but without the rivers and coastal rains that kept that land fertile. And, as in Bryhaine, after no great distance the scrubland gradually dwindled to bare and searing desert, save where the great rivers of the east flowed to the sea. Such relatively swift progressions were undoubtedly a product of the glacial "compression" of climatic zones, described in volume one. The Wastes were no better places for men than the chill deserts of the north, although, like them, they were not without other inhabitants.

THE EASTERN LANDS

The Eastern Mountains were not as high as either the Meneth Scahas or the Meneth Aithen. But—contrary to what almost everyone seems to have assumed—they proved to be, if anything, a more effective natural barrier, not only to the physical spread of the Ice, but also to its equally lethal climatic effects. They ran at a sharp angle to the Ice, and somewhat further south; it had reached only their northernmost peaks, and would have required an immense effort to spread further into warm climes, without snowcaps to act as its vanguard. Most important of all, however, they were very broad; the fell winters windborne from the Ice, which had so diminished both the harvests and the spirits of the people of Morvan, could scarely cross them. More, they rose in a series of stepped ridges, which broke the impact of the ill winds, and made them spend their furies upon barren peaks instead of the rich land beyond. So it was that the Eastlands were shielded by land, and their coasts were well warmed by sea currents. But amid the shock of Morvan's fall, few if any realized this, or saw the Eastlands as a potential successor to that great realm.

This was a legacy from the early days. Morvannec was the first settlement of men in Brasayhal; from there they had set out to discover the apparently more attractive lands west of the mountains, and founded Greater Morvan. Morvannec had dwindled as the fortunes of its descendant grew; when Morvan was at its height, it had become little more than a quiet and underpopulated port of passage for produce from the sea and the provincial farmlands. Even its princes spent more time in Morvan, necessarily so as the threat from the Ice appeared; Korentyn Rhudri was thought unusual in his care for Morvannec's interests. In this he was prompted by Vayde, who had a real affection for the town, and that is why his statue was set in the place of most honor by the harbor. Vayde may have been as farsighted in this as in other matters, for although they had been bypassed for the lands of Morvan, the Eastlands were potentially just as fertile. But craggy contours and woodland cover had made the Eastlands more suitable for a variety of smaller farms, rather than the rich monoculture the sothrans preferred; the plains of Morvan were flatter and easier to cultivate. Perhaps also the power of Tapiau was then stronger in the eastern woods, and his terrors guarded the trees. Certain it is that to the northern folk also the great expanses of hill and mountain north of the Waters, more thinly wooded, seemed more attractive places to settle.

But with these lost the Eastlands had much to offer. The floodplains of the many rivers could yield ample grain and soft grazing, and the low hills around rich pastures, while steeper slopes offered hill hardier grazing, great store of timber, and the hunting that the northerners had excelled in since the days of Kerys. The sea also was rich, since the Ice had driven much of its life further south. But only after the founding of the realm of Morvanhal was the wealth of the East recognized, and turned wisely to account.

THE ICE

The accounts of the Ice in the Book of the Helm reflect a very different aspect of it from the cramped valley glaciation Elof and Kermorvan previously crossed. Here for the first time Elof encountered the true icesheet, and the massive Walls of Winter, the Fasguaith, the glacial cliffs that spearheaded its terrifying advance. Ils' description of Ice movement is—as one would expect from the duergar—substantially correct, particularly in seaboard climates such as the City by the Waters enjoyed. However, it is somewhat oversimplified; many other factors may speed up or slow down glacial advance. One such is known as basal slip; the sheer weight of ice may melt a thin film of water below the glacier, upon which it may slide forward with greatly reduced friction—exactly the same principle as skaters use, concentrating their body weight into thin knife edges. The rather incoherent account of Morvan's fall attributed to Korentyn may suggest something of what this effect could achieve over an already frozen smooth surface; some areas of the modern Antarctic icesheet are afloat on buried lakes. Another factor is the season: oddly enough, the icesheet may have advanced more quickly in summer than in winter. In colder weather the pressure melting may lessen and the glacier freeze more firmly to the ground beneath; this slows its advance, but makes it vastly more damaging, tearing away vast blocks of hard rock. Many mountains were leveled and the majority of major lakes excavated in this fashion. The debris, borne along on or ahead of the glacier wall, created rockfalls such as the one where Raven left the travelers, and is generally known as glacial *till*.

MELTWATER

Equally accurate is the description of meltwater effects. The sheer force of the water in such outflows is astonishing, and is often aided by the large amounts of rock debris they carry, which grinds away the ice in its path. They may flow over the glaciers, or out from underneath, and in doing so create tunnels even larger than the travelers found, up to some 250 feet across; the water pressure has been known to slant them upslope, as Ils suggests. Often they carve deep channels in the surrounding rock. Volcanic action under a glacier, often triggered by its pressure on the rock, can result in a truly explosive outburst, an erupting torrent of water and debris known in Iceland as a *jökulhlaup*.

THE KING'S HILL (MORVAN)

Such isolated outcrops as this are in fact not uncommon in ice sheets; their technical name is *nunatak*. The ravaged surface is characteristic. Its sudden flowering, however, is equally probable; many species of small plants and even insects have been found thriving on *nunataks*, perhaps sustained by the concentration of sunlight reflected off the surrounding ice. It has even been suggested by some theorists that they acted as refuges for many subarctic species during major glaciations, but this is uncertain. It was probably the existence of the hill gates that helped preserve the Catacombs so well, by allowing a flow of dry cold air along the passages; grave goods in tombs in the Andes and elsewhere have been similarly preserved.

THE MAPS

As the Book of the Sword made clear, the peoples of the Western Land of Brasayhal had grown very insular in the thousand years since the fall of Kerbryhaine. For the kindreds of men, all that lay east of the Meneth Scahas was a memory of loss, grief and dangers almost beyond comprehension, and they chose to blot it from their minds, and keep no maps; they thought never to return. The Duergar were less blinkered, but age upon age had passed since their first flight west, and they also had expected never to go back. The map accompanying the first volume represents the approximate extent of even their knowledge, and it had grown vague and general. Thus Kermorvan's journey was in every sense an exploration, and he knew little or nothing of what lands and conditions he might expect to find. Only on this second map is the full extent of Brasayhal shown; or rather, Brasayhal free of the Ice. For the rest of that great land lay dead and buried for a long age, and longer yet was to pass ere it saw the sun's light once more; and, as with the long dead, its aspect then was sadly changed.

Some corrections have been made in the map—the full southward extent of the Meneth Scahas, for example, is shown, and the eastward margins of the Ice made clearer. For completeness' sake the main feature of the southeastern lands have been included, though they do not come into this tale.

FLORA AND FAUNA

The life of the Forest lands that dominate the Book of the Helm was undoubtedly much richer and more varied than the Westlands', but for the most part it still resembled modern forms closely enough to need little comment. Alongside them, however, many older and stranger creatures still dwelt, and not always by chance. At times, of course, the descriptions are not close enough to identify properly; for example, the flock of small birds through whom Tapiau spoke were very probably some variety of warbler, but it is impossible to tell. In one or two cases, however, some telling details can be picked out.

DOMESTIC ANIMALS

As a rule these are not described in detail, the authors no doubt assuming they would be familiar enough to readers. As they are; but a few exceptions remain.

PONIES (CHAPTER 2) There were many distinct species of horse, small and large, in the land at this time; a few, such as Kermorvan's warhorse, had been introduced from Kerys, but most were native, and only recently domesticated, if at all. Such the company's mounts must have been, and unusually primitive to have retained the small side-hooves mentioned. In most horses of this time these remnants of the ancestral three-hoofed foot had already dwindled to mere splint bones. It is possible that they were some pony-sized breed of the older genus *Hipparion,* which was superseded by the more modern genus *Equus* at around this time.

MUSK-OXEN (CHAPTER 9) There seems to be no significant difference between these creatures and their modern descendants, the species *Ovibos muschatus,* either in appearance or behavior. They are members of the subfamily *Caprinae,* or goat-antelopes, a hardy group which flourished particularly during the Long Winters, and in the case of the musk-ox and its little-known cousin, the takin, grew to relatively giant size. It is, however, possible that this growth was a product of deliberate breeding by the duergar, and perhaps even the species as such, descended from one or other of the varieties of mountain-adapted goats they kept. Certainly the musk-ox takes more quickly to limited domestication than many other species.

WILD ANIMALS

GIANT HORSES (CHAPTER 2) The chance reference to these creatures is in fact borne out by other books of the Chronicles. Such beasts undoubtedly existed; almost certainly they were of the species *Equus giganteus,* one of the wild strains native to Brasayhal, rather than brought by men from Kerys, and larger than any horse now living. Once they ran wild over the grasslands of Morvan, and their strength, fierceness and untameability became proverbial; their herds must have been an awesome sight. In latter days some might still be found among other wild horses in the Open Lands, where predators were few; hence Kermorvan's confidence about the ponies.

GIANT DEER (CHAPTER 4) These were undoubtedly true deer *Cervidae,* but not the most famous giant form, the so-called Irish "elk" *Megaceros;* it was never found in these lands. From the description, particularly the pendulous muzzle and cupped palmate antlers, the huge moose *Cervalces* is a more likely candidate; its antlers might have a span up to 12 feet.

DAGGERTEETH (CHAPTER 4) These fierce predators are more fully described than before, so they can be firmly identified as saber-toothed cats, and members of the long-toothed *Machairodontinae* rather than the ''scimitar-toothed'' *Homotheriini*. They appear to lack the lower-jaw ''sheaths'' characteristic of *Machairodus* itself, and their size, if unexaggerated, is too great for the later form *Megantereon;* almost certainly they were the archetypal ''saber-toothed tiger'' *Smilodon*. If so, Kermorvan's courage was all the more remarkable; *Smilodon* stood nearly four feet high at the shoulder, and far outweighed a genuine tiger. It was the most recent of its species to evolve, and the last; this again argues a relatively recent date for the Winter Chronicles.

ONEHORN (CHAPTER 7) This is undoubtedly a species of the so-called ''woolly'' rhinoceros. The great size, long horselike body and single, straight horn suggest *Elasmotherium*, the largest known rhinocerine species: its horn alone was about six feet long. Its shaggy coat and mane—and the characteristic tuft of ''beard'' below the jaw—undoubtedly gave this creature a horselike appearance which is very suggestive. Certainly memories of it would make a more credible source of folklore than modern rhinocerines.

OTHERS

The huge herbivore whose appearance so startled the company in Chapter 4 is not difficult to name, though it must have been near the north of its range. The shape of head and claws, the diet, and the dermal armor beneath a shaggy pelt identify it as one of the family *Mylodontidae*, the later giant ground sloths, and probably of the species *Glossotherium*, because neither flourished in these lands. Specimens of the skin have survived, complete with bony nodules which could well have turned arrowshot at long range.

The beast that lurked in the Catacombs of Morvan is much harder to identify. In appearance and behavior it seems closer to the *Mustelidae* than the bears, so very probably the travelers were right in thinking of it as some kind of giant wolverine. However, this raises a problem; such a beast did exist, but millions of years earlier, in the Miocene period. This would make it a startling anachronism in the time of the Chronicles, but not the only one. The Powers, and in particular the Ice, may well have maintained many such alive in their service long after their day had passed in the rest of the world, harboring them perhaps on or around the *nunataks*. If this is so, it raises an intriguing possibility for the *akszawan*, the lizardthing that in the course of the Book of the Sword surprised Elof and Kermorvan in their camp. Its reptilian aspect is hard to reconcile with its ability to survive and function in the cold climate of the Northland mountains. It might, however, have been a synapsid, or "paramammal," a transitional creature ancestral to all mammals, blending reptilian skeletal and body traits with the beginnings of mammalian dentition and a "warmblooded" physiology. But this family, whose best-known member is the sail-backed *Dimetrodon*, flourished as long ago as the late Permian—a period, interestingly enough, in which there may also have been severe glaciations. If it was a paramammal, therefore, its line had been kept alive for no less than 225 million years.

THE FOREST

The trees and plants of the Forest were, as far as can be told, very like modern forms, and where possible the modern names have been used in the text. It was the ecology in which they grew that was different. The Forest might have appeared the richest land in all Brasayhal, so vast and so energetic was the growth it bore. Yet, like the modern *selva*, this great pyramid of life grew from a very delicate foundation. Its ecological cycle was based on swift transmission of water and nutrients, leaving the topsoil beneath neither deep nor rich. Tapiau's fear of the incursions of the Ice on one hand, and on the other men, was therefore well founded. Once frozen, the ground could not support the Forest: once cleared, the Forest could not easily reestablish itself. In northern areas grassland swiftly took over, while in the south all too often the exposed topsoil simply dried up in summer and blew away. And to judge from the state of those lands today, this in the end was its fate. It may seem unlikely that so vast a woodland could perish so easily; yet great areas of the Sahara today were, not long since, the forests where Hannibal obtained his elephants.

• PEOPLES

THE PEOPLES OF THE EASTLANDS

At first sight it might seem from the Winter Chronicles that the folk who had remained in the Eastlands hardly differed from their kindred in the west, whether in language or customs. Bryhon had had little difficulty in passing himself off as one of them, and the travelers were easily understood and accepted. But there are indications that this surface similarity was deceptive; deeper differences did exist. For example, the Penruthya tongue was the dominant language, as it was in Bryhaine, but in a very different dialect, more archaic and adopting many wordforms from the Svarhath. If the travelers had not already had to adjust to the archaic tongue of the Forest dwellers, and been native or fluent Svarhath speakers, they would have had greater difficulty. Svarhath, as among the Forest folk, had changed much less, perhaps because of its stronger oral tradition, but chiefly because of its "minority" status. This was not forced on it, as it was in Kerbryhaine, but reflected the relative numbers of each people, and their involvement in public affairs.

Language thus points the way to an even deeper difference. The land of Morvannec maintained the blending of races that Kerys had achieved of old; it had not fragmented into distinct communities, as Morvan had begun to, or into separate countries, as did the Westlands to their own great loss. Northerners and sothrans, Svarhath and Penruthya, shared common communities throughout the land. Within the community, though, the northerners tended to be clannish, living in their own districts and monopolizing certain occupations such as sea fishing, small farming and crafts. The Penruthya dominated government, large landowning and trade, but such finance as there was lay in the hands of the Goldsmith's Guild, which was chiefly Svarhath. In general the two kindreds existed in goodhumored mutual toleration (though much of the good humor was at each other's expense). The disaster of Morvan had forced them together as sharply as it had divided the west.

THE ANCESTRAL FACTIONS

One casualty of this process in Morvannec appears to have been the ancestral political factions that so bedeviled the affairs of Kerbryhaine at this time. If earlier Chronicles are to be believed, they originated in the rise of Kerys, when, as so often happens, newly wealthy commoners found their interests conflicting with the ancestral landowning classes who had built up the country, and in a sense made that wealth possible. Many families became identified with one or another faction, and passed on that rivalry to their descendants. This is all too credible; it was the same conflict that first divided the patrician and plebeian classes in ancient Rome, and the lines of Guelph and Ghibelline at a later date. And as with them, it was handed down through so many generations that it lost sight of its origins. Inherited wealth soon gave the most powerful plebeians a thoroughly aristocratic outlook; many patrician families declined in wealth and status. And though the plebeian faction claimed to speak for the common people, very often the patrician faction was closer to them in spirit and interest, and enjoyed their support. The factions began among the Penruthya peoples, but intermarriage and common interests soon spread them among the Svarhath of the north.

The royal line of Kerys, the Ysmerien, usually remained aloof, striving to pacify and reconcile the factions, as they had the two peoples. Sometimes they would succeed for many generations together, yet sooner or later the old dissension would creep in once more. A younger son of the Ysmerien left Kerys for the new land of Brasayhal to found there a colony that would become Morvannec; his heirs established Morvan, and took the name of its central city, Kermorvan, for their new line. But even there they could not escape the old associations; the factions followed them. However, throughout the long centuries of Morvan's prosperity there was little serious cause for dissension, and the kings sternly repressed casual feuding; the factions faded into little more than familial rivalries, and among the Northerners died out altogether. But as the threat of the Ice grew, so the factions regained their meaning. It did not help that when the kings needed strong support they would always find it more readily among the patrician faction. Many plebeians sought to limit the royal power, or even substitute some "popular" form of government. Yet when they had their chance in Bryhaine they created the Syndicacy, as dependent on wealth as the old aristocracy and as autocratic as the kings had ever been.

The shifts of time and fortune ensured that no single family dominated either faction for very long; some even shifted from one to the other over the centuries. But for the Book of the Helm it is worth noting that the Herens were always strong among the plebeians. Like the royal line they blended the blood of both kindreds, but they were staunch populists and particular antagonists of the kings; in Morvan they added the prefix *Bry-*, meaning free, to the family name in protest against the new kingship. By and large they seem to have been a very honorable family, and at times more humane and peaceful than the stern kings they opposed. Yet undoubtedly it was within their kindred that the sinister cult of the Ice centered; doubtless it was passed on only to a carefully chosen and condi-

tioned few. Nevertheless, it is noticeable that it was Morvannec, where the Bryheren line was cut short by
accidental deaths a generation or two after the fall of Morvan, that managed to produce the most harmonious society
in the land. The High Kingdom of Morvanhal was to continue this tradition; the factions were forbidden by decree
and common consent, and never again acquired any sig-
nificance.

THE FOREST PEOPLE

No more need be said of the origins of these strange folk
than appears in the text, and of their eventual destiny little
is known. However, some deductions are possible. If they
used any name of themselves, it was *alfar,* but the duergar,
with customary clear sight, named them the Children of
Tapiau. For in truth they had been reduced to children,
dependent on him for all things. Though their bodies were
well adapted to life in a natural, primitive world, the picture of them in the Chronicles suggests that their minds
were not. For they appear to lack both the vices and virtues of truly primitive humans, that sheer raw energy which
allows them to survive and grow. They were dangerous
warriors, but only at Tapiau's behest; among themselves
they never fought, save in sport. This peaceable nature
may seem a virtue to civilized folk, yet even the most
manlike apes may murder and wage tribal war for no good
purpose; it may be an urge they need. Nor did the arts of
peace fare any better among the *alfar,* to judge by Morhuen's fate. How long could such a people survive in the
great changes that were to come? And could they ever
again climb up the same long slope? If enough of them
survived unaltered, it is possible they might manage to
endure. Certainly in other lands there survive legends of
a race of ageless, supernatural beings at once sylvan, rustic and strange, yet with courts and kings excelling in
splendor those of common men. Perhaps Tapiau had been
at work there also, with greater success. But where the
great forests of Brasayhal once ran no such traditions endure, nor is there any trace of the folk who roamed them.

Perhaps in the end the fabric of men proved tougher and less apt to Tapiau's hand than he suspected, and their descendants regained their manlike forms. But it may or may not be significant that in the jungles that endure far to the south there are legends of a man-sized arboreal ape, though no apes have ever lived on that continent; all that has ever been found are peculiarly large and long-limbed monkeys.

THE DWELLERS UNDER THE TREES

The other strange beings that Elof and his companions encountered should not, strictly speaking, be spoken of as people. They were as Tapiau described them, races of minor Powers. Yet their tasks and natures confined them to bodily form, and in those forms they lived, and even perhaps bred; and they undoubtedly had minds of some order, though very unlike those of men. In no account does Tapiau volunteer any more information to Elof about them; but in some texts passages are added which name them, apparently from duergar lore and traditions. Ils herself may have discovered these, though apparently she knew little or nothing of them at the time. The most human in shape, the creature who took Ermahal, is named *rhuzalkh* in the duergar speech. They did not think her wholly malign, for she did not seem to kill; and of those lost from the company Ermahal alone did not reappear among Taoune's shades. Yet they dreaded her, for she would ever provoke and strengthen dreams and illusions in an apparent need to share them, perhaps to feed on them. In doing so she would ensnare the dreamer wholly, luring him away down strange pathways from which few returned, and those lost and wandering in their wits. Always they were happy, which to the duergar seemed worst of all.

The monstrous lake-dwellers the duergar named *vadyanei*, and feared far less. In body they were as described, not unlike massive seals, yet with grasping forelimbs and huge heads. Formerly their dams had been found in many rivers and lakes, and it seems they were once set to watch and ward such places; they were simple of mind and savage of temper, though seldom dangerous unless disturbed.

When the duergar waterways under the mountains were
first made the *vadyanei* had often invaded them, endan-
gering ships and their crews, and been hard to displace;
but for thousands of years no more had been seen of them.

Both these creatures were unknown to men, and had no
names in their tongues. Not so the creatures of the Hunt;
they were known in the folklore of Bryhaine as one of the
principal terrors of Aithennec, where Tapiau no doubt set
them to deal with intruding men. As a group they were
named *helgorhyon,* probably meaning the Wild Hunt, but
the individual creatures were called *gourvlyth,* which
means approximately the same as the modern word were-
wolf; the duergar name *vrkalak* means as much also. That
implies some identity with men, yet by all accounts they
were twice the size of a man, and there is no tale of them
changing skin or shape; on the other hand, they were never
seen by day. But it is more likely the name refers to their
shape, and the mind that lay behind the brows of a beast.
Certainly they were of a fearsome intelligence, and once
on a scent no ruse or guile could turn them aside; Elof
and his companions were fortunate in their escape that
only *alfar* were nearby. Most probably the Hunt was still
west of the Meneth Aithen, to guard against Ekwesh incursions. Their original task was said to have been coun-
tering the creatures of the Ice, and as such they were
valued, even worshiped by the ancestors of the duergar,
who had suffered from it once before. That men knew
them only as terrors of the night and the treeshade was
perhaps unjust; it is worth noting that while they terrified
the company, it was only Kasse the wrong-doer they actually slew. And even his murderous bargain they justly
kept.

THE CONFLICT OF FORCES

In the Book of the Helm, for the first time, the two great
forces of the Long Winter come into direct conflict—
smithcraft in the hands of a man, albeit an extraordinary
man, against the controlling wills of the Powers them-

selves. And if there is no doubt to whom the first honors went, still there is more to be explained.

THE POWERS

The events of the Book of the Helm brought Elof into far closer contact with the Steerers of the World than any man in the memory of his times; though in the Chronicles accounts of others may be found. He learned much of their strengths and weaknesses, and, as the Chronicle suggests, he acquired much of this from Tapiau. No doubt the wily Forest lord, sensing that here was one on whom his usual allurements would have little hold, and divined the thirst for knowledge that was one of Elof's ruling passions, and sought to ensnare him with that instead. For though he might have held men by force, he preferred to give them at least an illusion of choice; the illusions he had woven for himself were the less disturbed thereby.

Yet it is improbable that Tapiau would reveal so much of crucial importance about himself and others as freely as the accounts have him do, and all at once. It is more likely that he let fall the information in tantalizing morsels, underestimating perhaps Elof's formidable mind and memory, and his ability to smelt and weld facts and truths as surely as he could metals. Also, many truths that Elof later learned from Kara may have been placed here by later compilers.

For the sake of concision many interesting speculations that are put into Tapiau's mouth have had to be omitted from the main text, but as one or two have a bearing on the tale they are worth repeating here. One concerns Louhi, and her need for the Tarnhelm. She was an immensely greater creature of her kind than Kara, and seemed able to shift in and out of human shape at will; why then could she not assume others as easily? The answer seems to lie chiefly in the great strain the Ice put upon her; human form came easiest to most Powers, having the capacity of mind closest to their own, and she had little energy to spare. Yet she now found she had to change, if only to keep up with Kara. The transforming powers of the helm were of a different order, masking rather than reconstituting the shape, and the power in the helm was not hers.

Another puzzling aspect of Louhi, or her true self Taounehtar, is her exact relationship to Taoune; by some accounts she was his daughter, but by others his consort. That is put in the voice of Raven, and carries all the more authority. That Taoune had long been reduced to an impotent shadow of his former power, as Tapiau suggests, is probably true. But the Chronicles tell that Tapiau had less share in that than he made out.

SMITHCRAFT

The accounts of smithcraft in the Book of the Helm confirm that in those years the sheer science of metalworking reached a height rarely if ever equaled—and not only in the remarkable person of Elof himself. The technique he used in the creation of the crown-helm is unmistakably that now known as electrolysis, or electroplating. This— as the account is careful to make clear—he did not discover for himself, but drew from the ancient lore of his craft. He was, however, probably the first to develop it for fine plating of metals; there is no evidence that the Elder folk had anticipated him. In assuming they had Ils lets slip that patronizing attitude to men typical of even the friendliest duergar. They did undoubtedly use electrolysis for refining rare metals; whether human smiths learned this of them or developed it independently cannot be said.

If it seems improbable to find electricity known and used in such an otherwise untechnical culture, we should remember that true smithcraft set very different values upon ordinary technology. Also, we should consider the skilled silversmiths of the ancient city of Baghdad on the river Tigris, who in the early years of this century were found electroplating with primitive batteries of copper and iron in ceramic jars of acid; they were assumed to have learned the technique from the west. There is now reason to doubt this. Among recent archaeological discoveries in the Middle East are small ceramic jars containing copper cylinders plugged with asphalt and containing corroded iron rods—in effect, batteries of much the same kind. They were found in at least three sites, all dating from the time of the Roman Empire, and all around the Tigris near Baghdad.

There is no doubt that the smiths of Elof's day understood at least something of the nature of electricity, though from a very different standpoint. When Elof set out to reforge his strange inheritance with lightning he undoubtedly knew what he was doing, though, encouraged by his mysterious visitor, he may have underestimated the appalling risk. But it is likely that little else would have allowed him to straighten so curious a blade; the glimpse he had of its content is curiously reminiscent of modern high-tensile materials such as carbon-fiber, which may be highly resistive to heat and impact. He had studied with a duergar mastersmith, and they, at least, had a very shrewd grasp of the forces at work with matter. Elof, in describing his hammer, shows that he had learned much from them, and in the greatest trial of his life, when all else seemed lost to him, it was this knowledge that was to prove crucial.

THE CHRONICLES

Why the Book of the Helm was so named is hard to say, whether for the strange crowned helm that broke the will of a Power, or the other, brought back into the world after long ages beneath the Ice, like a symbol of renewal and rebirth. But almost certainly it was for the Tarnhelm, second of Elof's youthful creations that were to haunt him throughout his turbulent life, and shape it as he had shaped them. For it was the Tarnhelm that lay behind all the conflicts and struggles of this time, that wrought for him both peril and final triumph, and brought him in the end to the fulfilling of his promise and his desire.